W9-BJP-310

PENITENT

More tales from Warhammer 40,000 by Dan Abnett

EISENHORN
BOOK 1: XENOS
BOOK 2: MALLEUS
BOOK 3: HERETICUS
BOOK 4: THE MAGOS

RAVENOR
BOOK 1: RAVENOR
BOOK 2: RAVENOR ROGUE
BOOK 3: RAVENOR RETURNED

BEQUIN
BOOK 1: PARIAH
BOOK 2: PENITENT

• GAUNT'S GHOSTS •

THE FOUNDING
BOOK 1: FIRST AND ONLY
BOOK 2: GHOSTMAKER
BOOK 3: NECROPOLIS

THE SAINT
BOOK 4: HONOUR GUARD
BOOK 5: THE GUNS OF TANITH
BOOK 6: STRAIGHT SILVER
BOOK 7: SABBAT MARTYR

THE LOST
BOOK 8: TRAITOR GENERAL
BOOK 9: HIS LAST COMMAND
BOOK 10: THE ARMOUR OF CONTEMPT
BOOK 11: ONLY IN DEATH

THE VICTORY
BOOK 12: BLOOD PACT
BOOK 13: SALVATION'S REACH
BOOK 14: THE WARMASTER
BOOK 15: ANARCH

THE SABBAT WORLDS CRUSADE
DOUBLE EAGLE

I AM SLAUGHTER
BROTHERS OF THE SNAKE
TITANICUS
LORD OF THE DARK MILLENNIUM

PENITENT

A BEQUIN NOVEL

DAN ABNETT

BLACK LIBRARY

A BLACK LIBRARY PUBLICATION

First published in Great Britain in 2021.
This edition published in 2021 by
Black Library,
Games Workshop Ltd.,
Nottingham, NG7 2WS, UK.

10 9 8 7 6 5 4 3 2 1

Produced by Games Workshop in Nottingham.
Cover illustration by Lorenzo Mastroianni.

A CIP record for this book is available from the British Library.

ISBN 13: 978-1-78999-851-1

Printed and bound in China.

Definitely for Jules Styles with thanks for the brainstorms, helping me with my maths homework (because maths is hard!), and introducing me to the original white box edition all those years ago.

For more than a hundred centuries the Emperor has sat immobile on the Golden Throne of Earth. He is the Master of Mankind. By the might of His inexhaustible armies a million worlds stand against the dark.

Yet, He is a rotting carcass, the Carrion Lord of the Imperium held in life by marvels from the Dark Age of Technology and the thousand souls sacrificed each day so that His may continue to burn.

To be a man in such times is to be one amongst untold billions. It is to live in the cruellest and most bloody regime imaginable. It is to suffer an eternity of carnage and slaughter. It is to have cries of anguish and sorrow drowned by the thirsting laughter of dark gods.

This is a dark and terrible era where you will find little comfort or hope. Forget the power of technology and science. Forget the promise of progress and advancement. Forget any notion of common humanity or compassion.

There is no peace amongst the stars, for in the grim darkness of the far future, there is only war.

The first section of the story,
which is called

KING DOOR

CHAPTER 1

Which is of the society one keeps,
and also of societies that keep you

My dreams had become sticky and black since I met the daemon.

It had been two months since he first visited me, and his immaterial presence had seeped into my dreams like tar, gumming all of my thoughts together so that nothing was clear or separate any more. Just one fused lump of black confusion, wherein ideas writhed, enfeebled, unable to pull themselves free or define themselves.

I had hoped for clarity. I believe, in fact, that clarity was the thing I had been seeking my whole life. I wished I had met, instead, an angel, whose essence would have flooded my mind like amber. This was, I confess, utter fancy. I had never met an angel, and I did not know if they existed, but that is what I imagined. Where a daemon's touch might drown my dreams like dark ooze, an angel's would fill them with golden resin, so that each thought and idea might be preserved, alone and intact, quite clearly presented, and I could make sense of them. Of everything.

I had seen amber on the market stalls below Toilgate. That was how I knew of the stuff: polished pebbles in hues of ochre, gamboge and orpiment, resembling glass, and within each one a lace fly or burnished beetle, set fast for eternity.

That is how I wished my mind was: each thought presented thus, available to the light from all sides, so clear that one might examine every smallest detail through an enlarging glass.

But the daemon had welled in, and all was black.

I say daemon, but I was told the correct term is *daemonhost*. His name was Cherubael. This sounded to me like the name of an angel, but as with all things in the city of Queen Mab, things and their names do not agree. They are, ineluctably, ciphers for each other. Through my sticky, black dreams, I had come at least to understand that Queen Mab was a city of profound contradiction. It was a place half-dead, or at least half-*other*, where one thing was in fact some opposite thing, and truth and lies interleaved, and people were not who they appeared to be, and even doors could not be trusted for, altogether quite too often, they opened between places that should not intersect.

The city was a dead thing inside a live thing, or the other way around. It was a place haunted by the ghost of itself, and few had the mediumship to negotiate between the two. The dead and the living questioned each other, but did not, or could not, listen to the answers. And those few who walked, aware, in the dark places between the two, the margin that divided the physical from the shadow it cast, seemed more concerned with consigning souls from one side to the other, sending the screaming living to their deaths, or plucking the purblind dead back to life.

Great Queen Mab and I had that in common. There was a dead-half part of me too, a silence within that made me pariah. I was a true citizen of Queen Mab, for I was a contradiction. I was shunned by all, an outcast orphan not fit for society, yet sought by all as a prize of some sort.

My name is Beta Bequin. Alizebeth was my given name, but no one called me that. Beta is a diminutive. It is said *Bay-tar*, with a long vowel, not *Better* or *Beater*, and I had always thought this was to distinguish it from the Eleniki letter that is commonly used in scientific ordinal notation. But now I began to think that was exactly what it was. I was Beta, the second on the list, the second version, the second-ranked, the lesser of two, the copy.

Or maybe not. Perhaps I was merely the next. Perhaps I was the alpha (though not, of course, the *Alpha* who stood with me in those days).

Perhaps, perhaps... *many* things. My name did not define me. That, at least, I learned from Cherubael, despite the gluey darkness of the dreams he spread. My name did not match me, just as his did not match him. We were both, like Queen Mab, contradictions from the outset. Names, as we will see, are infinitely untrustworthy, yet infinitely important.

I had become very sensitive to the distinction between what something is called and what it actually is. It had become my way, and I had learned it from the man Eisenhorn, who was by then, I suppose, my mentor. This practice of not trusting something by its surface was his very mode of being. He trusted nothing, but there was some value in this habit, for it had patently kept him alive for a very long time. A peculiarly long time.

It defined him too, for I did not know what he was any more than I knew what I was. He told me he was an inquisitor of the Holy Ordos, but another man, who claimed to hold that title with equal insistence, told me that Eisenhorn was, in fact, a renegade. Worse, a heretic. Worse, *Extremis Diabolus*. But perhaps that man – Ravenor, his name – perhaps *he* was the liar.

I knew so very little, I did not even know if *Eisenhorn* knew what he was. I wondered if he was like me, bewildered by the way the truth of the world could shift so suddenly. I thought I was an orphan, raised in the scholam of the Maze Undue to serve as an agent of the Ordos. But now it seemed I was a... a genetic copy and not an orphan at all. I have – *had* – no parents. There was no dead mother and father for me to mourn, though I had mourned and missed them my whole life, for they were a fabrication, just like the story of their tombstone in the marshland cemetery.

And I had been told the Maze Undue was not an Ordo scholam, but in fact an academy, run by a hermetic society called the Cognitae, which was of ancient standing, and served as a shadow-twin of the Inquisition.

I was expected now to decide my loyalty. Should I serve the Cognitae that bred me, or the Holy Ordos that I always believed I was a part of? Did I throw my lot in with Eisenhorn, who might be a servant of the Hallowed Throne, or a thrice-damned heretic? Did I turn to Ravenor, who claimed Imperial authority, yet may be the biggest liar of all?

And what of the other parties in this game? Not the least of them, the King in Yellow? Should I stand at *his* side?

I was resolved, for now, to walk with Gregor Eisenhorn. This, despite the fact he consorted with daemonhosts and a warrior of the Traitor Legions, and had been denounced to me for a heretic.

Why? Because of all the things I have just said. I trusted nothing. Not even Gregor Eisenhorn. But I was in his company and he had, I felt, been the most open with me.

I had my own principles, of course. Though it was done underhand by the Cognitae, I was raised to believe my destiny was to serve the Throne. That, at least, felt right. I knew I would rather pledge to the God-Emperor of us all than to any other power or faction. Where I would ultimately stand, I could not say, for, as I have stated, I could not identify any truth that could be relied on. At least in Eisenhorn's company I might learn some truths upon which I could base a decision, even if it was, in the end, to quit his side and join another.

I wished to learn, to make *true learning*, not the dissembling education of the Maze Undue. I wished to learn the truth about myself, and what part I played in the greater scheme of mystery. More than that, I wished to unravel the secrets of Queen Mab, and lay them bare to light, for plainly an existential menace lurked in the shadows of the world, and exposing it would be the greatest duty I could perform in the name of the God-Emperor.

These things I wished, though, as I came to reflect later, one must be careful what one wishes for. Nevertheless, revelation of the *entire truth*, in all clarity, was the purpose I had privately vowed to accomplish. Which is why, that cold night, I was Violetta Flyde, and I walked through the streets of Feygate Quarter at Eisenhorn's side to attend a meeting at the Lengmur Salon.

Yes, I know. Violetta Flyde was yet another veil, an untrue name, a false me, a role to play, something that the tutors of the Maze Undue used to call a *function*. But illumination might be earned from the play-acting, so I walked then, and for the time being, at Eisenhorn's side.

Also, I was fond of his daemon.

Cherubael was cordial. He called me 'little thing', and though he polluted my dreams, I fancied he was the most honest of my companions. It was as though he had nothing left to lose, and thus honesty would cost him nothing. There was no side to him.

Not all found him so bearable. Lucrea, a girl who I had brought with me into Eisenhorn's care, left after a short time. She slipped away into the streets one night, without a goodbye, and I am sure it was the daemonhost's company that had finally driven her away, despite all she had seen till then. But Lucrea had never been part of the intrigue, just a bystander. I could not blame her for wanting to be out of it.

Cherubael was a daemon, a thing of the immaterium, shackled inside a human body. I think the body had been dead for a long time. His true self, inside, stretched at his outer casing as if trying to get out. The shape of horns pushed at the skin of his brow, as though some forest stag or scree-slope ram was striving to butt its way out of him. This pulled taut the bloodless flesh of his face, giving him an unintentional sneer, an upturned nose, and eyes that blinked oddly and too seldom. I wondered sometimes if he would burst one day, and there would be nothing left but sprouting antlers and a grinning skull.

He was quite terrifying, but I found the fact of him reassuring. If he was a daemon, then such things existed. And Queen Mab constantly demonstrated that there was symmetry in all things: dead and alive, materia and immateria, truth and lies, name and false name, faithful and faithless, light and dark, inner and outer. So if he was a daemon, then surely there had to be angels too? Cherubael, cursed and wretched, was my proof that angels existed.

And perhaps, in time, one would come to me and fill my dreams with amber sap, and let me see things, golden and clear, for what they actually were.

'One may measure a city,' Eisenhorn remarked as we walked, 'by the number of metaphysical societies it harbours.'

'One may measure a circle,' I replied, 'starting anywhere.'

He looked at me, puzzled.

'Your point?'

'It's still a circle,' I said. 'No start, no finish. Infinite.'

'Yes. And this is still a city.'

'Is it, though?' I asked.

I was in a playful mood, and he didn't care for it. He meant, of course, the temperament and health of a city. A city in decline, one leaning towards corruption and malady of spirit, becomes home to curious beliefs. An interest in *the other* grows. This is basic Ordo teaching. A fashion for the occult and esoteric, a preponderance of fringe interests, these are the symptoms of a culture in dangerous deterioration.

If you do not know the city, the Lengmur Salon lies in a hollow of old streets beneath the flaking spire of Saint Celestine Feygate, whose bells chime at odd hours. On this night, upon the broad steps before the templum, many of the poor wretches known as the Curst loitered, begging for alms. I could not help but look to see if Renner Lightburn was among them. In the months since we had been separated, I had thought of him often, and wondered what fate had befallen him, for no trace of him could be found anywhere.

Nor was there trace here. Eisenhorn noticed my look, but made no comment. Though Lightburn had been brave and selfless during his time with me, his mind had been wiped by Ravenor's agents and he had been returned, mystified, to the streets. Eisenhorn believed I was better off without him and, most certainly, that Lightburn was better off without me.

Still, I had never had the chance to thank him.

All around that small, muddled quarter of Feygate there were salons, dining halls and meeting houses that were popular haunts for those of a metaphysical bent. I saw placards on the walls and notices in windows advertising spiritual lectures, quizzing glasses and table-turning evenings, or opportunities to hear noted speakers orate on many matters esoteric, such as 'Man's place in the Cosmos,' or 'The Secret Architecture of the Queen Mab Templums,' or 'The Hidden Potency of Numbers and Letters'. Several establishments advertised the reading of taroche, by appointment, and others promised spiritual healing and past-life revelation that would be delivered by expert practitioners.

The Lengmur Salon, its old windows glowing gold in the deepening evening, stood foremost among these. It was the meeting place of souls artistically and mystically inclined. It was said the celebrated poet Crookley dined here regularly, and that often he might be found drinking with the engraver Aulay or the beautiful opera singer Comena Den Sale. The place was famous for its lectures, both formal and informal, and its readings and performative events, as well as the provocative dialogues that flowed between the eclectic clientele.

'On another world,' Eisenhorn muttered as he held the door open for me, 'this place would have been closed by the Magistratum. By the Ordos. This whole district.'

There is a fine line, I believe, between what is permissible and what is not. The Imperium loves its lore and its mysteries, and there is always active interest in what might be considered fringe ideas. However, it is but a short step from those harmless and jolly diversions to outright heresy. Queen Mab, and establishments like this, teetered on that edge. There was an air of the occult to it, by which I mean the old definition of the word, the hidden and the unseen. It felt as though real secrets lay here, and true mysteries were discussed, mysteries beyond the innocuous fripperies and trifles tolerated on more upstanding worlds.

Queen Mab, indeed the whole world of Sancour, had slid into unwise, bohemian decay, falling from the strict and stern grasp of Imperial control into a state of end-times dissolution, which would only end in its decadent demise, or in a hasty and overdue purge by off-world authorities.

But the salon, ah such a place! Facing the street was its famous dining hall, a large, bright room that rang with the clatter of flatware and chatter of the customers. The place was packed, and people queued outside to get a supper-table.

Behind the hall and the kitchens lay the salon itself, a back-bar accessible by doors in the side lanes and through a curtained archway at the rear of the dining hall. This was the heart of the establishment. It was fusty, I would say, if you have never visited it, lit by old lumen globes in tinted glass hoods, the walls papered with an opulent pattern of black fern-leaves on a purple field. There was a long bar to the back, the heavy wood of it painted a dark green and ribbed with brass bands. The main space was filled with tables, and there were side booths around which black drapes could be drawn for private assignations.

The place was busy, thronging with patrons, many of whom had come through from the dining room to take a digestif after their supper. The air was full of voices and the waft of obscura smoke, but it was not lively, like a city tavern, or the busy dining hall without. There was a reserve here, a languor, as though these conversations were slow and involved matters of philosophy rather than the empty blather of drinkers finding evening recreation. Servitors, worked in brass and robed in green, weaved through the throng, serving trays of drinks and platters of food.

We took a booth to the side from where we could observe a decent part of the lounge. A servitor brought us joiliq in small, patterned glasses, and small plates of griddled gannek smeared with mustard, and keth-fruit flesh dipped in salt.

We watched.

I was intrigued by the clientele and their heady conversations.

'Is that Crookley?' I asked, eyeing a heavyset man who was sitting beneath a painting of the Tetrachtys, locked in conversation with a small woman in grey.

'No,' Eisenhorn replied. 'Crookley is taller, less meat on him.'

I am skilled at observation. It was part of my training. While caring to maintain the role of the prim young lady Violetta Flyde, I scanned the crowd, noting this visage and that, seeing whom I might recognise, and who it might be useful to recognise on another day. I saw a bearded caravan master from the Herrat, holding forth with three men – one who seemed to be a meek scholam master, another who was clearly a humble rubricator from his ink-stained hands, and a third who would not have seemed out of place at the head of a Heckaty Parish killgang.

At another table, three nurse-sisters from the Feygate Lazarhouse sat in silence, sharing a bottle of mint wine, identical in their tight-belted grey serge habits and white coifs. They did not speak or look at each other, and their tired faces read blank. I wondered if they were here by mistake, or if this was simply their nearest hostelry, and they tolerated the decadent society each evening for the sake of a restorative drink.

Beside the bar stood an elderly man with quite the longest arms and legs I have seen. He gangled awkwardly, as if he had never quite mastered the lengths to which his skinny frame had grown. He was dressed in a dark tailcoat and trousers, and peered through a silver pince-nez as he scribbled in a notebook. Alongside him at the bar, but apparently not of the elderly man's company, for they exchanged no words, sat a small, sad old man who was evidently blind. He sipped at drinks that the bartender slid into his grasp so he might find them.

I noted many others. I noted, too, any indication of weapons on their persons: a bulging pocket here, an underbelt there, a stiffness of posture that hinted at a concealed knife-girdle or disguised holster. I had no expectation that the evening would turn untoward, but if it did, I had already mapped the dangers, and knew from which directions threats would come.

Just before the lights started to flash, I saw two people at the side door, talking urgently. One was a young gentleman of means in a pinstriped suit and over-robe. The other was a woman in a rust-coloured gown. I was drawn by the quiet animation of their conversation. Though I could not hear the words, their manner was somewhat agitated, as if some serious personal matter was being discussed that was quite different in tone from the meandering debate in the rest of the salon.

The woman made a gesture of refusal, then turned to leave by the side door. The man took her arm – gently – to dissuade her, but she shook him off and stepped out. As she passed beneath the low lamp of the side door, I saw her profile, and felt at once that I knew her from somewhere.

But then she was out, and gone into the street, and the salon lights were flashing on and off.

Gurlan Lengmur, the patron of the establishment, stepped up onto the small stage and nodded to the barman, who ceased flicking the light switches now that attention and quiet had been achieved.

'My friends,' said Lengmur, 'welcome to this evening's diversion.'

His voice was soft and buttery. He was a small man, refined and well dressed, but otherwise quite bland in appearance, a fact that seemed to bother him, for his dark hair was shaved on the right side and then turned over long on the crown in a huge, oil-dressed lick as the latest society fashion prescribed. I felt he had embraced this modern style less because it was modish and more because it afforded his person some specific feature of interest.

'There will be taroche later, in the back room,' he said, 'and then a talk by Master Edvark Nadrich on the significance of the Uraeon and the Labyrine in Early Angelican tomb sites. Those of you who have heard Master Nadrich's talks before will know to expect a riveting and educational treat. Afterwards, then, an open discussion. First, though, on this small stage, Mamzel Gleena Tontelle, the feted voicer, will share her mediumship with us.'

There was a warm round of applause, and some clinking of butter knives against the rims of glassware. Lengmur stepped back, extending a gesture of welcome as he bowed his head, and handed up onto the foot-stage a dowdy woman in a pearl-grey silk dress of a style that had been out of fashion for some decades.

Her plump face was pinched. I guessed her age to be about fifty years. She accepted the amiable applause with a nod and a gentle sweep of her hand.

'Her dress,' Eisenhorn whispered. 'Styled old to remind us of generations past. A common trick.'

I nodded. Mamzel Tontelle indeed looked like a society lady from the glittering ballrooms of the previous century, a time when Queen Mab had been a grander place. I had seen such things in pict-books. Even her mannerisms had something of the old-fashioned about them. This was an act, a role, and I had a great interest in those who performed roles well. She had, I think, applied some costuming powder to her skin and dress.

'Powdered like a ghost,' Eisenhorn grumbled. 'Voicers call it "phantomiming", and it's yet another stale conceit.'

Mam Tontelle had done herself up like some mournful shade, the light powder making it seem as though she had stood, unmoving, through the passage of decades as dust settled upon her. It was understated and, for my part, I thought it most amusing.

She clasped one hand to the shelf of her bosom and spread the fingers of the other across her brow, furrowing in concentration.

'There is a boy here,' she said. 'A small boy. I see the letter "H".'

In the crowd, some shaking of heads.

'Definitely a boy,' Mamzel Tontelle continued. Her voice was thin and colourless. 'And the letter "H". Or perhaps a "T".'

'Cold reading,' muttered Eisenhorn. 'The oldest trick of all. Fishing for reception.'

And of course it was. I saw it for what it was, and shared Eisenhorn's scepticism, but not his disdain. I had always been charmed by such distractions, and was entertained to watch an actor at work. More so, a trickster who was, through performance, fabricating something out of nothing.

Mam Tontelle tried another letter, a 'G', as I remember, and a man at the back took her up on it, and presently had become convinced that he was receiving a message from his godson, long dead. The man was quite astounded by this, though he had provided all the facts that had made it convincing, offering them innocently in response to Mam Tontelle's deft suggestion.

'He was young when he died. But ten years old.'

'Eight,' the man replied, eyes bright.

'Yes, I see it. Eight years. And drowned, poor soul.'

'He fell under a cart,' the man sighed.

'Oh, the cart! I hear the rattle of it. It was not water upon the poor child's lips, but blood. He loved so a pet, a hound or–'

'A bird,' murmured the man, 'a little tricefinch in a silver cage. It could sing the song of the bells at Saint Martyr's.'

'I see the silver bars, and bright feathers too,' said Mam Tontelle, hand to head as if in exquisite pain from a migraine, 'and so it sings...'

And so it continued. The man was beside himself, and the crowd much impressed. I could tell Eisenhorn was quickly losing patience. But we had not come to watch the voicer ply her tricks, nor had we come to hear a lecture or have our taroche read.

We were here to find an astronomer who had either gone mad, or had seen a great secret that many in the city would kill to learn.

Or possibly both.

CHAPTER 2

Of a visitation

His name was Fredrik Dance. For many years, his prodigious gifts as a magos mathematicae had taken him across the entire Scarus Sector, lecturing at the finest academic institutions, and publishing a series of important works on astromathematic application. Eventually, he had retired to Sancour, where his polymath genius in the sciences had led to him holding the office of Astronomer Elect in the court of the Prefect, Baron Hecuba, whose palace lay in the north of the city. Then he had left office, in circumstances that were not entirely clear, and shortly thereafter published another work entitled *Of the Stars in the Heaven (with ephemeris)*.

This had been privately issued, and had found no audience, but Medea Betancourt had turned up a copy on a remainder stall in the Toilgate market, and brought it to Eisenhorn's attention. You must remember that Eisenhorn's small team had been in Queen Mab for over twenty years, conducting a painstaking investigation, and in that time, all manner of small evidences had been discovered, pursued and then discarded.

But the book had been unusual. Written in Low Gothic, with a parallel text in formal Enmabic, it purported to be an accurate gazette of the constellations visible from Sancour, in both northern and southern hemispheres. The details it presented, however, had very little to do with the actual facts in the night sky. Eisenhorn initially dismissed this as the work of a madman or incompetent, until Medea pointed out certain curious details, not the least of which was Dance's significant credentials as a mathematical savant, and a capable and learned observer.

To expand, our work on Sancour pursued many things, chiefly the Yellow King, but also the concept of a 'City of Dust' that lay close by, invisible, a shadow-twin of Queen Mab.

I had grown up believing the City of Dust was a myth, and if it wasn't a myth, then it was a ruined and antique place that lay somewhere beyond the Crimson Desert. But as I had become embroiled in the intrigue between Cognitae and Ordos and any manner of other factions, I had learned there was more than myth to it.

Eisenhorn said that the so-called City of Dust was an 'extimate' space, which is to say an artificial non-place, quite real, that existed outside our reality and, so to speak, overlapped the physical. So, if you might imagine, Queen Mab and its twin were simultaneous, occupying the same location, but present to each other only as ghosts. As I did, you will find this notion quite fantastical and without merit, along with Eisenhorn's insistence that he had once entered just such a place, on a world called Gershom, but I ask your indulgence, for now I too have seen it. For a brief time, during a visit to the house called Feverfugue, out beyond the dreary expanse of the city district known as Wastewater, I entered the extimate space, and saw that it was real. I was in Queen Mab and yet I was not.

The idea still alarms me. Our working theory was the Cognitae had constructed the City of Dust, just as they constructed the place on Gershom, as an occulted hiding place for the Yellow King, where he could go about his infernal work, unchallenged. Why this should be the case, or what the Yellow King Orphaeus was doing, we will come to.

For now, let me focus on Fredrik Dance. His lunatic work suggested he had somehow observed the other heavens, which is to say the star fields that shone over the City of Dust, quite contrary to those that twinkled above Queen Mab. The City of Dust, whatever it is, is virtually impossible to find or access. Many, including the dread scions of the Traitor Legions, have been trying to find a way in. My own access was quite accidental, and though we had revisited Feverfugue – now a derelict ruin – I was not able to repeat it.

Finding an access point to the City of Dust had become our priority.

So, Fredrik Dance. The mad savant-astronomer. Him we would question, and him we could not find. Since his departure from the baron's court, he had been of no fixed abode, and our search for him had been fruitless. It seemed he lodged with friends, and never stayed long in one place. We had a pictotint portrait of him, taken from the frontis of one of his more respectable works, and Harlon Nayl had conducted extensive streetwork to track his whereabouts. The same answer kept turning up: wherever he might be living was a mystery, but he had been seen regularly at Lengmur's salon, drawn, perhaps, to the society of others who shared his fringe beliefs.

Mam Tontelle's performance continued apace, and I had now scanned the premises three times.

'Only one person here even comes close to matching his description,' I whispered to Eisenhorn. 'The old fellow at the bar there.'

Eisenhorn frowned. 'Then we've wasted our night and endured this pantomime for nothing. We'll try again tomorrow, or the night after.'

'So that's not him?'

He looked at me, and raised his eyebrows with a sarcastic air. When I had first met him, Eisenhorn had claimed that his countenance was incapable of expression, but this, I had discovered, was a bluff. His almost perpetual lack of facial gesture was a matter of habit, and a conditioned desire to give nothing away.

'No, Beta,' he said.

'Because?'

'I thought you were a sharp wit,' he said. 'We're looking for an astronomer.'

'And you discount him, though he fairly matches the description, because he's blind?'

'It seems reasonable to do so.'

'A blind astronomer is not the most unlikely notion I have had to entertain since meeting you,' I said. 'I have seen words break bones, and been carried over rooftops by daemons. Just saying.'

He sighed, and turned to look again at the small man seated at the bar.

'It's not him,' he said. 'I have just scanned his thoughts. He is drunk, and of very fuddled inclination. There is no shred of science or learning in him, and the only name that circles there is Unvence.'

I sighed. 'Poor Unvence,' I said. 'He is dejected and alone. I suppose he just comes here to listen.'

'He comes here to drink,' Eisenhorn replied. 'I can hear his mind, staggering around, trying to count from memory the coins left in his pockets to calculate how many more amasecs he can purchase.'

Eisenhorn made to get up and leave. I placed my hand on his arm to stay him.

'What now?' he asked.

'Listen to her,' I hissed.

Mam Tontelle was addressing her audience again, beginning another of her fishing expeditions.

'No one?' she asked. 'The number I see is clear to me. One-one-nine. One hundred and nineteen. Oh, it is very clear. A letter too. The letter "L".'

No one responded.

'Let's go,' Eisenhorn snapped at me.

'One hundred and nineteen,' I whispered back.

He hesitated.

'No, she's just a charlatan,' he said.

'Her affect has changed,' I replied. 'Look at her.'

Mam Tontelle was trembling slightly, and looking to the crowd with some anxious hope. The pitch of her voice had altered. If this was an act, it was unexpectedly good, and had taken a strangely agitated turn that seemed unlikely to entertain the gathering.

'Is there another letter, mam?' I called out. I heard Eisenhorn growl in frustration.

Mam Tontelle turned to look at me.

'Do you know?' she asked.

She would not cold-read me.

'Another letter, mam?' I repeated.

'Yes,' she said. She swallowed hard. 'A "C". The other letter is "C".'

There had been a book, a notebook. I had borrowed it from the Blackwards emporium... I say 'borrowed', but in truth 'purloined' is a better word. It had been in my possession until I fell into Ravenor's custody. It had been small, bound in blue and handwritten in a ciphered language that no one seemed to recognise. On the inside cover had been inscribed the number '119', and it had appeared to be a commonplace book belonging to Lilean Chase, the Cognitae heretic, an individual Eisenhorn had been pursuing for more years than I had been alive.

I had never managed to crack the cipher, nor identify the number '119', which I felt might be a key to decryption.

And here was Mam Tontelle, the parlour voicer and false medium, linking that number with Lilean Chase's initials.

I glanced at Eisenhorn, and saw him settle back with a frown on his face. Whatever the fakery here, he was caught by the significance too. He saw my glance and acknowledged it with a little nod that admonished, 'Proceed – with caution.'

'Do you have a whole name, mam?' I asked.

Mam Tontelle shook her head.

'You must tell *me*, dear,' she said. She looked most uncomfortable. She kept licking her lips as though she was parched.

'I am wary of tricks,' I replied. 'To engage with your act here, I would need a name. A provenance.'

An ugly leer contorted her face, and she flushed with anger. But this was not her, I felt. It was her face responding to some alien emotion that had seized her.

'Provenance?' she hissed. 'You have provenance enough! The letters! The numbers! And here, more... A colour. Blue. A commonplace colour, I think you'll agree. What more would you have? The name cannot be spoken. Not here. Not in public company.'

Four clues now, exceeding all coincidence. The colour, the stress of the word 'commonplace'.

'Very well, mam,' I said. 'Then what is the message that you are obliged to transmit?'

'I think Mamzel Tontelle is growing tired,' said Gurlan Lengmur, stepping forward. He had an eye on the crowd, and saw the disquiet growing in his genteel establishment. 'I feel this session is now at an end.'

'I would hear the message first, sir,' I said.

Lengmur favoured me with a poisonous look.

'We have a code of decorum here, young lady,' he said. 'Mam Tontelle is becoming unwell.'

I looked past him at the voicer. Her gaze found mine. There was a blankness there, a vacancy. It was not Gleena Tontelle looking back at me.

'The message is simple,' she said. 'In the name of all that is and all that will be, *help me*. Help me, before they detect this effort to–'

Two things happened, both at once. Mam Tontelle cut off, mid-sentence, as though her throat had closed or been plugged. She gagged, and stumbled sideways into Lengmur's waiting arms.

Then the salon was bathed in light. It came from outside, on both sides of the building, shafting in through the windows that looked out onto the side lanes. To the left of the building, the light was pale green, to the right it was the hot orange of an elderly star. Both lights drifted outside, moving along the windows as though trying to peer inside.

An agitation gripped the room. People got to their feet. A few glasses were bumped over. Voices rose. The coloured ghost-lights burned in at us all, fiercely. Most present were mystified and aghast. But I felt at once that I knew what this was. Eisenhorn grabbed my wrist. He knew too.

The lights outside were graels, the abominable forces of the Eight that served the Yellow King. I had encountered one, and knew from that encounter that a grael's warping power was terrifying.

And here, upon us, were two of them.

CHAPTER 3

Unexpected opportunities

'Everyone?' cried Gurlan Lengmur. 'Let's all move, without delay, out through the dining hall, and away from this room.'

Few present needed this direction. The air had taken on a chill like a winter morning, and specks of frost twinkled on the tabletops. With a rising clamour of alarm, the patrons began to hurry towards the dining hall exit, knocking into one another in their haste.

'Stay still!' Eisenhorn ordered, rising to his feet. Movement and panic might excite and aggravate the graels, but no one heeded him. He could have stayed the whole room by the use of his will, but he refrained. Such a display, I knew, might goad the graels even more. He shouldered through the patrons flooding past him, and made to take Mam Tontelle, who was now swooning, from Lengmur's arms.

Before he could reach them, a tiny ball of orange light, like a willerwhip, flew into the room. It passed clean through the wall and circled the salon like a firefly that has flown indoors and cannot find a way out. It sped towards the stricken Mam Tontelle, struck her between the eyes, and vanished.

Mam Tontelle let out a shriek. She tore away from Lengmur's support, fell headlong across the foot-stage, and began to writhe. The strings of pearls around her throat broke, and the stones scattered, wayward, in all directions, rolling and bouncing and pattering.

Then she issued a horrible, wheezing rattle, and died. She lay, sprawled and undignified, across the edge of the foot-stage. Lengmur uttered a cry of dismay. I was on my feet, my hand on my limiter cuff, ready to switch it off. I did not know if my blankness could nullify a grael, let alone two, but I was prepared to try, if it came to it.

However, the lights outside shivered, and then faded. Their work complete, the graels departed.

'I would know, mam,' said Gurlan Lengmur, 'your name. And yours, sir.'

He had placed a tablecloth over poor Mam Tontelle. Most of his clientele had fled, and those that remained were dulled by shock, and drinking spirits to fortify their nerves.

'Violetta Flyde, sir,' I answered.

'What was this business?' he demanded. 'This malice–'

'I know nothing of it, sir,' I replied.

'She voiced to you, and you knew the business of which she spoke!'

'I knew nothing,' I said. 'I was enjoying the show, and participating in the act as you encourage people to do.'

'You dissemble!' he snapped. His fashionable coiffure had become dislodged, and he batted away unruly strands that had flopped across his face. 'You knew what this was–'

Eisenhorn loomed over him.

'She knows nothing,' he said. 'Neither of us do. We were amused by the entertainment, and engaged with it.'

Lengmur glowered at him.

'I have never known her work like that,' he said. 'Such specificity, and one *you* recognised.'

'Cold reading can fish out anything,' Eisenhorn told him. 'My wife believed the letters corresponded to the name of a maiden aunt, who died when she was one hundred and nineteen.'

'You see, then? This malevolence *does* link to you,' Lengmur exclaimed.

'But no,' I said. 'My... *dear husband* is incorrect. My aunt died aged one hundred and eighteen. We had hoped she would make the next birthday, but she did not. I admit I was taken with the poor lady's words for a moment, but the specificity was not there.'

'Let the girl be, Gurlan,' said a man as he joined us. It was the heavyset individual I had noticed earlier near the painting of the Tetrachtys. He was a bulky, slabby man, and his eyes were somewhat hooded, suggesting he had been drinking from an early hour. 'You can see she's shaken,' he said. 'And she had no part in this. No more than any present. I had a friend with those very initials, and he once lived at Parnassos 119. I'm saying it could just have easily applied to me.'

'But you didn't speak up, Oztin,' Lengmur replied.

'Because I've seen Gleena's act a dozen times, bless her toes, and I know it's all a farce,' the heavyset man replied. He looked down at the cloth-covered body, and sighed, making a half-hearted sign of the aquila. 'Poor old girl. It was ever just a parlour trick.'

'Not tonight it wasn't,' said Lengmur. He shrugged. 'This is ruination,' he said. 'The salon's reputation will be in tatters–'

'I think the reverse, in fact,' I said. 'Your customers have fled for now, but come tomorrow...'

'What are you saying?'

'I'm saying, sir, that people come to this quarter, and to your fine establishment, to taste the mysteries of the shadowed world. And, for the most part, I feel you serve nothing but mumble-jumble. Play-acts and diversions. Now, this is a tragic occurrence, but word will spread. Lengmur's will be known as the place of real mysteries and supernatural happenings. Fear won't keep customers out. Not the customers you like. It will bring them in, despite themselves, and your reputation will be enhanced.'

Lengmur stared at me.

'I would advise your suppliers to bring you food and wine in larger quantities than usual tomorrow,' I said, 'to meet with demand. You might also sell apotropaeic charms on the door, to reassure the timid, and spice your establishment with the prospect of genuine manifestation.'

Lengmur gawped. The heavyset man bellowed with laughter.

'I like this young lady!' he chuckled. 'She's not wrong, and she has a canny grasp of your business. Apotropaeic charms indeed! Now that's the thinking of a true promoter. A killing to be made from a killing, yes?'

He laughed again, a rich, booming laugh. Lengmur scowled.

'You're obnoxious as always, Oztin,' he said. 'I can have you barred.'

'Again?' the heavy man asked.

Lengmur turned smartly, and stalked off. 'The Magistratum has been summoned,' he declared over his shoulder. 'I must await their arrival.'

'Well, that's my cue to withdraw,' the big man announced. 'I've no truck with the Magistratum. We could lose the night answering questions.'

'Especially with your reputation,' I said. He grinned, and held out his hand.

'My fame precedes me, does it?' he asked.

'It does, Mr Crookley,' I replied, shaking his hand. I had known it the moment Lengmur had used the name Oztin. This was the infamous poet-rake. My earlier identification had been correct.

'I know a place down the street,' he said. 'If you'd care to join me, and avoid the impertinent fuss?'

I looked at Eisenhorn.

'My apologies, sir,' Crookley said, holding out his hand to Eisenhorn. 'I meant you both. Oztin Crookley.'

'Daesum Flyde,' Eisenhorn replied, accepting the handshake.

'Will you join me?' Crookley asked.

Eisenhorn nodded.

'I have no wish to be here any longer,' he said. I was sure he did wish to stay, but the imminent arrival of the Magistratum would be an inconvenience.

'Excellent,' Crookley declared. 'We'll all go together.' He turned, and raised his voice to the clientele nearby. 'We're repairing to the Two Gogs. Are you coming? Aulay? Unvence?'

'I'll come, if you're paying,' said the man with the ink-stained hands I had before taken to be a rubricator.

'Unvence?' Crookley called. The elderly man with the gangling arms and legs stood up and nodded. Eisenhorn and I exchanged quick looks.

'That's Unvence?' I asked.

'Yes,' said Crookley. 'Lynel Unvence. You know him?'

'No,' I answered. 'I just thought the blind fellow sitting beside him was Unvence.'

Crookley shook his head.

'Him?' he said. 'No, that's his mad friend Freddy. Freddy Dance.'

CHAPTER 4

A conversation

My mentor and I had achieved our evening's objective, that of locating the missing astronomer. I wondered if it might be time to lie low again, but Eisenhorn intended to press on. He believed the night might yet have more to reveal.

As we followed Crookley's stragglers, a rowdy band, down the street to the Two Gogs, Eisenhorn sent quick psykanic messages to the rest of the team, all of whom were close at hand and shadowing us. To Nayl, Medea and the lurking Deathrow, he issued instructions to stay on us and identify Fredrik Dance, who was with Unvence in Crookley's company. He was to be watched from this point on, and tracked so that we might question him later. To the daemonhost, he sent an order of collection, which I did not fully understand until later.

Then we walked, following Crookley's revellers, but held back so we would not be overheard.

'Is there more to be learned?' I asked.

'I doubt it, but we'll stay with Dance until Nayl and the others confirm acquisition,' he replied. 'It'll be useful to make a friend of Crookley, I think. He knows everyone in these circles, and can open doors we might find barred to us.'

'Do you mean "friend"?' I asked.

'Euphemistically,' he replied.

'Ah,' I said. 'Because I didn't think you made friends.'

'I make them well enough,' he replied. 'I just don't seem to be able to keep them. Watch Crookley. He's odious and dissolute. His mind is a lascivious mire. But he might be useful.'

'Does he know anything of the King?' I asked him.

'No more than any of them,' Eisenhorn replied. 'I read the name in his thoughts, and in the thoughts of his entourage. But the King in Yellow, King Orphaeus, is a local myth. I doubt there's a soul in the city who hasn't heard the term at some point. It's folklore to them. They do not consider it real in any way. Crookley and his hangers-on are far more interested in the half-baked esoterica they meet to discuss, imagining themselves illuminated initiates of secret lore.'

'What's this with Unvence and Dance?' I asked. 'It's not like you to read incorrectly.'

'I can't explain it,' said Eisenhorn. 'Perhaps my insight was fogged and confused. Some psi-field precursing the graels.'

'And there's the real thing,' I said. 'Two graels. Right upon us. How did they find us?'

'They didn't. They found the voicer, to silence her. We weren't their quarry, which is why we're still intact.'

'But she was a hoaxer. Surely–'

'I agree, Mam Tontelle had little or no psykana in her.' There was a puzzled look upon his face that I found unsettling, and his eyes flashed violet. 'Perhaps just enough to make a career from her fakery. No, Beta, that was possession. Something jumped into her. It used the vantage of her compliant mind to speak to us.'

'To us?' I asked.

'Lengmur was right about the specificity. Those details were offered up, and only a few would know them. You, most of all. They were given to prove the veracity of the message.'

'Which was never completed.'

'The graels shut down her voice,' he agreed, 'but it was a message for us.'

'A request for help? From whom?'

'I don't know,' he said.

'Lilean Chase?'

'Don't be foolish.'

'Then Balthus Blackwards, if he lives yet? Or perhaps his family? He knew the particulars of the book.'

'Perhaps.'

'But why?' I asked. 'He's no friend of mine.'

'Unless you mean it euphemistically, there are no friends here,' he said. 'No clear enemies either. Everyone is neither or both.'

'This much I realise from being in your company.'

He looked at me as if I had scolded him, or wounded him somehow. If you have not met Gregor Eisenhorn, and I can think of no sane reason why you would have, it is perhaps difficult to picture him. I don't mean the look of him, for that is straightforward: a strikingly tall man of powerful build, despite the fact he has been ravaged by age and injury. He wears, most times as that night, a long, heavy coat. His back and legs are braced by augmetic frames of metal, and there are other signs, such as neural plugs that reach up from under his collar and insert into the base of his skull, that he has weathered much. He never told me how he came by these injuries, or if they occurred all in one dire moment or were the accumulated results of a long life walking a dark path. I suspect the latter.

I mean more his demeanour. He is frightening, and intimidating in the size of him, but there is often a melancholy that laces his grim, obsessive deportment. More than once, I felt sorry for him. Sorry that he had to be him. Whether by choice or happenstance, he had committed to a life that would never set him free.

I have known him laugh, usually in the company of Nayl or Medea. It was rare, but it happened. Medea told me, confidentially, that since the mission to Gershom twenty years before, he had been able to smile sometimes, something he hadn't been able to do for many years. She implied this was due to the correction of some neurological palsy, a paralysis, but I sensed there was more to it than that. Something happened to him on Gershom, a world quite far away. Something that made his eyes gleam with that odd violet hue.

I don't know what this 'thing' was. Again, the truth was veiled from me, and only alluded to. But it set him on his path to Sancour. He was already chasing the Cognitae by then – he had been for years – but

Gershom narrowed his focus. Whatever transpired there located for him the hiding place of the King in Yellow, and threaded together the bare elements that we knew: the King, the City of Dust, the eudaemonic forces of the graels that served the King as familiars, known as the Eight; Enuncia, and the connections to Chase, the Cognitae, and their infernal works of extimate engineering.

It also led him to me. It was by then clear that the forces ranged against us believed nulls, such as myself (which is to say untouchables or 'blanks', who are naturally psi-inert), to be vital instruments in whatever Great Work they were engaged upon. The Cognitae indeed, under the guise of the Maze Undue, had reared a whole school of them.

But I was clearly more than just one of these instruments. Eisenhorn had learned of me, on Gershom, before I was ever born. He had come to find me and, I think, protect me. I was, it had been confirmed, the clone or cloned daughter of a dead woman also called Alizebeth Bequin. She had been a null too, and had served with Eisenhorn. Medea implied they had been especially close, perhaps even in love, if such a human concept had any meaning to a man as generally inhuman and closed as him. Eisenhorn had a mission to complete on Sancour, perhaps the last and greatest of his life, and I was part of that, but I was also a second mission. He intended to watch over me, not because I was part of the Great Work, but because I was me.

I reflected earlier in this narrative on why I had chosen to side with him at this time, when there were many good reasons not to, not the least being the company of daemons and Traitor Astartes that he kept. This was it. He cared for me. Others did: Medea, poor Lightburn, and perhaps Nayl. But Eisenhorn cared for nothing and no one except his duty, so this spark of humanity seemed more significant, more true.

I wondered if it was because I reminded him of his lost Alizebeth, for many had remarked how like her I was. Sometimes I even wondered if he felt I was somehow a surrogate daughter. There was no other bond of affection between us. I am as certain as the sky is blue that he did not see me as a substitute for his lost love, his Alizebeth miraculously reborn and returned to him. There was never anything like that. I suppose, for a time, he was the closest thing to an actual father I had ever had, though the distance between him and an actual father was somewhat further than the distance between Sancour and Holy Terra.

My brief meeting with the man Ravenor had added one more piece to the puzzle of Sancour. He claimed the King in Yellow was trying to rebuild the lost language of power known as Enuncia. This language was something Ravenor had spent most of *his* career pursuing. The King wanted Enuncia so it could allow him to govern the very operation of the Universal Reality. And, most particularly, he wanted to learn a single word that would grant him unrivalled power: the one, true name of the God-Emperor of Mankind.

Sometimes, I wondered if the curious text, handwritten in the commonplace book, the one mentioned by the late Mam Tontelle, was some glyphic representation of Enuncia, though it did not resemble any other written traces of that language known to us. I wondered if it was an encrypted form of Enuncia, and if it in fact hid, within itself, that singular, authentic name of the Imperial Majesty.

'What are you thinking?' Eisenhorn asked me.

'Idle thoughts,' I replied.

'No room for those,' he said. 'Whoever used Mam Tontelle so cruelly was a psyker, or had a psyker in their employ. We–'

'What about Ravenor?' I asked. 'You said he was a psyker of near-unmatched power, and he hunts for you.'

'Not him,' he said.

'Not to draw you out? He has Chase's commonplace book now. He knows the details enough to use them. He–'

'You think that was a trick, then?' he asked. 'An attempt to lure me out?'

'Could it not have been?' I asked.

'No,' he said firmly. 'Such scheming is beneath him. I know him well.'

'Do you really, though?'

'Yes,' he said. 'He was my pupil.'

'Ah,' I said, for there was nothing more I could say to that.

'Gideon knows to stay out of my way and leave me alone,' he said. 'For if our paths cross, that will be the end. He is sworn to burn me, and I will not submit. If he chose... *when he chooses*... to move against me, it will be direct and bloody. It will not involve games and tricks.'

'Good to know,' I said.

'If the graels were sent to stop Mam Tontelle delivering her message,' I added as an afterthought, 'it suggests the message was of genuine import. That it was not a trick to beguile us, but a true thing they didn't want us to hear.'

'Or anyone to hear,' he replied.

'But the message was for us,' I said, smiling. 'You said so.'

'Violetta! Daesum! Hurry along!' Crookley called to us, laughing the while. 'We're there!'

We had arrived at the Two Gogs.

CHAPTER 5

Which is of numbers

The Two Gogs was a drinking hall two streets from the salon, a shabby corner building at the bend of Feygate Road where it became Little Heckaty Street. Perhaps you have passed it, if you have paid a visit to Queen Mab?

More properly *The Yagoch and Magoch*, it is named after the mythic daemon giants who sundered the primordial void and split materium from immaterium, and its doorway is overmounted by two figures of carved fepen wood, portraits of the twin brutes entwined and roaring. These figures, something of a local landmark, are repainted regularly to protect the ageing wood from the elements, though evidently this is done with whatever surplus paint is to hand at the time. That night, they were, for the most part, a lurid green, familiar from infirmary wards, their limbs and beaks the stale blue of barge-hull undercoat, and their talons, teeth and buckled chainmail a caustic yellow. In truth, I cannot think of anything that would ever be painted that colour for there to be any paint left over.

Perhaps a madman king?

They had held weapons once, to beat each other with, or at least something raised in their hands, but these objects are long gone to decay and vandalism. Yagoch clutched a wreath of dead flowers stolen from some city cenotaph, and Magoch held up a battered hat that had probably been tossed there for sport. It looked as though he was welcoming us in with a strenuous wave of his cap.

We entered. The place was not busy, and smelled strongly of spilled ale and unbathed bodies. Oztin Crookley, who clearly loved to be the centre of all things, loudly hailed the staff in overfamiliar terms, and roused them to bring refreshment for all those in his train.

We took tables, and conversations begun in the street became louder and more animated. As at Lengmur's salon, I took a moment to mark the room. At a side bar, I saw a large man flirting with two waiting staff. His back was turned, but I knew it was Harlon Nayl. He was in place already, and I knew he knew we had come in.

My attention turned to the rest of the party, Crookley's 'gang', an ill-assorted bunch of almost twenty, who evidently hung around him like a fan club retinue, delighting in his every word and basking in the tarnished glory of his celebrity. I do not know what he was more famous for, his verse, some of which, I admit, was very fine, or his scandalous reputation for debauchery, bedding anything that moved, consorting with dubious types, and proclaiming himself a master – a *magus*, no less – of occult practice.

He was no disciple of Chaos, though he prided himself on his wicked reputation as a charismatic rake. He was nearing his dotage by then, overweight, alcoholic, his mind and health ruined by decades of substance abuse. He seemed to me a man determined to prove he still had potency in all things, when those things in actuality had long since decayed. He clung to the idea of what he used to be, intent on never letting go.

In this, I am ashamed to say, he reminded me of Eisenhorn.

As to the others, most were of no consequence: sycophants and hangers-on, or merely dypsomaniac chancers who knew from experience that if Crookley was around, the drink would flow.

But some were of interest. Aulay, the ink-stained engraver, was a quiet soul, whose work had made him very famous. His attire showed that his career had rendered him prosperous, but his hands shook, and it was clear he was a hopeless lush. His role was as Crookley's partner in crime, a duty he undertook with reasonable patience. I think Crookley kept him around because he liked to be seen in the company of famous men, but also because Aulay was boundlessly wealthy and could underwrite most evenings out of his own pocket. For Aulay's part, I think he simply disliked drinking alone.

Then there was Timurlin, who was – for he told everyone several times – 'the' Connort Timurlin, a concert clavierist of great merit. He played the edge of the table like the keys of his instrument. He was a young man, the very same young man, I realised, in pinstriped suit and over-robe I had seen in altercation with the woman in the rust-coloured gown at Lengmur's.

Near him sat Mam Matichek, a tutor and linguist from the Academy Hecula. She was a stern, vulpine woman, who had once been a great beauty, and retained a haunted glamour in her declining years. Whether by choice or a lack of income, she had never elected for juvenat work. I took her to be at least sixty years old, and her expressive face wore its lines well, like a diagram of her excessive youthful beauty. Nor did she colour her hair, but left it – in a long bob – the colour of first frost on dead winter grass. She dressed in black crepe and lace gloves, and lacked a smile of any kind. She smoked lho-sticks in a silver pinch-holder, and was prone to correcting, without warning, the grammar of those around her. When Crookley held forth on the initiatic path that had led him to the level of magus – apparently a long and penitential pilgrimage into the Crimson Desert, where the daemon simurghs of the Herrat came to him and bestowed the gifts of nekuomanteia, pharmaka, mageia and goteia – Mam Matichek chided him that the simurghs should use Eleniki terms rather than Enmabic words, and wondered too why they mixed this with the Chaldean term *makus* – for magus – and, further to this, puzzled that the entities of the warp should be so fluent in the dead languages of Terra, languages that were dust before even Old Night.

'Did they not have languages of their own, these daemons?' she asked.

'They did, mam!' Crookley laughed. 'But not any I knew! Nor had they the inclination to teach me, nor I the mouth to speak them!'

'So, Oztin,' she remarked, 'you were fluent in Eleniki and Old Chaldean *before* you went into the desert?'

'Oh, dearest Aelsa,' Crookley cried out, amused, 'do you not like a good story?'

'I delight in them, sir,' she replied. 'I just wonder why Sancour is such a reef of shipwrecks. It seems to me that more debris, more pieces of old, old Terra, wash up here and mingle all together than in any other corner of the great Imperium. It is as though we are the high water mark, and the Current of Time sweeps all the litter of the past in and heaps it here for us to pick at.'

And, of course, there was Fredrik Dance, the object of our interest. He spoke very little, no matter the rowdy talk around him, and seemed at ease in his own thoughts, provided there was a drink in his grip. The elderly man with the spider-long limbs sat at his side. This, as we had learned, was Lynel Unvence, a senior clerk with the Helican Shipping Line. I did not know that existed still, or that anything was ever shipped anywhere.

In the salon, though they had sat side by side at the bar, they had not acknowledged each other, but in the Two Gogs there was some kind of relationship, even if it didn't match what Crookley had described as 'friends'. Unvence made sure Dance was supplied with drinks, and even seemed to be listening to him, though I never saw Dance speak at all. Sometimes, Unvence adjusted his silver pince-nez, and scribbled something in his notebook, quite as though Dance had said something worth noting.

+Interesting.+

Eisenhorn hissed into my mind on the most confidential level of psykana. I raised my eyebrows.

+This Unvence. Now I understand it. He's a psyker. Low level, and of a very specific type.+

'Really?' I whispered, raising my chipped glass of joiliq to hide my response.

+Type D-theta-D, as the Ordos notate it on the standard Gaumonic Scale. Passive and singular.+

'Like one of Mam Matichek's grammatical rules?' I murmured.

+No. It means he can read, but not send. And specifically from only one mind at a time. It's rare. Very limited. He can't hear me now, for example, nor the minds of any others around. His focus is entirely on Dance. He's listening to his mind. Reading it. The relationship is odd, almost symbiotic. Unvence is Dance's eyes and mouth. He... writes down what Dance is thinking, like a stenographist. It would not surprise me to learn that Unvence wrote the mad book of stars for Dance, taking dictation.+

'And what is the blind astronomer thinking now?' I asked very quietly.

+I can't say. Unvence is so locked to Dance's mind, it's closed. A private conversation. That's strong for a D-theta-D. It suggests a long familiarity, almost a dependence.+

'Well,' I whispered, 'let's find out what they're saying.'

Eisenhorn looked at me sharply.

'I hear you work in shipping,' I said, leaning forward to Unvence. Down the table, most of the party were hanging on the details of Crookley's latest smutty tale, which he had stood up to deliver.

'I do, mam,' Unvence replied. 'It is dull work, I'm sure a fine young lady like you would find it very tedious to relate.'

'I find shiftships most exhilarating,' I replied. 'To go beyond this world, to reach other stars...'

'Well,' he said, 'my work is mainly in manifests, for cargo, you see. It is just pen-pushing. I have never left Sancour myself, though I have seen shiftships in the docks and at high anchor.'

'They must be very splendid things,' I said.

'You are the lady who spoke,' said Fredrik Dance suddenly. He cocked his head my way, though his eyes remained as unseeing as ever. 'You spoke to Mam Tontelle during her voicing.'

'I did,' I said.

'Yes, I know your voice. She's dead, I hear. Just dropped dead.'

'Sadly true, sir,' I said.

'She hooked you with a number,' said Dance. 'One-one-nine. One hundred and nineteen. An interesting number. I thought that at the time. A natural number, of course, semiprime, surprisingly large totient. The sum of five consecutive primes.'

'Really?' I said.

'Yes. Seventeen plus nineteen plus twenty-three plus twenty-nine plus thirty-one. It is the fourth number in the Shepralon Sequence, and the smallest composite number that is one less than a factorial. It–'

'Oh, hush now, Freddy,' said Unvence, placing a caring hand over Dance's wrist. But Freddy Dance was in the mood to talk.

'One hundred and nineteen is the order of the largest cyclic subgroup in the Benchian Master Group,' he went on, 'and also the midpoint in the Leukamiss Scale. It is the number of stars in the constellation Antiko, and the angle, in degrees, of Sycax at Midwinter sunrise. It is the number of steps in the tower of Saint Zoroast, and the number of rail posts on the western side of the Parnassos Bridge. It was the tail number of the Thunderbolt flown at Iprus Defile by Commander Dorian Cazlo, during the Fifth Orphaeonic. His wingman, Vieve Laratt, made one hundred and nineteen kills during that campaign. It is the number given to Phantasmagor in Clinides' *Bestiarie Of All Daemonkind*. It is the age your aunt would have reached, had she seen another birthday. Is she dead?'

'My aunt?' I asked.

'No, Mam Tontelle.'

'She is, I'm afraid.'

'"L" and "C"... those were the letters that followed. I wonder–'

'I wonder too, sir,' I said. 'You are a man of numbers. How might you employ one-one-nine as a key in, say, a written cipher?'

CHAPTER 6

A private matter

A great storm rolled down onto Queen Mab during the week that followed, a beast that lumbered in from the mountains, and whipped at the city for days with its gales, rattling the shutters and making the weathervanes spin. We kept to ourselves at the house called Bifrost, which had become our lair, of sorts. Eisenhorn and I had parted company with Crookley's coterie that night at the Two Gogs on good terms, with a promise to revisit, and I had established a bond with Freddy Dance. He seemed intrigued by the problem of a cipher key, and promised to think about it if I cared to return and visit him. Unvence seemed wary, but admitted it would do his friend good to have a puzzle to occupy his mind. Despite the gales, Eisenhorn set Nayl and Deathrow the task of surveilling Dance, to learn his habits and frequencies. They were not to let him out of their sight.

Bifrost stood in the Talltown district, west of Feygate, its fine mansions and hab blocks degraded by the fumes of the Farek Tang manufactories nearby. The house was a fine place of great size with room enough for a roof dock to house Medea's gun-cutter. I think it had once been a habitation block for many families. Entire floors of it, at one time fine apartments, stood empty. Nayl had made the place secure with extensive autodefences, and Eisenhorn had warded it inside and out with protective hypersigils. I felt safe there, as safe as anywhere.

But it was not a friendly place. It was spare and serviceable, and lacked personality. It was never a home. It felt like a hotel, which we might vacate at short notice and without regret. Eisenhorn, I guessed, never made a home anywhere for long, and was always ready to cut his losses and run.

I thought, as I waited out the storm in Bifrost's cheerless interior, of Mam Matichek and her comment about Sancour being like a junk room of Old Terra, an attic where such a curious melange of oddments had wound up. I had no experience of worlds beyond Sancour, but both Medea and Eisenhorn had separately remarked on this quality. There were remarkable survivals here, all thrown together, both as word memory and physical artefact, so much of Old Earth and mankind's beginning, as if Sancour was a drain around which human culture's dirt had circled and lodged. I knew that Bifrost was a name from ancient Terran myth, the Yggscandik legends, and referred to a bridge between realms, a bridge that spanned the void between the material world and a divine kingdom. This struck me as odd, for it described the very thing we were seeking. I wondered if Bifrost might, of all strange coincidences, be a door or a bridge to the City of Dust. I looked to find out, but was quickly disappointed. As with all things in Queen Mab, including me, nothing matched its name. The truth was writ in flaking paint across the loading dock behind the house: 'Bi[*ochemical*] Fr[*aternity*] O[*f*] S[*outh*] T[*alltown*]'. The name was made from the letters left visible on the wall.

'How will you test Mr Dance's key, if he makes one for you?' Medea asked me. She had just brought me caffeine and sweet, baked rodas for breakfast. She was wearing a simple white shift and trousers, but her hands were as ever clad in red gloves. There was a smudge of powdered sugar on the dark skin of her cheek. Rain rippled down the tall windows, making the light shift as though we were behind a waterfall. It was very early, still dark, three days after the night at Lengmur's and the Two Gogs. I was not sleeping long or well, because of the dark, oozing dreams.

I showed her, opening a notebook I had purchased the day before.

'You wrote this from memory?' she asked as she read.

I had. My memory is good, if not quite the eidetic skill of old Mentor Murlees at the Maze Undue, but he had taught me tricks of recollection and recomposition. I had studied the commonplace book extensively while it had been in my possession, and had managed to reproduce a fair copy of the first few pages, though I did not know any of the characters I was making. I had shown them to Eisenhorn, thinking that perhaps he might recognise them. They seemed, in part, to be numeric, and I fancied they might relate to binaric, the data-cant used by the mysterious Adeptus Mechanicus, but Eisenhorn assured me they resembled no binaric script he had ever seen, nor any language he knew of.

'I'll show these to Mr Dance,' I said, 'and see if he can make sense of them.'

Medea pursed her lips and nodded.

'And if he can?' she asked. 'If he devises a key that works? Will you write out the rest from memory?'

'Oh no,' I said. 'That's beyond my skills. This is all I can manage.'

'So then?'

'So then if he *can* decrypt them, we'll need the original.'

Medea looked at me with mischief.

'And how, my dear Beta, might we get hold of that?'

I shrugged. 'The way I got it in the first place,' I said. 'I'll steal it.'

'From Gideon?'

I nodded.

'I think you're capable of great deeds, Beta, but that sounds unlikely.'

'I don't know,' I said. 'Perhaps it's time I escaped the clutches of the cruel heretic and his minions who keep me imprisoned here, and fled back to the safety of the brave inquisitor who offered me salvation.'

Medea laughed. I had always liked her laugh.

'You would double on him?' she asked. 'Make pretence of turning loyalties?'

'What is loyalty in this city?' I asked. 'Besides, it would be just another function. The playing of a role. I've done many, and I'm trained for it.'

Medea shook her head. 'Gideon would see through it in a second,' she said. 'He'd read it.'

'Not in the mind of a null he wouldn't,' I replied.

She thought about this. I took a bite from a piping hot roda.

'Do not,' she said, 'attempt this. Not without consulting me or Gregor first.'

When she had gone, I went to the rack and took down weapons – a salinter and a cutro – to drill for a while.

'You are so like your other, little thing,' said Cherubael.

I turned and saw him. I think he might have been there all along. He was hovering, adrift, in the corner of the room with chains trailing from his twisted ankles, like a child's lost balloon. He made a small and constant sound, a faint fizzing hum, like a fluorescent vapour bulb whose starter is beginning to burn out.

'You mean my mother?' I asked.

'I know what I mean,' he said. 'Mother, other, what you will. You are brave and you are reckless, just like her. I liked her.'

He grinned down at me, but then he always grinned. I don't believe his stretched face could relax.

'Did she like you?' I asked, making practice swings in the air with the cutro.

'Of course not,' he said. 'No one likes me.'

His hanging chains shivered slightly.

'Do you need something?' I asked.

'Many things,' he said. 'Things no one can give me. Freedom. Peace. Release. Liberty. A fresh-baked roda.'

'You can have a roda,' I said, gesturing to the plate Medea had left.

Cherubael patted his tattooed, washboard belly with a taloned hand, and shook his head.

'They don't agree with me,' he said. 'Not with my... present constitution. The butter in the pastry flake gives me wind.'

'Well, that would make you truly awful,' I said.

'I know.'

'Then... you are unoccupied?' I asked, setting down the cutro and trying the salinter instead.

'Yes,' he said, drifting slightly. 'I wait. Always wait. It is my lot. I wait for instructions, for tasks. I wait to be summoned and used. Meantimes, I drift and think.'

'Of what?'

'You don't want to know, little thing.'

'You're saying you're bored, then?' I asked.

'Always,' he purred. 'I have been bored forever. I have no idea how your kind wastes so much time given the brief spans of life allotted to you. Me, I'm always busy, always doing this and that. When I was free, I mean. When my time and bidding was my own.'

'Well, I'm sorry to hear that,' I told him.

'I know.'

I heard the chains shiver again, and saw him turn slowly to drift out of the room, a child's lost balloon caught in a draught.

'Goodbye then,' I said.

He paused and looked back at me. I knew he was an infinitely dangerous entity, though in our company he was regarded more as a strange pet. Both Medea and Harlon had intimated that, following the mission to Gershom, Eisenhorn's command of Cherubael had become absolute, as though the daemonhost was entirely constrained by the inquisitor's will. His apparent timidity made it easy to forget what a horror he was.

'Oh,' he said. 'I remember something. I saw your man.'

'My man?'

'The other day when I was loose abroad on an errand. I saw him on the steps of Saint Nodens' Undercroft in Ropeburn.'

'What man do you mean, Cherubael?'

He raised his right hand, and waved it with slow distraction.

'The man. Your man. I'm not good at names. Render, is it?'

'Renner? Renner Lightburn?'

'That's it,' he said. 'The Curst boy. He begs there now. It's become his patch. Poor fellow, with all his woes. I feel he is more damned than I am.'

He looked at me. His eyes flashed.

'That was a joke,' he said.

'I know,' I said. 'You're nearly getting the hang of them.'

'Practice,' he replied. 'I've got plenty of time. Anyway, I thought you'd want to know. You were looking for him, weren't you?'

'Is he there still?' I asked.

'Now, you mean?'

'Yes, daemonhost.'

He tilted his head thoughtfully, and sniffed the air.

'Yes,' he said.

* * *

The gale had not eased, and rain was still washing the streets when I went out. It was early still. I told Medea where I was going, that a sighting had been made of Lightburn.

She sighed. I could tell she thought it a bad idea to renew contact, but she also knew I was set upon it. She told me to be back by midnight.

'What's happening then?' I asked.

'With luck, some answers,' she replied.

I walked as far as Alohim Court, glad of my hooded overcloak. The rain was fierce, and the wind was lifting litter and tossing it about. Shutters banged on their hinges, and the signs of emporia squealed as they swung to and fro on their chains. The businesses were shut, and the streets were empty. It was past dawn, but the storm had cast the town like twilight, and the gloom refused to lift. This should have been the hour when the city woke up, emporia opened their doors, eating halls clattered with the bustle of breakfast service, and people shuffled off to work or devotion. I fancied that, for yet another day, the gales would keep citizens indoors, and most businesses closed for the duration.

I had hoped to hail a fly at Alohim Court, but none were around, and the stand on the west side of the drenched square was vacant. The cabmen, lacking fares because of the weather, had retreated to the stable depot with their traps and flies and hansoms to brew caffeine, sit around the braziers and complain about lost income.

Instead, I crossed beneath the viaduct at Hearthill Rise, braved the narrow lanes there with my head down, and reached the top of the Ropeburn Quarter in time to catch a tram down the hill of the avenue. The tramcar was as old as any in the city, painted blue and white, and strapped in bare brass. Its hinged pantograph collected voltaic power from the overhead lines, and somewhat spat and fizzled in the heavy rain. Inside, it was warm, and lit by lumen hoods above the seat backs. It should have been a busy commuter trolley, but I was one of only two or three passengers, all sodden and sorry for themselves, and the grumpy conductor didn't speak as he took my coin and ratcheted a ticket from his machine.

I watched the dead, black city go by through a window distorted by raindrops. The tram moaned and hummed its way with a slowly rising, slowly falling song, punctuated by the squeal of the rails.

I wondered what I would say to Renner. How do you reunite with a person who has had all his memories of you stolen?

CHAPTER 7

Upon a day like night

Of the poor breed known as the Curst, you should know they are penitents, shunned by the society of the city. They are more properly known as 'burdeners', for they each carry the burden of great sins or crimes for which the Ecclesiarchy courts have damned them. The manner of their sin is marked upon their flesh in ink, and they are banished to live in the streets, surviving on charity, in order to spend the rest of their lives making atonement. This they do by offering aid to any in need, without thought for their own safety, so to defray their burdens. They may also take on the sins and crimes of others, absolving those persons of their wrongs. This does not damn the Curst further: the moral value of sparing another man from sin counts for more.

In truth, this means they can become little more than unpaid mercenaries, for the greater the wrong they take on, the greater the redemption. They will, it is reckoned, do almost anything for anyone.

Renner Lightburn had done much for me. He came upon me when I was in plight, and did his best to protect me. His own crime, when he finally confessed it to me, was the ill-judged act of defending a latent psyker, a young girl, from the temple hierarchs. In me, a latent *anti-psyker*, he saw some agreeable symmetry, as if my salvation would out-balance his original sin.

I later learned he had been set upon this duty by Mam Mordaunt, the headmistress of the Maze Undue, who I now believe to be an agent of the Cognitae. Renner had no idea – nor would he have truly cared – that he was working on behalf of darker forces, though in truth it was later revealed that the Mam Mordaunt who had engaged him was not *the* Mam Mordaunt, but in fact an agent of the inquisitor Ravenor, posing as her. Having delivered me to Ravenor, Lightburn's memories had been expunged, and he was returned to the city streets.

No matter his original crime (which, I must say, I had much sympathy for), he did not deserve this. Curst or not, he had been staunch and valiant. I had been concerned for his welfare since. And I wanted to thank him for his duty personally, for we had been parted abruptly.

With this course in mind, I crossed the wide boulevard of Ropeburn in the sheeting rain, and approached the undercroft of Saint Nodens'.

The temple is old, dark and very plain, like a towered bunker of the Munitorum, and on this day, the bulk of it could scarcely be picked out against the blackness of the heavens. There was a wide, paved court before it where beggars normally gathered, but this area was empty, aside from a few discarded blanket rags, and the sousing rain plashed everywhere with such force it threw spray back up into the air. I spied a figure in the entrance arch, fighting in the wind to secure the donation boxes before they could be carried off to tumble down the street. It was a deacon of the temple, who told me beggars and Curst had been seen in the yard, but several days of storm had driven them off, in search of shelter. He suggested I tried the arches beneath the viaduct, or perhaps the almshouse that occupied part of the precinct's undercroft. I could tell he was baffled as to the reason for my enquiry.

The almshouse lay down some stone steps to the side of the court. It was little more than a soup kitchen, and stank of boiled cabbage. An almoner and his novice helper were making some thin breakfast in the dank interior, and the place was crowded with destitute souls, who had come there as much to be out of the gale and rain as to get a bowl of food.

I was by then wet to the bone, and so dishevelled I passed for a street wretch myself. I asked the almoner if he had seen any of the Curst that day, and he replied he had seen some, but did not recognise Lightburn from my description. To him, I think, all Curst and vagabonds were alike, and passed him by in the soup line without him remarking on any of them.

Lightburn was not there. I wondered if Cherubael had lied to me, or if he had been pranking me, sending me out into the storm on a fool's errand. But he had never shown me any malice – an odd thing to say, I know, when speaking of a daemon – so it seemed strange that he would make wilful mischief for me.

I spoke instead to some of the paupers and ruffians. Several had seen Curst that morning, and two thought they knew Lightburn from my talk of him. The outcast of Queen Mab do not see each other as anonymous and uniform, though I feel this had more to do with their constant wariness of strangers, potential dangers, and outsiders encroaching on their patches.

'A man come in,' said one. 'He was a Curst himself, and he took them away. Early this day, it was.'

'Took them away?' I asked.

'He come in every few days, offers coin or food to those who will help him in his burden. Some take him up, some don't.'

'How do they help him?' I asked.

'I think,' said another, 'that they fight for him. For them as come back are often cut or bloody. That's why I never gone.'

I knew that fight rings existed in the city, illegal bouts for wager and sport. It did not surprise me that those used for this underground vice were recruited – for a few paltry coins or a crust of bread – from the beggars and the Curst. The city has a dark core, and it is distressing to encounter proof of its meagre-hearted cruelty.

'Where do they go?' I asked.

'Down the bonehall, so it's said.'

The bonehall was the Ossuary of St Belpheg, a catacomb where the bones of the dead from the Orphaeonic War were stacked like kindling. It lay across the temple pavement beneath the bell tower and the Old Burn Wall, and by the time I reached it, even though I ran, I was soaked through, yet again. The storm seemed quite committed to drowning the city in water and gloom.

There was a small gate, which I passed through, and beyond, a narrow hall, quite plunged in darkness, which stank of damp. Through sad archways to either side, I could discern the first of the chambers in which the bones were racked, the old bones of the war dead, brave souls and cowards mingled without distinction. Thus are we all levelled in the end, so the parable says, where a life's virtue weighs no more or less than a life's unvirtue.

Beyond the stone hall, steps led down into the earth, and I groped my way. Here, mould and lichen both inhabited the walls, and where the stonework was bare, it had been polished like glass by the calcified downrun of water from the surface. This was a frontier, where the living city above ceased and became a dead and buried foundation made of crushed yesterdays. I was entering the rubble and spoil of the city's roots, the stratum of compacted ruin on which the present city stood. It was the past down here, the compressed layers of previous Queen Mabs that had been folded under, reduced to the rubble on which the city built and rebuilt itself, like a weary swimmer struggling to stay afloat. Down here were the broken things, the things that no one needed or wanted or remembered any more. I fancied that down here might be found all the things that had ever been lost, and all the things that had ever been forgotten. Down here was where they slipped and fell, and lay hidden from the day.

I hoped Lightburn might be one of them.

Each flight of the steps showed me shadowed galleries of the bone-hall, where bundles of long bones were heaped on stone shelves, and skulls, tobacco-brown, sat watching on ledges. The darkness was enveloping, and water ran from the ceiling in many places, for the rain finds its way down into the darkness just as surely as things forgotten. I wondered how much longer it would have to rain before these stone cavities began to fill.

I came to another crypt tunnel, which I followed. There was no one around, but the iron covers of the lanterns along the wall were still warm to the touch, as if they had been not long put out. There was a smell of tallow, of gutter-smoke, and also the cold scent of 'roma, that heady blend of lho that was now so popular a vice.

Presently, I heard voices. I tucked myself against the deepest shadows of the wall, and peered into the blue gloom. I had apprehension, certainly. I also had a quad-snub fastened in a holster under my coat, and spare shells in my belt. Harlon Nayl, whose life had taught him such things, had insisted that none of us go abroad beyond the walls of Bifrost unarmed.

In a chamber not far on, there were some seven or eight persons, chatting to each other as they closed their business for the day. One, an elder officer of the watch by his uniform coat, was hooking a glow-globe to a pole, so as to light his comrades' way back to the surface now the lanterns were out. By the globe's sallow glare, I saw the others: a vagabond woman in an apron, gathering together a box of herb-salves and bandages, and brown-ply aid kits that had surely been stolen from some medicae office; another woman, older and folded in a threadbare shawl, who was tossing items into a battered metal pail; two men of the roughest disposition, who were collecting up old billhooks, short-blades, cudgels and such, and returning them to a large dresser-cupboard that had clearly once stood grandly in some monastic prefectory for the storage of surplices, candles and altar-cloths. A third man, little more than a youth, was wiping chalkboards fixed to the wall, to clear what was writ upon them, while a fourth, an elderly fellow, had placed himself on a nursing stool, and was assisting his comrades by means of strenuous advice and instruction. This old fellow was a veteran, and still wore his patched Militarum greatcoat. His voice was thick with the phlegmy cough and rattle of a 'romatik, and he was filling a clay pipe with more of the pungent weed.

A final soul, a tall and surly burdener by his sleeves of tattooed sins, was occupied with the chaining up of a gate of iron bars.

'Am I too late for the sport?' I asked in street Mabiçoise, stepping into the lamplight.

They all looked at me in surprise, and some measure of unfriendliness.

'You sho'n't be here, missy,' said the older woman.

'This is no place for you,' agreed the old soldier, turning on his stool to fix me with a mean stare. 'Be on.' His eyes were glazed drowsy from the 'roma he had partaken of.

I saw the tall burdener stiffen, and reach his hand behind his hip, surely to rest upon some weapon. He was the one I would need to watch.

'But I wish to have a wager,' I said, all innocence. 'Is this not where the sport is done?'

'Yes, but it's done already,' said the youth, still clutching the chalkboard's dirty sponge in his fingers. 'They've gone in, half-hour ago already. There's no more sport today.'

'Gone in?' I asked. I glanced at the barred gate that the burdener had locked. 'I thought it was a wager-bout, for spectators?'

'No, it is travail,' the boy replied. 'They go in by number, and come out under Limehall. And them as come out first are the winners on which wagers are paid out.'

'And them as come out at all are lucky,' chuckled the old veteran.

'Close up your mouths,' the burdener said, his voice bearing the hard accent of the Herrat. 'She's no wagerer. Look at her.' He stared at me. 'What is your true game?' he asked.

'Is there one called Renner?' I asked, changing my approach quickly. I described Lightburn to them in simple terms.

'Him, aye,' the veteran said. 'Renner-boy. Him's a good lad. Done it three time, so he has, and won the purse each go.'

'That's why he took number three,' said the old woman with the pail. I saw that it contained many tokens cut from plastek wafers, each one inscribed with a number.

'Our champion, is Renner,' the other woman agreed.

'So he has gone in?' I asked. I already knew the answer. The boy had not yet sponged away all the words written on the boards, and I saw Renner's name chalk-written alongside other names, each with a number and odds marked against them.

'And you should go off,' the burdener hissed. 'Be away, or we will fetch you away.'

It was not the worst threat I have ever been issued, but the menace was more in his bearing than his words. He took a step forward, his hidden hand preparing to draw. I read the hunch in his shoulder as he braced to engage. He had fought before, and knew how it was done.

I turned my limiter cuff off before he could demonstrate. The cold emptiness of my blankness washed into them hard, magnified in the small chamber. It was as though all warmth had imploded. They all recoiled in distaste at the *un*-ness of my presence. Even to those not psychically sensitive, the pariah state can come as an unsettling shock, especially when delivered suddenly. The two men who had been stacking weapons fled at once, but the rest could not, or dared not, pass close to me to reach the exit. They were reluctant to touch what was untouchable, and flinched back.

The veteran slipped off his stool, the old woman gasped and drew her shawl up to her lips, and the boy started backwards into the chalkboard.

The burdener was wrong-footed. In his hesitation, I grabbed his face and shoved, sweeping out his legs at the same moment. He fell on his back. I relieved him of his hook-knife, and put my foot upon his chest.

'Where do they go?' I asked.

None of them wanted to answer me, for they were all too disarmed by an uncanny *lack* they could not explain.

'Where?' I insisted.

'Through the underworld,' the veteran stammered. 'Down in the below, in the old catacombs.'

The lowest and oldest part of the bonehall.

'It's a race?' I asked.

'There are no rules,' the veteran said. 'It's travail. You find your way, or you get lost. It's a maze down there.'

'But the first to find their way to Limehall wins?'

He nodded anxiously.

'Are there hazards?' I asked. 'You arm them.'

'No rules say you cannot afflict your competitors in the dark,' said the woman with the apron. 'It's catch as catch can. And there are holes, mind. Sinkholes. Pits.' Apprehension of me wavered in her voice.

'So, it's first one to Limehall by whatever means necessary?' I asked. 'What else lies below?'

'Who knows?' mumbled the boy. 'But so many go in and so few come out, as I can't explain by pit-holes or a knife in the ribs.'

'They come out in Limehall?' I asked.

'We're going there now,' the militiaman said, holding the lightpole with a shivering hand. 'It never takes less than three hour for them to come out. The wagerers will be gathering, to see who first emerges.'

I considered going to Limehall. It was, perhaps, a mile away. If Renner came through, I could greet him there. It would be a risk, if the gamblers were assembling at the finish line. The kind of men who wagered on such human blood sports would not be hale company. They would be armed, or accompanied by lifewards, and they would not take well to an interloper in their midst.

My choice was then decided for me. A man's cry of pain, distant but clear, rang up from the depths through the cage gate.

I felt sure that it was Renner Lightburn.

'Give me the keys,' I said to the burdener.

Prone, with my foot on his sternum, he grudgingly held the key-bunch up.

'And give me that,' I said to the militiaman, reaching for the lightpole.

'We need the light to find our way back up,' he said, with some concern.

'Find another,' I snapped. 'Light a lamp.'

I stepped off the ruffian's chest, and unlocked the cage gate. It was heavy on its hinges, and opened with a squeal that sounded like another distant cry of pain. Lightpole in my hand, I peered in.

'You can't go down there,' said the old woman.

'Watch me,' I replied.

CHAPTER 8

Which is of the Below

I entered the underworld, and did so with unease.

I had read books, perhaps too many, and could easily recount the many myths of travellers who ventured into underworld realms. It was said even Orphaeus himself, whose name ran through the very fabric of the world, had made a pilgrimage into darkness. Such journeys were fraught. In not one single myth did the traveller undertake a crossing without paying a toll or making some sacrifice. There was always a price for admission, and another price for exit.

But that was myths. This was merely underground, the subcore of Queen Mab. But the 'romatik veteran's choice of word had bothered me. Queen Mab was a place where myths seemed more real, hiding just beneath the skin, and I well knew that, however hard it was to find access, the City of Dust overlapped the City of Mab. I felt as though I was descending into a real underworld of myth, not some benighted catacomb. I shivered to think I was embarking on some soul-quest into the otherworld, a safe return from which would require some existential penalty. I felt I should have brought a lyre, or coins to pay the boatman.

I tried to dispel such whimsical fears.

I had the lightpole, and the field of waxy, yellow light it cast around me. I had my sidearm, and I still had the burdener's ugly hook-knife. I turned my limiter back on, for I did not wish to rile up the lemures and spirits of the dead with my null state.

That which they had called the Below was a dire place. The steps down were ragged, and worn slick by run-off. The walls were dripping wet, like the black cliffs of thawing glaciers. Shadows bobbed and weaved, and everywhere, in side chambers and pits, bones were piled like matchsticks. There were heaps of femurs, and bundles of ribs, and pyramids of skulls. It felt like the True Hell of the infernally damned, except that the tormenting fires had gone out. It also resembled some vault of spare parts, where raw components had been sorted and stored according to type, like screws and washers, from which an artisan god could reassemble men and send them back into the light to live additional lives.

The darkness beyond the compass of my lamplight was heavy. It seemed to throb like a living thing. It was like pitch midnight, distilled down to a concentrated syrup. I could hear the constant drip of water, but I felt I could *hear* the darkness too, hear what an old poet had called the weird sound of its own stillness.

Down here were the bones of men, the bones of lives, the bones of dreams, the skeletal remains of things forgotten and neglected. They had all fallen here, but I had chosen to come, and I quickly began to regret that choice.

I walked with tentative steps. My boots were good, but still they slipped and skidded on the wet calcite. My light sparked back to me off glinting rock crystal in the shadows, mere reflections, but they seemed like the tapetum flash of observing eyes. The stacks of old bones were endless, heaped by the unreliable path, or piled in pits, or crammed into stone alcoves of ancient manufacture so that they spilled out underfoot. As before, they were compulsively sorted by type. This, I knew, was the habit of bonehouses like St Belpheg's Ossuary, and of long barrows and kiln graves too. The bodies of the dead were left on the stone shelves of the upper galleries until age had taken the flesh and tissue all to dust. Then the attendants of the ossuary would gather the loose and now anonymous bones, and remove them to the catacombs below, sorting them type by type so they might be packed and stored with more economy. Thus the upper vaults were kept clear for new arrivals, and the irreducible bones were archived in smaller and yet smaller spaces.

Thus skulls were stacked in niches, and longbones piled end to end in alcoves, and spines were entwined in stone basins until the last gristle had decayed, whereupon the loose vertebrae could be tipped like seashells into ouslite urns or marble coffers.

These I saw along the way: boxes of bones, stone jars brimful of knucklebones, urns of phalanges and tarsals. I saw old push-barrows too, and handcarts and brooms and rakes, the tools of the attendants' trade. I wondered what such a trade, a constant nocturnal administration of bone, did to a person's mind. Did they lose all disquiet of death, or did they become more prey to superstition than most?

Beyond the next rambling gallery, filled with baskets of loose ribs bound into bundles like corn sheaves, or quivers of bent arrows, I found an answer of sorts. Before me stood a gateway made of human ivories, its frame of thigh bones braced with wooden collars, its arch of shoulder blades crowned with jawless skulls. The mind, it seemed, became deranged, or so inured to the material of the deceased that it was prompted to disrespectful sport. More bone sculptures loomed into my light as I went on: grotesque constructions of impossible anatomies. Some were huge, towering ten metres tall or more, and many of the bones they had been wrought from had evidently been selected for their unusual qualities. There were fragile wands of osteoporotic wastage, bones knurled with old and long-healed fractures, and others distended by the overgrowth of acromegaly. The sculptures were made more awful by the fact they had no meaning, none I could discern, and served no purpose. They were not even gates or arches, just ivory confections raised like the altars of the mad. More awful still was the vacant stare of the empty sockets: bare skulls whose constant grins betrayed no mirth, and whose deep orbits seemed to plead for dignity. A ribcage with four heads, upon a platform of ulnae; a rostrum of pelvic halves, surmounted by ten skulls bound into one; a death-knight mounted upon a whole horse, both fashioned from human fragments, both armoured with scale mantles of overlapping scapulae and sacrums, and strung with necklaces of teeth.

I fancied I should not like to meet the ossuary workers, above or below ground, and wondered if they were one of the hazards that the wager-sport participants were obliged to evade.

Ghost sounds came from the breathing dark, not just the patter of seeped water. I heard, more than once, dry bones scatter and rattle, as if settling, and thought they might have been disturbed by intrepid rats, except I saw no rats, for there was no meat or marrow to draw them down. I heard, twice, a distant cry, but I could not judge the direction, and once I distinctly heard the sound of running, of hasty footsteps that approached and resolved to nothing.

At the base of more steps, which could not have been riskier to descend if they had been hewn from ice, I found a yellow disc. It was a plastek token, like those the old woman had held in her pail. Near it, on the gleaming floor, I saw spots of fresh blood. I picked up the token, and saw it bore the number '7'. Not Renner, but seven had been an unlucky number for someone.

Just then, my luck seemed to end too. I almost pitched into a sheer pit, the bottom of which my light could not reach. The wet stone floor was almost black, and the mouth of the pit black too, and only at the very last moment did I notice the black was no longer reflecting the gleam of my glow-globe.

I started back, then stooped, feeling the ground until my fingers found the invisible lip, the line where black rock became black air. One more step, and I would have plunged. I looked for a way around, for none was clear even by lamplight. I used the base of the lightpole to prod and test what was stone and what was not. I found, at length, a narrow path, little more than a ledge, that skirted the pit beneath the gable of a stone colonnade where each recess was packed with jumbled skulls, like market wareboxes piled with dry-husk fruit.

Again, I heard a far-off cry that made me tense, and I drew back against the alcove arch. I waited for a moment, and as I did, I noticed that some of the skulls there had been turned so they faced – out of the haphazard heap – in the same direction. This was true in the adjacent alcove, and the next along, suggesting it was not random. Someone had turned the skulls, perhaps to mark the route, and indicate the safe way forward with their vacant stares.

In the crypt beyond, several femurs had been extracted from their stacks and laid out along the same plane. More markers, deliberately set, though not obvious in this desert of bones. Once I had noticed them, I began to find more, little moments of linear precision in the scattered litter. Who had set them so, and where did they lead? It was reasonable to suspect they marked the way to some trap or misfortune, yet there was nothing else I could trust, because I could not see far into the darkness, and my sense of direction was scrambled by the catacomb's twists, descents and turns.

The thought took me by surprise. For a moment, I had to work to control rising anxiety. I had been focused on the way ahead, and finding poor Renner. Now, I realised, I wasn't certain I could easily retrace my steps if the need arose. I imagined Medea chiding me for my rashness, and Harlon beginning a blunt lecture on tracking practices and proper field preparation.

This, in every myth, was how visitors to the underworld came astray. The underworld swallowed them and, despite their confidence or determination upon setting out, they lost their way. The myths always ended in the same manner, no matter their cultural derivation: the visitors only ever emerged from the underworld if they had a guide, or if there was divine intercession, or if they paid the boatman's price to be shown the way. They never, ever found their own way out, and some part of them, at bitter cost, was always left behind. I thought of coins upon dead eyelids, the ferry-fee.

I was lost. The furtive signposts of bone were my only aid. I hoped they were, perhaps, *my* divine intercession. I placed my trust in them, and followed their morbid lead.

'Give me your light,' a voice called out.

It startled me a little. So many odd sounds had occurred since I began my descent, I had begun to dismiss them all as imagination, but this was abruptly real.

'I will not,' I replied, turning and raising my lightpole to squint at the shadows.

'Give it me.'

A man's voice. Out of breath and, from the tone, scared. I smelled rank sweat.

He edged into the lamplight. He was a street vagabond, clad in poor and dirty clothing. He was short but heavyset, his face blotched with an old las-burn. In his hand, he clutched a rusty cutro, the tip towards me. My lamp was meagre, but his eyes creased at the glare of it.

'Give me it,' he said. 'I need it.'

'Are you of the game?' I asked, keeping an eye on his small sword.

'What?'

'The game? Do you play it?'

He nodded, and patted at his chest. There, a green token was pinned like a medal, and on it, the numeral '9'.

'What's your name?' I asked.

'Never mind my name, girl. Give me the lamp.'

'I will not,' I replied, 'for I need it to find my way. But if you give me your name, I will share my light. You look lost too.'

His expression was pained, from nothing but fear.

'Eyling,' he said.

'We both need a way out, Eyling,' I said. 'We do not belong here, nor should we have entered.'

Eyling nodded. 'Play the game for a few pennies,' he replied ruefully. 'I thought it would be easy. But there's something down here in this damn pit.'

'The other players?'

'No, not them. The anatomists. Forsaken freaks. You've seen their work, you must have done.'

Eyling, a Militarum veteran of the war, had been living in poverty on the city streets, his circumstances miserably reduced when his pension was denied. He had joined the game in a desperate bid to make coin. The anatomists, he told me, were the workers of the ossuary, who dwelt in the deepest parts of the catacomb, and shunned the surface. They had become a tribe to themselves, living in a world of human bone that had long since demented them and driven them feral.

These, and many other things, he told me as we made our way by the light of my lamp. He acted bold, as though he had taken me prisoner and was now in charge, but I could tell he was simply glad of my company. He talked without my prompting, chattering eagerly now he had light again and a person to talk to. He'd only been in the Below for two hours, but the solitude and heavy darkness had already punished him badly.

'Do you know Renner?' I asked him.

'Renner?'

'Number three?'

'Oh,' he said, 'Lightburn. Yes. Him, I know. He's played before. He told me not to join the game, but I need the pay. It's hard, he said, hard on the mind, and I said to him, I said, I was at Caston Field with the Sixty-First, I know hard.

'I was wrong,' he added, after a pause. 'It *is* hard on the mind. To be alone, and in such weight of darkness. I believe this is how it feels to be dead.'

'I do not think being dead feels like anything,' I replied.

He shrugged. Eyling was a poor wretch, but I was strengthened by his presence. He was the lost soul now, and I had become his light and his divine intercession, and that suggested my myth might play out in a quite different fashion.

We came to a long gallery where many more macabre sculpture displays had been raised from the bone litter. Skulls mounted on serpentine trunks of braided spines leered at us like lamia out of the fossorial gloom. Skulls hung inside baskets of ribs, like birds in cages. A skeletal beast, with far too many legs, each of which was far too long, lurked like a titanic spider. It wore an intricate clavicle crown.

'It's different today,' he said, then glanced at me. 'Today? Tonight? I have no clue of the hour. Is it night yet?'

'It's always night here,' I answered. 'Why do you say it's different?'

'Something has stirred them up,' he said. 'The anatomists. Lightburn said they keep to themselves, and avoid the players when they come through. But not tonight. They've moved up to these levels. I've glimpsed them and heard them. I think they're picking us off.'

'Why would they do so?' I asked.

'I think something has risen up from the very deepmost places,' he said, 'and scared them towards the light. It has driven them before it.'

I put no store by this. His mind had been playing pranks with him.

'Why do you say that, Eyling?' I asked.

'I've heard the rushing,' he said. 'Have you not? Now and then, a great rushing sound, like... Like the wind through trees. Or the crash of waves on a sea.'

'There's no sea here,' I assured him. 'Or any trees.'

'But I've heard it,' he insisted. 'The rushing of a sea. I think the city is sinking into a great and hidden sea, and the flood tides have drowned the deep, and driven the anatomists up to these levels.'

He stopped then. We both did. Another rat-skitter of bone in the darkness.

'Do you know the way out?' he asked, his voice very small and tight.

'I cannot say yes to that,' I replied, 'but I have a hope.'

I had been following the markers. Those odd and deliberate bones still seemed to me to point the way, though now I was beginning to suspect that, like Eyling, my mind was simply imposing order where there was none. That tibia – had it been placed there on purpose to point the way, or was it simply lying where it had fallen?

Was I tracing a pattern that my mind had invented? I did not tell him so.

Eyling grabbed my sleeve suddenly.

'Is that a light?' he asked.

The chthonic blackness ahead was indeed invested with a pallor, and it was no trick of the eye. It was a lambent glow, like limelight, and as we hurried towards it across a shingle of metacarpals, it grew brighter. A light at last.

It glared at us, a soft white radiance tinged with green. We passed under a high archway of vertebrae, and through a longbone colonnade where every upright femur was capped with a jawbone finial.

The chamber beyond was vast, but it was not the outside we had hoped for. Some algae afflicted the dripping walls, and issued a photoluminescent haze that filled the place with snow-soft light. Wooden pews, taken from some temple, and rotting with age and mildew, had been placed in rows along the cavern floor. They were occupied. A congregation of skeletons, wired and screwed into their seats, all faced forwards, with decayed hymnals in their fleshless laps or hooked upon their finger bones. There were hundreds, filling all the pews in silent worship.

I saw what they faced, what they had all been wired to gaze at.

My heart broke a little. After all this time, I had found an angel, that which I had yearned for to bring me clarity, and balance out the daemons that polluted my life.

But it was long dead.

CHAPTER 9

Of angels and anatomists

The angel hung upon a cross at the front of the anatomists' parody of a temple. It had been crucified, with iron pins driven through its arms, ankles and outspread wings. Algae had invested its bones so that they glowed with frosty light, like the cavern walls.

'Their minds are twisted,' Eyling muttered. 'This is their greatest desecration.'

I nodded. The anatomists had constructed abominations throughout the chambers of the ossuary, things that were perverse and bizarre, and a disgrace to the ways of nature. But this seemed a greater disgrace, because it was, in a way, more beautiful: a magnificent winged figure, nailed to timber beams.

So yes, I nodded in agreement with the vagabond, but I had noticed details that he had not.

Every sculpture we had seen thus far had been built of human bone in defiance of anatomical sense. But I could not tell how this angel had been made. The bones were assembled in what seemed like natural order. This was no mix of parts thrown together. And even given the disfigured and abnormal nature of many bones the anatomists chose and favoured, I could not discern where these had come from.

I approached the crucifixion and gazed up at it. The figure was a giant, well over two metres tall. Where did bones of such magnitude originate? They seemed to match, as if this was no sculpture but a whole body preserved. There was something odd and shell-like about the massive thorax and heavy sternum. And the wings were not crafted from pilfered human longbones. They seemed like the bones of real wings. What avian creature possessed wings with a four-metre spread, and where could its remains have been found? How had they been attached in such a seemingly authentic way?

Close up, I saw that the giant's bones were clad in a flaking husk, like old parchment, the sorry vestiges of skin and tissue. It was not an artful construct of depraved anatomists. It had been real and whole, a winged giant that had once been alive.

'They make sick mockery of the Brightest One,' said Eyling, who knew the myths too. He did not dare speak the name aloud, but I knew it. The Great Angel was a saint of ancient legend, who had fought at the side of the God-Emperor in the Last Conflict of Terra, and had fallen in sacrifice to a vengeful spirit in the final hours.

This was sacrilege indeed, certainly as Eyling saw it. But he, in his outrage, had no eye for the forensic detail. To me, it was worse than blasphemy, for I was sure it was real. An angel, murdered and crucified, proof of the divine that infuses the One Faith, displayed as a grim trophy.

I felt I might weep.

'It is Astartes,' I said.

'It is not,' he refused, with a sharp shake of his head.

'It is, Eyling. Look at the bones of it. The scale of them is more than human.'

'Astartes are a myth!' he snapped.

'We are in a realm of myths here,' I replied, then added, 'Besides, they are not.'

'They are,' he returned, 'and any fool-child can tell you they do not have wings.'

'The primarch did–'

'Speak not to me his name!' Eyling said, raising his hands to stopper his ears. 'And even if he did, blessed be his might, Astartes do not.'

I stepped forward again, and knelt, sifting through the litter and refuse at the base of the cross. Old books had been piled up, gone to dust and mulch, along with other pitiful tributes.

'I thought it was daylight,' Eyling murmured from behind me.

'I did too,' I answered.

'The glow, I thought it was a way out, but no. Just shining slime in a hellpit. Why does it make light?'

'It is a chemical process, Eyling,' I replied, still sifting. I had found something, a large object under the heap of dead books, hard and metal.

'Tricked by slime, that is my life,' Eyling cursed.

It was a warhelm of some size, too large for human use. It was caked in grave-mould and dirt, and its lustre was gone, but it had once been red.

'We must move on, girl,' Eyling said behind me, paying no attention. 'I saw light, and it gave me hope, but it was a deceit. We must move on.'

'We will,' I replied. I scraped dirt off the helm's dome, and picked crusts of mould from the eyepieces. I knew this pattern, for I had seen it in variation. Astartes armour, without doubt. Upon the brow was marked, in black, the numeral 'IX'.

'Nine,' I murmured.

'Yes, I am nine,' Eyling said. 'Nine is my number. What of it?'

'And you led me here,' I mused. 'To the light.'

'What?' He grew exasperated.

The myths of Queen Mab and its underworld were toying with me. I had sought the light, and it had been false. I had traversed the underworld, and found no exit, but instead the angel I had prayed for, except that it was dead. Myths only linger if they have meaning. They are knowledge encoded in story so that they can be passed down through generations. I was surrounded by the symbols of myth, and yet could not extract a meaning.

I decided there was none, and there never had been. I was seeing patterns that were not patterns, and appreciating symbols that were not symbols, just as I had done with the bone markers. All my life, I had wanted to make sense of the world, and that desire had become so desperate, I was manufacturing sense. There were no myths. I was a woman lost in a bonehouse, bewildered by the darkness. The world had no sense to offer me, for it had none, and all the signs and signifiers were not symbols for *anything*.

I heard a smack, like the impact of a bullet.

I looked to Eyling. He turned to me with an expression of puzzlement on his face. There was a hole in his neck from which blood was flowing in great quantities. He was already dead.

There came a second crack. Eyling lurched as something struck his temple, and the impact dropped him on his back. His legs twitched as the life went out of him. On his head, where he had been struck the second time, a huge weal had raised.

More impacts struck around me, one scattering bone chips near my feet. I could hear no report of gunfire, but I was being shot at. An impact took out my lamp, shattering the glow-globe. I dropped the pole and ducked for cover. Further impacts splintered the edge of the pew I had chosen for shelter. One missile hit hard, and bounced off the wood, its force spent. I saw that it was a human knucklebone. Slingshots, catapults… bones were being used as ammunition to fire at me.

I saw the first anatomist when he rushed me down the length of the pew. He was hunched low in a scurrying gait, a spavined thing, emaciated and clad in dirt-black rags. His skin was caked with white bone-dust, like an aristocrat's face powder, and his sunken eyes were filmy and glazed. He hissed through a mouth of broken yellow teeth and decayed gums, and swung an axe to cleave my head. The blade of the axe was a sharpened human scapula, the haft a femur.

I sprawled on my back to evade the blow, and the axe missed my face by a whisker and bit into the pew. There was no time to regain my footing. I arched onto my shoulders, and caught his arm between my legs, then scissored, snapping the limb. As he staggered backwards, squealing, I made a back-spring onto my feet, and felled him with the heel of my hand.

A second anatomist hurled himself across the pews to get at me, knocking free the heads of several of the skeletal congregation. I ducked aside, avoiding his grasp, and he tumbled to the ground. By the time he got up, I had drawn the burdener's old hook-knife, which I rammed into his chest. He fell, but the blade had wedged fast, and his body took the knife with it.

Lethal shots were whipping at me. Under the bone arch through which Eyling and I had entered, I spied half a dozen anatomists spinning slings and loosing knucklebone pellets. The missiles struck the pews, puffing splinters, and rattling the seated skeletons. One shot hit a skull, blowing it apart like old crockery. I dropped back low, hearing the pew thump and shake with impacts. If there was another way out of this place of crucifixion, I did not know it, and I dared not raise my head to look.

I drew my quad-snub. It was a compact piece with a rubberised grip and a short, square snout of blued steel, with four barrels set like the pips on a die. A squeeze of the trigger fired each shot, clockwise from top right, but if the trigger was held, all four rounds would fire in such rapid succession as to be almost simultaneous. I reached to my belt for spare bullets, so that I might reload quickly when the first salvo was fired.

Something struck the back of my head with great force. I blacked out, briefly, and came to on the ground with my cheek in the powder dust. I could smell blood in my sinuses, and the rear part of my skull throbbed with a stinging, radiating pain. My vision swam back into focus and I saw, on the ground, right in front of my nose, a human knucklebone that was wet on one side with blood.

A slingshot had found its mark.

I tried to rise. My body was sluggish. The impact had quite denied me sense. I could hear the anatomists calling out and approaching, and knew I would be dead if I did not stir quickly.

But I was still too dazed.

Then came a great, echoing detonation that seemed to lift the dust from the ground in front of my eyes with its shiver.

A hand seized my shoulder.

'Can you get up? Are you killed dead?' a man asked, before firing another blast. 'Can you move, woman?' he demanded, shaking at me.

I knew the voice. It was Renner Lightburn. I had come all this way to save him, but he had, once again, saved me.

CHAPTER 10

Which is of ways out

Lightburn no longer had the great Thousander pistol that had been his pride. He fired a long-barrelled autopistol, a Gulet-P, that had seen better days.

'Can you get up?' he cried again, forcing the anatomists to dive and shelter with his steady shots.

I could, though I was far from steady.

'That's twice now,' I said.

'Twice what?'

'You've saved me.'

'What?'

Of course, he didn't know. In the moment, I had forgotten that *he* had forgotten. One of Ravenor's agents, Patience Kys, had put a telekine spear through his short-term memory so that he remembered nothing.

His gun was out. He ducked to reload.

'There's a passage back there,' he said, indicating with a jerk of his head. 'When I make 'em cower again, run for it.'

I took out the quad.

'Let's run now,' I suggested.

I swung up, my head woozy, and discharged all four loads. The quad-snub's recoil jolted my hand. The shots blew the end off a pew, and smashed part of the vertebrae arch.

We ran, as fast as we were able. He hooked his hand under my upper arm to steady me. A few bone missiles chased us. The passage was where he said it would be. We sped along its darkness, loose bones kicking out under our feet.

'We have no light!' I cried, stumbling.

'Stay with me,' he insisted.

We ran into another vault space. More mould grew here, emitting light, though far less than in the eerie chamber we had exited.

'In here,' he said, and yanked me into the shelter of a dank culvert. We waited for sounds of pursuit. He quietly reloaded his pistol. His beard had grown in, and his hair was longer than before. He was also thinner, but he was the man I remembered. The tattooed litany of his Curst burden showed on his skin.

I opened the break action of the quad, and a spring clip automatically ejected the warm shell casings. I slotted four more rounds in place, and snapped the quad shut.

'That's a decent piece,' he said.

'It is,' I agreed, and slid around to watch for movement.

'I'd ask how it come to belong to you,' he said, 'but a bigger conundrum is what you're doing here. Did you enter the bonehouse by mistake?'

'No,' I said.

'You ain't no vagabond,' he said, 'and your clothes are good. I can't think of no reason that a woman like you would be down here.'

'You do not know what kind of woman I am like,' I said.

'True,' he said. 'But I look like a worthless Curst, for I'm exactly that, while you–'

'I was looking for you,' I told him.

He squinted at me, baffled. 'Do I know you?' he asked.

'Do you?' I returned.

'Not at all,' he said. 'I think you've gone an' mistaken me for someone, mamzel. I'm but a Curst.'

'You are number three,' I said, 'and your name is Renner Lightburn.'

He was alarmed by this, and I couldn't blame him.

'You have forgotten all about me,' I said. 'Your memory was taken.

But you knew me once, months ago. And you helped me, according to your burden.'

He looked most doubtful and troubled, but I sensed I had struck something.

'A few months back,' he said quietly, but with some stern anger, 'I woke in the street near the Coalgate. I couldn't remember how I'd got there, or anything of the hours or days precedin' that awakening. I wondered if I had drunk meself stupid on 'still juice, but I've never been no drinker. Well, I *believe* I've never been no drinker. I supposed then that I had been mugged, or had suffered some malady-fit. But a man such as me isn't able to seek the expertise of a fancy medicae.'

'What did you do?' I asked.

'I continued with what I presumed had been me life,' he said. He paused. 'We knew each other?'

'Yes,' I said. 'You carried a Thousander when last we met.'

'That I remember,' he said. 'It was with me a while. I ain't got no idea where I lost it.'

'The same night as your memory,' I said.

He stared at me in the blue gloom for so long, I began to feel uncomfortable.

'I don't know your face,' he said at length. 'Is this a trick? Are you tricking me?'

'I am not,' I said.

'The gun. Your mention of the gun. That feels convincing. Few if any would know of that. I'm not a man much noticed. I ain't a man of acquaintances.'

'I mentioned the pistol for that very reason,' I said.

He shrugged. He glanced out of the culvert again, but there was no sign of the wild-man anatomists.

'Why'd you come seeking for me?' he asked.

'I have been looking for you for some time,' I replied. 'Today, at last, I got a lead. Some intelligence that said you were here, so I came, and when I found you had partaken in this foolish blood sport, I followed you into the ossuary.'

'Well, that was damn foolish in itself.'

'I concur.'

'What...' he began.

'What?' I asked.

'Well, now you've done and found me, mamzel. And at some effort. What've you found me *for*, exactly?'

Now I felt stupid.

'I felt that I needed to... To thank you.'

'Thank me?'

'For your service to me.'

'Did I do great deeds?' he asked.

'You were courageous when you had no cause to be, so yes.'

He pursed his lips, and nodded thoughtfully.

'Well, mamzel, now you've thanked me. And I thank you for your thanks. What else?'

'Well, that was all, really,' I said.

He laughed quietly. 'That were a lot of risk and effort for two words,' he remarked. 'I think there's more.'

'More, sir?'

'Were we lovers?'

'No,' I said.

'Well, only lovers make such rash gestures.'

'We were friends, Renner,' I said.

'I don't even know your name,' he said.

I told him what it was. I told him *Beta*.

We waited a while, until we were confident the anatomists were not nearby, then we set off again, following a route away from the hall of crucifixion. My head ached badly. I had a contusion on the back of my scalp the size of a bird's egg, and blood matted my hair.

Lightburn traced our route by way of the bone markers. Their placement had not been my imagination.

'Why do you play this game?' I asked.

'I'm good at it,' he said. 'I make coin by it. The winner's take is decent. It beats sittin' with a bowl. The first time, that were easy enough. Yes, the dark is daunting, but where the other chancers rushed headlong, I tracked a way and left markers what I could retrace if I had to. The second time, easier. I followed me own marks. Third time, easier yet. There are hazards, true, like sink'oles, and the others in the game can cut rough, and seek to eliminate the competition.'

'And this time?'

'I brought a gun to keep safe. They gives you weapons, but they lets you take your own if you have 'em. And I'm glad I did.'

'Why?'

'This time it's changed,' he said. 'The bone-keepers've come up. I think it's the storm. I think the rain has flooded out their levels.'

'That's what Eyling said,' I remarked.

'Eyling?'

'Number nine.'

'Ah,' he nodded. 'Well, they warned us the bone-keepers could make trouble, but this run is the first time I've seen 'em.'

'They are murderous,' I said.

'They are,' he agreed.

'Eyling reckoned they had been driven up here by something in the very depths.'

'The rain.'

'No, something. He was not specific.'

'The dark plays tricks,' Lightburn said. 'After just a few minutes, the mind starts to spin. It were Eyling's first run.'

'And his last.'

'Indeed. He 'ad rattled his wits, that's all.'

We walked on. Some spaces were lit by the luminescent growth, but other passages were entirely lightless, and we were obliged to feel our way along cold, wet stone.

'That thing,' I said.

'What thing?'

'The winged man, on the cross–'

'That?' Lightburn sniffed. 'Them bone-keepers build things. You musta seen. Awful things, made out of the helpless dead. They are peculiar-mad, I think.'

I did not tell him what I thought. I had only just won from him some limited trust. I chose not to tell him that I thought the winged man was real.

'Have you heard the sea?' I asked instead.

'Yes,' he replied.

'Really?'

'Yes. It's just another trick o' the dark. Some sound of air, or water perhaps. Echoing and magnified. Yes, I've heard it. It ain't the sea, but I confess it do sound like it.'

'Is it not the sea?' I asked.

'We're a long ways away from the coast, Beta Bequin,' he replied, 'and there ain't no sea under Queen Mab.'

I asked him how far we had to go. He told me some little way more. Our sojourn in the dark had been longer than either of his previous experiences.

'Limehall is to the north, and our way is marked,' he said. 'I wonder if I'll be the first back. There's a decent purse in it if I am.'

'But you may have lost the lead.'

'I may have.'

'Because you stopped to help me.'

'I heard the commotion. You was in trouble.'

'But you didn't know who I was.'

He looked at me.

'You was in trouble,' he repeated. 'My burden asks me to help others, and shoulder their burdens as my own. And my burden is more important to me than a bag o' coins.'

'Still...' I said.

'I does what I does as a penitent soul in the gaze of the God-Emperor,' he said. 'And see how He rewards me? He sends me a friend what I didn't know I had, one who'll wilfully brave the dark to say a thank you. And one who, despite her modest and meek looks, like your rubricator or your steward's secretary, can take down two bone-keepers hand-to-hand, and carries a gun of fine crafting.'

He smiled.

'I'm interested to know who me new old friend is,' he said, 'and what profession she follows.'

'I will tell you,' I said, 'but not now.'

I took his sleeve, and pulled him into the shadows of a stone pier. Water dripped on our heads and ran down our collars. I winced as the cold touched my head wound.

'What?' he whispered.

I pointed. Ahead, along the cold and ruined gallery, anatomists were visible, a great many of them, entirely blocking our pathway to the surface.

* * *

We agreed there were too many to rush and take on. Gangs of them were gathering, whooping and calling. The posted way out was closed, and I believed it would not be long before they would start to move back in our direction. I wondered if I might disperse them with my null, but I feared their communal fervour might insulate them against the effect, and that Lightburn, even forewarned, might choose to quit my company.

Lightburn, for all his plain courage, was askance at the bone-keepers' massing. I told him we had no choice except to find a way around. This he shook off.

'There ain't no way,' he stated. 'No way marked, or that I know. We could get most truly lost.'

'It's that or go back the way we came,' I said. Retracing our steps might take hours, and would not be without considerable danger.

He followed me then with great reluctance and misgiving. I found a side passage through the narrowest of stone slots, which obliged us to turn sideways and shuffle in order to squeeze through. The tight space pressed upon us, and forced us to draw shallow breaths, which further ratcheted our claustrophobic anxieties. The slot seemed endless. As we edged along, I feared it would continue to narrow until we were quite stuck. I tried not to dwell upon this possibility.

The slender defile brought us at last to a low gallery built of old and heavy stone. A torrent of brackish water flowed along its floor trench, and everywhere grew profuse and horrid fungi, with meaty bulbs and vase bodies, fat stalks, and heavy caps like leather. The air stank, but the open gallery was such a welcome relief from our prolonged compression, we were glad of it. Lightburn flexed his shoulders and stretched.

'Where now?' he asked.

I pointed. I was sure the narrow slot had not curved, so the gallery we had reached ran parallel to our original route. We splashed along the lightless brook, for the fungal growth choked the narrow stepways on either side, and neither of us wished to touch the ugly colony. Some caps and stalks were so huge, they resembled the nursing stool the old veteran had sat on.

'I think they might eat 'em,' Lightburn remarked.

'Who?' I asked.

'The bone-keepers,' he said. 'They must eat something.'

It was a disgusting thought, for the meaty caps and pitchers looked foul, and exuded a carrion reek, but I believed he was right. Further, it might well explain the derangement of the anatomist enclave. Any doctor or physik will warn against the ingestion of mycological substances, for the flesh of mushrooms conceals all variety of lethal toxins, and many psychotropic properties besides. The anatomists, deprived of other vittles, may have learned – through grim trial and error, I presumed – which forms were deadly, and which were edible. Those they fed upon would conjure visions, convulsions and phantasms, a practice they may have come to ritualise, as I had read some other cultures do. The anatomists lived in a constant hallucinogenic state, which would account for their awful creations. I wondered what they saw us as. Night-bred monsters, perhaps, which would prompt their homicidal attacks.

The gallery led on without end, like an underground canal. There was some light, from odd luminous growths, and from the flowing water, which flashed like silver around our ankles, phosphorescent. The fungal colonies leaked matter and spores into the flow, I had no doubt, causing this effect. Lightburn and I were soaked from the knees down. I worried that the madnesses of the cave-growth might be absorbed through the skin.

'This runs too long,' Lightburn complained, after some minutes. 'This gallery, it's passed way beyond the turn north for Limehall.'

I judged his estimation accurate, but there was no turn or exit we could take. Then I felt a cold breeze upon my face.

After another forty paces, the gallery opened into a dark and open space. The ground fell away, and the flowing brook poured down jagged black slabs into the darkness below. I could see the water flash and glow as it cascaded, like a string of cold fire. Of the space itself, there was nothing but darkness, but we could sense by the airiness and cold that it was vast.

'Where now?' Lightburn asked as we paused upon the brink.

I could see little. Lightburn reached into his pocket, drew out a small glow-globe, and lit it.

'You have a *light*?' I asked reprovingly.

'Only a fool comes Below without a light,' he answered.

'Then why have you not produced it before?'

'Because its charge is low, and I won't have it run dry,' he replied. 'Gloom is one thing. I saves the globe for true dark.'

He held the glow-globe up. Its light was indeed paltry.

'*This* is true dark,' he said.

We still could not make adequate sense of the scale, for the globe's sepia aura lit but a modest cone around us. But it was enough to see that, to our left hand, rude steps were cut into the rock beside the gallery's mouth. They led downwards.

I went first, with him close behind, holding the globe above us so we both might see. The steps were narrow – two persons could not pass on them, even chest to chest – and either old or poor-hewn. They were chiselled from the cavern wall, so that to our left was sheer wet rock and to our right an open drop into nothing. There was no railing, or hand-hold.

We descended slowly, and with great trepidation. The footing was worn and slick. We hunched our left shoulders to the rock face, pawing with our left hands for some semblance of support, and took the narrow way one step at a time, left foot down, right foot to it, left down, right to it, painstaking and measured, tilting our weight and balance to our left sides, left legs, and the wall. It was another grim effort of concentration and anxiety, like the narrow slot we had braved. Here, the slot's crushing claustrophobia was replaced by a sick fear of falling, of slipping and plunging into a measureless abyss.

At first, I counted the steps under my breath, but gave up after seventy for it took all my will to concentrate.

'There,' whispered Lightburn at my ear, a flutter of fear in his tone, 'look there.'

Below us, the steps came to an end on a black platform, a floor of sorts. We reached it, and stood for a moment, letting our heart rates calm.

Lightburn raised his little lamp.

'Where do you–' he began and then stopped. His words had echoed at once, an odd repeat that seemed cold and mocking.

'Just echoes,' I said, echoing myself.

'Some space,' he said, and the walls repeated. 'It feels large.'

He was right. There was only blackness, and it was curious how some blacknesses, identical to the eye, could feel impossibly large or oppressively tight.

We ventured ahead, across jumbled stone blocks. I felt the breeze again, cold, and from our right.

'Turn off the lamp,' I said, and so did the echoes.

He did so, puzzled.

The darkness was complete, so utter, that I could not see my own raised hand. But, as we waited, I began to feel the breath of the breeze more strongly, and sensed its origin more clearly.

We waited a minute longer.

'You see?' I asked.

You see? said the space.

'I see nothing,' he replied.

...nothing.

I groped for him, and found his face, and turned it. Our eyes were adjusting to the engulfing darkness. There was a faint blue light far away, barely traceable. Light, in fact, was too strong a word. It was a pale blue smudge, like a scrap of moonbeam. The breeze was coming from the same direction.

'Praise be your good eyes,' said Lightburn.

...your good eyes.

'You just have to use the darkness sometimes,' I replied.

...use the darkness sometimes, use the darkness sometimes.

He turned the globe back on, and it seemed dazzling to our dark-accustomed sight. Though we could no longer see the fuzz of moonlight, we were sure of its position. We set off across the giant blocks, helping each other step up and across from one uneven slope to the next.

'The roots of the city,' he said.

...roots of the city.

'Or of older cities that came before,' I replied.

...cities that came before, the darkness teased.

Queen Mab was as old as anywhere, and it had risen across the ages, layer upon layer, building its foundations on the strata of the past. These blocks were of immense age, and they had been fashioned by masons long before they slumped. What walls had they been? The bulwarks of what towers? What name had they owned? What lords and rulers had they known? This was not, I felt certain, the *other* city, the City of Dust. That was extimate, a simultaneous reality. This was the deep past, the buried relic of the eras that had preceded mine.

The moonlight shone to us, a pale gap. When we came to it at last, tired and short of breath, it revealed itself as a great archway, a stone gate of cyclopean columns. Cold air issued from its mouth. I could hear a distant rushing, a rolling crash, like the beating of giant wings, or–

Or the sea. The rolling of an ocean.

I stepped towards the immense arch. Beyond its frame lay an endless void. I sensed a tide below me, a great weight of water lapping at invisible rocks. I smelled salt-air, and could just make out a line of horizon, very far away. The source of the light we had followed was not apparent, but it seemed to swell, ethereal, from whatever clouded sky hung above the unseen sea.

It was a way out, or a way to *elsewhere* at least. It was no sea, for that would have been an impossibility. An underground lagoon, perhaps, or the vast cistern of some previous metropolis. I wondered how Lightburn and I might pass across it, for we had no boat. I wondered, too, why I shrank from it. I had longed for a way out of the underworld, but this did not seem to be it. Beyond the ancient arch was not 'out', it was deeper still.

I heard a cry, from out in the gloom, like the wail of a seabird turning in the air above the invisible waters. It was the most lonely sound I had ever heard. Whatever lay beyond the arch, it was a voyage I had no wish to undertake. It felt, though I could not fully articulate the reason, that only terror lay beyond that threshold.

But we had come too far to be thwarted. I looked around. More fashioned blocks lay around the mouth of the arch, great slabs of ouslite. One, chipped and haggard, taller than me, seemed set as a marker. Inscriptions had been carved into it, and these then deliberately defaced, leaving only a few letters behind. I peered at it in the cold gloom.

Whatever had been inscribed originally was gone. What remained, worn by ages yet still discernibly in the fine style of classical Enmabic, read:

KIN G DO OR

Was that the name of the arch? The name of the monarch who had raised it? It was not any name I knew from Sancour's history, but seemed more a nursery name, from fairy tale. But then, so is 'Queen Mab'.

Besides, 'King Door' was not what had been writ here originally. An afterwards hand had struck away the original text, and left these few letters as a riddle, or a joke. And the handiwork of those who habituated this underworld place was manifestly mad, and without reason or logic.

The cry came again, but this was Lightburn.

'Here, Beta Bequin!' he called. He was nearby, to the left of the massive archway. Like me, it seemed, he had felt no wish to step through the portal called the King Door.

By the light of his upraised globe, I saw what he had found. It was a staircase, leading upwards. And it was no narrow or rough flight like the one that we had descended with our hearts in our mouths. It was a grand thing of great majesty, ten metres wide, with fine, wide marble steps. Dirt and dust cluttered it, but its noble scale had not faded. The walls were proud masonic masterpieces of columns and ornate acanthus, that still showed the residue of the gold leaf that had once adorned it. This was a passageway of state, a ceremonial staircase by which some great monarchs might descend in all pomp, flanked by lifeward guards and chancellors, from their palace to their royal docks, or by which high ambassadors of foreign lands might be admitted, with fanfare and solemn drum, to a regal court.

'I like this better,' Lightburn said.

'Better than the arch?'

'Infinitely,' he replied. 'That arch leads nowhere I want to go. I feels it in my bones.'

'Agreed,' I said, 'and I cannot say for why. That vista, and the sound of the sea, it frightens me.'

'Me too,' he said. 'But this... This way goes *up*.'

I smiled, and took his hand, so that we might ascend together, but the seabird cry came again, now very loud. We turned and saw, to our amazement, a great bird fly in through the towering arch, and come to rest upon the inscribed block. Its wings were mighty, silk-white, and fully five metres in span, furling as it perched to rest.

But it was no bird.

It was a winged man. No, a winged giant. No, an angel. My mind could not reason it. It was the living cousin of the dead thing I had seen.

Naked, he seemed a god. His corded physique was that of the legend-heroes whose statues supported the portico of the Prefect's mansion. His skin was porcelain white, his hair long, black and bedraggled. He crouched upon the King Door block like a perfect messenger of the divine. He seemed almost twice the size of a mortal human.

Lightburn and I had both frozen on the bottom step, astounded by the vision, but my heart lifted. Here, here, *here* was the angel, the *living* angel, I had yearned to find. Here, I was sure, was truth and answers, the clear and golden light that would banish the daemon-darkness of my life.

The angel slowly turned its head to look at us. Its wild black mane hung down, almost across its eyes, framing its face. A beautiful face, quite the most beautiful I have ever seen: high cheekbones, a patrician's nose, a wise and solemn mouth. I wondered what words it would speak to us.

The angel sniffed the air, its head bobbing like a falcon at hunt. Its eyes widened. They were entirely glossy and black within.

Its mouth opened. Its long fangs were like that of a wolf or carnodon. A drop of blood trickled from its lip down its alabaster chin.

With a cold howl of malice, it sprang, and flew at us.

CHAPTER 11

Of blood and fire

I know nothing. My life is built of contradictions. This I had suspected for a long while. On the decayed steps in the Below, it was confirmed, in a split second, with such a savage flourish as to seem almost spiteful.

Dark is light. Good is bad. I am and I am not. I walk with a man who seems loyal to the Throne and is yet branded a heretic. I shun another who I am told is my enemy, yet is also a stalwart servant of the highest powers. The Maze Undue was an Inquisitorial school, and yet it was the Cognitae, and yet the Cognitae and the Inquisition cannot easily be untied. Orphaeus was a lord hero, but yet the King in Yellow is dark menace. Queen Mab is a city, and yet it is also another, and neither are whole or together. I am hunted by many, yet I am a pariah. I have made a friend, or at least amiable company, of a daemon, and yet a bright angel seeks to rip out my throat.

All is deceit. Nothing wears a true face or uses a true name. Nothing is as it appears to be, as if the whole universe were busily playing out a function, 'guised in cunning. The mad are sane, the blind can see, the sane are otherwise demented, good is evil, and up, for all I care, is down.

The angel, the beautiful angel, flew at me, screaming, fangs bared. It flew at me not just as a predator, not just as some instrument of murder, but as the brittle punchline of some elaborate joke. An angel of death. A lightness of dark. A beautiful horror.

Look upon me! it seemed to scream. *Look upon me and see the utter folly of your mind! You longed for me, and searched for me, and here I am, nothing more than death!*

Its speed was that of a whip's crack, a winter owl stooping upon its hapless prey. Its power was ungodly. I knew I could neither move aside, nor fight it, even if there had been time or means to do either.

There was not. And I was frozen, besides, in abject terror.

It smashed poor Lightburn aside like a twig. I scarcely felt the impact of its strike. It bore me backwards, up the old, grand steps, clutched in its grip, its scream in my ears. I felt the stone density of it, the heat of its skin, the sting of its wet hair lashing my face. I smelled the scent of it, clean but sour, like a raptor, and the copper gust of its bloody breath.

It landed halfway up the flight, and cradled me in hands that could have enveloped my head. I heard the rippling crack of its wingbeat. It had my head in its long fingers, twisting it roughly as if to snap my neck. I felt it sniff the back of my skull.

It could smell the blood there. It had smelled it from across the chamber.

An animal growl rose in its throat, like fierce lava bubbling up a volcanic flue.

Blind, I snapped off my cuff.

The ravening angel shrieked and recoiled, dropping me like a white-hot ingot. I landed hard across the edges of the marble steps, bruising thigh and hip and ribs, and striking the back of my head. Sharp pain detonated like a grenade as the contusion hit against marble. I cried out, blinded by bright-coloured spots and sparks of light.

My senses swam. I sat up. The angel was falling backwards down the steps, bouncing and rolling, folded almost in a ball, and clawing at its own face.

It did not like my blankness at all.

As for Lightburn, he lay nearby, propped awkwardly on the steps where he had been knocked down, his back against the wall, gashes bleeding on his cheek and behind his ear. His glow-globe lay at his feet. He gazed in vacant dread at the killer angel now coiled in pain and mewling at the foot of the steps.

'Renner–'

He did not reply.

'Renner, get up! We have to go!'

He turned to the sound of my voice, and shuddered. The angel's assault had shocked him deeply, and left him especially vulnerable to the effect of my blankness. My proximity was distressing him very much.

I could not turn the cuff back on, for I was sure my null was all that was driving the angel off, but I would not leave Lightburn. I clattered down several steps until I was below Lightburn on the staircase, and that was enough. The cold focus of my nullity was now between him and the angel of death. He sprang up, galvanised by repulsion, and began to half run, half stumble up the steps to get away from the emptiness that chilled his soul.

I grabbed the light, and ran after him. I was, I knew full well, driving him, herding him like a piece of frightened livestock. He would run all the while the deadness of me was at his back.

The staircase was immense. At the very top was a lofty portico and a pair of huge and ancient gilded doors that faced the head of the stairs. The doors were six metres high. They stood ajar, and light shafted through the narrow gap.

Lightburn, still gripped in panic, burst through them. He turned, and scrabbled to shut them in my face, to keep the atrocity of me at bay.

I turned on my cuff.

'Renner, let me through!'

He backed off, and I slipped through. The doors were immensely heavy, but there were iron slide-bolts on the inside.

'Help me!' I yelled, trying to heave the doors shut.

He stared at me, uncertain, and then moved to my assistance. We closed the doors, pushed home the bolts, and then dropped into its brackets a hefty bar.

I turned to him. He was ashen.

'I am a blank, Lightburn,' I said directly. 'I am a null, what is called an untouchable. It is my curse, and now you have tasted the miserable *lack* of my presence when it is not limited. I'm sorry.'

He opened his mouth, but found there was nothing he could say.

'I'm sorry,' I said again. 'I would have told you of this, and perhaps warned you what it could be like, but there was no time. Thus, it was an ugly shock.'

'Did I know this about you?' he asked.

'You did.'

'Was I all right with it?'

'It was, I think, why you stood by me in the first place,' I said. 'I am an outcast of the world as much as any psyker.'

He swallowed hard.

'All right,' he said. He looked at the bolted doors.

'And... that?' he asked.

'An angel,' I replied.

'I would say there ain't no such thing,' he murmured, 'except for that I saw it and felt its rage...'

He paused and gingerly touched his wounds.

'I think it was a Blood Angel,' I said.

'What?'

'An Astartes warrior, of the Old Ninth Legion.'

'Are Astartes real?' he asked. Then he shook his head and laughed grimly. 'Why ask? After today, *anythin'* is possible. Are *angels* real? Are daemons–'

He stopped and looked at me sharply.

'Are *daemons* real too?' he asked.

I chose not to answer. He had been traumatised enough for one day.

'We must go,' I said. I turned and started to walk, and he followed. We were in a vast and ruined hall, perhaps the reception chamber of what once had been a stately residence. Stained glow-globes, still functioning on low power, hung from the arched ceiling on long chains.

'Someone dwells here still,' he said.

'Or the power is maintained, perhaps on automatic,' I replied. 'Do you recognise the place?'

He shook his head.

'I do not know if we've even reached street level yet.'

The walls were decorated with elaborate frescos that were too dimmed by grime to understand. I thought they were scenes of triumphs and Imperial glories, for I could just make out noble figures in gold and crimson, swords brandished aloft, and revelling putti cavorting in blue skies. I did not intend to stop and study it in more detail. We picked our way between ormolu furniture left to rot, and pieces of ceiling plasterwork that had fallen in disrepair and shattered across the polished ouslite floor.

'Ninth Legion,' Lightburn muttered. 'They wore red, didn't they?'

'According to the stories.'

'But they didn't have no wings...'

'This from a man who, until two minutes ago, swore they did not exist. Now you are an expert?'

'What Astartes have wings?' he replied.

'Their sire did,' I answered.

'Their sire, yes...' Lightburn shuddered. 'Sanguinus.'

'*Sanguinius*,' I corrected.

'But...' he pressed, 'acceptin' that they *are* real, the Astartes were heroes of the Throne. The mightiest of all. They weren't no... blood-thirsting beasts.'

'They were not, so the myths report,' I said, 'but up is down.'

'It's what?'

I held up my hand sharply. We were not alone.

Their approach had been as silent as the darkness they dwelt in. They had been lying in wait, perhaps, or drawn by our voices. The anatomists edged out of the shadows, or emerged from behind decayed chairs and side tables. Some had slings ready, others clutched bone axes or stabbing spears. They snuffled and growled, perhaps forty in total, and we were pinned, for they were both ahead of us and behind.

We drew our guns and swung back to back.

'I have six rounds,' Lightburn said.

'I have three loads of four,' I replied, though I knew there would be no reloading in the chaos of a fray.

'Make 'em count,' he advised, 'then take one of their weapons when you're out.'

The anatomists surged. Lightburn's pistol barked, putting two on the floor. I fired my quad, aiming for body mass, and firing only one shot at a touch. My first bullet exploded a chest in a gout of blood. The quad's ammunition was built for stopping power.

I checked, and put a second shot through a belly. The bone-keeper was spun off his feet before he could loose his spear, his blood dappling the white-powdered skin of the men behind him. My third shot took down two: it eviscerated the first, and then slug fragments struck the anatomist to his left, and he fell too, bleeding from the calf and wrist.

Our shots were overlapping, one boom-and-flash across the next.

I had lost count of Renner's firing. I thought he was out, then heard another boom.

But it was not Lightburn's gun discharging.

It was the double doors splintering open, bolts sheared, bar snapped.

The killer angel burst into the hall, snarling. Two racing strides, and it was airborne, swooping the length of the ancient hall with titanic wing-beats that stirred the air like the rushing of breaking waves. It uttered a strigine shriek.

It swept into the rear of the anatomist pack charging me, striking like a giant hawk. As it had been when it assaulted us, the angel's speed was beyond measure, too quick for the eye. The anatomists had barely turned before it commenced their destruction. Its strength was beyond measure, too. With bare hands alone, it tore limbs clean off, dug fingers through meat to rip out spines, crushed skulls. In seconds, it was drenched in blood, clamping teeth into the throats of flailing wretches, tearing.

Drinking.

It was drinking their blood as it killed them, like a raging sot demolishing half-finished glasses at a bar, tossing them aside to reach the next. It was the most appalling slaughter I had ever witnessed. The most barbaric extermination, a blind rending of flesh and cracking of bone.

The anatomist throng facing Lightburn beheld this dread scene, and turned tail. Perhaps they had seen its predation before, or the predation of its angelic kind. Perhaps that was why they had nailed its brother angel to a cross. The bone-keepers must have discovered that one dead, or sick, for there was no way they could ever have overcome such a killer.

I grabbed Lightburn's arm and dragged him to run after the fleeing anatomists. The angel was almost done with the rest of them. A lake of blood spread from the mangled bodies surrounding him as it gorged upon the last. Lightburn could barely look away. He gazed in horrid fascination at the angel's massacre.

'Run!' I cried.

He began to, but I knew we would not get far.

'Renner,' I said. 'Renner! Look at me!'

He tore his gaze away from the spectacle of murder, and found my eyes.

'I'm going to turn off my cuff. My limiter cuff. It is our only hope, but you must brace yourself.'

He nodded.

I turned off the cuff. I felt him tremble at my side, and I heard him stifle a murmur of discomfort.

The angel stopped killing. It let go of the shredded corpse it was feeding on, and let it drop with a splash. The angel was washed in gore, its face, its chest, its hands. Blood spats flecked the white skin of its massive arms, and hung like rubies on the frosty fibres of its feathers. Blood drops swung like garnets from the strands of its lank black hair.

Hunched, it turned to look at me. It grunted and growled, short barks like yelps of pain that aspirated blood from its nostrils and lips.

'Go back,' I said.

I took a step towards it. The angel took a step back, splashing blood underfoot.

'You must go back,' I said.

It shook its head, sending blood drops flying.

'You must.'

It spoke. Its voice was too quiet to hear, as if it had not been used in a very long time.

'What did you say?' I asked. I took another step.

The angel coughed, and spat out black clots.

'You take it away,' it said. Its tone was flat, no more than a whisper.

'What do I take away?'

'The Thirst. The Rage and the Thirst.'

'Are you Astartes, a Blood Angel?' I asked.

The angel hesitated, as though it didn't know how to answer, or did not understand the words.

'Comus,' it said.

'Comus?'

'Comus Nocturnus. That is my name. Was my name.'

It... or I should say, *he*, regarded me again, and brushed the blood-soaked hair from his face. He straightened up from his hunch. He was demigod tall, and the tips of the folded wings at his back made him taller.

'Are you a null?' he asked.

I nodded. 'You say that calms you?'

'It is... uncomfortable,' he replied. 'But I crave it too. My mind has not felt such peace for...' He shrugged, an oddly emphatic gesture when one is in possession of giant wings. 'I know not how long. What year is it?'

Before I could answer, the angel frowned.

'I tried to kill you,' he said. 'You and the man beside you.'

'Yes,' I said. 'And I fear you will do so again if I unblank.'

'No,' he replied. 'I have slaked my thirst. Years of craving. It will not return for a while.'

He looked down at the grisly mess around him in what seemed like utter disgust.

'I want nothing except to see the light again. Liberty from the darkness that has bound me. Do you know the way out?'

'I think I can find it,' I said.

'We can't–' I heard Lightburn hiss.

'What?' I said, aside.

'We can't let that thing into the city,' he said between clenched teeth. He was plainly terrified of the monstrous angel, but could barely bring himself to look at me.

'Renner, I don't think we can prevent *that thing* from doing anything,' I said.

I kept my cuff set *off*.

The angel followed us, just walking, a few paces at our backs. He seemed oblivious to his own nakedness, or his impossibility.

Lightburn kept glancing back, and walked at a good distance apart from me.

'What is your story?' I asked, over my shoulder.

'I have none,' the angel rumbled.

'Surely–'

'I existed in the darkness, and the darkness was endless. I did not live, I just existed. I was in the darkness, chained to a rock, and wracked by maddening thirst. Whole ages of the world turned, I'm sure, while I suffered that torment. What world is this?'

'Sancour, in Angelus,' I replied.

'And the date?'

I told him that too.

'Those things mean nothing,' the angel said. 'I remember nothing.'

'You know your name,' I said. 'And you know about nulls.'

'Yes,' he admitted. 'But it is all a fog. There was a war. No beginning or end. I was wrought in it and for it, my rage bred to be turned upon the foe. A calamitous thing. The end of all things. I wore red.'

'Who fought?'

'I did.'

'But for what cause, and against–'

'I do not know, null. Just a blur of red. Of flame. Of death. My enemy was whatever I saw. Thus I was commanded.'

'By whom?' I asked.

I looked back at him. He had halted. He eyed me sadly, and shook his head.

'I have no idea,' he replied.

'Well,' I said, 'your name is Comus Nocturnus. I believe you are of the Ninth Legion Astartes, called the Blood Angels. I do not know why you are winged, or driven by blood-thirst. I *do* know you are not the only one of your kind. In Queen Mab, we will find you some answers.'

'Who is Queen Mab?' he asked.

'The city,' said Lightburn.

'And who are you?' he asked.

'I am Beta,' I said, 'and this is Renner. I would ask you note us both well, and do us no harm.'

'If you command it,' said the angel. 'I was bred to obey.'

'Then I command it,' I said.

The angel nodded. I turned my cuff on.

'Are you mad, woman?' Lightburn gasped.

The angel sighed. The madness in his black eyes did not return.

'I have been commanded,' he said. He sniffed.

'Is that rain?' he asked.

We emerged into the downpour in the shadow of the old Gault Manufactory east of Highgate Hill. The last hour had been a climb up mouldering steps and ragged slopes, leaving the buried palace underground as we tracked through sewers and storm drains to the surface proper.

It was dark, and the storm had not abated. Lightburn sat on a low brick wall to ease his feet. Comus stood in the rain, his head tilted back, eyes closed, and let the water wash the blood off his skin. Lightburn watched him.

'What kind o' life do you lead,' he asked me quietly, 'that such things are everyday to you?'

'They are not.'

'Yet you take 'em in your stride. And I still don't know nothing about you, nor your line of work.'

'I am an agent of the Throne,' I said. No matter which side I stood on, I knew that to be true. 'There's a man I want you to meet,' I said to the angel. 'I believe he might be able to help you.'

'Can he help me?' Lightburn asked.

'You he already knows, so stay by my side and keep your counsel. I will vouch for you.'

'Does he not like me?' Lightburn wondered.

'He will like you because I will tell him to,' I said. 'Now, come on. We're going to Talltown.'

'On foot?' Lightburn asked, getting up. 'We're to walk through the streets with...'

He didn't finish the sentence, merely gestured to the naked, winged giant.

'If we have to,' I said.

So we did. The storm and the hour had entirely emptied the streets. Rain belted, and lights shone behind window shutters. Once, a lit tram rattled past in the distance. I saw the faces of half a dozen sleepy or drunken passengers gawp in our direction, but then we were gone from their view, and I knew they would disbelieve themselves come morning. Lightburn pulled up his hood and trudged with his hands in his pockets. The angel padded behind us, without modesty, marvelling at the empty streets and the city buildings.

'This city,' he remarked, 'it smells new.'

'It is the oldest place I know,' I said.

'Fresh and new,' the angel insisted, 'as if it was built yesterday.'

We were crossing Eelhigh Square, empty of any other people at this hour, when I heard a familiar crackle in the driving rain.

'There you are.'

Cherubael drifted into view like a sad, lost kite, and bounced weightlessly off the pavement in front of us. He had appeared without warning. When he travelled abroad in the city, his daemonic gifts cloaked him from casual gaze.

'Ooooh,' said the daemonhost with some concern, 'little thing, what *have* you found?'

Lightburn was speechless. Terrified, in fact. I regretted not confirming the existence of daemons to him earlier. The angel tensed, and narrowed his eyes.

'Daemon,' he murmured.

'Daemonhost,' I specified. 'And chained. Your protection is not needed.' I looked at Cherubael, 'Nor is yours.'

'But the sight of him offends me,' Cherubael said mildly.

'Control yourself.'

The daemonhost pouted, disappointed.

'I've been looking for you,' he said. 'He told me to. You're late, little thing, and it is almost midnight. He may start without you. I see you found the Curst boy. Was he where I said he would be? I don't know why you had to find *that* too.' The daemonhost glared at the angel.

'I do not much care for the company you keep, Beta,' Comus said.

I turned to him. 'I'm sorry, but work demands it. I ask your patience, and your tolerance. If I am to help you–'

The angel shook his head sadly.

'You have helped me already,' he said. He held out a hand, palm up, and let the raindrops strike it. 'Rain,' he said, with a child's simple delight, 'and a sky.'

He looked up.

And was gone. His great wings took him aloft before I could speak. He soared, a dart of white against the low night sky, banked around the tower of St Phaedra-Over-Keep, and vanished.

'Well, thank gods *he's* gone,' said Cherubael. '*That* was awkward.'

Way past midnight, we came to Talltown, the daemonhost trailing above us like a windblown banner on a length of chain. Just streets away from Bifrost, I knew something was wrong.

Cherubael did too. Without a word, the daemonhost sped away ahead of us.

I started to run. Lightburn held back. He had kept his distance from the daemonhost, and his fear of Cherubael was very raw. He had no wish to follow the thing anywhere.

'What is it?' Lightburn yelled.

'Keep up!'

'What is it, Beta?'

I came to the street. I had not been mistaken. The amber glow I had seen, shivering behind the nearby habs, was a raging blaze.

Bifrost was on fire.

The second section of the story,
which is called

MY WARBAND

CHAPTER 12

Which is of embers

The flames leapt to the top of all the world. They were not like, as one might say, mortal flames, such as might devour a dry forest after a thunderstrike, or burn through a kitchen from an unwatched grate. They were tongued blue with subliming heat, and green with the vapours of oxides. The heat of them was as a furnace, transforming metal to liquid, evaporating all that was organic, a daemon-fire that ate into the very earth, and baked it, and split it, so that the world cracked open, and the ranges of high mountains crumbled and fell, and millions died, engulfed in the firestorms and the blizzards of cinders, and in the sleet of las-fire that rained from the skies, loosed from the hands of predatory angels. They flocked like keening white vultures in the endless smoke, and fell upon the burning planet to administer its destruction entire, on the booming command of a giant King in Yellow, daemon-dogs leashed at his heels, his hand outstretched, armoured in matchless gold, to signal doom, and the War which would abolish all wars and–

So, I awoke, and I knew that the dream had repeated, a loop of dreams that played unbidden every night. Four days had passed since Bifrost's immolation. Fire kept me awake, then ignited my dreams, so that I woke, crying out with fear, with sweat upon my brow.

Four days, four nights. The bunker was quiet. I rose from my cot. It was early. Renner had gone out. An empty cup stood on the table. This had become his sign, so that I would know he would be returning. He slipped away to the markets at dawn, to fetch food and hot caffeine, and the cup said he would come back to fill it. In this way, he did not have to wake me.

Bifrost had burned, wholly. We had raced to it that night, but the heat had been too great, and there was no way to enter the blaze. I stood in horror and watched the building's destruction. Crowds gathered. Fire-watch brigades rushed from six boroughs with their bowser-wagons and hatchets, but they could not fight it.

It spread from Bifrost into the adjoining properties, and by the next morning, six whole blocks of Talltown mansions were ablaze. Hundreds fled their homes. Firebreaks were set. Smoke choked the city as far as Feygate. The old curfew chains were hung across the thoroughfares to keep the crowds back. The Baron Prefect came in person, with a detachment of city militia, to observe in disapproval from a safe distance. In the news sheets and handbills, it stated that he abhorred the loss, and that he pledged investigation by the Arbites and District Watch to find the cause and prevent a further such tragedy. Some spoke of arson, most agreed that the chronic decrepitude of Queen Mab's ragged and unsafe infrastructure was the likely culprit.

During the second day, there were general fears that the monstrous Talltown blaze might carry out of control, and set light the whole city, and that Queen Mab might suffer another Great Fire, like that which had roared through it in 677. But the long and angry storm that the city had endured finally did some good, and the ceaseless rains began to rob the fire of force.

By the third day, the fire was out, all except for Bifrost itself, the original seat, which was by then a blackened collapse. All was lost. Even the daemonhost, which had run on ahead of us when the fire was first sighted, and had never returned.

Alone, except for Lightburn, I waited in the vicinity the first night, then took myself away when it was evident I could do nothing. Eisenhorn's warband had been operating in Queen Mab for two decades, and there were standing plans for emergencies, such as an attack on the house. We were to repair to one of several locations arranged and secured in advance of need. I had been told of one, and trusted with the code of its lock. Medea had told me to go there if need arose or contact was lost.

The place was a basement beneath merchant properties near the Pauper's Field Commercia in Shorthalls. At street level, there was a butchery, a flower stall, a vintner's, and the premises of a maker of hats and, above those, the shabby offices of bookkeepers, practitioners of jurisprudence, a mender-tailor, and a physik who treated ailments of the eyes and ground lenses for spectacles. The basement could be accessed by a side gate and an underyard. It was a three-room bunker, no more, no less, without windows or much in the way of amenities, except cots, a table, some damp bedding and a cargo trunk. Inside the trunk were various weapons wrapped in oilcloth, and a vox-caster unit.

I set the 'caster up, and tried repeated contact using the channels and codes I had been taught. There was no answer from Eisenhorn, from Medea or from Nayl. For Deathrow and Cherubael, there was no code.

I continued with the code-sends, every half-hour.

Late on the second day, just as I was readying the 'caster for the next send, the bunker door opened. Lightburn and I turned to it rapidly, weapons aimed.

'You're here, then,' said Harlon Nayl.

He came in, begrimed with soot, and evidently exhausted. We fetched him broth, and he barely acknowledged Lightburn.

I asked Nayl what had occurred. He but shrugged.

'Eisenhorn had planned an interrogation,' he said. 'It was to begin at midnight. He was frustrated that you'd gone out, and annoyed that you were late back. He wanted you there. He delayed the start.'

'An interrogation of whom?' I asked him.

'Mam Tontelle,' Nayl replied.

'Harlon, Mam Tontelle is dead,' I said.

'So?' he asked.

'Well...'

'It's a thing that can be done,' he said, with a dismissive flick of his hand. 'Psykana. It's a technique the boss has done before, now and then. You can get decent answers from the recently dead. They have nothing to lose, I guess.'

'Are you... Do you mean a séance?' Lightburn asked, with much incredulity.

Nayl looked at the Curst.

'You're back, then?' he said. 'Yes, a séance. A para-audience. He wanted to know who or what had spoken through the old girl that night in the salon. He sent Cherubael to sneak her body from the coroner. Anyway, Eisenhorn waited a while, then ordered the daemonhost out to take one last look for you. Then he decided to waste no more time, and started.'

'Did it work?' I asked.

Nayl sniffed. 'Yeah. Always does. It's some sick shit, but yes. It gets results.'

'Such as?'

He shrugged. 'Names, I think. Couple o' names. The poor old bird was gabbling. I don't think she had fully grasped the situation. She was worried about her missing pearls.'

He glanced at us. Nayl looked old, and more burdened by woe than Lightburn.

'Then a house alarm went off,' he said, monotone. 'Perimeter. Cherubael was still out, so I went to check. I figured it was a fault. Interrogations, see, they can drop temperatures fast. Cause ice to form. I thought a sensor had tripped. So I went down, to the street at the back. There was nothing. I was about to go back in when...' Nayl made a 'pop' with his lips, and drew his hands apart, fingers splayed. 'Place went up like a torch,' he said. 'So hot, so fast, I couldn't get back inside.'

'What of Eisenhorn? And Medea?' I asked.

Nayl shook his head.

'Dead?' I asked.

The bounty hunter shrugged again.

'Was it a device?' Lightburn asked. 'A bomb?'

'Something,' said Nayl. 'No accident. Bifrost cooked from inside. And the heat, it was beyond a natural blaze. It roasted like a flamer was on it, and it spread so damn fast. I went around from the south end, and tried to get in through the next building along. But that was a furnace too. Then I saw the daemonhost. He went into the flames–'

'He was with us,' I said. 'He rushed ahead–'

'Well, he didn't come out again. That's some fire that burns the likes of him.'

'Could they have escaped using the gun-cutter?' I asked.

'I don't know,' said Nayl. 'I saw nothing.' He looked at the vox-set. 'But if they had, we'd have heard something. You've got nothing on that?'

'Nothing,' I said.

Nayl took a comm-pack out of his jacket and put it on the table.

'Me neither,' he said. He rose to his feet.

'So, it was an attack?' I asked. 'A strike against us?'

'I'm sure of it,' he replied. 'Because Deathrow's gone dark too.'

Deathrow was a satellite operator, independently active. Even Nayl knew very little about him, or how he had come to be in Eisenhorn's cohort, but Nayl's read was correct. If Deathrow had gone dark, someone or something had targeted the entire group. There was a chance that Deathrow had seen what had occurred at Bifrost, and gone under deep to maintain security, but he would have answered Nayl's code-sends.

No, the team had been targeted, Nayl had survived by happenstance, and I had only escaped because I had been delayed elsewhere.

I tried to talk to Nayl more, to establish some game plan, but he would not be drawn. He insisted we wait a few days, to see if belated contact came. I concurred. I think I had only wanted to talk some more so I didn't have to think about the loss. The end of Eisenhorn was a tragedy for the Throne. The loss of Medea hurt me worse. I had known her by far the longest, for in her role as Sister Bismillah at the Scholam Orbus, she had all but raised me until the age of twelve.

On that fourth morning, then, I awoke in the bunker. The dreams of fire and cataclysm tormented me. The visions were terrible, and augured grave disaster to come. But their fires had replaced the darkness and noxious dreams the daemon had conjured.

For those cloying dreams to have gone, though I had wished it, meant the daemon was gone too.

I ran the code-sends, then went up to the street to wait for Lightburn. Down the road, the market was setting up. The neighbourhood air still smelled of smoke. I knew we had a choice to make, Nayl and I.

Lightburn returned, and Nayl not long after. He was filthy with soot again. We went down into the bunker, and sat around the table, drinking caffeine from the flask Lightburn had bought.

'I got onto the site,' Nayl said. 'Still hot, but I raked around. There's nothing left. I thought if the cutter had been caught, I might find parts of it. Debris. But nothing.'

'So, they got out?' I asked.

Nayl looked dubious.

'That craft was heavily armoured,' I said. 'It was built to endure combat. You would have seen debris, at least. Armour plate–'

'The fire was not natural, Beta,' he said. 'I told you that. Far too hot. The girders of the building, ferrocast, had melted down. Imagine that. They're wrought to withstand burning. So the cutter may have been consumed too.'

'Then we must–' I began.

'What? What must we?' Nayl asked.

'Act on the presumption they are dead,' I said. He looked bitterly surprised. 'We waste time otherwise, Nayl,' I said. 'It's what he would expect of us, isn't it?'

'Of course–'

'And if he returns,' I said, 'if *they* return, then we will have work to show them.'

Nayl sat back.

'Say your mind then,' he said. 'But know we are poorly provided, and there's just the two of us.'

'Three,' I said, indicating Lightburn.

Nayl sneered.

'Your Curst there can be handy, I'll admit,' he said.

'You're too kind,' said Lightburn.

'*But*,' Nayl went on, 'he knows nothing of this. Throne, you and I, Beta, we know shit-all either. Gregor had the overview.'

'Then let us consider what we *do* know,' I suggested. 'First… Who struck at Bifrost?'

Nayl laughed, an ugly sound.

'How long do you have?' he asked.

'Yes, there are plenty of parties in the frame, and we won't exclude any, but I think there are two chief suspects.'

'The Cognitae,' said Nayl.

'The Cognitae,' I agreed. 'They were the cause of this operation, and they are Gregor's oldest foes. Some of their people escaped the Maze Undue… Mam Mordaunt, perhaps Saur and Murlees, perhaps even the Secretary. My point is they are still potentially active, and Undue was surely not their only stronghold here.'

'They haven't shown up since,' said Nayl, 'and they've probably gone to ground after Gideon hit them so damn hard.'

'So, they've waited,' I said. 'The Cognitae play the long game–'

'The longest,' he agreed.

'And they are a large operation. They may have got word out, and had reinforcement sent. It's only been months, not that long. And we know the Cognitae's work was grooming and procurement, through the scholams, to find suitable grael vessels for the Yellow King. At the Lengmur Salon, someone tried to pass information to us via Mam Tontelle, and she was silenced by graels. Then Eisenhorn pushes that with his séance, to get the truth from Mam Tontelle's remains, and Bifrost is hit. Another silencing.'

'The old girl's message concerned Chase's blue book, didn't it?' Nayl asked.

'My reconstruction of which is now lost in the fire,' I nodded.

'So, the Cognitae,' Nayl said. 'And that makes your second suspect the King himself.'

'No,' I said. 'Not him. The King, whoever and whatever he is, keeps himself apart. It almost feels as if we are too small for his bother. The Cognitae handles such matters on his behalf. He does not intervene directly–'

'The graels–' Nayl protested.

'Even the graels of the so-called Eight, Harlon. They are his servants, yes, but I think they operate through the Cognitae too.'

'You don't know that,' he said.

'I don't. But I think the King is only involved in as much as others have come after his adversaries for him. I really think he operates on another level entirely.'

'So who is your second suspect?' Nayl asked.

'Ravenor,' I said.

'No,' he said.

'Ravenor's operation is almost the twin of ours,' I said. 'He seeks the King, and all the King's men. The difference is, Ravenor believes Eisenhorn is one of them. We know he seeks to apprehend or destroy Eisenhorn. We know the Ordos have only permitted him to continue as an inquisitor if he brings down his old master.'

'No,' Nayl repeated.

'No? Because he was once your friend, and you cannot bear to think he would do so?'

'He wouldn't strike so bluntly,' said Nayl. My suggestion had got him annoyed. 'It's not his way. So direct, and with such force.'

'Eisenhorn fully expected he would,' I said. 'He told me so.'

'You're wrong–' said Nayl.

'The Ravenor I met was both strong-willed *and* direct,' I replied. 'If he had a chance, he would strike, and do the job he was sent to do. He would not flinch because of sentiment. He and Eisenhorn may have been close once–'

Nayl slapped his hand on the table and made me jump.

'No,' he said. 'I was in Gideon's band for a long time. I know his workings. He loves Eisenhorn. He cannot, I believe, accept that Eisenhorn has turned. Listen to me, Ravenor knows the day must come, some time. But I think he is putting the inevitable off. He wants no clash. And if the Ordos ask why he dallies and delays, then his answer is simple. He is observing. Gregor's been in this struggle longer. Gideon's best route to the King is through Eisenhorn. He's cunning, Beta. He would not shut that lead down by killing it. Think about it. Ravenor sent you back to infiltrate us, not kill us. He shadows us. He learns what Eisenhorn knows, then uses that to bring the full weight of the Ordos down and topple the King. And maybe, in that hoo-ha, he can take Gregor alive. His job gets done, and perhaps then he can plead Gregor's case to the Lords of the Inquisition. Leniency, because Eisenhorn has led them to the King.'

'And they would spare him?'

'They might.'

I sighed. 'It's academic, anyway. The deed's done. Your loyalty, Harlon, is admirable, but it's split. You're Eisenhorn's man, not Ravenor's, not any more. You love them both. I think that love makes you forget they are both inquisitors. *Inquisitors*, Harlon! Souls bred to be hard, to be ruthless, to be merciless to the point of cruelty. It is the only way they can perform the task the Emperor has set them. Ravenor would kill Eisenhorn without remorse. Eisenhorn would kill Ravenor. You're a hunter, Harlon, a sell-sword. Throne knows how many lives you've taken in your career. A stone killer. Yet, compared to them, you are a gentle and forgiving soul.'

'Screw you,' said Nayl, and got up with a screech of chair legs. He strode across the room and found the bottle of amasec he'd purchased the night before. He poured a heavy measure into a tin cup, and downed it.

'You're right,' he murmured at last, staring at the bunker's dank wall. 'This damn life takes a toll. It breaks you, no matter how hard you're made. Only the strongest – and for that you may read "cruellest" – prevail, and that's why they are given the rosette. Inquisitors. I hate the bastards. Hate 'em, and love 'em the same. There is ruthless, and there is them.'

He glanced at me.

'Yes, I'm a killer,' he said. 'A fighter. So was Medea. So was Midas. So are sweet Kara, and crazy Kys. So were all of them that came before. Misfits, killers, warriors, specialists. Toughest folk you'd meet, or not care to, on any world. But just fodder to them. Instruments. Agents of use. But even the most black-hearted and brutal of us... *fah*! We didn't have a scrap of their merciless resolve.'

He raised the cup, a mocking salute.

'To fighters,' he said. 'All of 'em, your mother amongst them.'

Nayl poured another measure, and stared at it as he swished it around in the cup.

'I think I'm in your way,' he said. 'You can't trust me.'

'I know I can,' I said.

Nayl shook his head and took a swig.

'You think like him, you know that?' he said. 'Just like him. Clarity. Razor focus. No sentiment to cloud you. I don't know if it's your mother's blood, or the way the Cognitae shaped your temper. Anyway, you see through me. I'm torn, and I have been for years. Two masters. Yes, I made a choice, but I'm damned either way. In this rivalry, my judgement is bad. I can't see the game for the people in it. So I think it's better I walk. Now, before I do some real harm with a poor decision. If I stay, I'll mess this up.'

'A poor decision?' asked Lightburn mildly. 'Like that one?'

Nayl eyed him.

'Shut your trap,' he said.

'You go,' said Lightburn, 'you'll diminish this party by a third.'

'A third, is it?' said Nayl archly. 'You're not a part of anything, Curst. Just a hanger-on. A stray. Part of nothing, and not much use.'

'Well, if I'm nothing, and you go,' said Lightburn, 'she'll be alone.'

Nayl stared at him. He was going to say something, but the words didn't form. He put the cup down.

'Sorry,' he said, and walked out.

CHAPTER 13

Names and tactics

'Will he come back, d'you think?' Lightburn asked.

I made a face.

'Thank you for trying to speak some reason, though,' I said.

'Weren't nothing,' he replied.

'Renner,' I said, 'you can go too. Whenever you like. You know that, don't you? You're not part of this if you don't want to be.'

'Reckon as I'll stay, for a while,' he said. 'See, I don't have anything. Not a thing, apart from a burden and one friend. So I'll stay.'

'You do not like to bear your friend when the truth of her pariah soul is open to you,' I ventured, 'and I understand that.'

'I've borne worse,' he said. 'Just try not to do it too much.'

I left him to do the code-sends, the way of which I had taught to him, and went out. Late morning, and the rain had eased for the first time in days, as though the storm clouds had exhausted themselves in putting out the Talltown fire. The Pauper's Field Commercia was in full swing, and bustling with trade. I went on through Shorthalls, past the packing plants and the rusted silos of the derelict orbital wharf.

I walked to clear my head, and straighten my thoughts. It was, it seemed, all down to me, now. There was a mission of great importance to be accomplished, and it was in my hands. It was perhaps, I decided, now my time to take the role of the *alpha*. Only out past Clerestory Rise did it occur to me that I had placed myself in the open. Those who had struck at Bifrost, and perhaps at Deathrow too, were still out there, and here I was, full of bold thoughts of strategy and approach, thinking like I was some interrogator taking charge of a case, yet acting like an untrained amateur.

I turned my cuff at once to *dead*, so that I might walk less noticed, or at least deter the interest and approach of any undesirables, and turned back, making my way home by a different route, my pace quicker, and my vigilance sharper. If I was going to be the lead on this now, I had to raise my game, and remember all of my training. All of the skills and all of the temper that had been forged in me by the Cognitae, now in the service of the Inquisition.

Returning to the bunker through the other end of Shorthalls, I saw him sitting in a commercia tavern, the Starry-Gazey. The front doors were open to the noon street to welcome thirsty market traders. There he sat, just inside, alone in a patch of the day's weak sunshine. I had seen him before he noticed me.

I restored the limiter, went in, and sat down, facing him. Nayl looked up.

'I was coming back,' he said.

'I know.'

'I was.'

'Because you've had time to think,' I said.

'In truth,' he said, 'I was coming back because I'd remembered something. But I was coming back. I can't leave you to this, because I know damn well you'll keep on.'

'I will.'

He nodded. 'Well,' he said, 'this game will kill me. I know it. But something's got to.'

'What did you remember?' I asked.

'Names,' he said. 'They came to me, sitting here. It's all been so much since the fire. Zoya. And Connort.'

'And who are they?'

'The two names spoken by Mam Tontelle's chattering corpse during the interrogation. I wasn't playing close attention, because those sessions turn your stomach, but I heard her dead lips say 'em before I left the room.'

I thought on it.

'Zoya... I don't know. But Connort...'

'It's a common name,' said Nayl.

'Yes, and I know one. Connort. Connort Timurlin. "The" famous musician. One of Crookley's entourage at the Two Gogs.'

'So he was there that night?' Nayl asked. 'The night Tontelle turned up her toes?'

'Yes,' I said. 'He was at Lengmur's before he went to the Gogs with us. That's not all. Just before Tontelle's act started, I saw him in conversation with a woman at the salon door. It was a serious matter, whatever it was. I didn't know him at the time, we were only introduced later. But the woman he was with...'

'What about her?'

'I knew her from somewhere.'

'You knew her?'

I nodded.

'Well, *where*, Beta? I know what your recall's like. You see a face, you know it.'

'That's the thing,' I said. 'I knew that I knew her, but I could not place her or give her a name.'

'So?'

I smiled at him.

'It means she was in disguise, Harlon. A very good disguise. I did not know who she was pretending to be, but I could still recognise the actor beneath.'

'A disguise?' He raised his eyebrows.

'I'm not talking about dress-up, Nayl. I mean *trained* disguise. She was performing a function. She was someone's agent.'

'Bet you all the coins in my pocket I know whose,' he said.

We walked back together through the market.

'We have options,' I said, 'but I know the one I mean to take first.'

'Go to the Two Gogs?' he suggested.

'That's second,' I said. 'First, I go with the plan I have been considering since Cherubael fetched me back to Bifrost.'

'*We* go with the plan, you mean?' he said.

'Yes.'

'And what is this plan?'

'I'm going to Ravenor,' I said.

'Oh no,' he replied. 'Medea told me of your notion. Go back to him and pretend you're turning? The double-cross? Worm your way in? It's too late for that.'

'It is,' I said. 'And I think Talon would see right through it anyway, no matter how well I played my function.'

'So what then?'

We had reached the side gate and walked down the steps to the bunker's door.

'We just go to him,' I said. 'No pretence. We tell him what happened. We tell him what's at stake. We share what we have. He's an agent of the Ordos, Harlon. One of the best. We have a mutual enemy. And *we* need a warband.'

We went inside. Lightburn looked up, and casually nodded to Nayl as though nothing had passed earlier in the day.

'All right?' he said.

'Fine,' said Nayl, with equal nonchalance. 'Help me talk some sense into her.'

Lightburn sat up.

'Her plan,' said Nayl, pulling up a chair, 'her plan, to glorify it with such a name, is to go to Ravenor.'

'Under what pretence?'

'Under no pretence,' Nayl told him.

'This is Ravenor, who hunts for us as heretics?' Lightburn said.

'The very same,' said Nayl.

'Well, I ain't never met him,' said Lightburn, 'except that I have, but I don't remember nothing of it, because Ravenor, so I am told, burned my memory out like a poker through paper so, yeah, I'd say that's a stupid bloody plan.'

Nayl turned to me with a grin.

'See?' he said. 'Even he thinks so, and he doesn't even matter.'

I smiled. 'Ravenor wants the King, we want the King,' I said. 'The city is rife with enemies, or at least factions that are hostile to both of us. We are outnumbered, and so is Ravenor. I say we face him, and lay our cards on the table. A truce, a unity. Throne knows, they have both ever bent the rules. Eisenhorn *and* Ravenor. Necessary compromise. That's why one's called a heretic and the other is labelled a rogue. They bend the rules for the greater goal. Indeed, they are above the rules. That is the power of an inquisitor. They side with that which serves... Like daemons. So, a truce, and a pooling of knowledge and resources... That would far outweigh the differences.'

'I'd just point out,' said Lightburn, 'that earlier you were the one namin' Ravenor a chief suspect in the murder of your friends. Convincingly so.'

'And I still think it may have been him,' I conceded. 'But inquisitors see the bigger picture, and that's the Yellow King, not us. We have knowledge Ravenor lacks, leads he knows nothing of. He'll see the advantage of siding with us, at least on a temporary basis.'

Nayl opened his mouth to speak, but I wasn't done.

'And further,' I said, hand up, 'face to face, we'll know. We'll know if it was him. We'll know if he's the enemy that burned Bifrost. We'll meet with him and make friends, or claim some vengeance.'

'You reckon we can take him?' Nayl asked, amused. 'Him and Kara and Patience?'

'I've beaten Kys before. We're one-all, in fact. But yes, I think we can. You know their plays, and you're no slouch. And I am a blacksoul blank, and *that* trumps his dreaded psykana.'

'I also have a gun,' said Lightburn, raising his hand.

Nayl and I looked at him, and we both nodded eagerly to humour him.

'I don't relish the idea of this coming to blood,' Nayl said. 'But it's inevitable. So... Maybe it's best to get it done and over with.'

He glanced at me.

'Is there nothing I can do to talk you out of this?' he asked. 'I mean, technically, you hold no rank over me. In terms of seniority–'

'And yet here we are,' I said.

'Still and all,' said Nayl. 'Do you really–'

'My call,' I said. 'We established this morning that you are torn, and thus cannot be relied on to make good decisions. You admitted it.'

'You kind o' did,' said Lightburn.

'You can't be objective, Harlon,' I said. 'I can. My judgement is... This is what we're doing.'

Nayl sat for a moment, exhaled wearily, then got to his feet. He walked over to the vox-caster, set the dials carefully, and picked up the mic, letting the spiral cord dangle.

He threw the 'send' switch.

'Thorn wishes Talon,' he said.

CHAPTER 14

Upon the slipway

Thus it was that a meeting was arranged. I cannot pretend I was not apprehensive. My dealings with Gideon Ravenor had been brief, but I was in no doubt of his power. In many ways, he was to me a more alarming and dangerous prospect than Eisenhorn. So often, the pupil exceeds the mentor.

In truth, I know, as I had told Nayl, that they were *both* immeasurably dangerous and ruthless. But with Gregor Eisenhorn, I had always felt I had a small advantage: his uncharacteristic affection for the late Alizebeth Bequin, and my connection to her. It was a rare fingerhold of emotional loyalty, an unspoken bond that he tacitly acknowledged in his dealings with me, and which preserved me somewhat. Eisenhorn had gone through life showing no regard, ultimately, for any human soul, except for my mother, and thus, for me.

With Ravenor, I felt I had no such card to play.

But there were other safeguards and checks that I could employ. I knew I was playing with a weak hand, and from a position of severe disadvantage, but my mentors – no matter if they had been good people or bad – had taught me well. It was almost liberating. I answered to no one now, and used my years of training to prepare as well as I could. At last, I felt as though I was a player in the game, and not a mere pawn on the regicide board.

Nayl had set the meeting up, through vox exchanges coded in Glossia. He accessed private funds laid down in some of the city's counting houses, emergency deposits left by Eisenhorn over the years in case of extremity, and furnished us with some goods through the black market. I visited the municipality records archive at the City Chambers, and acquired copies of the site plans, which Nayl and I studied. Renner supplied his own, local knowledge. We devised the terms of the meeting, means of securement, and methods of exit should it go bad.

On the night before, I went up to the roof of the buildings beneath which the bunker was hidden, slipping up the dingy common staircase, past the landings of the bookkeepers and the mender-tailor, and the eye-doctor, until I faced the little roof door, painted shut, at the top of an unlit staircase. I forced it open, causing a little flurry of old paint chips, and went out onto the ragged, mossy tiles overlooking the Pauper's Field Commercia and Shorthalls in the fading light. I had told Nayl and Renner that I was going for a walk, to clear my head, and perhaps raise a prayer to the God-Emperor for His safekeeping.

That was a lie. I took a small blade with me.

The meeting was to take place on a slipway in the old shipyards south of Toilgate's crumbling mass. The day was not promising. The storm had shambled back into its lair, leaving lank, grey-smudged skies from which light rain fell in a desultory fashion. The sky was so wan and empty, it felt as though it had set itself to default, a vacant space awaiting new weather patterns to be programmed in and activated.

We were on the verge of the great river, on its tidal plain where once great industry had seethed to fill the coffers of Queen Mab. The throngs of shipyard workers no longer poured in and out of Toilgate every day, and the rockcrete roads were cracked and overtaken with weeds, and had not rung with the clump of hobnail boots for centuries. It was a very flat place, and wet. The old river, very wide at this point, lay like a grey strip along the horizon, and had taken back much of the land that industry had stolen from it. Old causeways ran out into watery nothing. Silted marshes had invaded the area for kilometres around, and lay stubbled with wretched trees and the mossy shells of derelict buildings. This was the marshland belt where, in some fabricated history, I had been born, and where my imaginary parents had died. From the slipway, I could see, across the marshes, the small and impoverished communities that still clung to the river's course: little dwellings, and the spire of a small templum church, all with blotted reflections. I fancied that its tiny, waterlogged yard might be the site of my parents' gravestone, but I did not pause to visit it, for that, I am sure, is all quite a fiction, and I did not know which would bother me more: to find no gravestone in the cemetery, or to find one after all, placed there to cement the lie.

Besides, I had work to do.

We went on foot, the three of us, via the holloways, and then on beyond the decaying city gate. The huge sheds of the shipyards stood at intervals along the wide marsh plain. They were buildings of ridiculous scale, raised in precast rockcrete, though in the great flatness they looked small. Within their walls, great ships had been wrought by armies of expert craftsmen, ships that would sail to other continents and other worlds. The sheds were ruined now, of course, and empty, though their sheer scale had allowed them to survive the generations of weather and neglect. The service buildings, annexes, store-blocks and canteens that must have once clustered around their flanks like little towns were long since gone, reduced to mudflats, weed-banks, beds of salt-willow or bare rockcrete platforms.

We had chosen Shed One Hundred & Nineteen. They were most all alike, but the number had appealed to me. It towered, a rotting monolith, from the marsh levels, fringed by morning mist. Everything was grey, like ink running in water, and the very air was damp, even in the breaks between showers. From the mouth of the shed, a giant slipway ran down to the river shore and the muddy bounds. Ships had once rolled out, along that great stone avenue, before cheering crowds.

We came two hours early, and reconnoitred. Neither Harlon nor I doubted that Ravenor's team might have scouted ahead, or even sent an advance into position. But the shed and its environs were vacant. Inside, it was a realm of wet shadow, dripping with rain from the incomplete roof, and piled with items of bulk engineering so black with corrosion it was impossible to determine what they had once been. There were great coils of metal chain, the links of quite fantastic size, too heavy for a man to shift, and lengths of this chain ran out from the shed's mouth and down the causeway like mighty marine serpents laid out as fishermen's trophies. Weeds nodded in the breeze. Out on the grey plain of the estuary, I could make out the grim shapes of the distant prison hulks: dead ships neutered, stripped of masts and engines and vanes, and moored in the river as exile gaols.

Satisfied the ground was ours to command, we took up our positions. Nayl secured himself on top of a giant engine block inside the shed doorway, which gave him a commanding view of the slipway. He had purchased a Militarum long-las rifle, along with scope, from some backstreet dealer, a marksman's weapon that would assure him a clear field of fire across the open rockcrete. Renner, armed with a reconditioned assault autorifle, laid in at the rear of the shed, out in the rain, with keen sight back across the approach roads and the marsh, all the way back to the ghostly mass of distant Toilgate. He would spot anything moving in our direction. We were linked by small vox headsets, again ex-Militarum, that Nayl called micro-beads. We checked in with each other on a timed schedule, for the space, and our placing, was so considerable we were almost out of contact by eyes alone.

I waited on the slipway, out in the open. My bodyglove was reinforced by a waistcoat of flak-mesh that Nayl had provided, and over this I wore a long coat with a hood collar. My quad-snub was in a belt holster, and a pair of stab-dirks – short, sharp knives for hand-combat or throwing called *sluca* – were strapped flat, one to each forearm. I had a short-pattern lascarbine on a sling over my shoulder. I had my cuff.

The cuff, set to *off*, was all that mattered. Without it, Ravenor's mind, and his minions, would overcome us in a trice, no matter what arsenal we fielded. I almost dreaded encountering the lethal telekine Kys again, as much as I did Ravenor.

I waited. I watched the distant flats of the river, the wind bristling the marsh grass. I smelled the cold, the wet. I felt the rain, and notched up the heating elements of my bodyglove. My mind would not be still. It jittered. I looked again, and saw the lonely little spire of the templum church once more, far away. I focused on that. For a moment, it troubled me, for it made me think of the memories I had grown up believing, memories I had been taught to regard as sad. But they were gone, and false, and there was nothing to mourn, at least not in that distant cemetery. Instead, I used the distant spire as a focal point, a *drishti*, as Mam

Mordaunt had called it, citing the ancient teachings of the Indus practices. Using it as a focus, I ran through my old tempering litany to still my mind and my nerves. It seemed quite odd to use what was most certainly a Cognitae mind-tool, but it had always served me well. Each of us at the Maze Undue had selected a calming memory as the basis of our tempering litany. Mine had been a passage from *The Heretikhameron*, that ancient verse epic that declaims the War of the Primarchs, *'... the Nine Sons Who Stood, and the Nine Who Turned'*.

But my tempering litany had never been just the words, it had also been Sister Bismillah's voice reciting them. She had often read the poem to me in the dormitory of the Scholam Orbus, so the memory of her gentle voice was an essential part of the meditation.

I stopped, almost at once, feeling a pang of true sadness, not the mendacious sadness of the distant spire. Sister Bismillah had been Medea, and Medea was lost. That was an honest and keen loss, far greater than anything I had grown up believing, and it was still raw.

My micro-bead clicked.

'Are you all right?' Nayl's voice murmured in my ear.

'Yes, Harlon,' I answered.

'Sure?'

'Yes.'

'I have eyes on you, Beta. You just seemed to falter there, for a moment. Something in your posture–'

'I'm fine,' I said.

I paced on the slipway. I thought to quit the litany, for its worth was now tainted with sadness. Then I thought of Eisenhorn, and of Ravenor too. They were men whose lives had been devoid of emotion, who had trained themselves to care not for anything, or allow feelings to weaken them. But it was not weakness. To care for another, that was not weakness. To feel, that was not weakness. Emotional response was what made us human, what gave us character and worth. I resolved I would not become like them, not ever. I would hold on to what I was and what made me – what *truly* made me, and not some marshland lie – even if it hurt.

I returned to my litany, allowing now for the loss it bore, and embraced it, and let it settle my mind. Even gone forever, Medea would be at my side to steady me.

'Nine Sons who stood, and Nine who turned, Nine for the Eight, and Nine against the Eight, Eighteen all to make the Great Cosmos or bring it crashing down...'

My 'bead clicked again.

'Are you talking to me?'

'No, Harlon. Stay vigilant.'

A moment later, Renner came over the link.

'Looks like it's showtime,' he said.

A cargo-8 came down the circuit road from Toilgate, and then turned onto the feedway that led to Shed One Hundred & Nineteen. Renner, from his vantage, saw it first, long before I did, and kept his weapon trained on it, staying out of sight.

It came down the eastern side of the shed, jolting over the weeds and ruptured rockcrete on its heavy wheels. I heard the rumble of its engine before it came into view. I checked, for the umpteenth time, that my cuff was set correctly and my blankness unmasked, but it would have been too late by then if I had made an error. Ravenor's mind, or the human puppets he would oftentimes 'ware, would already have taken us down.

'Check in,' I said, 'then settle and follow the plan, and my lead.'

'Acknowledged,' crackled Nayl.

'Understood,' said Renner's voice.

I stayed put on the open slipway, a lone figure on acres of rainswept 'crete. I undid the catch on one of the sluca scabbards.

The truck came into view, toiling along slowly. It was, from the look of it, an ex-Arbites vehicle, a cargo-8 with small, reinforced window panes and a closed payload space. Sections of its bodywork were armoured with metal plating, including skirts that covered the tops of the wheel arches, and it had been painted pale blue, the colour of a marshchaff's eggs. It drove onto the slipway, tyres hissing in the greasy wet, and came to a halt facing me, twenty metres away. I waited.

'Covering the doors,' Nayl voxed. From his position, the truck was almost side-on, and easily in range of his hotshot loadouts. I was confident that military-grade kill-shots could defeat even Arbites body-plating.

'Re-setting,' Renner reported. I could not see him, but I knew that he, according to our predetermined plan, was moving along the side of the shed from the rear to cover the truck from behind. Between him and

Nayl, we had the vehicle in a one-eighty fire-field. Of course, I had no cover at all. I hoped that would not become something I regretted. But I had to present myself in the open.

Nothing stirred for a while, and then the cab door swung open, and a figure jumped down. I knew it at once: the tall, lithe form of Patience Kys in her rich brown bodyglove. Her black hair was pinned up with those deadly silver needles. Her telekine abilities were damped by my raw presence, but she moved with feline grace, and I knew she was entirely formidable, even bereft of the psychokinetic talents of her mind.

She stood and looked at me, then strode across the slipway from the pale blue truck until she was twenty paces from me.

'I have the shot,' Nayl voxed.

'Copy,' I replied.

Patience looked at me. There was ever a cynical air to her expression.

'Beta,' she said.

'Patience.'

She looked around casually, as if disapproving of the weather.

'A wide open space,' she remarked.

'In which we both stand.'

'Yes, but you have me at a disadvantage,' she said, and smiled. 'You have at least two shooters on me.'

'And you don't?'

'Don't you know?' she asked, with a glint of mischief. 'Mm, perhaps you're not as prepared for this meeting as you should be. Where's Harlon? Was it him I glimpsed at the back of the shed as we drove through? No, he'd be closer.'

She looked at the dark, cavernous mouth of the shed. In its dark gulf, Nayl was invisible, but she waved cheerily anyway.

'Morning, Harlon!' she called out. 'Head or heart, please! I don't want to suffer!'

She looked back at me.

'You left us so soon, Beta,' she said.

'I had little choice, as I'm sure you're aware.'

'Cherubael,' she said, and nodded. 'He left his stink behind. But you could have returned.'

'Perhaps I couldn't,' I said. 'Perhaps I was under duress.'

'Perhaps.'

'Or perhaps I was doing your master's work all along, as requested, and infiltrated Eisenhorn's retinue.'

'That seems unlikely,' she replied, 'given how long it's been, and the nature of this meeting. For whatever reason you went silent, things have clearly changed. Do we have something to discuss?'

I nodded. 'Yes, but not with you. I'm waiting.'

'For?'

'For him,' I said. 'And to see what furious surprises you might unleash.'

She raised her gloved hands, open, wide.

'I'm just here to start the conversation,' she said, 'and to estimate your furious surprises too.'

'You know I have none,' I said. 'We do not have the kind of resources that you do.'

'Resources?'

'The manpower and gunships that took down the Maze Undue. Your master has the full backing of the Imperium at his beck and call.'

Kys gave a little sniff of a laugh.

'Not so much,' she said. 'That raid was undertaken with the cooperation of local Arbites, and the office of the Baron Prefect. They supplied the muscle and vehicles, in the expectation of a significant haul. And that, Beta, we didn't get. Oh, we closed the place down, but the Prefect was expecting a round-up of arch heretics that could be paraded through the courts to put him in good odour with the Sector Ordos. It was not to be. So he is disgruntled with us, and less inclined to assist our operation these days.'

She looked at the sky, and closed her eyes, letting the raindrops fleck her face.

'There will be no flights of gunships descending on us today,' she said. 'This is a quiet meeting, just as you requested.'

'Then let us begin it,' I said.

She nodded again, turned, and walked back to the truck. She seemed in no rush. I waited, listening to her heels click across the rockcrete pan. She went to the back of the cargo-8 and unfastened the rear doors. I heard the whine of a hydraulic cargo lift.

'Something's coming out,' Renner voxed.

'Stay put,' I replied.

'It's him,' crackled Nayl.

'Hold steady on the targets.'

Kys reappeared from behind the vehicle. She was walking beside the heavy, armoured object known as *the Chair*. It was part box, part throne, entirely enclosed, hovering softly on its gravitic assemblies. It looked like a small glide-tank. I knew that the bulges and pods lacing the sculpted plate of its hull concealed more than just scanners and optic systems. Some were weapon modules that could shutter open at any moment and unleash streams of psycannon fire.

The modules remained shut.

The Chair moved towards me, Kys walking at its side, and came to a halt on the spot where Kys had previously stood.

'Just you,' I said.

I heard a little vox click over the patter of rain, and Kys shrugged. She stepped back, and returned to the cargo-8. She leant back against the cab, folded her arms, and stood watching.

'You have me at a disadvantage,' the Chair's transponders said.

'Well, sir, that's the point,' I replied. 'That mind of yours... I apologise for the discomfort my blankness may be causing you, but the advantage would be very much *yours* if my cuff was not set the way it is. I have not come to fight, or issue terms. I am simply here to talk.'

'You wish to talk?' the Chair said. Hovering, it turned slightly, to one side then the other, as though looking around. A pure affectation. Ravenor's sensor systems were global sweep. He was trying to reassure me by giving his very inhuman form the mannerisms of a person. 'Where is Gregor?'

'He's gone,' I said.

'Perhaps you could define that?'

'I doubt I have to,' I said. 'I am fairly sure it was your doing.'

There was a silence, broken only by the spitting of rain.

'I have done nothing,' said the Chair. 'I have done nothing to Gregor. I can only give you my word of that, but I give it sincerely. Beta, please... What has happened?'

His voice was merely augmetic, a machine simulation broadcast through cowled speakers, yet I sensed a tone of concern in it.

I took a few steps forward.

'A few nights ago, our safehold was attacked and destroyed,' I said.

'Destroyed?'

'Entirely, sir.'

'By?'

'You,' I said. 'You were my first thought. Making a move, at last, against Eisenhorn after your years of games.'

'I swear it was not me,' he said. 'I had not even determined your location. Gregor was always very good at concealing his tracks.'

'Not this time,' I said. 'I only escaped it by odd chance.'

'Where was this?'

There was no value in deflecting.

'Talltown,' I said.

'Great Throne... That blaze?'

'That very one, sir.'

There was another pause. I saw that Kys had straightened up, and was no longer leaning with such studied indifference against the cab. She had unfolded her arms, and stood looking at me with a frown of what seemed genuine surprise. She had heard it all.

'Who was lost?' she called out.

I ignored her.

'Who was lost, Beta?' Ravenor asked firmly.

'Medea, the daemonhost and Gregor,' I replied.

If Ravenor had been a man, I might have seen his response, a reaction in expression or body attitude. I could read it in Kys. She betrayed little, but I could see she was taken aback. The Chair did not move, or make a sound, and suddenly that felt far worse. This news had truly pained him. I felt that with great certainty.

'I'm sorry,' he said at length.

'I believe you are,' I replied.

'You brought me here to tell me this?'

'In part.'

'What else?' he asked.

I gestured to him, and turned to walk down the slipway. After a second, he skimmed slowly after me, leaving Kys at the truck. Much more alone now, further out in the open, I stopped and turned to face him again. He swung up just a few metres short of me, imposing and brutal, the Chair's hull beaded with raindrops.

'There are many sides at war here,' I said. 'Many factions, many interests, all playing against each other. From my own experience, I can count off nine or ten at least. It seems odd to me that *two* of them, in opposition, are Inquisitorial retinues.'

'You know it's not as simple as that, Beta–' he began.

'I know he was deemed a heretic, and accused of acting beyond the Ordo's remit,' I said. 'I also know you had no stomach for this pursuit, and that you were only hunting him to make peace with your masters for fear of them branding *you* heretic too.'

'Again, you oversimplify–' he said.

'Do I?'

A pause.

'No, perhaps not. Understand me well, Beta, I will not excuse his actions. He has operated beyond Imperial Law and without the grace of the Throne of Terra for decades. No matter the reasons, he has crossed the line.'

'*Had*,' I corrected.

'Yes. And I cannot pretend I have not crossed a line or two myself. He taught me perhaps too well. I took instruction from the Ordos, and committed to his apprehension with great reservation. Politically, I was obliged–'

'I care not,' I said.

'Understand me, *please*. I saw the pursuit of Gregor Eisenhorn as the means to a greater end. He was not my target. Not my *true* target. He was an excuse to get at something else, and he was also the way of finding it. We were hunting the same thing.'

'I know,' I said. 'I'm not a fool. That's why I took this risk to talk with you. I don't want to burn as a heretic, or burn for association with one. Your target is mine too. There are too many sides here, some of them of great malice. Now one player, your main rival, has vanished from the board. You can concentrate on what really matters.'

'The King,' he said.

'The King, indeed.'

'And you?' he asked.

'I have accumulated what little is left of Eisenhorn's warband, and we have gathered intelligence and leads that I believe you do not possess.'

I looked at the Chair.

'And vice versa,' I added. 'You and Eisenhorn worked at cross purposes, for years. Now he's gone. There can be focus at last, and a pooling of resources. I am underpowered, but I have value. That's why I asked for this meeting.'

'To work together?'

'To work as one. Ravenor, there are only two sides in this, when all is said and done. Forget the factions and the disparate interests. There is *us*, and there is the *Archenemy*. Not to work together would be foolish and negligent.'

'You are very like her,' he said.

'That's what people keep telling me.'

The Chair turned slowly, and faced the looming bulk of the shed.

'Shed One Hundred and Nineteen,' he observed. 'That number was not a coincidental choice.'

'It was not.'

'You want access to the book, to Chase's book?'

'It's a vital lead,' I said, 'but it's not the only one.'

'Beta,' the Chair said. 'You realise it is very difficult to trust you. Almost impossible. You are Cognitae product. You may be following an agenda even *you* don't appreciate. I have only your word that Gregor's dead. You have with you a mercenary of whom I am truly fond, but who has changed sides more than too many times. And I know he's not the only operative you have on-site today.'

'For our security only,' I said. 'I agree, there is little trust yet. If I armed my cuff, you could take us in an instant. And Kys is not *your* only operative. Where is the other woman?'

'We must establish trust if this is going to work,' he said.

'We must, and you haven't answered my question.'

He made a sound that I think was some kind of rueful sigh.

'Kara has a gun to the back of Harlon's head,' he said.

I stiffened, and touched my micro-bead.

'Nayl?'

'He can't reply right now, Beta,' a woman's voice answered.

'This is how you demonstrate trust?' I asked Ravenor.

'I'm showing you my hand,' he said. 'You think we'd walk into this without being ready for you? This meeting could have been any kind of trap.'

'But it is not.'

'So it would appear,' said Ravenor. 'Which is why I am showing you my hand. Kys, at the transport. Kara, in position behind Nayl. As for your other man, Mr Lightburn–'

I reached for my throat mic, but stopped. Renner had come into view around the end of the shed. He was walking with his hands on his head. A heavyset man in a visor and jack-armour was walking behind him, covering him with a laspistol.

Ravenor had a third agent.

'I mean them no harm,' said Ravenor, 'but they are contained. It is just you, Beta, and I do not fancy your chances against me, even blanked. So, do we continue this discussion with some moderate measure of trust, or do I let the three of you walk away? Now. No second chances?'

I was both impressed and angry. I thought we had been thorough, despite our limited means, but he had outplayed us. That third operative had been his wildcard.

'You'd let us walk?' I asked.

'Rules of parley, as Harlon negotiated,' he replied. 'I'm not a monster. But if you choose to walk, that would be it.'

'Then we should talk,' I said simply, and started to stride back towards the shed.

He followed me. Kys wandered from the truck and stood watching Renner, who looked most exercised by his capture. The visored man lowered his pistol, and said something to Kys I couldn't catch. Nayl walked out of the shed, the long-las resting across his shoulder with the powercell removed. He too looked most put out. Behind him came Kara Swole, an amused grin on her face, tossing the powercell up and down in her hand like a plaything.

'So, do we execute them for heresy?' Kys asked Ravenor as we approached. She grinned at me. 'Joking,' she said.

I did not smile back.

'Sorry,' Nayl said to me.

'Forget it,' I replied.

'It's good to see you again, Beta,' said Kara. Her smile seemed genuine and warm, but she had taken Harlon Nayl down without a shot fired. My estimation of her had increased considerably.

'What happens now?' asked Kys.

'We withdraw to safety and talk,' said Ravenor. 'You will consider Beta, Harlon and Mr Lightburn as allies unless I say otherwise. Put your weapons away.'

'You think we can trust them?' asked the man in the visor.

'Funny bloody question from a man in a mask,' spat Renner.

'Shut up,' the man replied.

'I won't give my instructions again,' said Ravenor.

'As we're brokering trust,' I said, 'let's see your face.' I was looking at the man in the visor. There was something about his build and voice that was oddly familiar. He glanced doubtfully at Ravenor.

'Do so,' said the Chair. 'We cannot have secrets if we are to engineer a collaboration. Do not react to this poorly, please,' Ravenor added to me.

I wasn't sure what he meant by that until the man in the mask unbuckled his visor and took it off.

My heart skipped and I went cold. It was Thaddeus Saur. It was Mentor Saur of the Maze Undue.

'This is how you trick us?' I exclaimed.

'Whoa, whoa!' Kys cried, her hands raised.

'Beta–' said Ravenor.

'We are walking,' I said. 'Saur is Cognitae! You know that!'

'Was,' said Saur sullenly.

'Thaddeus was apprehended during the raid on the Maze Undue,' said Ravenor. 'I will explain in greater detail, but know he is now assisting me in this investigation.'

'That is in no way reasonable,' I declared. 'He is Cognitae, and tied to the Eight. At best, he is a spy among you. What kind of idiot are you?'

Kys stifled a laugh of surprise to hear me rebuke her master so.

'Saur's brain had been wiped and blocked when we found him,' said Ravenor calmly. 'I have spent weeks probing him with psykana to ascertain his motives and status. I have scanned him for even subliminal codings. There are none. He is a dangerous man, but his connections are cut. He is quite anxious to assist me.'

'I swear it, Bequin,' Saur said to me. 'I don't know what I was part of, or what was done to me, but I want answers. They say you know me, but I have no recall. I understand your reservation, I do. They told me plain I was an agent against the power of the Throne, and that I can scarce believe. I swear to you, I just want answers, and the chance to undo any wrong I might have done.'

'He murdered your agent Voriet,' I said.

There was a silence. Kara looked at the ground uneasily. Kys pursed her lips.

'They know that,' said Saur.

'We know,' said Ravenor.

'They know that, and I don't,' said Saur.

I sniffed. 'If his mind is wiped, what use is he?' I asked.

'I know faces when I see them,' said Saur. 'Faces I don't know I've ever seen. Yours, as you walked up. Soon as I saw you, I knew your face. I have uses. Perhaps to spot Cognitae before you do.'

He glared at me. I could not forget the cruel and intimidating mentor I had known. He was a thug, a brute, and I could not believe his lifetime of work for the enemy had been erased.

But Ravenor was a great psykana talent, and he had probed. And we were into this now. Collaborative effort was what mattered. I would not let a wretch like Saur disrupt a valuable pact that might serve us well.

'We will discuss this further,' I said. 'I will, I assure you, require more convincing. But I wish our arrangement to stand.'

I slipped the sluca from my forearm sheath, let it drop into my hand, and quickly cut the flesh of my left palm. I raised my hand, letting drops of blood drip into the estuary wind.

'The hell are you doing?' Kys asked, stepping forward quickly.

There was a crack, like the sails of a clipper catching the wind, followed by a rushing sound. Comus Nocturnus landed on the rockcrete behind me, and slowly rose upright, his vast snowy wings extended and heaving. He was still quite naked, and his alabaster bulk towered over us all. Ravenor's people took a step back in dismay. Nayl flinched in surprise. Even the impassive Chair seemed to recoil slightly.

'What is this?' Ravenor asked.

'I'm just showing you my hand,' I said. 'In the spirit of trust. You had outplayed me with a third operative, but if it had come down to it, sir, a fight would not have gone the way you expected.'

CHAPTER 15

The Shoulder

I looked upon myself and, in the golden candlelight, reflected upon my situation as constantly as the looking glass reflected my face.

I studied the features of that face, a face that was soon not to be mine any more. My hair was pinned back, for it had yet to be styled, and my powder was not fully applied. I looked at my eyes, my nose, the line of my mouth, the set of my throat. It was simply the face I had always had, and I wondered that others saw so much else there: histories, past deeds, definitions of loyalty.

Kara had shown me a pict of Alizebeth. It affected me less than I had expected, though I saw how alike we were. This ordinary face of mine had currency, as it had done with Gregor's team. It secured me a degree of trust. It carried the past in it, a past I didn't know, but which meant something to all of them. I had underestimated the affection Ravenor's team held for Alizebeth Bequin. Ravenor could not help but see Alizebeth in me, and be prompted to recall his association with her and, even unconsciously, grant me greater allowance than I had anticipated. This was a source of some relief.

But I was concerned what I might lose, now the time had come to cover it.

The mirror, round and convex in the style of the Mid-Orphaeonic cabinet makers, could not show me the answer to that. It showed me only myself and the room I sat in, all pulled in around my shoulders and bent by its fisheye bulge: the surface of the dresser on which the mirror stood, laden with powders, brushes, cosmetic paints and salves, all borrowed from Kara, a hairbrush, a pot of pins, the hundred candles all around, warming the dark room amber; and me, bare to the shoulders, a cloth tied across my breast to stop powder falling on my clean, linen undershirt, the grubby band and hairpins holding my hair back from my face. I was framed like a cameo by Tizzley or Carnach, the little portrait masterpieces where perspective is bellied out so that every last facet of the surroundings may be included to display the painter's finesse for miniature detail.

Behind me, a room, a room in a house, a house in the city, a city at evening. I had been living here a week in the company of Ravenor's band.

'What about this one?' Kara asked, entering the chamber behind me, and holding out a bottle of lip paint. She had been coming and going for some minutes, helping me prepare, while she got herself ready. She was naked apart from a short slip, uninhibited like a fellow performer in a dressing room. Or, perhaps, a sister. 'This shade, perhaps?'

'Perhaps.'

'What do you stare at?' she asked, pausing to glance at the looking glass too.

'Just thinking,' I replied. I chose not to be specific, but the focus of my thoughts since the slipway had been Saur. I could not reason a way of trusting him, no matter his story of stolen memory. Just as my face made them trust me more, his face made me trust them less.

A tension had lingered all week. Ravenor had brought us – myself, Nayl and Renner, at least – to his seat of operations, this elderly townhouse near Feygate. It was, it seemed, three buildings in one, all of them old, that had over time spilled into each other to become one thing. At the west was a low, half-timbered hall of the Pre-Orphaeonic era, into which had been at some time stitched an agreeable, modest villa of three storeys and stone floors, well dressed with good plaster and large grates. At the east, a more modern extension in the Antebellum style, with diamond-paned windows and curled staircases, which seemed permanently cold. The house had no name.

Neither did the feeling that had gnawed at me since our arrival. Unease, perhaps? Discomfit. There were questions on both sides, questions of active intelligence and also more nebulous issues of caution. To handle the former, we had met for hours at a time in a large room in the villa part of the house, and gone through all that we knew. The latter issues were harder to address. I had a problem with Saur, and I made that plain, but Ravenor was insistent that Thaddeus Saur was no more than a useful pawn. Saur was kept out of the strategy meetings, and in person, he was amiable with me, as if anxious to demonstrate his innocence. There was no innocence there. At best, I hoped, there was simply an absence of malice.

Ravenor's own nagging lines of enquiry revolved around two things: the demise of Bifrost, of which I spared no detail, and the nature of Comus, of which I said as little as possible. After the meeting on the slipway, I had sent the angel away, knowing that my blood could call him back at any time. Comus would, once more, hide himself from human sight up in the rooftops and lonely spires of Queen Mab. Ravenor, of course, recognised what Comus was, and that begged more questions in him, as it had in me.

'This shade then? Too red?' Kara asked. Her fingers smelled of floral perfume. She had been trying several fragrances, to find one that would suit her 'guise.

'Yes,' I said, reaching for the powder pot. 'Perhaps something less operatic.'

'I think I have something,' she replied. She looked at my reflection, and found my eyes. 'You can trust us,' she said.

I nodded.

'I know you believe that,' I replied. 'I think in this city, there is very little trust to share around, and it must be rationed.'

Kara's face fell a little. The right strap of her slip had slid off her shoulder, and she hoiked it up.

'I believe I can trust you,' I said, seeing her look. Indeed, I thought so. She was more boisterous and energetic than Medea, and had a deep and surprisingly dirty laugh when amused, but I had come to feel that Kara fulfilled a role equivalent to Medea's in this outfit. She was the warm heart and the glue.

A grin re-lit upon her face.

'Something less operatic,' she said. 'I think that can be done.'

She bounded out of the room, her bare feet swift as a cat's, and the candle flames jiggled in her wake. In a moment, I could hear her rattling through a cosmetic case in the room next door.

Trust had, in fact, now been imposed to a degree. On the third day of our operation in the house, I had finally relented and turned on my cuff. This had been an act of faith on my part, for it gave Ravenor full sway, but it was clear foolishness to restrain our greatest asset.

'I will not look without your permission,' he had said.

'I do not know how a mere word from me would prevent you,' I had replied.

'There can be civility in all things, even for a psyker,' he said.

I had shrugged, hands wide.

'Look for yourself,' I said. 'For how would I tell if you were looking anyway?'

In fact, it *was* possible to tell. Facing the Chair on that third day, I felt his mind sweep into mine, as though someone had opened a door somewhere and let through a breeze. I felt he was a polite visitor, entering the rooms of my mind and looking around, not rifling through every cupboard and drawer. Still, it was an uncanny sensation, and I knew full well that he would not have to dig down the back of a drawer or a blanket box to locate my distrust of him.

He said nothing of that.

'The ossuary,' he said, at last. 'That's where you found him? This Comus?'

I had known that would be the goal of his first search.

'Under that, even. The depths of Below.'

'And you think him of the Ninth Legion?'

'Don't you?'

'King Door,' he mused.

'A gate to another realm, I think,' I replied. 'I could not explain it. The angel came from there, and could tell me little of it. It may be an open path to the City of Dust, though I could not see how one could cross it. It seemed impassable, except, perhaps, to an angel.'

'King Door,' he said again. 'If one examines that name–'

'And thinks, as with the Maze Undue, of the Old Franc,' I cut in, 'then one arrives at "D'or", and thus "gold" and thus "yellow". Yes, sir, that had occurred to me.'

'I see that.'

Ravenor paused. I smelled a wash of neurohormones.

'What have you found now?' I asked.

'I...' He hesitated, as though processing details that were startling to him. 'I am bewildered by these glimpses, Beta. Things you have seen in the last year or so. Traitor Astartes of the Word Bearers...'

'Inveigled with the Pontifex of the Ministorum–'

'The elders of this city seem hungry for their own destruction. I had no idea such parties were involved. The Word Bearers are... It is insanity to try to deal with them.'

I nodded.

'And the Baron Prefect,' he added, 'has deep ties with the Ecclesiarchy, so this pact might explain why the Baron is less forthcoming in his aid to us, of late. The Ministorum has great political influence. And what's this now? One of the Emperor's Children too?'

'Just so,' I replied. 'Two Traitor Legions I know of stalk this city, hunting for a way into the Yellow King's domain.'

'What I see here of this Teke, I am amazed you survived.'

'I am too.'

'And now I see how you did,' he said. 'Deathrow.'

'Ah, yes. Him. I accept I have omitted to mention him.'

'So, your estimate was incorrect, Beta. *Three* Traitor Legions. In all fairness, I must ask – did Gregor's open affiliation with the Alpha Legion not impress upon you the extremity of his heretical leanings?'

'Look into my head, sir, into my soul, and tell me how clearly delineated good and evil seem to me. Nothing can be trusted, nothing aligns where it should align, and archenemies make friends of each other–'

'The sad truth is,' he replied, 'that is the story of our cosmos. I do not say that to alarm you, but my experience has ever been that our Imperium, behind its bright banners and proud sermons, is far from the solid edifice we like to imagine. It is, at best, decayed and stagnant, and at worst rotten through.'

'Then you answer your own question, sir, I think.' I took a seat and perched facing him. 'The Endless War of Mankind is most acutely realised here in this city – parties and powers of all kinds and breeds, intermixed in a broil of murky intrigue. The issue, as it seems to me, is that none of us have any idea of the war's nature. Not here. We impose our own rules of good and evil, of Throne and Infernal, because we have been raised to understand that reassuring binary concept, and our faith in the Imperium depends upon it. But in Queen Mab, everything is ravelled and knotted. I fear our greatest weakness, sir, is that we do not even begin to understand the scheme or scope of the war. We do not know who opposes who, or why. We do not know which side we are supposed to be on. We do not even know on which side we currently stand.'

'No,' he agreed. 'The true prize is unknown to us, so we can only guess at where all the players fall in relation to it.'

'Your theory is that it's a quest to find the God-Emperor's true name through Enuncia,' I said.

'And thus command power over all things,' he said.

'But that may not be it at all,' I said.

'I agree,' he replied. 'And a true determination of that scheme has been my objective since I arrived here on Sancour. That is why I tolerate the company of a known Cognitae killer, and it's why you consort with murderous angels–'

'And Gregor was content to keep a daemon and Alpharius in his retinue,' I finished. 'We are all heretics, sir, or none of us are. This war dissolves all differentiation, and is of such import, clearly, that it demands we consider anything a potential ally. I ask you to remember that, should Gregor have survived and we chance to meet him again.'

'I do not need to be convinced,' said Ravenor. 'And although I can see you take it seriously, Beta, I advise even greater caution from you. I sift through your memories and see other faces. You have learned how dangerous the Blackwards are–'

'Their alignment?'

'Self-interest,' he replied, 'as it has always been, as far as I can see. They are, in the old sense of the term, rogue traders. They are above nothing when it comes to preserving their legacy. And this face in your mind, whom you seem to regard with only minor caution – Alace Quatorze. She is of the Glaw dynasty.'

'So she said.'

'And the name means nothing to you?'

'Not really.'

'The most reviled heretics, Beta. You had no idea who you were dealing with at Feverfugue. I am only thankful she was but a minor and worthless branch of that foul dynasty.'

'What is the next step you intend to take?' I asked him.

'There are options,' he replied. I realised only then that his voice was soft and very reassuring. For the first time, I was hearing it, his true tone, directly in my mind as it had once spoken in life, and not manufactured by crude transponders. 'I see one appeals to you.'

I could not deny it.

'I have shared my mind with you, Gideon,' I replied. 'Now will you share the book with me?'

The commonplace book of Lilean Chase, so small, and so innocent in its pale blue cover. It lay beside me in the candlelight as I made myself up, Kara fussing in and out behind me. Ravenor had handed it over after that conversation, and had confessed that he had made no headway with it.

Like me, and like Gregor, Gideon had not been able to determine the significance of the number 119, nor the linguistic nature of the dense text inside the book. Gideon had not seen its like before, anywhere, and he had made a long and detailed study of languages and cants. He agreed with my conjecture that the script seemed numerical, in some form, almost like a very long string of numbers. But his expert knowledge, far greater than Gregor's, aligned with Gregor's: it was not binaric, or any other version of number-based data-code known to be used by the Adeptus Mechanicus. And though the characters seemed more like numerals than letters to both of us, there was no way of knowing their corresponding values. We needed to know the language it was written in before we could decrypt it.

Even with the original book to study, I had made no progress, but I was increasingly certain that 119, rather than denoting the number of the book in some sequence, somehow described its contents, like a title, and furthermore represented a key to its decipherment. I know Gideon had worked hard at the decoding, and was a man of no mean intelligence, but his small team lacked a dedicated savant. They had, to begin with, used the resources of the Baron Prefect's court, but that was now withheld, and I believed Gideon was reluctant to trust such material to unreliable parties anyway. I believed, and Ravenor agreed, that it was time to exploit the odd and eccentric relicts of the city as our helpmates. I had come to feel that the city's outcast and overlooked souls were the most, or perhaps only, trustworthy allies at our disposal. In truth, I had come to feel myself as one of them. I would find poor, mad Freddy Dance again, and I would consort with his quirky circle.

Or, at least, a face they recognised would. Therefore, before the looking glass, I put on the identity and mantle of Violetta Flyde once again.

'Is this a better colour?' Kara asked. She had returned with an enamel tube of lip-lacquer in her hands. Now she was wearing nothing but a silk robe, open and untied. She had a dancer's frankness, which startled me, a confidence in her own flesh, though I confess, if I had her body, I would be unashamed to show it.

'Yes, much better,' I answered. 'Are you not dressed yet?'

'It will only take a moment,' she said. 'I am choosing a bodyglove. Crimson, or green, do you think?' She held up a garment in each hand for consideration.

'It depends,' I said. 'What would your guise wear?'

Kara frowned, a crease between her plucked eyebrows.

'I don't... know what you mean,' she said.

I started to explain, but she stopped me at once.

'Your voice is different, Beta,' she said. 'A little softer, and more clipped with the tone of the aristo classes.'

'That is Violetta's voice,' I replied, using it. 'I am sinking into character, so I can be ready, to speak like her, and think like her. Are you not doing the same?'

'I just dress up and improvise,' she said. She chuckled. 'If I get lost, Gideon can always drop a useful hint into my mind. Is this what you call a function?'

'It is,' I said.

'Full immersion in a character? One you know backwards and forwards, from birth day to–'

'Yes.'

She shrugged. 'I have worked undercover many times,' she said. 'I have lived as other people, but never with such calculation or study.'

'I find that strange,' I said. 'I was taught – *trained* – that the development of functions was a primary field tool of Ordo agents, that it was a skill all needed to possess.'

'You were trained by the Cognitae,' she admonished with a wink.

'Is there a difference?' I asked, and that made her laugh her dirty laugh.

'I'll learn from you, then,' she said. 'Already, you seem like a different person. It is quite disconcerting.'

'I'm not there yet, but Violetta is almost in place.'

'At least my poverty in such precise play-acting is not an issue tonight,' she replied. She had chosen the green bodyglove, and dropped her robe to the floor to pull it on. 'I have no starring role tonight. I'm just background colour and backup. I'll have eyes on you from a distance.'

'How's your Mabiçoise?' I asked.

'Decent enough to buy a drink and chat up a barfly,' she replied, in passing good Mabiçoise.

'And how is Patience when it comes to functions?' I asked.

'She, I'm afraid, is always Patience,' Kara replied, balancing on one foot to wriggle the tight 'glove on. 'But that will serve tonight, I think.'

I hoped it would. Patience Kys, for better or for worse, was to be my lead partner in the night's endeavour. I trusted she had the talent for such a duty. At least, I felt, she was exactly the kind of exotic creature who might fairly fascinate the likes of Oztin Crookley.

We tried, first, the salons and meeting houses of the bohemian quarter around Saint Celestine Feygate, which thronged with the usual permissive society. It was mid-evening, the street lamps were all lit, and the dining rooms were on their second or third service, with patrons still to seat. There was no sign of Crookley's circle at Lengmur's, nor at Zabrat's, nor at the caffeine house adjoining the Old Almanac Booksellers.

From there, we turned to the Two Gogs, only to find it closed, for the most part. The Gogs, it appeared, had suffered in the late storm, like so many properties in the city. It had lost a good many roof tiles to the plundering wind, and a fierce quantity of rain had got in, drowning the fore-bar and the kitchens. Regular business was suspended, though the owner was clearly so keen to resume trade that, even by evening lamplight, a small gang of labourers was at work, on double-pay, up ladders to patch the roof and make good the gutters. Carpets, rugs and table linen had been hung up outside to dry. I noticed one workman occupied repainting the trademark figures at the door in yet another range of gruesomely unsuitable colours. I wondered how the colours of the carvings had been compromised by the heavy rain, but perhaps it was just a thing that was done from time to time, not when repair was warranted, but upon the mercurial whim of the owner. Perhaps he had merely come into another job lot of unwanted paint.

A modicum of service had been maintained in the yard and street before the Two Gogs. Plank benches had been set up, and casks of sack dragged out, the bar staff selling by the mug out of doors to a gathering crowd. A fire, of some concerning ferocity, had been lit in the yard, and over it a half-grox was roasting, the spit turned by a blackened kitchen servitor. Flat breads stuffed with slices of the roast meat were selling well. A fire-spitter entertained the crowd, pacing the flame-lit yard in his motley, lighting his wands off the roast-fire, and belching great plumes of rushing combustion to the *oooohs* and *aaaahs* of those watching, especially those standing close enough to be in danger of ignition. Tumblers and dally-dancers cavorted about the place, some in a most lewd and suggestive display, while an old woman played the helicon and a boy thumped a tambor, and the crowd clapped. The dancers were all masqued in the carnival style, very garish and merry, and some performed alarming tricks of contortion. They gathered coins in their caps and bowls from the onlookers.

As Violetta, I scanned the firelit crowd, but could see no familiar faces in its mass. I glanced at Kys and Renner, by my side.

'Where next then?' Kys asked.

'Perhaps The Physik?' I ventured. 'Or–'

Kys held up a slender hand to cut me off, and nodded at the crowd. Kys, as Kara had suggested, was just Kys, though she had chosen a lustrous black bodyglove for this evening excursion. Her guise was as my lifeward, so her regular demeanour was entirely appropriate.

'Wait,' she said.

One of the masked dancers, quite the most limber and gymnastic, had cartwheeled close to us, and was pausing to gather tips in a tin cup. She came to us, cup out, and I saw that it was Kara behind the mask.

'A coin for good chance, a coin for thanks?' she said, rattling her tin.

'You'll be lucky,' Kys replied.

Kara winked at me from behind her fox-head mask.

'The pot-boy says Crookley cares not to sup in the evening air,' she whispered, 'and he finds the rowdy-dow-dow of the crowd boorish. He's taken off to The Shoulder for the night.'

I plunked a couple of coins in her cup.

'Thank you, fine mamzel!' Kara cried aloud. 'May the angels of the Throne watch over you!' She turned, and bounded away into a handspring.

'The Shoulder,' I said. 'That's on Mereside Row, isn't it?'

'I know where it is,' said Renner.

The Shoulder – more properly, The Shoulder Of Orion Amid The Sundry Stars – lay a short walk away, and we went there through busy streets of the quarter. Renner and Kys, in the role of a fine young lady's bodyguards, walked alert, Kys at my side, and Renner a few paces behind. My cuff, for now, was on, so that Kys would not be encumbered.

'Why is it you don't like me?' I asked Kys as we walked.

'I never said I didn't,' she replied. 'I tend not to like people much, generally.'

'No, it is a particular thing,' I said.

'I have not met a blank I liked,' she said. 'We had one. Frauka. He was odious.'

'What happened to him?'

'Long gone,' she said.

'So it's that I am a blacksoul?'

'And you tried to kill me.'

'Likewise, but that is behind us. I hold no grudge,' I said.

'Nor I,' she said and looked at me. 'But your past is a trouble to me. And I believe Gideon's great weakness is Eisenhorn. You are clearly of Eisenhorn's part in all this.'

'He's dead.'

Kys shrugged. 'The old bastard's evaded death many times,' she said, 'so I'll believe it when I see a corpse. And even if he is, his legacy lingers. Those true to his cause, like you. Like Nayl.'

'You distrust Nayl too?' I asked. 'I thought he was an old friend?'

'He is, but...' Her voice trailed off.

'What?' I asked.

'Harlon was Eisenhorn's man for a long time,' she mused. 'Then he came to Gideon's team, like Kara. He's a good man, I'll grant you, a good fighter. But he is getting old. Slow. Not the force he was. We are friends, I suppose.'

'But?'

'When Eisenhorn reappeared, Nayl went back to him. I dislike those who can switch masters so easily.'

'Kara–'

'Kara didn't go back,' Kys said. 'Once she had stood with Gideon, there she stayed. And I have been with Gideon since my start. But not Harlon. He's a strong brute, but to flip back and forth... That speaks of a weak character.'

'Or a torn one,' I countered. 'I think he's loyal to them both, but their rivalry has put him in an impossible place. And he's only come back now because of circumstance. Might I suggest, in all reason, that Nayl serves one true master... Not Gregor or Gideon, but the Throne itself?'

Kys snorted.

'He's a sell-sword, you silly girl,' she said. 'Besides, I only care to trust what I know. Not some faraway concept. I'll trust only those I can look in the eye.'

'And how do you look Ravenor in the eye?' I asked.

She scowled.

'You are new to this, Bequin,' she said. 'You have not walked the dark places as we have. You have not learned that trust is earned through adversity. Only yesterday, you stood four-square with the Cognitae.'

'I would not have, had I known,' I said. 'But it's odd. I am told we are much alike, you and me. Both orphans, born with outcast gifts, raised in cruel scholams–'

'Kara had no right to tell you such things.'

'It wasn't Kara,' I replied. 'It was Harlon. He spoke of you when we first met, when we both believed I had killed you at the Maze Undue. He mourned you, Patience. Your friendship towards him may be cool these days, but his respect and affection for you remains strong.'

She made no answer.

'Be reassured–' I pressed.

'There's nothing reassuring about this work,' Kys said. 'You're all under the influence of the great Gregor Eisenhorn – you, Nayl, Kara, even Gideon. You're all in awe of him. I'm not. I'm the one thing that will keep you true.'

The Shoulder was a sprawling tavern, much lit with glow-globes and hanging lamps. It was crowded too, but we could hear Crookley's guffaws even as we entered.

He was holding court with his coterie in a private side parlour, some twenty people in all, and many I did not recognise, but they were surely the usual strays and hangers-on that his notoriety, and Aulay's purse, attached to him of an evening. They enjoyed the frisson of being a temporary friend of the infamous poet, and the transgressive thrill that they might become party to some discussion of forbidden occult mysteries, but most of all they liked the fact that someone else was paying for their night out. The table was piled with the remains of a hearty dinner, and serving girls were running in with fresh bottles.

'Mamzel Flyde!' Crookley boomed the moment he saw me in the doorway. He was already half-cut, his mouth greasy from the haunch of gannek he had but recently devoured. 'You are too long from our company! We have missed you!'

He came to me at once, to kiss me upon the cheeks, a greeting that I was spared by the figure of Kys, who interposed herself and stared down Crookley with no little disdain.

'And, who,' exclaimed Crookley, not at all put out, and his eyes fair straining as he took in Kys, 'is this delightful creature?'

'This is Patience, Oztin,' I replied. 'She is one of my lifewards. I fear my husband is away on business, and he insists that I not go abroad in society without some safeguard. It is, I think, unseemly for a young married lady to step out without proper escort.'

'Quite right,' said Crookley. 'Quite apart from propriety, one might encounter the most unsavoury types in these benighted streets.'

He turned to Kys, who, as I had expected, had captivated him at once. That she was beautiful I had no doubt, but it was the menace in her that I knew would matter more. Pretty girls were ten a penny to the likes of Crookley, but a sense of danger and the prospect of a true challenge quite entranced a man of his transgressive character. He immediately offered her a glass of amasec, insisted she took the seat beside him, and plied her with questions: where had she trained? How many arts of killing did she know? Could she kill with her bare hands? How many men had she done away with? All the while, his gaze was fixed upon her face. I fancied he thought he was beguiling her, or mesmerising her with some weird gift he believed he possessed, taught to him by the spirits of the air. He was, after all, a magus, empowered with dark cunnings and esoteric tricks of sex and magic.

Kys played along, of course. Crookley was no direct use to me, for he talked much, especially in his cups, and said nothing of merit or truth. He had to be distracted and occupied while I went to work.

The room was busy, with much laughter and chatter. I spotted Aulay, but knew he was of no particular use, for he was very drunk as ever, and never spoke much to begin with. I pushed through several of the guests, and located the stern Academy tutor, Mam Matichek.

'My dear,' she said, and pecked my cheek. 'Have a seat with me. Oztin says he is to recite his new odes tonight, so there is much excitement, though I doubt the grammar will be any better than last time. And your girl, it seems, has delayed him further.'

She nodded meaningfully across the busy table, to where Crookley was gazing into Patience's eyes while she answered his incessant questions in a fashion that was, I was sure, both brutally glib and seductively mysterious.

'You come alone?' enquired Mam Matichek.

'Daesum is away,' I said.

'On business?'

'It can't be helped.'

'And he lends you lifewards?'

'I can hardly look after myself in the streets of Feygate,' I replied. She shot me a look that suggested, just for a second, that she believed quite the opposite.

'The woman I get,' she remarked, 'a high-class 'ward. Sunderer Martial School? Or Wayfarer's Agency?'

'Kresper House,' I said.

'Oh, the very best service. Which makes the other even odder. A Curst?'

Renner was lingering by the door, his eyes on me.

'Indeed, yes,' I said. 'Daesum is rather funny. He believes that burdeners make for the best guardians, because of their sworn duty. He takes them into service. I am rather obliged to accept my husband's notions. That man has almost become part of the household.'

'What's his name?' she asked.

'Why,' I said, answering as Violetta would, 'I have no idea at all. We call him "Curst", and he answers.'

Mam Matichek poured me a flute of joiliq. Through my function, I was presenting to her exactly the person she assumed I was: a wealthy, bored, privileged young gentlewoman, amusing herself by slumming with rakish intellectuals and would-be illuminates of 'secret lore'.

'I see very few of the faces from last time,' I remarked.

'Such as?'

'I was quite taken by Mr Dance,' I said.

'And he with you,' she replied. 'I hear you set him a mathematical test.'

'Oh, nothing so formal,' I replied. 'We were talking of numbers, and I asked the implications of one.'

'And we have not seen him since,' said Mam Matichek. 'According to Unvence, our Freddy has been locked away, night and day, quite obsessed.'

'I am sorry to hear it,' I replied. 'I had not meant to set him fast on some task.'

'Sadly,' she said, 'that is his way. His mind is fragile. Poor Freddy. He has a habit of seizing on something and fetishising it. Obsession is the right word, quite compulsive. Unvence says Freddy can't be torn away from his books, not even for the promise of liquor, and has almost forgotten to eat or bathe. I confess, my dear Mam Flyde, I am quite glad to see you tonight. I was hoping I might ask a favour.'

'Ask,' I said.

'I was wondering if you might come, perhaps tomorrow, and call upon Freddy with me? Unvence can arrange it. You see, I think if you visited him, and listened to his findings for a quarter-hour, and expressed satisfaction, he might cease this current bout of obsession, or at least be eased of his burden. He may ease back if he thinks he has satisfactorily resolved an issue raised by a pretty young lady. I do fear for his health.'

'I would be glad to do it,' I said. 'I am most sorry to hear I have derailed him with such a trivial matter.'

'At four tomorrow, then,' she said. 'In the courtyard of the Academy. You know it, I suppose?'

'I do. I will meet you there.'

'That's very kind,' she replied, and took a small silver case from her black crepe purse. She handed me a neatly embossed calling card. 'But I appreciate you are a very busy young lady. If you are unable to make the appointment, send word to me, and we will rearrange.'

Not long after that, Renner came to me, and drew me to one side. The rowdy merrymaking in the parlour continued, and was so loud, he had to lean close to my ear and whisper.

'I have seen him,' he said.

'Seen who?'

'The man. The musician,' he replied. 'Connort Timurlin, the one you said you wished to find.'

'Where?'

'Why, out in the main saloon, playing on the clavier.'

We stepped out of the private room. I cast a nod to Kys, letting her know I would not be long, and that she should stay put and occupy Crookley.

There was a narrow serving hall between the parlour and the main saloon. It was chilly there, and harried-looking serving staff bustled past us. From the saloon beyond, I could hear the fine playing of a keyboard above the noise of the bar. The Milankovich Variations in A.

I paused, and looked at Renner Lightburn.

'What?' he asked.

'How did you know?' I asked.

'Know what?'

'You say you saw him, but you've never seen him, not to know his face.'

He shrugged.

'The inquisitor put it there,' he replied, tapping his forehead. 'He'd seen the faces from your memories, and he shared it with all of us so we'd know who to look for. Timurlin, the Dance chap, and all the rest of note in this crowd. Their faces all popped up. Fair creepy, it was. I little like these psykana doings.'

He looked at me, and noticed my mood.

'Did he not tell you?' he asked.

Ravenor had not told me. It was not an abuse of trust, exactly, and it made great sense in terms of the efficiency of our work. I imagined it was standard practice for his warband: he would routinely copy visual information from one mind to another, so that all could be aware. But I couldn't help but feel as if he had cheated me, somehow. I had let him into my mind and stood with him, so to speak, as he politely looked around. Now he was sharing my thoughts with others, without permission. I wondered what else of me he had shared. I wondered what else he might have taken without my knowing.

I reminded myself that this was probably habit, and simply an everyday thing for so potent a psyker and the people he worked with. I imagined

Ravenor might be mortified to realise my offence at the casual intrusion, and apologise most genuinely.

But it rankled, and weakened my trust in him, a trust that was not yet strongly grown.

'Stay back and shadow me,' I told Renner.

I pushed through the padded swing doors into The Shoulder's main public saloon. It was warm and well lit, very busy, and the air stank of lho smoke and spilled liquor. Small tables stood to one side, where hot suppers were still being served. The night crowd was packed four deep at the long bar, and most other bar-tables and booths were filled.

At the far end, beyond the bar, an old clavier stood before the alcove that led to the cellars. Timurlin was sitting at it, playing, amusing a small crowd who were paying for his amasecs. The music was fine, despite the odd dull notes of the old instrument's raddled keys.

When I arrived at his side, he glanced up quickly with a smile, expecting to see another admirer, then did a double take and stopped playing.

'Mamzel!' he said.

'Mr Timurlin,' I said, smiling. 'When I heard the music, I knew it could only be you. *The* Connort Timurlin.'

He got up, and bowed.

'Please, don't let me interrupt,' I said.

'I'm just playing for fun,' he said with a smile. I could sense he was nervous.

'And for modest payment,' I said, and helped myself to one of the amasecs his audience had lined up along the top of the clavier's case. 'I was looking for you,' I said, taking a sip and keeping my stare fixed on him.

'Why, whatever for?' he asked. His body language was off. It was more than nerves, or surprise. He was wearing a green hanymet suit and half-cape of quality. I studied him for concealed weapons, and detected none.

'I was meaning to ask you,' I said, 'and I quite forgot last time we met. How is Zoya?'

'Zoya?'

I nodded. 'How is she?'

A change settled upon his face. A hard look, the look of a man who is unexpectedly caught out and cornered.

'I don't know any Zo–'

I raised one finger to hush him, knocked back the amasec, and set the empty glass down. My eyes did not leave his.

'Please don't,' I said. 'I'm in no mood for a game of pretend. We both know you know Zoya. How is she?'

'Why do you ask?' he said, apprehensive.

'Mam Tontelle sends her regards,' I said.

At that, he snapped, and made to kill me.

CHAPTER 16

Which is of pursuit

He swung his fist at my head.

It seemed the wild thrash of a desperate man, but it was not impulsive. I had fought, and been schooled in fighting, enough to read the blow, and the fact that it was not telegraphed. There was no microexpression of warning, of prior tension or bracing. It just came, expert and fluid. Just as fast, I dipped down to avoid it. But even as I did so, I was puzzled, for it was not a blow that anyone would strike with the hand, especially not a man who was clearly proficient. The move was more a sword-stroke, aimed at the side of my neck. Why strike so, with a fist?

All this I relate now in a hundred, perhaps a thousand, times the instant it took for the blow to come. It was fast, and I barely avoided it.

And in avoiding it, I found my answer.

A sword's blade missed my head and buried itself in the side of the old clavier. It buried itself deep. The impact shook the instrument, and knocked over the glasses of amasec standing along its top.

There had not been a sword in his hand a half-second before. There had not been a *place* for him to conceal a sword. It had just appeared in his grip.

I knew what it was, and thus knew what he was.

I could do nothing but throw myself aside as he ripped the blade out of the wood case, and sliced at me again. I had to spin to avoid, and then sidestep to dodge the murderous third strike. The sword – a straight cutro with a metre-long blade – cut through the silks and lace of my skirts and underskirts. The crowd cried out, backed away, some dropping the glasses they were holding. I darted aside again, and the tip of the chasing blade punched through the back of an empty chair. He was driving straight at me, and without ability to parry, I had to create space. I grabbed the rim of a small round table, and threw the whole thing at him, the drinks upon it and all. Timurlin staggered back against the clavier. The table had bought me a second, time to cross my arms and unfasten my slucas from their forearm sheaths. As Timurlin re-addressed, I threw my arms wide, gravity sliding the knives out of my sleeves and into my hands. I deflected his thrust with the blade in my right hand.

Timurlin was relentless. He had committed to murder, and would not back off, even now his target was armed. He hammered thrusts and slices at me with expert skill and dizzying speed. Now I closed, cutting down the distance between us, and endeavouring to both command the space, and control his blade. I parried, with one blade or the other, or both crossed in a V, or else danced out of his line as best as Violetta's gown would allow.

He was committed to it indeed, despite the roaring disapproval of the tavern crowd, who were aghast that he should attack a young lady of fine bearing so savagely, and yet too afeared of their own wounding to intervene.

He was committed because he was Cognitae. His sword, which had come from nowhere as if by magic, was a blinkblade. I had never seen one, but I had read of them. At the Maze Undue, Mentor Saur had warned us that such rare dangers existed. They were blades held in scabbards of what I now know is called extimate space. Bidden by their masters, they appear in corporeal reality, conjured from pocket-space. Saur, of course, had said that these were weapons wielded by what was called the *perfecti*, the 'high guard' of the Ordos, specialist lifeward killers who guarded the most senior Inquisitorial worthies.

But Saur's tale, as I now knew, was upside down. The perfecti, whatever that meant, were not Ordo, they were the Cognitae elite.

So I was certain, in that frantic moment, that Connort Timurlin was Cognitae, and that he was of the Cognitae's very best lifetakers.

I gave a good account, for had I not been trained by the same organisation? My knives whipped and clashed, blocking and repelling his every stroke, or wrapping them aside. I kept line, claimed space, and used both hands and both blades to control his sword and find a movement of conclusion. For a moment, I was almost thankful to odious Thaddeus Saur for training me so well. My staunch defence clearly bothered Timurlin. It was much more than he had anticipated. He had been expecting to make a quick kill, and then to bolt out of the tavern, and be gone into the night. Now he was hemmed in, and caught in a bitter fight he regretted starting.

I heard Renner yelling. He had lunged forward the moment Timurlin went for me, and was forcing his way through the stunned crowd to reach me.

Timurlin heard him too. Distracted, his eyes switched aside to gauge the approach of a second assailant. I plunged at him, knocked his guard up with my right sluca, and caught him across the flank with my left.

Timurlin yelped. He suddenly, impossibly, had his sword in a reverse grip, stabbing with it like a dagger's downstroke, and it caught the corner of my right shoulder. I felt no pain, but my right arm was suddenly running hot and wet.

By then, Renner had tired of the crowd's reluctance to part for him. He drew his handgun and fired into the ceiling. The shot, loud as a cannon salute as it seemed, brought down a cascade of plaster and one of the hanging lamps. The patrons scattered in terror, heads down, screaming. Two men vaulted the bar to find cover.

'Don't you bloody move!' Renner yelled, aiming the gun at Timurlin across the suddenly emptied saloon.

'Screw you, Curst!' Timurlin roared, swinging to attack.

'You first,' Lightburn replied, and shot him.

Renner's aim was good. The bullet would have struck Timurlin in the breastbone, and blown out his spine. But Timurlin – I can see it now in my mind's eye, for it was so memorable and so improbable – Timurlin flipped his sword around and dashed the bullet out of the air before it could impact. The bullet flicked sideways, tumbling, and destroyed a shelf of bottles behind the bar.

Then, *then* Timurlin was out the door. He took off like a startled stag, kicking the street doors out of his path. I gathered my skirts and gave chase. Renner ran after me.

'You're cut!' he cried.

'Shut up! Where did he go?'

The night was cold, the street dark and empty, despite the pools of lamplight. How could he have vanished, as magically as his blinkblade had materialised?

'There!' I yelled.

There were spots of blood on the cobbles. I had stabbed his flank, and he was leaving a trail. I began to run again, then stopped, and used my slucas to slice Violetta's torn gown off me. I cast it aside. In the body-glove beneath, untrammelled by the weight and volume of silk and lace, I could run much faster.

We reached the street corner, where Mereside Row turned down into Cavalry Parade. Renner and I ran down either side of the empty street, hunting for more telltale splashes of blood. I was leaving a trail of my own. The sword had cut through my gown and my bodyglove, and into the meat of my right shoulder. My right arm was sore, and growing numb, and blood was dribbling from my right hand.

At the public pump at Cavalry Cross, we stopped again, and looked left and right.

'I have no idea,' Renner said to me.

Kys appeared between us, cat-silent.

'What?' she demanded. Her silver kine blades were floating either side of her like nectar-birds.

'Timurlin,' I said.

'Did that to you?' Kys asked.

'Yes. He's Cognitae.'

'Gideon!' Kys snapped.

Ravenor's voice was in our heads.

+Turn left. He flees towards Saint Kallean's.+

We started to run. I realised Kys was barely touching the ground and quickly outpacing us. Buoyed by her telekine force, she ran as though she were bounding across some weightless world.

'Can't you drop him?' she yelled.

+He's shielded. Perhaps a cuff of some sort. But I can read the heat of him. He's gone left again, onto Little Orphic Street. We're close. We'll shut off his routes.+

We ran past the steps of Saint Kallean's Vow-house, and down the cobbled slope of Little Orphic. Late carousers at the street taverns watched in bafflement as we sped past.

+He's turned back.+

Timurlin came out of the dark, thrusting his blade at Kys. She cleared him, and his sword, and two and a half metres of air besides, cartwheeling with almost lingering slowness in mid-air. Kine-force brought her down on her feet behind him.

Panting, Renner put his fist into Timurlin's face. Timurlin staggered backwards, and fell sideways against a stone drinking trough.

'You needn't have bothered,' Kys said to Lightburn. She looked at Timurlin, and picked him up with her mind. She slammed him into the wall of a grain merchants, and smashed the wind out of him. As he started to slide, the twin kine blades whistled out of the night air, and pinned him to the wall, one through each sleeve.

'We have him,' she said.

But we did not. Like an escapologist, he twisted out of his coat, cape and shirt and broke free, leaving his garments pinned to the wall. In a second, he was gone down the mouth of a side-alley.

'Should have put them through his arms, not his clothes,' Renner said to Kys, though there was a slight wobble in his voice that betrayed his disquiet at her frightening gifts.

'Ha, ha,' she replied, and took off again, following Timurlin into the unlit passage. Her kine blades followed her like chase-hounds, chinking out of the bricks and letting Timurlin's shirt and jacket drop.

Ahead of us, we saw Timurlin's silhouette as he scrambled over a high wooden fence. Kys cleared the fence with ease, and landed on its top like a rope-walker, gazing down the far side.

'Oh, you stupid fool,' I heard her say.

We got over the fence. On the far side, in the muck and refuse of another backlane, Timurlin lay on his back. There was a sword wound through his heart. His eyes were open.

Saur stood over him, a salinter in his hand.

'What?' he said to us. 'You saw him. He had a sword.'

* * *

Ravenor arrived, flanked by Nayl and Kara. They looked grim. Saur was protesting that he'd had no choice. Kys told him to shut up.

'That was a mistake, Saur,' said Ravenor through his transponders. 'We wanted him alive. He will not answer questions now.'

'My apologies, sir,' Saur replied, sullen. 'He had a cutro out, and–'

'Convenient,' I said, 'that you should silence him and allow him to keep Cognitae secrets.'

'Now look here, you little wretch,' Saur snapped, turning on me. 'I just did what I could. Don't start accusing me of any–'

'Why not?' I asked.

'I am not a part of it!' Saur protested. 'I didn't even know him! Not even his face! I was just trying to help–'

'We will consider your actions later,' said Ravenor.

'And take that sword from you now,' said Nayl.

Kara came forward to examine my wound, and was about to tear strips from her bodyglove to bind it.

'No need,' said Kys. She twitched her lip, and I felt the wound pinch shut, clamped by telekine force. 'I'll stop her bleeding. You can dress it when we get back.'

I looked down at Timurlin's body.

'We may yet get his secrets,' I said.

'How so?' asked Kara.

'The same way Gregor got secrets from Mam Tontelle,' I said.

They looked at me.

'No,' said Nayl.

'You told me yourself that it could be done, Harlon,' I said. 'You've seen it done, and it's been done many times. Gregor had the knack of it. I'm sure Gideon does too.'

'It's not a technique I care to practise,' said Ravenor.

'You've done it before, I'll bet,' I said. 'Needs must. Nothing we do here on Sancour is orthodox, or risk-free.'

'Even so,' said Nayl, 'the last time... I mean, when Gregor did it, there was hell to pay. I would advise against such a show. We have no idea what danger it could bring down.'

'Gregor did it,' I repeated. 'And as I am often reminded, Gideon is a far superior practitioner of psykana. One of the most powerful in the ranks of the Ordo.'

I looked at the Chair.

'Yet you seem to withhold,' I said, 'and seldom use your gifts to anything like their potential. Why is that, Gideon? Are you afraid of yourself?'

'Hey!' exclaimed Kara, horrified.

'Beta is simply trying to goad me into a course of action,' said Ravenor flatly. 'Crude psychological persuasion. I am both offended and amused. Insulting my pride and daring me to show off will not work, Beta. I have weathered worse.'

'I'm sure,' I said. 'But give me one good reason why you won't do it anyway.'

CHAPTER 17

The revelation of dead whispers

The nameless house was silent.

When that which had been Connort Timurlin spoke, it came as a reluctant gust of breath, like a fretful draught blowing beneath an ill-fitted door, or a dry wheeze of air forced from old, leather bellows.

Gideon asked him his name.

'Connort Timurlin,' the sigh said. '*The* Connort Timurlin.'

+That identity was a function. I mean your real name.+

The flames of the candles arranged in a precise pattern around the corpse fluttered outwards, as though a breeze was stirring within the cold body.

'Do not make me tell you, please,' the dead voice whispered.

+I am afraid you must.+

'And I am afraid too. It is dark here, and I don't know where I am, and I cannot find my way out.'

To hear something of death's sombre realm, from one who is witnessing it, bothered me greatly. The voice sounded so desperately lost and disappointed. The description, though slight, also reminded me too much of how I had felt in the Below while searching for Lightburn, the incarcerating darkness and lack of dimension. I had lost all sense of myself, and all ability to see, and had felt that my connection to the world had gone forever. All hope and sight and meaning had been taken from me. The memory of that fear struck me, and I hoped that death was not like that.

I knew, like all of us, I would find out one day.

It was late, which is also to say, brutally early: the deepest part of the night, two hours before the first hint of dawn. Nayl had urged that we wait until the following evening to perform the auto-séance, so that we might have time to rest and prepare, but Gideon had gainsaid him, arguing that the longer we waited, the further Timurlin's essence would have drained from his cooling body. To have hope of any coherent answers, we had to act at once.

We conveyed the body back to Ravenor's nameless house in Feygate, and laid it out on the flagstones of the old muniment room, the largest chamber in the half-timbered Pre-Orphaeonic section at the western end, and a chamber we barely used. Nayl and Renner swept the room clean of dust and cobwebs. Under Gideon's direction, Kara and Kys marked out certain symbols on the floor around it in chalk and trickled sand, and arranged fresh candles at measured intervals. The drapes had been closed, and the frames of the windows, doors, and even the grate itself, had been warded with herbs such as fellwort, bindsap, asafoetida and rosemary, along with sigils in chalk, and brass cups of shaellic gum incense. I was charged to tie sprigs of lammasberry and gorax to the door handles and window latches with bows of black ribbon.

Once the preparations were complete, Gideon ordered everyone except Kara and me to repair to the Antebellum eastern end of the house, furthest away, and to bolt the doors. They were not to emerge, but at his direct command. They were to ignore any noises or odd phenomena, and not answer any knocks at the door until after sunrise.

He instructed Kara and me to bathe scrupulously and dress ourselves in clean clothes, all white or undyed, no colour. We were to assist him. He chose Kara because she had no psykana gift that could be annexed, and also because he found her the easiest to ware in an emergency. And, of course, I think he trusted her the most, and thought of her as the most stable and reliable.

Me, he chose primarily because I had insisted on the matter being done, and wished to witness it and participate in it. But I was also the safeguard. My cuff was set to limit me, but could be adjusted in an instant if the dampening force of an untouchable was required to shut the practice down.

Before I went down to join him, I opened the little window of my bedroom. The blood I had spilled earlier in the night, thanks to Timurlin's blinksword, had drawn Comus to me in the aftermath, much to the concern of the group. I had assured him all was well, and instructed him to wait.

As I opened the little window-light, I found the angel perched on the tiled eaves outside, hidden from the street in the shadow of the ridge tiles.

'You were hurt,' he said. 'I smelled it.'

'I was cut in a fight,' I told him. 'The wound is cleaned and bound now.'

'Should I find and kill the soul responsible?'

His voice was soft. He was a snowy shape in the darkness, like a looming chunk of sea-ice spied from the porthole of a ship at midnight.

'The culprit is dead already,' I said. 'We are about to perform a psykanic interrogation. You may want to depart from here. I fear the conditions might alarm you.'

I had no real way to judge the robustness of the angel's mind, but I was concerned that the outwash of a psyker's power might agitate him untowardly.

'I will stay,' he said.

'Then stay outside, Comus Nocturnus, and stay hidden. Keep watch on the house, but do not come in. If things become difficult, I ask you to withdraw until I call you again.'

The vague, pale shape in the darkness nodded.

'But if things become difficult…' he said.

'Then I will make sure to call you,' I said. 'Then you may enter. But it will not be necessary.'

'So be it,' he replied.

I was about to close the window when a question occurred to me. It was the first opportunity I'd had to ask it. I stepped back into the room, and fetched the commonplace book.

'Do you know this number?' I asked, leaning out of the window to show him the inside cover. 'The number, here, or the name writ beneath it?'

His large hands took the book from me and made it look like a miniature hymnal or chapbook. I could barely see much besides his spectral shape in the night's darkness, but his eyes were evidently better than mine.

'No,' he said. 'I know neither name nor number.'

'But you can read them?'

'Yes,' he said, and glanced at me. 'I did not know I could read.'

'Can you read the text?' I asked. 'The main body of the book?'

He turned some of the leaves slowly.

'No,' he said, after a moment's consideration. 'But I know the script,' he added. 'Not to read, or comprehend, but I recognise the marks. When I was chained, in the dark place under the world, this was the script used there.'

'Used? Used how?'

'I remember little,' said the angel, 'but I know these marks. They were used to make the hexes which bound us and made us serve. A language of command. I'm sorry, I know no more than that, and I cannot tell you what the words say.'

He passed the book back to me.

'Thank you,' I said. 'Now, remember... If things become unruly, do not enter. And if you become troubled, withdraw from here until I call you again. Gideon knows what he is doing.'

'If that is your command, null,' he replied.

I closed the window. The angel, a faint ghost, was still there when I went downstairs.

I was certain Gideon Ravenor *did* know what he was doing. His psychic abilities were monumental. Even Gregor had spoken of them in awe. I found myself wondering, yet again, why Ravenor used them so sparingly, mostly on what seemed like modest or routine purposes. With such keen gifts bestowed, by the God-Emperor Himself no doubt, he could surely smite down every foe and heretic and enemy of the Imperium. Had I been right to think he was afraid of his own power?

My needling of him had worked, at least, because he had agreed to the séance, though I sensed it was something he had considered himself. As Kara and I joined him in the muniment room, I began to understand some of his reservations.

His chair sat facing the feet of the prepared body. He was deep in contemplation, perhaps performing tempering litanies of his own to prepare his mind. There was an odd silence in the room that seemed to muffle even the ambient sounds of our breathing and our footsteps. That too reminded me of the ossuary's underworld. We closed the doors, and checked that the wards and totems were all still in place. Then Kara lit the candles, one by one, with a white taper, and I lit the cups of incense with a red one.

The warm spice of shaellic filled the air, and vague blue veils of smoke drifted through the candlelight.

Connort Timurlin, dead now four hours, stared at the ceiling. His flesh looked like white marble so that, but for his breeches, he resembled a graven image on the lid of some templum tomb, the carved likeness commemorating some ancient worthy. Kara had marked certain sigils on his cheeks, forehead, chest and palms with ash, according to Ravenor's direction. I could make no sense of the designs, nor of any of the sigils writ on the floor, nor even of the pattern in which the candles had been laid out, but some of the shapes and symmetries made me uneasy. Kara had told me that the act was to be performed according to old lore contained in something called the *Malus Codicium*, an ancient tome of abomination that had once been owned by Gregor Eisenhorn, and extracts of which were saved in the databanks of Gideon's chair.

This was daemon-craft, warp-lore. I saw it now, and I saw the distinct difference, beyond the very obvious, between Gregor and Gideon. Gideon was, above all, a creature of science, a student of enlightenment and technoscientific knowledge. He trod the narrow but bright golden path that led from the foot of the Holy Throne into the future, a way lit by genius and discovery. Whenever he had strayed from it, into the dark off the golden track, calamity had followed.

Gregor, Gideon's great mentor, had chosen instead to walk in the dark places, from perhaps the earliest days of his career. He had deliberately gone into the dark, and parleyed, dealt and contested with the nether-things it contained, often stealing their secrets from them and turning those tricks against them.

This act, this auto-séance, lay too much in that realm of the arcane that Gregor favoured. It was of the warp, a thing so great and terrible that no man, not even a posthuman champion like Ravenor, could ever hope to control or conquer it. The few times Ravenor had faced such dark immensity directly, it had almost overwhelmed him, and those times had, almost always, been as a consequence of him following Eisenhorn's footsteps.

Our work smacked of magic, of necromantik dabbling. It reeked of forbidden lore, and of the ravings of mad heretics and doomed sorcerers. There was no cold science in it, no golden path, no trusted fact or true knowledge. Ravenor feared it, and he despised it. He knew how seductive it could be, how beguiling, how addictive. He knew how easily it could go wrong, and how badly. He knew that to toy with it was hubris, that to pretend mastery of that which was infinite and masterless, was to begin a plunge into a midnight pit from which no one could return.

There was a line, past which insanity and damnation awaited. Gideon had crossed it a number of times in the course of his work, always unwillingly or in extremis. Gregor crossed it willingly and eagerly every day of his life.

In the pair of them, the Imperium itself was represented, the impossible balance. To know and use the warp was essential for mankind's survival; to know it and use it too well or too much... was to tempt the annihilation of our species.

We stood behind Ravenor's chair, at either side. The silence bred like fog.

+Speak, Connort Timurlin.+

For a long while, there was nothing, and Ravenor repeated his telepathic summons several times. Then the candle flames began to bob and dance, and the rasping voice began to answer.

+Tell us your real name.+

'I beg you, do not ask that of me.'

+Then tell me, who do you serve? Understand, Connort Timurlin, the symbols that mark you prevent you from uttering anything but the truth. Your soul is bound.+

'My soul is lost,' the sigh replied. 'Lost and damned. I am dead, aren't I?'

+You are.+

A choking rattle issued from the dead man's throat. I wondered if he could see. His eyes were open, but they did not blink. I glanced over at Kara, and saw she was watching carefully. She had Timurlin's blink-sword at her side. According to lore, a dead man's weapon was the most efficacious way of slaying him again. I wondered, bleakly, who had first found that out, and under what circumstances. The thought almost made me laugh, mainly because our nerves were heightened, but this was in no way a time for mirth.

'I serve the Cognitae,' the corpse whispered. 'I stand in service of the one truth.'

+You were what they call a perfecti? One of the Cognitae's warrior cadre.+

'Yes.'

+There are few like you. The Cognitae seem to prefer professional retainers and sell-swords.+

'There are few like me now,' the whisper answered. 'Once there were many. In the old days, before the Crusade and the Great Heresy, the perfecti were a secret army. But our numbers dwindle.'

'So in this day and age, a perfecti is a precious resource,' said Kara, 'used only for particular missions?'

It seemed odd at first to hear her speak, but Ravenor had instructed us to share the questioning, in moderation, for the contacted dead can become resistant to one, repeating voice. We would learn more if our questions came from different voices.

'That is so,' the corpse replied.

'What was your particular mission?'

'I was the personal guardian of my mistress, who is an exalted senior of the Cognitae order.'

I took a step forward.

'The woman I saw you with that night at Lengmur's salon?'

He did not reply.

'This was the night Mam Tontelle perished.'

'Yes,' he replied, with a reluctant sigh.

+Was it you and your mistress who co-opted Mam Tontelle's performance so? Used her to communicate?+

'Yes. We dared not approach directly. We thought to use Mam Tontelle as an unwitting intermediary, to gauge your willingness to talk. But… it went wrong. Our efforts were discovered by the King, and the Eight came to silence us.'

'Why would you wish to communicate–' Kara began.

+A better question – with whom were you trying to communicate?+

'With me?' I asked.

'With you... Yes. More particularly, with Eisenhorn.'

+Why?+

'In the hope that he might help us, or side with us.'

Kara and I exchanged perplexed looks.

+A senior of the Cognitae wished to reach out to an inquisitor, and ask for help?+

'No. Eisenhorn.'

I nodded.

'That's why you tried to kill me, isn't it, Timurlin? You reached out to me and Eisenhorn, but now Eisenhorn is gone, and you know I stand with Ravenor. When we met again tonight, you tried to kill me and escape, for now I was in the service of the Ordos.'

'Yes.'

I tried to keep the anxiety out of my voice. It meant, for all my care, they had been watching me all along. It also revealed a stark difference and a painful reminder: the Cognitae considered Ravenor true Inquisition, and thus something to be feared and shunned. The Inquisition was, and had always been, their enemy.

But Gregor Eisenhorn, for all he hunted the Cognitae, perhaps more ruthlessly and doggedly than any man in the last few centuries, was no longer Inquisition to them. He was an adversary, a scourge perhaps, but nevertheless, they felt they might deal with him.

And that he might understand why.

'You thought Eisenhorn might be receptive?'

The whisper exhaled in answer. 'Against a mutual foe.'

+Who is that foe?+

Silence. Then the merest sound.

'The Yellow King.'

We did not speak for a moment. Kara looked at me, alarm in her eyes.

+The Cognitae serve the Yellow King.+

'We do not. We have aided him, for a long time. But we are not his.'

'Explain,' said Kara.

'His goal,' the corpse sighed, 'his mission... For the longest time, it seemed the same as ours. A shared ambition. So, for a long while, we worked with him, lending our talents and our secrets to help accomplish it. For a long time. All the ages of the stars.'

+How long?+

'Centuries, and more. The project has lasted almost as long as the Imperium.'

'And now you fall out? You are at odds with him?' I asked.

'The King is all-powerful. We have helped him every step of the way, but he has used us up. He has stripped us of every asset, every secret. He no longer needs us. We presumed he would honour the ancient debt he owes to us, that he would respect our centuries of toil on his behalf. That he would, as befits the magnanimity of a king, keep us close, and reward our loyalty by sharing his power with us. This, he promised. He comes close to fruition. The City of Dust is built, and his hosts assembled. The hour of his triumph is upon us. The universe that you know, and that I know, is about to change forever. But he has reneged. He keeps all power to himself, all authority and command, all secrets and instruments of transmutation, all reins and harnesses of Pandaemonium. He shuts us out. We are of little further use.'

+And this is unacceptable to the Cognitae?+

'It is not,' the whisper said, 'what was promised us. The goal was, forever, to remake the Imperium, to build it anew, to tear down the mockery that is the Corpse-God, and begin again, for the glory of mankind. To make the Imperium as it should have been, not as the petulant and arrogant False Emperor devised it.'

The whisper died away, and the corpse on the flagstones shuddered slightly. When the voice returned, it was a dry rasp, like stirring leaves, and barely audible.

'But that... that is not enough for the King in Yellow. He wants more. He wants a greater prize still. And we have given him the keys to claim it, and he shuts us out. Our ambitions are no longer harmonious. Worse, he sanctions us when we object. He purges the seniors of the Cognitae from his dusty court, casts us out of favour, and hunts down, with murderous intent, any who try to oppose him. The Cognitae is broken, and is persecuted by both the Inquisition *and* the Yellow King.'

'This is why you attempted contact with Eisenhorn?' I asked. 'As a potential ally?'

'The Inquisition could not be bargained with,' replied the whisper, 'but we thought he could be made to see reason. We know him of old. An enemy, yet we hold him in high regard. He is capable. He has damaged our cause many times. He found and destroyed our operation on Gershom–'

'Things must be bleak for the Cognitae to turn to a sworn enemy for help,' said Kara.

'Not the Cognitae. Merely my mistress. I told you. The Cognitae is broken, scattered and in hiding. It no longer operates with one mind. My mistress, fearing for her life, made the decision to approach Eisenhorn. Other parties were considered, but–'

'So the Cognitae was not behind the Talltown attack?' I asked.

'No.'

'Who was?'

'I know not.'

+You said others. Other parties. What do you mean?+

The corpse made an odd, rattling noise. After a moment, I realised with distaste that it was laughing.

'Almost every force, every faction, every power in the galaxy opposes the Yellow King,' the whisper said. 'Not all of them for the same reason, of course. But they all want him stopped. Other forces gather here on Sancour, seeking his destruction.'

'Such as the Traitor Legion known as the Word Bearers?' I asked.

'Oh, yes.'

'With such eagerness, they would side with the Ecclesiarchy?'

'And vice versa?' added Kara.

'Yes.'

'And the Emperor's Children?' I asked.

'Yes, them too. The Smiling One and his hideous-beautiful warriors. So many come to the court of the Yellow King, to overthrow him, to stop him, or to forge an alliance to share in his coming glory. All are denied. There are many we could turn to who would share our intent, but most are too dangerous to deal with.'

'And Eisenhorn was not?' I asked.

'Comparatively. My mistress considered him, and one other faction. But the other was not receptive.'

+Who was that?+

'I will not speak their name.'

+Then speak yours now. What is your true name?+

'I would not say it.'

+You have no choice.+

'It is Verner Chase.'

The corpse began to sob. Dry sobs. It was hard to listen to.

+Chase? A relation?+

'Yes. Lilean Chase was my grandmother.'

'Where is she?' asked Kara.

'I know not.'

+Is Chase your mistress?+

'No! No.'

'In what language did your grandmother compose her commonplace book?' I asked.

'What?' Timurlin seemed now puzzled.

'Her commonplace books, the journals she kept,' I pressed, running with the guess we had made that the numbered book was just one of many. 'What private cipher or language did she use?'

'She kept many notebooks,' he replied. 'I do not know.'

+You do.+

'A hex!' he cried. 'A hex, that is all I know. She wrote in a secret hex!'

A *hex*. Just as my angel had said.

'What does that mean?' asked Kara. 'A hex?'

'She never said. Some kind of spell, some hexcraft, I supposed. A magical alphabet.'

+What is the significance of the number 119?+

'It means nothing to me.'

'Who is your mistress?' I asked.

'I guard her name and her life, even dead. I will not say.'

'Where may she be found?'

'I will not say.'

'In these circumstances, Verner,' said Kara, 'I suggest you relent. If she is prepared to cooperate, as she intended with Eisenhorn, she will be treated fairly by the Inquisition. We can be her allies, strange as that may sound, if she shares what she knows. Where may she be found?'

'I will not say. I will guard her. You Ordo murderers cannot be trusted.'

+What was the other party?+

'No!'

'What is her name?' Kara asked.

The corpse resisted again. I saw the technique now, standard Ordo interrogation. The subject was weakening, and his resistance failing. Kara and Ravenor were switching their lines of questioning rapidly, so that Timurlin could not build a hard barrier against any in particular. They were probing his failing mind with varying jabs and thrusts, so he could not shield or block them all, like two swordsmen cornering one.

A third would weaken him further.

'What is the name of your mistress?' I asked.

'No–'

'Say it!' I snapped.

'Zoya Farnessa!'

+Her *true* name.+

'I will not tell!'

'Where is she?' I asked.

'I will not say!'

+Who is the other party?+

'You do not want me to say it. I swear, you do not!'

'What is her true name?' asked Kara.

'Who killed Eisenhorn?' I asked.

+Where can she be found?+

'Stop! Stop it!'

'What is her true name?' I asked.

'Who is the other party?' Kara snapped.

'I beg you, stop!'

+Who killed Gregor Eisenhorn?+

'Please!'

'What was the other party?' I asked.

'The College!' The whisper broke, brittle. 'The Immaterial College!'

Then the whispers stopped. The air went cold and soundless. The candle flames dipped very low, almost out, and started to issue ribbons of smoke.

+He has gone. I could not hold him.+

I sagged a little. All energy seemed to have been squeezed from us, and the room – and the night outside – seemed darker than ever.

'What is the Immaterial College?' Kara asked. 'I've never heard of it. What did he mean?'

+I don't know, Kara.+

'Have you heard of it, Beta?' Kara asked, glancing over at me. I opened my mouth to reply in the negative, but Ravenor cut me off.

+Wait.+

CHAPTER 18

In the muniment room

We were no longer alone.

Though it was very dark, and the drapes drawn, a shadow seemed to pass by the windows of the muniment room. How a shadow could be detected under such circumstances, I cannot imagine, but there it was, crossing the end window. I heard a footstep or two, and the shadow paused, as if trying to peer in at us.

We waited. After a moment, a shadow passed the side window. I felt at first that the shadow was circling us, prowling around the house. But it seemed as though something was still peering in through the end window. Two shadows, then, two visitors lurking outside.

In the oppressive silence, Kara flexed her grip on the blinksword. I reached to my wrist.

'Cuff?' I whispered.

'Not yet,' Ravenor responded, his voice issued by the Chair's transponders at very low volume. 'We are warded. Let us see who we have beckoned to us.'

The shadows outside seemed to have stilled. I fancied they had been tricks of the eye, until one moved again, the second, or perhaps now a third. After a moment, the end window rattled slightly in its frame, as if someone was trying it to see if it was loose.

'Stay within the outer circle, both of you,' Ravenor said. Timurlin's body had been placed at the centre of a chalk-and-sand diagram on the floor, but a wider circle of poured salt formed a full circumference around us, almost to the walls of the room. We remained obediently inside it. The air had gone cold, making the afterscent of the shaellic seem stale and sour.

The window rattled again. Then, distinctly, something tapped on the glass. *Tap-tap-tap*. Not the brisk knuckle-rap of a caller at a door, but the furtive pattering of fingertips, the gentle knock of an illicit lover at a bedroom casement.

Tap-tap-tap.

'Do not respond,' said Ravenor.

The tapping came again. Three of the candles around Timurlin's corpse died into feeble strings of smoke.

'They test our bindings,' said Ravenor. 'Kara?'

She nodded, and moved quickly to relight the candles that had failed. Like me, she was unnerved. Her hands fumbled with her little tinderbox as she struck and lit a taper. The candles began to glow again, but the light from them, from all of them, was frail, their flames a very pale yellow, as though the air was growing thin.

I glanced around as the tapping came again, now from a different window pane. The window bumped in its frame, as if pressed by hands seeking to unseat the latch.

Then silence again.

We heard a flutter suddenly, from the direction of the grate, and all turned. Some soot and grit scattered down the chimney into the hearth, as though the very chimney pot had been probed and tested as a means of entry. Another rattle, and another fall of grit. Then, quite quickly, footsteps again, circling the muniment room on the pavement outside.

'Remain calm,' said Ravenor softly.

'I am calm,' I replied.

'I meant Kara,' he said.

Kara nodded, and forced up a cheery grin that did not convince.

'We have come to someone's attention,' Ravenor whispered. 'I would know who we have drawn out.'

Footsteps came again, heavy but soft. They seemed to pass the end window. A shadow flitted. Then the tone of the footsteps changed. They were moving slowly, upon floorboards, not the pavers of the street. They were in the house, in the hall outside the room. They seemed to have passed from street to hall without ever a door opening, and certainly there was no exterior door in the hall at the end of the muniment room.

The footsteps came, and went, then came again. We heard a faint noise, the sound of palms sliding gently across the panelled wall between hall and muniment room, either side of the main door, testing, feeling for some catch or hinge.

Then the footsteps resumed. Someone, something, walked the hall outside from one end to the other, then returned to the main door. The handle rattled as someone tried to turn it.

'The way is barred,' said Ravenor very clearly.

The handle stopped its rattling. A second later, the brass knob of the side door tried to turn instead. It quivered and clicked, but the door remained shut. The footsteps walked back down the hall.

A hand knocked on the main door. Four, heavy knocks.

'You may not enter,' said Ravenor.

A pause, then another series of four knocks.

'The way in is closed to you,' said Ravenor. 'But you may identify yourself.'

Something slid against the outside of the heavy main door, fingertips perhaps.

'You know us,' said a voice from outside. It was muffled by the thickness of the door, but quite remarkable: a low, bass voice, like that of some giant, dense and heavy as iron yet somehow also hollow.

'I do not,' Ravenor replied.

'You do,' said the voice from outside. 'You called to us.' The voice had such oppressive weight, like lead pressing down upon us. It was also marked by a distinct accent that reminded me of the speech of the dry Herrat, but it was not that. It was an accent of some faraway place, and I did not know it. It spoke in formal Enmabic, but with the careful precision of someone using a learned tongue or a second language.

'I called to no one and no thing,' said Ravenor.

'You did. Our name, you have spoken. Our name, we have heard. We have come to find who calls us. Let us in.'

'I called to no one.'

'Our name was spoken and we heard it.'

'I spoke no name,' said Ravenor. 'Not any with power. None that should draw anyone.'

'You have little wit, then, and little lore,' replied the voice.

Both door handles rattled at the same moment.

'This is my house,' said Ravenor. 'No guests may enter uninvited, and I invite in only those I know. I know you not, and have not spoken your name.'

'You have!' said a voice at the side door. It was a different voice, crisp and brittle, like flaking ice, an angry hiss.

'You have,' agreed the first voice, from behind the main door. 'We are of the College.'

The side door shivered in its frame: a more frustrated and annoyed effort to open it.

'I see,' said Ravenor calmly. 'The name was mentioned. But it is just a name. Two words, both quite common, neither a word of power. Even in conjunction, they could not have summoned you.'

'The working of vile sorcery can invest any words with power,' said a third voice from outside the end window. It was solemn and stern. 'This much I have learned. You are a fool to think otherwise, and lacking in talent.'

'Cease your prattle and let us in!' snarled a fourth voice from the side window. It was a deep growl, like that of a predator.

'I do not think I will,' said Ravenor. 'The way is barred, and you are not invited. So, you have charged the name of your fraternity by means of sorcery, such that it lights like a signal-fire when uttered. I see how that may be done... by those unwise enough to tinker with magics.'

'We are no fraternity,' declared the solemn voice at the end window.

'Let us in!' hissed the voice at the side door.

'Let us in now,' demanded a new voice, the sharp tone of a carrion bird, which echoed from the grate. Dust and soot showered down the chimney.

'We grow tired of your lack of compliance,' came the snarling tone at the side window.

'What is your business?' asked Ravenor.

'Our business is to know you for what you are,' said the heavy, hollow voice outside the main door. 'To know why you spoke our name. To know what part you play.'

'My business is my own,' replied Ravenor.

'We will enter if we please. No door is closed to us.'

This was a new voice, a sixth voice, as distinct as all the others. It was as solid and dull as a block of rockcrete. It too came from the main door.

'I can assure you, it is–' Ravenor began.

The main door shook in its frame, as though it had been dealt a huge blow. More came, rapidly, fierce pounding blows of immense force. The old wooden door seemed to bulge and distort in its frame, bending like a reflection in a trick-glass. I flinched, and knew without doubt that whatever was striking the door was doing so with such inhuman power, it should have splintered the wood into kindling. It was not the physical door that was withstanding the assault, it was the wards of power that Ravenor had placed upon it.

The hammering continued for almost a minute. Kara and I jumped involuntarily at every impact.

I glanced at Ravenor.

'Not yet,' he said mildly.

The hammering stopped abruptly.

The icy, hissing voice at the side door laughed cruelly.

'You idiot,' it said.

'Shut up!' replied the dull, rockcrete tones of the voice at the main door. I sensed anger simmering.

'Enough, both,' said the hollow voice in its curious accent. It seemed, despite its ominous calm, to hold some authority over them. Footsteps shifted.

'Let us in, or we will enter anyway,' it said to us.

'Unless you state your business in less enigmatic terms, and identify yourselves by more than a meaningless name,' said Ravenor, 'you are denied.'

'You are in no position to deny us,' said the hollow voice.

A creeping sense of dread began to ooze into the muniment room. I felt my hairs stand up, and gooseflesh rise. Cold sweat came, unbidden, to the small of my back.

'Brace yourselves,' Ravenor said to both of us.

The air became drowsy and charged, like a late afternoon before a storm. The darkness thickened. One by one, the candles around Timurlin's corpse went out. They did not flutter and extinguish: they burned down rapidly. Thick templum candles made to burn for days exhausted themselves in a matter of seconds, descending unnaturally into puddles of molten wax until the struggling wicks drowned and the flames vanished. All the windows and door handles began to quiver and shake. The charms of herb sprigs on the window latches, door handles and grate began to wither, drying and shrivelling away to dust, as though an entire autumn and winter had flown past in a few seconds. The air filled with the scent of mould and decay, of rotting leaves and spoiled herbs. Then a fouler stench came.

I looked, and saw that Timurlin's corpse was decaying too. It was shrivelling and rotting, first bloating, then shrinking into an emaciated, twisted rigor. Then the flesh submitted to putrefaction, blotched green and puce, and liquefied, like the wax of the ruined candles. Rotting organs shrivelled like the sprigs of herb, and reduced to sticky tar. The smell was brief but noisome. In less than thirty seconds, mere bones remained, blackened, then bleached, then clattering apart into disarticulation; then even those loose parts eroded and became dust.

A wind arose from nowhere that chilled our faces, and fluttered my hair, and Kara's too. It eddied the dust that had once been bones; then it began to blow up the sand and salt, and even the dust of the chalk, like a sea-wind fretting a beach. The lines of the ritual diagram blew away, and so did the outer circle. Only the faint trace of chalk marks remained on the old floor.

The main door twisted. It did not open, nor did it break or collapse or burn. The old, heavy wood that composed it simply flowed like water, like the surface of a still pool as something deep below rises up into the air. It rippled like quicksilver around a figure that was slowly but inexorably pushing through it.

A face first, then chest and shoulders, then one hand, straining to pass through the barrier. The figure was tall, huge, in fact, a being of titanic stature. It looked as though it was made of glass, or lead crystal, a smooth, milky white with a bluish, lambent glow within. It reminded me of the pretty ornamental perfume bottles in Kara's collection.

There was little detail to it, except a noble formation to its head, and a sense of concentration to its features. It strained against the barrier, forcing more and more of itself through into the muniment room. A foot appeared, part of a leg. It had the bulk and physique of Comus Nocturnus, and the strength too, for it was heaving its way through a warp-warded perimeter by sheer force of will.

Half through, the door rippling around it, it stared at us.

'I see you,' it announced in its hollow voice, with some slight sign of effort and struggle. 'I see you. Three human souls who defy us. You are nothing. Inconsequential. A disappointment.'

'Then why do you struggle so to reach us?' asked Ravenor.

'Because you defied us,' it replied. It made another surge, and brought more of itself through the door.

It was not alone. A second figure, of similar stature and milky-glass countenance, was sliding its way through the side door. Its long fingers were hooked like glass claws. A third began to lean through the window and wall at the end of the room, and a fourth through the side window. A fifth, quite the largest and most broad, began to slide through the panels of the wall beside the main door. From the grate, dust and stones scattered down, and the fireplace itself began to bulge and distort as the sixth made entry.

'Gideon!' Kara gasped.

'Keep your place,' he replied.

'They are coming in,' I said. I had a Hecuter auto holstered at my hip, but thought not to draw it, for what good would a hard-round gun do against such an invasion?

'Keep your place,' Ravenor repeated steadily.

The Chair was facing the main figure as it bulged through the door.

'You test me well,' Ravenor said to it. 'Your command of sorcery is profound, and dismaying in its heresy. Nevertheless, you are not invited, and you are not welcome. By edict of the Holy Inquisition, your entry is forbidden.'

'The Inquisition be damned,' the glassy figure replied with utter venom.

'Most likely,' said Ravenor, 'but not today. You were warned.'

Until that moment, I had known Gideon's power, and been impressed by it, though I had wondered why he used it with such restraint. Now, he set restraint aside. I became one of very few people to witness him unleash his full potency.

And thus, I came to understand why he kept it in check, and rationed its use, and doled it out sparingly. It was the most terrible thing.

The air burned, as though we had plunged suddenly into the blinding heart of a main sequence star. There was a brightness that was impossible to bear. A screaming filled the room, so loud it shattered window glass and cracked flagstones. Gideon's power, may the Emperor protect me, was a monstrous force, more monstrous even than the dreadful figures clawing and straining their way into the muniment room to reach us.

A beam of radiant energy seared out from Ravenor's armoured chair, and struck the advancing figure in the chest. The beam was constant, like a column of light, a glistening rod of silver power that crackled and sizzled.

The advancing figure shuddered, stopped in its tracks. It pressed against the unstinting beam, but could not staunch its flow. Its white crystal form began to bubble and melt where the beam touched it, flowing and spattering like superheated glass at a blower's furnace.

The figure roared, and redoubled its efforts. The intensity of Ravenor's beam increased. Around the besieged room, the other figures faltered and began to writhe. The one with the icy, hissing voice shrieked in pain or rage. Invisible power forced each of them back through the walls, doors and windows, their forms contorting and undulating, spattering into drips and blobs that fell to the ground, and seethed like spats of magma. One by one they were driven out in anguish, deformed and distorted. As each one was forced back, it disappeared with a pop of decompression, as though spat through the bending skin of one reality back into another. The huge figure bearing in through the wall was the last to go, and then only the main intruder, speared by Ravenor's beam, remained.

It would not desist. Impossibly, with staggering determination, it took a step forward, driving itself into the torching force of the beam. It reached out a hand to try to block or cap the relentless psykanic ray, but its fingers and part of its palm melted like ice where it came into contact.

Still, it did not desist. It managed another, superhuman step, stooping into the beam like a man fighting into a hurricane.

'Beta?' Ravenor said in a small voice I could barely hear above the screeching roar of psykanic fire.

'Yes, Gideon?'

'Now, please.'

I switched my cuff to *off*.

The slap of pressure shook the room, throwing both Kara and me to the ground. What was left of any window glass blew out. The light vanished, and the terrible beam of energy flicked off. The muniment room was plunged into an ice-cold vapour.

The advancing figure squealed in rage, and disintegrated, the shards and fragments of its form showering to the ground and vanishing.

I rose, my ears ringing with overpressure. The intruders had all disappeared. The drapes had collapsed from the broken windows, their poles buckled, and the pale light of dawn washed in. Steam wisped from the hull of Ravenor's chair.

The main door opened. Kara and I snapped around, weapons raised.

Nayl stood there, with a heavy assault las in his hands.

'What the hell's going on in here?' he asked.

CHAPTER 19

Upon an empty pathway

'What does this change?' I asked.

'It changes almost everything,' Gideon replied.

'How so?'

'If what Timurlin told us is correct–'

'And is it?'

'I believe so,' he replied, 'for it is almost impossible for a soul to lie under those conditions. Between my mind and the charms we inscribed, almost all scope for mendacity and evasion had been stripped from his mind. Connort Timurlin couldn't lie, and indeed was clearly distressed by some of the things he was being forced to confess.'

'You mean Verner Chase,' I said.

'Indeed, him. One of the elusive Chase dynasty, brought to light for the first time.'

'It seemed–' I began.

'What?'

'Rather cruel,' I said. 'We tormented his soul.'

The Chair turned to me gently. Once again, I found it curious that Ravenor made such efforts to use his armoured physicality as one might use one's face or body. He was trying, I believe, to remind us all that he was still human, though the opportunities for expressive body language were limited.

'I have come to think much of you, Beta,' he said, 'even in the short time we have been in collaboration. You are clearly highly trained and very competent, and you seem to possess a level of determination and composure that rivals that of Patience. Perhaps the mentors of the Ordos have much to learn from Cognitae training regimens.'

'A low blow,' I replied.

'My apologies. My point was, you seem to have true steel in you. Yet, from time to time, you seem to display a dismaying weakness – a level of sympathy for–'

'A level of compassion, I prefer to think,' I returned.

'Call it what you will,' he replied. 'Connort Timurlin, or Verner Chase, was an agent of heresy, and his life's work was predicated on the overthrow of the Imperium. That much he admitted. Yes, we dealt with him ruthlessly. But the Inquisition cannot falter. It cannot. The constant threat we face, and the traitors we pursue, are dedicated to the destruction of our way of life. The Ordos are harsh. The Inquisition is no one's friend. Emotion plays no part in our work. No one ever said this would be easy or pleasant.'

'Harlon said as much,' I replied. 'And I have seen it for myself enough times now. In the end, none of us matter in the face of the cause. I will consider myself reprimanded. But do not mistake my compassion for heretical sympathy. I may have been schooled by heretics, but by their twisted logic I was raised to believe in the Throne. I am a servant of the God-Emperor, Gideon, and out of my past, I come to you, and to Him, a penitent.'

We had gone out of the nameless house into the small gardens behind it. It was early still, the sun yet rising across the rooftops and spires of the city. The gardens, once ornamental, had run wild through years of neglect, but the light was the colour of spun gold, and there was mist and some birdsong. It seemed almost tranquil, as though no menace had been at our door but an hour before.

I had expected him to seem tired, and in need of rest and recuperation after his monumental display of force, but he was vital and eager, as though he had expended but a tiny fraction of his strength.

'You see,' he remarked, 'why I prefer to use my mind with restraint.

Here in Queen Mab... indeed everywhere... any manipulation of the warp causes ripples. The more you use such powers, the greater the force of them, then the greater the reaction. I am a weapon against the dark, Beta, but I am also a beacon that summons it. We must keep ourselves guarded and hidden, for we have few friends on Sancour. I would appreciate it if you would not chide me on such matters again.'

'Who were they?' I asked. 'The–'

'I think we are wise to avoid saying the name,' he replied. 'Through sorcery, they had charged the very words with power, so that their very title could not be taken in vain. Let us call them... the visitors.'

'So they were sorcerers? The... visitors.'

'One of them, at least,' he said. 'Of significant ability.'

'Do you know who they were, though?'

'Not precisely. But the accent of their leader was distinctive.'

'Yes, I thought so.'

'I have heard it before,' he said. 'It was the accent of a soul born and raised in a city called Tizca.'

'Where is that?' I asked, for I was sure I knew the names of all the cities on Sancour.

'Not on this world,' Ravenor said. 'It stood on a world far away, a long time ago. The city is gone, and the world is dead. The planet was called Prospero.'

I felt cold suddenly, despite the coat Nayl had lent me.

'But that–'

'Indeed,' he said.

'That was a traitor-world of the ancient days,' I said. 'You speak of the infamous Fifteenth Legion.'

'I do.'

'Then... he was Astartes?'

'Perhaps,' Ravenor replied. 'I do not know what form or guise the men of Prospero take these days, but the accent was assuredly that of Tizca, and the Fifteenth were notorious sorcerers. We know other Traitor Legions are afoot on Sancour, rivalling each other in their attempts to either deny or join the Yellow King.'

'Chase said as much.'

'He did. I am alarmed, but not at all surprised, that the Thousand Sons of Magnus are part of that intrigue.'

At the rear part of the small gardens, beyond a crumbling wall, a flight of weathered and overgrown steps led down to the Footstep Lane holloway that ran behind the back of the property. We descended into that phantom and abandoned pathway, where empty buildings gazed upon us silently from either side. It was, perhaps, too early for the vicious warblind gangs to be abroad. In the pale, low sunlight, the holloway was eerily peaceful, the derelict ghost of a city that had once been.

'Verner Chase's admissions were the most important,' Ravenor said. 'He spoke of the Cognitae as all but dissolved, put to flight by the Yellow King. The balance of power has changed, and our enemy is recomposing his forces, which suggests the Yellow King is on the verge of accomplishing his great work. Chase stated he was.'

'So?'

'So our timetable has changed,' he replied, drifting slowly across the weeds and broken cobbles. 'Our investigation here has lasted years, and has been patient and careful. Eisenhorn's was too. Years of work have got us this far. The unravelling of this mystery has been going on for more than the span of your life. And it has been the only safe way to proceed. But if the King's work is close to fruition, then we are running out of time. We are, I think, now obliged to act with greater urgency and directness, though I am loath to do so. We must apply brute force.'

'We would risk exposure,' I said. 'And we may find ourselves helpless in the face of the King's power.'

'Yes,' he said. 'But we must trust ourselves. And each other.'

Something odd happened to the holloway as he spoke. It seemed to me that the light around us smudged, and for a moment I saw the world as though through a window pane smeared with grease. Then the derelict structures of the holloway, and the narrow sunken lane itself, disappeared and we were walking, instead, down the wide and magnificent boulevard of a towering city in bright sunlight. Behind us, some towering monument stood against the clear sky.

'Do not be alarmed,' he said.

'Did you do that?' I asked.

'I did. Forgive me. Sometimes I find it reassuring to walk in places where I have walked before.'

'This is a memory?'

'Yes, Beta.'

'You have brought me into your memories?'

'I have entered my memories to compose my mind. I have brought you with me, for I thought you might enjoy the view.'

I smiled. 'This is not Sancour,' I said. 'Is it... Tizca?'

'No, no,' he replied. 'It is, I suppose, the world on which I grew up. The world that made me. This is how I remember it, all those years ago.'

'In such detail!' I marvelled.

'Beta, I have left many details out. But I find it reassuring, and I thought it only fair. You have allowed me to pass into your mind, and examine your memories. I am returning the favour. Regard it as a gesture of trust.'

I breathed in. The air was cool, and smelled nothing like the city air of Queen Mab.

'So, what do we do?' I asked. 'Surely the first goal is still to find a way into the City of Dust?'

'It is. And we know that is possible, because of your experience in Alace Quatorze's house.'

'But Feverfugue is gone to fire,' I said, 'and I have not been able to duplicate the effort anywhere else. Freddy Dance, and his visions of other stars, seems a more profitable line of–'

'Perhaps,' said Ravenor, 'but there is no telling if he knows anything, or is able by any means to show us a way in. The Dance investigation was promising, but it was taking too long, and I fear it is no longer viable.'

'So, then? What?'

'There are two lines of possibility that I believe may be more fruitful and more immediate,' he replied. 'The first is the Cognitae. From Chase's confession, it's clear that the Cognitae enjoyed, at least until recently, direct dealings with the Yellow King. This suggests they had some access to the City of Dust.'

'Yes, but that may now be denied.'

'It may. But Chase's mistress, this "Zoya Farnessa", the woman he died protecting, is now so out of favour with the King that she dared to seek the aid of Eisenhorn. She is senior Cognitae. If anyone might know a way in, it's her.'

'And I know who she is,' I said.

The Chair's transponders made a noise that I understood as chuckling.

'Yes, I thought as much,' he said. 'I saw a stirring of it in your thoughts. You recognise her now?'

'I didn't at first,' I admitted. 'Not when I first glimpsed her. But I have become certain it was someone I knew, disguised in a very skilled function. After hearing Chase speak, I am convinced. I believe his mistress was once mine too. I believe she is Eusebe dea Mordaunt, once Mam Mordaunt of the Maze Undue.'

'I think so too,' he replied. 'She raised you, trained you, trusted you even, and when she saw you placing your confidence in Eisenhorn, she believed he could be approached.'

Yes, she raised me, and honed me, but she was never more than a stepmother to me, and a distant one at that. I wondered if Gideon was right, and Mam Mordaunt had trusted me more than I ever realised. Perhaps, even, had been more fond of me than I ever realised.

'It's possible I could serve as a key,' I suggested, 'and convince her that she must work with you. From Timurlin's actions, it's plain that the Cognitae have utter animus for the Inquisition, even in their hour of need. But we don't know where she may be found.'

'Not entirely true,' Ravenor replied. 'Timurlin refused to answer us, and resisted our efforts to make him reveal her whereabouts or even identity. His mind was strong, even in death, trained in psychologik techniques to deflect interrogation, and even the probing of a psyker.'

'We were all taught such things,' I said. 'I would imagine the perfecti were schooled to an even higher degree.'

'Quite so. But I was in his mind, and I am rather more capable than the interrogation psykers routinely used by the Inquisition. He would not answer, but as we pressed him on her identity, he could not help but think of the very thing he was fiercely guarding. It is a basic trait of human consciousness, a subliminal thing. Your mind is strong, Beta – try not to think about the scholam where you were raised.'

I frowned, and did so. It was, of course, impossible. To cast what I wished not to think of out of my mind automatically made me think of it so I could focus on that which I wished to remove. The useless effort made me laugh.

'You see?' he said. 'That mind function may be diminished by intense training, and the use of technique... mind-blocking, Tanser partitioning, the Galantine Method, even a fortified memory palace... but it cannot be removed entirely. Timurlin resisted to a very high degree, but I could see the shadows behind him.'

'Behind him?'

'In his mind. No face. He kept his mistress hidden with great skill, nothing more than a silhouette. He was so dedicated to her protection, other things seeped through.'

'Like?'

'If you'll permit me?'

I nodded.

A picture slipped into my mind, like a slide into a magic lantern. I closed my eyes. It was quite distressing, for it was edged with pain, and distorted by Timurlin's suffering. I could smell blood and fear. I saw a silhouette, perhaps female, it was hard to tell. It was a fuzzy patch of darkness. But there was something behind it. I focused on the image Gideon was sharing with me, ignoring the discomfort that accompanied it and the generally distressing sensation that something as live and slippery as a Toilgate eel had slithered into me through one ear and was roiling and squirming inside my skull.

That which lay behind the silhouette was a place, like a poorly focused and overexposed pict: a haze of sunlight on a bright day, the smudged impression of rooftops, a spire here, a steeple there. It was hard to make anything out. It could have been any city, anywhere.

'That tower,' I asked, eyes tight shut, 'is it Saint Clavin's?'

'I don't think so,' he replied. 'But there are other things of interest. Two, in fact. Regard the steeple further away, to the left.'

'I can barely make it out.'

'But the shape of it, Beta?'

'One tall steeple... with a flanking bell tower to the side. Is that Saint Marzom Martyr?'

'I think it is. It's very distinctive.'

'Then we're seeing it from the north...'

'And what's the other thing?' he asked.

'I don't know, I... We're seeing it from very high up. It's a view from very high up, right across the city.'

I opened my eyes.

'So what's north of Saint Marzom Martyr, and of sufficient altitude?' he asked.

'Stanchion House,' I replied, with a smile.

'Good,' he said. 'You see now the granular detail in which even matters of great scope must be inspected. The merest shadows and whispers, barely limned, can yet betray considerable truths.'

The sunlight was warm on my face, though it was not Sancour's sun. The great boulevard around us, a kilometre wide, majestic and empty, seemed a fine place, a place of hope, a great city of the Imperium. I wondered where it was and when it had been. It struck me that it was a place that represented the Imperium of Man at its best, a prosperous and dignified city, contained within strong bounds of law and justice, robustly free of the canker and decay that gnaws at the hem of our ancient civilisation. This remembered city, and every great place like it, on every Imperial world, exemplified the potential of the Imperium, and thus precisely represented the cultural ideal we worked to protect. All our efforts, and our pain, and our sacrifices, were given to safeguard such places, and to maintain the peace and aspiration of humanity. We toiled and struggled in the dark to keep these places safe. It was a salutary reminder of our cause, and I was grateful Ravenor had shared it with me. I imagined it was why he liked to visit it in his mind, to remind himself when work seemed exhausting and impossible.

I had wondered why there were no people abroad in the place, on such a fine day, but now I saw some, just a few dots, indistinct, at the edges of the wide avenue. One figure stood where we were, out in the centre of the broad boulevard, and seemed to be walking towards us, but was yet far away.

'So, we go to Stanchion House?' I asked.

'I believe it is worth the effort,' Ravenor replied. 'We'll do it at once, today. If our suppositions are correct, and we can secure Mordaunt, or any senior of the Cognitae, then it will be of value.'

'Agreed,' I said.

'But we will not waste long on it,' he added. 'If she's not there, or other impediments are placed in our way, we abort, and give it up as a bad job. We don't have the time for persistence.'

'So then,' I asked, 'we would turn our attention to the second line of possibility. You said there were two.'

'I did.'

'And?' I pressed.

'The King Door,' he answered.

I raised my eyebrows.

'I think that's unwise,' I said.

'I know you do.'

'I do not think it is a way into the City of Dust,' I said, 'or rather, I do not think it is a *safe* way in.'

'I fancy there are no safe ways,' he replied. 'But a way in must be found, without delay, and it is by far the most promising option.'

I sighed. His mind was set. In his way, Gideon could be quite as obdurate as Gregor. I looked around. The lone figure was closer now, wandering towards us, a long coat rippling in the wind.

'You've seen into my mind,' I said to Ravenor. 'I let you do it. You saw the King Door–'

'Yes, Beta.'

'Then you must also have felt what I felt. It is hard to place in words, but that opening was not a... Not a place of entry. I felt a great dread of it, and Renner did too. We were anxious to escape the Below, Gideon, madly anxious, yet there was a doorway, and a dim vista beyond, and neither of us dared to step through it.'

'I am aware,' he said. 'I have studied the impression it left upon you. Not so much a door as a window, perhaps? A vantage from which one may view what is beyond. But it was barred physically, it seems, by some ocean or sea. And by other things too. Nameless sensations of dread and foreboding that made you both recoil. It was a glimpse of an inhospitable and dangerous boundary.'

'Then it should be left alone,' I insisted. 'I came from it with the unshakeable feeling that it could not be crossed, by any means, and that to try would be to invite doom.'

The wind gusted on the boulevard. I heard banners flap and snap on the great monument behind us.

'Yet, it was crossed,' Ravenor said. 'By your angel.'

'One, he is not "mine",' I said. 'Two, he is wrought of stuff beyond our mortality, and I think can endure much that we could not. Three, I think the effort all but killed him. He was blood-mad when he came to me, exhausted and tormented. He had been driven to escape, and had braved a crossing that was otherwise utter folly. I think he only made it by some miracle of chance or fortitude. Gideon, it was a hell that the likes of an angel risked everything to escape, and the effort drove him insane. I do not think we can duplicate his feat, and I believe it is reckless to try. I think the King Door was not made for mortal humans.'

'Show me a better option,' he said.

'I can't, but Comus was desperate and–'

'And we are not?'

I shrugged in frustration.

'I have not pressed you, Beta,' he said, 'but you have kept the angel to yourself. I would like to talk to him directly, and examine his mind.'

'He knows nothing, Gideon.'

'Nothing he has told you. But from what you've said of him, I believe that his experiences, the undoubted suffering, has stifled his memory. He has made himself forget, so as to cling to what sanity is left him. I think he knows more than he realises, and through careful sifting of his thoughts–'

'If you reach into his mind and try to unlock his memories, I fear you would tip him back into frenzied madness. We cannot risk that fury in our midst.'

'No,' he agreed. 'I would have no choice but to terminate him.'

I looked at the Chair sharply. He was not joking. In pursuit of his goal, he would think nothing of executing an angel, if that angel did not suit his needs. I wasn't sure what was more troubling: that he would so calmly admit he would kill an Astartes-angel, or that he so confidently thought it was something he could do at all.

'The King Door is a dismal option,' he said, 'but it may be our only one. I will make preparations to investigate and, if possible, penetrate it. I would at least like to see it for myself. If you can, by any gentle means, extract more knowledge of it from your angel friend, then I urge you to do so. In the meantime, let us hope that Stanchion House provides us with a better route and better intelligence. Believe me, I pray it does.'

'I will need to lead,' I said. 'If we are to make peaceful contact with Mam Mordaunt, it has to be me. She will trust no other of us.'

'Except Thaddeus Saur,' he said.

'I doubt that,' I replied. 'And he should not be charged with such a vital task.'

'I agree,' said Ravenor. 'I expected you to take lead, Beta. I hoped you would. Thus, I must acknowledge the formal capacity in which you work at my side.'

The lone figure that had been approaching all this while was suddenly with us, as if he had transported the last few hundred metres in a blink while my back was to him. He nodded to the Chair, and then smiled at me. Then he held something out for me to take.

I had never seen him before. I did not know him. And yet I did; I knew the smile as though it had been bestowed upon me several times before. In truth, it had been, I had just never seen it.

The man was young, tall and strong, and very handsome. With his fiercely grey, fiercely kind eyes, high cheekbones and long black hair tied back, he reminded me oddly of the pict-book images of aeldari I had seen as a child. But he was human.

'These are for you, Beta,' he said. I knew his voice. It had come from his lips and throat and tongue out into the air, but it was the same as the one that had been speaking inside my head.

I saw the things he held out to me. A small leather case, and a silver necklace.

I took them from him. The necklace bore an amulet of wraithbone. All the members of Gideon's warband wore one, for the psychoactive material facilitated his waring of them, should the need arise. It was a tool, an instrument of team operation, but it was also a badge of belonging that proclaimed membership of a small family. An odd family, but a family nevertheless.

'Let me,' said the young man, and gently clasped it around my neck as I held back my hair. His face was very close to mine.

'For you, it is more a symbol than anything,' the Chair said. 'I would not choose to ware you, except in extremity, and I cannot ware you with your cuff inactive. As a pariah, even limited, I may not be able to function through you as fluidly as I can Kara or Kys.'

I nodded, and let my hair fall back.

The leather case was heavy. The leather was a fitted cover for a small, flat box of perfectly machined obsidian. I opened it and looked at the Inquisitorial rosette that rested on the blue silk cushion inside.

Ordo Hereticus, Officio Thracian Primaris, Scarus Sector.

'To act in my name, you must carry my authority,' said the Chair. 'Your trained ability is beyond doubt, despite its bastard origins. This is a discretionary field appointment. My choice, by my command, and temporary, of course.'

'Of course,' I said, smiling.

'By which I mean, pending,' said the young man.

I closed the box and case, and slipped it into my coat pocket.

'I will not fail you,' I said.

'Don't worry about failing me,' said the Chair. 'It's not me you're serving.'

'It's not you I was talking to,' I replied. The young man laughed.

'Thank you,' I said to both of them. I placed my hand, flat, upon the warm hull of the Chair for a moment, then turned and kissed the young man on the cheek. He grinned, bashfully.

'I hope I haven't broken protocol already?' I asked the Chair.

'I'll allow it,' the Chair replied.

I became aware of music, the rising boom of martial bands. There was cheering, as though the whole city had woken up to celebrate my investment.

Crowds now lined the boulevard, huge, roaring crowds. Streamers and banners flew. I had no idea where they had come from.

'I have let some details slot back into place,' said the Chair. 'Not just the location, but parts of the things that were in it that day.'

'Was this the day you became an inquisitor?' I asked. 'Did the crowds come out to cheer your election?'

'No,' said the Chair. 'It was for something else. A Holy Novena. A great triumph, to commemorate a military victory. Crowds like this do not celebrate the election of inquisitors, Beta. Such matters happen in the dark, in private rooms. This was not the day of my appointment, but it was the day I became the inquisitor you know.'

The young man looked at the Chair.

'It was the day I became him,' he said.

I looked around. There were petals in the air, blossom falling and whirling like snowflakes. We were in the midst of a vast parade that had just appeared around us. Marching regiments of Astra Militarum, war machines, gleaming ranks of Adeptus Astartes giants. The noise was deafening, a roar of marching feet, of mass cheering, of thundering engines, of drums and cymbals and brass and pipes playing the *March of the Primarchs*. My diaphragm shook. Overhead, low and fast, warcraft shrieked by in fly-past formation. The air vibrated with the noise and motion.

The young man looked at me. Petals fluttered between us.

'This is the Hive Primaris, Thracian Primaris,' he said. 'The great Avenue of the Victor Bellum. This day happened about one hundred and fifty years ago. That monument that rises behind us, whose shadow falls across us, that is the Spatian Gate. I want you to remember, as I remember, that the greatest danger can strike when all seems safe, and when harm is least expected.'

He smiled again, but the smile was sad, or perhaps full of some longing. He looked into my eyes, and touched my cheek for a moment, then brushed loose petals off my shoulder.

'It's nearly time,' he said. I could barely hear him above the howl of the warcraft flying by above. 'I have to go now.'

A fleeting shadow passed across us, something flickering overhead in the bright sunlight–

And the Footstep Lane holloway was empty. The deserted quiet of early morning, with nothing but birdsong and the low golden sunlight of dawn.

'I'll see you in the house,' said Ravenor, and the Chair turned away, floating silently back to the steps. I was left alone on the weed-fringed cobbles of the sunken street, with the weight of the rosette in my pocket.

The third section of the story,
which is called

TRUE LEARNING

CHAPTER 20

Which is of the House of Webs

The warblind gangs are not to be trifled with.

Three of the warblind blocked my path, and I sensed at least one more step into the ruined hallway at my back, denying me retreat. From the scarified brands and inks on their shaven scalps, they were of the Marzom Cross killgang, the most notorious of the northern bands. They carried blades and, more, they carried bulk. Under the cake of filth and rags, they were all enhanced muscle and reinforced bones, the relics of their combat engineering.

'I would pass here,' I said, clearly and in the low dialect of the street.

One uttered a growl in answer, the most coherent sound, I feared, he was able to articulate. I could smell the metallic stink of the aggression stimulants flooding their blood. The feral warblind of Queen Mab could never be reasoned with, but sometimes one could slip past them if one remained calm and quiet and made no abrupt movement, or if, by luck, they happened to be at the low point of their aggression cycles.

Not these. There would be no talking, no reasoning. They were already twitching, synthetic hormones drenching their systems and rousing them to mindless rage. Their secondary eyelids began to flutter and blink: nictitating lids that had once flashed target lock displays onto their retinas.

These augmetics were long since broken, but the rising hyperstimms were triggering their military implants to fire up, as they had done lifetimes ago in the warzone. This hall was their warzone now. This life. A brutal life where there was only ever war.

I gauged I would have time to move my right hand just once before they struck. To the gun at my hip, a heavy Tronsvasse Kal40 that Harlon had armed me with? Or to my cuff, which, when off, had rendered me blank to the warblind in the past?

I made my choice, but it was academic anyway.

Someone lunged out of an archway to my right, and slammed into the trio. A razor-edged severaka struck body mass with a crunch like splitting wood, and whirled a ganger clean off his feet in a spray of blood. The ganger rotated in the air like a dancer, bounced off the wall behind him, and crumpled, sliced open.

Thaddeus Saur had only begun.

Saur was a powerful man. I knew that much from years of training under him at the scholam. He had bulk and he had speed, but nothing like the enhanced mass or reflex of the warblind. However, Saur also possessed daunting skill, a honed finesse, which he employed with lethal precision. Big as he was, with his shock of dirty-white hair and his oxblood-red bodyglove, he seemed to slide like oil between his hulking opponents, yet each time he struck, it was with bone-fracturing force. The first ganger had not yet hit the floor before Saur had engaged the next, blocking a vicious blow with his left forearm – a second impact that sounded like a cleaver chopping root vegetables – in order to make a gap in his enemy's untutored guard. The severaka came up through that space, driving hilt and blade-base into the ganger's face and neck. There was a wet smack of meat and gristle. The ganger was hurt, but too stimmed to fall down. He swung again, raking with his dirty blade, but Saur went in under him, using a shoulder barge as leverage to flip the wounded ganger up and over, and slam him onto the ground on his back.

There was no time to finish him. The third ganger piled into Saur, snarling. Saur, his crocodilian eyes hooded, blocked him twice, paused to savagely back-kick the second ganger who was beginning to rise again, then returned to the third once more, cutting him three times with successive sword thrusts.

Saur was a master. Perhaps, of the people I had met in my life, only Harlon Nayl was his equal or superior in the trade of physical combat. Unlike Harlon, who cut loose with measured fury only when necessary, Saur relished his craft. After semi-imprisonment in Ravenor's care, Saur was venting his frustration. I had seen this unfettered brutality in him only once before, the day he had killed Voriet in front of me, and begun the process by which my life would unravel.

The fourth ganger, lurking at my heels, was about to launch forward now that violence had erupted, and I was ready to tackle him. But Saur, locked with the third and apparently not even looking, hurled his severaka sideways. The blade whistled past me like a javelin and staked the fourth ganger to the wall behind me.

It was, I confess, a superb demonstration of skill. I fancied Saur was showing off, reminding me of his talents, reminding me of his seniority. He was, and intended to remain, my superior.

He was now fighting the third ganger, unarmed. This seemed no disadvantage, nor did the ganger's combat knives, nor the ganger's greater size and strength. Saur ducked a hissing blade, then drove his fist into one of the wounds his sword had left. The pain response folded the ganger's right side involuntarily, tilting him away. Saur grabbed the ganger's left fist, twisted, and drove the combat knife it gripped into the ganger's face.

The ganger toppled backwards, his own blade buried to the ricasso between his eyes. Saur didn't even watch him go down. He turned away, and stamped on the throat of the second ganger to finish the bout.

He looked at me, the thin line of his mouth bent in a sneer. How I despised his stump of a nose, his small, heavy eyes, and his unruly yellow-white hair.

'The way's clear,' he said.

'Very accomplished, Thaddeus,' I replied, knowing that he hated me addressing him as though he was an equal, 'but also entirely unnecessary. They are dead, and therefore cannot provide us with any information.'

'Information?' he replied, with open disdain. 'From the warblind?' He retrieved his sword.

'I don't think they were here by accident,' I replied. 'I think they were left down here in the same way one might chain dogs in a yard.'

I heard footsteps. Renner Lightburn came up the hall behind me. He was carrying a Mastoff assault-auto with a heavy bulk mag, another loan from Harlon's cache. He glanced at the bodies and winced.

'What happened here?' he asked.

'Thaddeus decided to show off,' I replied.

Saur was wiping blood and grease off his blade. He looked at me, sidelong.

'Not at all,' he said. 'Close combat was called for. You won't let me have a gun.'

This was true. I had been reluctant to allow Saur to come to Stanchion House with me, but Gideon had required me to. Not providing Saur with a firearm was the only concession I'd won.

'If there are more of these animals around,' he remarked, 'you'll want me armed with more than a blade and my fists.'

'I don't want you full stop,' I replied. 'If I'd had my way, you wouldn't be anywhere near this.'

He shrugged, and I regretted the remark. I had seen the flash in his eyes. We had not told him who we expected our quarry to be. I had felt it too sensitive. Gideon had thought it a useful test of Saur's conditioning and memory. If, and how, he recognised Mam Mordaunt, should we locate her, might teach us a lot about the manner in which his mind had been edited. My remark had let slip that we were seeking something or someone that might hold significance for him. Thaddeus Saur was not stupid. He'd noticed it.

He passed no comment. Instead, he sheathed his sword and nodded towards a hatchway ahead.

'We don't need answers from the warblind,' he said. 'The place is guarded. Use your eyes, Bequin.'

Like I taught you, was the unspoken end of that sentence.

There were marks scratched into the frame of the old hatch. Sigils of disturbingly arcane design.

'Witch-marks,' I said.

'Witch-marks,' he agreed. 'The way ahead is warded.'

He turned, and rolled one of the bodies over with the toe of his boot.

'And, you see here? The same kind of mark has been made on their flesh, and here, on the collar. Fresh scarification. They were dogs on chains, all right, and they don't need to be alive to tell you that.'

'You know these marks?' asked Renner. Saur nodded.

'From where?' I asked.

'I've seen them somewhere,' said Saur. 'I recognise them. Phantoms of the memories stolen from me.'

'That all?' I asked.

'They're Cognitae glyphs,' he said, with a little reluctance. 'The forms are older, from hermetic lore, but these are done in the way the perfecti are taught to make them.'

I peered at the marks more closely, but I was disappointed. They in no way resembled the script in the commonplace book. This was another arcane alphabet entirely.

'And their meaning?' I asked.

'These on the men, they're glyphs of control. To keep them here, in this place, as sentries. Those on the doorway… I don't know, but I wouldn't want to step through that hatch.'

'A pain door?' I asked.

'Maybe. Or worse.'

'Can you counter them, Thaddeus, or undo them?'

Saur shook his head.

'I think I could have done that, once upon a time. I think I was trained in their use. But that skill's been taken. I'll not tamper with them, and I advise you don't either.'

He looked at me.

'The Cognitae, eh? That's who we seek here?'

'You're no fool, Thaddeus. You've worked that out already.'

'Maybe. Who?'

'You can work that out for yourself too,' I replied. 'Consider it a test. Any ideas?'

'No,' he said, and looked genuinely miserable. 'I don't even remember their names.'

There were rare moments, like this one, when I felt pity for him. As a mentor of the Maze Undue, Saur had been a strong and bold force, and a senior, privileged member of the Cognitae. To have that all removed, the power, the knowledge, the authority; to be burned out and abandoned by those you had been loyal to, that was a bitter and ungrateful fate. I reminded myself that Saur was a killer, and had been a cruel mentor to me, and that thanks to him and his order, my life had similarly been stripped of meaning and truth.

'Secure the area,' I told them both. 'Make sure there are no more warblind in the vicinity. I will consult.'

Stanchion House stood in the north-western part of the city. In its former days of Imperial splendour, Queen Mab had been served by several towering starports and elevated dock facilities where, along with the shipyards, shiftships could make low anchor. Trade had thus thrived, and visitors had poured to the city in their millions, and proud regiments had embarked for war and foreign service.

Few ports now remained. High Carlo was gone, torn down, and Anchor Gate was a sorry ruin. Marheight was a derelict spire that only the wind visited. Diminished in size, power and influence, Queen Mab was sustained now by only one port of significance, Queensport, which more than coped with subsector traffic. Stanchion House, as it is now known, had once been Galeside Port, one of the last to be decommissioned some forty years earlier. It was an enormous bulwark, a cube of girders and scaffold-work, that towered above the north-western quarters. During its long life as a working port, the inner frames of the scaffold structure had been filled with interlocking STC modules to provide accommodation, freight and service areas, and offices for the port authority, the Munitorum and the Administratum. I am told that those compartment units at the highest level, affording the best views of the fine city, were of luxurious appointment, and served as state apartments for visitors of wealth, for diplomatic envoys, and for merchant princes.

Like so many parts of Queen Mab, Galeside had fallen into disrepair in its sad afterlife. Abandoned, it decayed, and some parts of it were boarded off, for fear of structural collapse. The lower levels and old street-side markets were colonised by the poor and the homeless, the Curst and the warblind, forming a vertical slum that was, in general wisdom, to be avoided. Over the years since, the slum had sprouted upwards within the stanchion frame, through the addition of salvaged compartment modules that had been hoisted and stacked in place. Some of these were precarious indeed, barely supported by girder bracing or tension cable supports. Others were rudimentary things of ingenious if rickety design, improvised from scrap plate, flakboard and wood, strung along the horizontal beams like nests or hanging baskets. Gangways, suspended bridges and teetering staircases linked them together. Some said Stanchion House looked like a gnarled tree-stump overtaken by bark fungus, or some sprouting tower of propagating dwellings, where each chamber or module was a bud that germinated offspring on the beams around it.

For my part, I had always thought it resembled a child's toy, a pile of assorted building blocks stacked carelessly and without skill or design within a cage of metal ribs. It could be seen – and indeed smelled – from many streets away, forever looking like it was about to topple down. On its uppermost levels, more than half a kilometre from the street, the port structures of cranes and derricks and anchor masts rusted against the sky. One old ship, known locally as *The Lyre*, still creaked and rotted in the topside graving docks, never to sail again, though I do not know if that is the vessel's true name, or some colourful invention of city folklore.

The glimpse of Timurlin's secret mistress that Gideon had shared with me had evidently looked out from the ruin's south face, and from the highest possible vantage for it to have enjoyed that particular prospect of Saint Marzom Martyr. We had concluded that it must be one of the high apartments that had once served the gentry and the well-to-do. Accessing it from above was beyond our means, for we had no transport that could carry us up there. Thus I had led the way up to it from the street, braving the filth and lawless gloom of the stacked slum, and the treacherous nature of its construction.

Now this approach too seemed barred to us.

I did not like Stanchion House at all. It was a grim and squalid place, full of blind corners and illogical, makeshift architecture. The air was rank, and some of the lower halls had become choked with foul middens of refuse and decomposing waste. The walls were thick with grease and crusted dirt. Occupants scurried away from our intrusion like vermin, and we could hear voices and whispers in the darkness. The further up we went, the more unstable things seemed to become. Some modules swayed or shook as we walked through them, as though barely balanced or poorly suspended. In places, the deck or wall had rotted through to such an extent it would have been foolish to test them with our weight, and in others they had fallen away completely, presenting sudden and giddying views down to nest habitats below, or even all the way down to the distant streets. Cook-smoke filled some narrow passageways and stairwells like bottled fog, or plumed through derelict galleries on the penetrating breeze, like rancid djinn new-released from lamps.

I had expected to find the warblind here, for their gang territories included the whole district, but I had not expected to find them harnessed by means of bonding sigils to guard the place. Nor had I expected the route upwards to be so thoroughly warded against intrusion. My only consolation was that the manner and thoroughness of the defences spoke to considerable ability. Whoever hid in the upper reaches of the place was plainly a senior member of the Cognitae, or someone of comparable learning.

I stepped away from Renner and Saur as they began a sweep of the landing stage we had reached. We were perhaps a third of the way up the ragged bulk of Stanchion House. It was a bright, hazy day, with little wind, but at this height, the breezes and draughts moaned through chinks in the walls or broken window lights, or sighed between floorboards. Drop curtains and ragged tarps, strung up to further weatherproof the place, swayed and rippled. Clumsy totems of thread and feathers and bird skulls clattered in archways as the breeze stirred them, and crude wind chimes tinkled like handbells. The impoverished dwellers had made little windmills, bladed discs of paper, punched tin and plycard, that whirred and puttered along sills, driven by the draughts so hard that their rotating spokes raised a buzzing drone.

I tried my micro-bead.

'Penitent wishes Talon,' I said. 'Aspirant pathway confounded.'

There was no answer, just a hiss of static, barely audible above the chatter of spinning vanes. I repeated the signal. Gideon had insisted we use the informal argot Glossia for communication, and Harlon had taught me the basics. Indeed, I had already learned some while in the company of Eisenhorn. Glossia was an informal cant that had originated in his service, and used oblique metaphors and pre-agreed substitutions so that brief, inscrutable exchanges could be made even on open channels. It also served to confirm the identity of an otherwise anonymous responder. I had thought it a little old-fashioned, and vulnerable to anyone with half a wit, but it was effective in its simplicity, and sidestepped the need for elaborate and often cumbersome vox-coding and encryption. In truth, I had been quietly delighted to have been assigned a keyword of my own.

'Penitent wishes Talon,' I repeated.

Still there was no response. I wondered if the haphazard structure of the edifice was confounding comms, or somehow reducing active range. I moved further down the makeshift hallway. Daylight spilled in ahead, from beyond a threadbare drape. I drew my sidearm, and held it braced, prepared for surprises. The rough boards groaned beneath my feet, and the windvanes chattered.

'Penitent wishes Talon,' I said. 'Penitent wishes Talon, aspirant pathway confounded.'

I pulled the drape aside, and stepped through. A little alcove, littered with broken bottles, let out onto an exterior gantry suspended over the south face of the house. Built of reclaimed lumber, and strung to the nearest cross-beam by fraying steel cables, it wallowed gently in the soft breeze.

I was on the outside of the building. A better signal here, surely?

'Penitent wishes Talon,' I said.

The city lay below, far below, a vast patchwork of rooftops, chimneys, masts and steeples stretching away in the yellow haze of the afternoon. I could hear, on the wind, the distant drone of traffic, the sound of horns, the hollowed cries of street vendors and market hawkers at the Strange Square Commercia. It was a long drop. I could see the hazed shape of Saint Marzom's to my right. The angle of view was wrong, and I was still far too low. I leant back against the wooden rail, and craned upwards. The ragged, rickety face of the old port's south aspect soared above me, a cliff-face of suspended containers and decaying shacks against a sky that was trying to be almost blue.

I cursed to myself quietly, for we could not afford delays. I touched the wraithbone pendant around my throat.

'Gideon,' I said. 'Gideon? Where in Throne's name are you?'

Renner, Saur and I had been assigned to lead the ascent. Nayl and Kara were supposed to follow us in, with Ravenor and Kys bringing up the rear, once access was achieved.

'Gideon? Penitent awaits, frustrated.'

Still no reply. I turned to go back in, then heard a whisper at the back of my head.

+Penitent.+

'Gideon? Where are you? What's wrong with the comms?'

+Nothing. Wait, please.+

I waited as instructed. Two minutes passed.

+Penitent. The situation has changed.+

'Well, we need you here. Our advance up the tower is blocked. The doorways have been warded, and Saur is either unable or unwilling to disarm them.'

+Unfortunate.+

'Indeed. We need your expertise.'

+I'm sorry. The situation has changed. Something has come up, and I am unable to join you.+

'What do you mean? What has changed?'

There was another silence that seemed to stretch out unendurably.

'Gideon? At least advance the support team. Nayl and Kara–'

+I can't. I need them both, and Skewer too. Circumstances have arisen that require my immediate attention. I need to pull the three of them back.+

'Please explain. What is so significant that we compromise an operation after it is under way?'

+I can't send freely, Penitent, nor can I explain via vox. I am under observation. I think it best we consider the operation aborted. Withdraw to a safe place and await my further instruction.+

'We are already in this, Gideon–'

+I appreciate that. But if you cannot go any further, and I am prevented from assisting you, then we must stand down. If you wish to proceed, and you are able to, then do so, but I can't render support. You will be on your own. I advise you to withdraw and wait. I will contact you again in due course.+

'In due course? What does that mean? Gideon?'

Nothing.

'Gideon? Speak to me. Gideon?'

I waited a full ten minutes, but no further word came. I could not conceive of what might have distracted Ravenor so. If it was a new and more promising lead, he would have simply summoned us back. I reviewed his words in my mind, and reflected how careful they had seemed. He had expressed only basic things, with few specifics. No mention of our location, or his, and he had used only the key words of Glossia – *Penitent* for me and *Skewer* for Kys – rather than personal names. He had been guarding his words and the degree of content. Under observation, that's what he'd said.

But by whom? Clearly someone with both the technical skill to monitor comms and the psykanic ability to eavesdrop thoughts. Why else would he have masked identities in Glossia, even when sending? Perhaps old habits, the accustomed reliance on Glossia in the field. But his thoughts had not only been tight and guarded, there had been a background wash of... something. A distinct and deliberate sensory mood intended to convey meaning wordlessly. High-function psykers can do that, framing an emotional context around their communiqués, as one might alter the font style of a written message to communicate urgency or affection.

His sends to me had conveyed the tight-lipped feeling of tension. Of apprehension. Perhaps even anxiety.

If he had been cornered or surprised by an adversary, then who? As the God-Emperor is my witness, we were not short of such in Queen Mab. Enemies, and friends of enemies, lurked in every shadow. I composed a quick list of the most likely, headed by the graels, and by the Cognitae perfecti. Then I thought of another. Even now, all this time later, I am reluctant to write their name here. I was thinking of the ones Gideon had called 'the visitors', those who had stalked us in the muniment room and had been led by a voice from ancient Tizca. They placed specific and unholy significance in the power of true names, for their title alone had drawn them upon us.

Was it them? Had they returned? Was that why Gideon had avoided using our names, for fear of marking us out to them?

Of course, I would not learn the answers to these questions for a while, so I will state what happened next simply as it was known to me then. On that precarious wooden gantry, I considered my options and tried to allay my fears. The mission was derailed, but not yet impossible. If I withdrew, it could only be to shelter, for I could not locate Gideon to help him, and our chance to secure our target might vanish forever. To continue alone and unsupported, however, would take lateral thinking.

And greater risk.

I made my decision. I holstered my pistol, and reached into the pocket of my leather coat.

'Lightburn?'

'Where are you?' Renner answered over the link.

'Close by. Talk to me.'

'Well, we've swept the galleries here. No more warblind, but three more doorways guarded by those damn symbols. We think every staircase up from here is protected.'

I took the phial out of my pocket: one of Kara's pretty little scent bottles borrowed and repurposed.

'Renner, I'm going to make the ascent from here, alone.'

'What?' he said.

'You heard. Stay put, and keep an eye on Saur. We have no backup. Don't ask me why. If you can find a safe way of advancing, follow me up, but otherwise stay where you are until I signal again.'

Lightburn began to protest in no uncertain terms. I deactivated the micro-bead, and silenced his reproachful voice.

I unscrewed the phial and held it up, open. I had half-filled it with my own blood before the wound I had taken from Timurlin had been dressed. I had no wish to keep cutting myself, though the drops in the little bottle had become cloudy and turgid. I hoped, though not fresh, they would suffice.

I heard the heavy beat of wings almost at once.

Comus Nocturnus landed on the gantry before me. He alighted with great care, his huge bulk barely disturbing the precarious ledge, and crouched with his great wings furled behind his back. He did not speak. I saw there were what seemed to be two or three tiny specks of blood on his chin and at the corner of his lip. I did not want to know why, but his eyes were fierce-bright, and I feared the angel had begun to lapse again, sliding back into the predatory madness that tormented him. I turned off my cuff.

The angel sighed, and the pent-up tension fled from his shoulders.

'How is your mind?' I asked.

'Better now,' he replied. 'The open air pleases me, and the freedom... But the fury is never far away. I thought I had out-flown it, but it lingers and sometimes...'

'Sometimes?'

'Sometimes I forget who I am, and time blacks out.'

'You are Comus Nocturnus,' I said.

He nodded. 'And you are solace, null.'

'There is blood upon your face,' I said cautiously.

He frowned, and raised a giant, marmorial hand to his mouth.

'Oh,' he said.

'Should I be concerned?'

'Pigeons,' he said, ashamed. 'And I caught a raven over the church-yard yonder. My thirst is hard to–'

I raised a hand to quiet him.

'Are you still mine to command, Comus Nocturnus?' I asked.

He nodded. 'Of course.'

'Then I wish to ascend,' I said to him, pointing up at the stack above.

He rose fully upright and towered over me.

'That can be done,' he said.

Without hesitation or ceremony, he took me in his arms. I was swallowed in a tight embrace, but it had none of the fury with which he had enfolded me on the steps above the King Door. There was barely a moment to review the wisdom of my request, or to prepare myself. His arms firmly around me, he slid from the gantry.

We fell. Wind clapped at my ears. The world rotated around me, fisheyed and panoramic, an inverted curve of horizon, diagonal steeples, the carpet of the city rushing up with such aggressive speed I closed my eyes and buried my face in his chest. I may have involuntarily uttered some yelp, or a word frowned upon in polite company. Then we were no longer falling. I heard the crack of inhuman wings as they beat and ploughed the air. I felt the huge power of the muscles in his chest, his sternum and his flanks moving like a seismic flow against me. I clung to him, regretting everything.

We had weight again, gravity dragging upon us, but confounded by his wings. We tilted and soared. Sunlight flooded my clenched eyelids. I felt the heat of him, the tight power of his cradling arms. I smelled the un-scent of his white flesh, like the powder smell of fine travertine or ouslite in a cold temple.

The wind was in my face. I opened my eyes. Beyond the clenching curve of his monumental chest, I saw the face of Stanchion House flashing past, a descending whirl of windows and walls, jetties and balconies, cables and beams, scaffolds and girders. I couldn't breathe, the wind was buffeting with such force. How did he breathe?

How did he ever come to the ground again when this freedom was his?

We climbed above the summit of Stanchion House, higher than the whole world. I glimpsed the ruined landscape of the upper platforms, the rusted barrens of dead ships, cranes and freight yards. I saw the corroded bones of vessels that had once plied between the stars, and rows of disintegrating Militarum drop-ships waiting where they had been left on flight decks like fossil birds in a museum case. Beyond that, the whole bowl of the world and sky. I could see Queen Mab entire, every edge and limit of it, as only the God-Emperor may regard it from the height of His Golden Throne. Then we dipped, weightless again, inverted, and swooped in beneath the lip of the high yards, into shadow and out of the sun, soaring between bulk girders and around the oiled columns of hanging chains so vast in scale they could have dragged the world. They hung dead, like the stopped pendulums of giant clocks. Another burst of wings, and we shot forward, an acceleration that prompted another helpless yelp from me. In we swept, under a low and mighty arch of cast iron, across the tops of close-riveted containers, through a gap in adamantine bracework.

And then he set me down.

I stepped back, finding my balance, remembering my own weight. He looked at me with an enquiring frown. I could not help but laugh.

'Why?' he asked.

'I fancy I will not do that ever again,' I said.

'Did I hurt you?'

'No, Comus. It was an experience I doubt I shall ever get to repeat. I am a creature of the ground, not the sky, like you. It is... unnerving and terrifying. But I also see the joy of it.'

The angel nodded slowly.

'It is the only escape I know,' he said, 'apart from you. The sky, and you, null. The only companions I can trust. Is this the place?'

I glanced around. We were on a broad balcony beneath the lip of the port, perhaps the remains of what had once been a roof terrace for a private apartment.

'Yes,' I said. I paused, considering the prospect. 'I think–' I turned.

The angel had already gone.

I went to the rail. I tried my link, but there was no response from Renner or Saur now either. Either the beads lacked decent range, or the mass of cast metal and other materials between me and them was denying a signal.

I looked for Saint Marzom Martyr. It was almost directly ahead of me, and the angle of view approximated that of the image in my mind. If anything, I was now a little too high.

I drew the Tronsvasse, checked its load, then made my way into the apartment behind the roof garden. The glass was all gone from the windows and doors, and the hab was a rotting ruin. Years of rain, storm and long winters had reduced what had once been a luxurious residence to a cave of liquescent filth, where books and drapes and upholstery had been rendered down to mulch and black slime. The air was pungent. I advanced carefully, checking surfaces and frames for signs of warding sigils. A door, swollen to fibrous pulp in its frame, thanks to water damage, gave way after a couple of sturdy shoves, and I let myself into the interior hall. This was a gloomy realm, for the few windows were crazed with dirt. The smell of cold damp was strong, and water plinked from the ceiling.

It was like the landing of a grand hotel, with a black iron staircase descending to the floors below. At least here, things were more steady underfoot. These once elegant residences were part of the port's original structure, not makeshift additions raised at a later time with scant regard for safety.

I made my way down the iron steps, my pistol raised. I flexed my shoulder, realising how sore it had become. Timurlin's blade had caught me just the night before, and though the wound had been cleaned, dressed and closed with a plastek seal, it was deep. The exertion of my trip as an angel's cargo had flexed it, perhaps even opened the wound that was newly healing.

The apartments on the next level down were all ruined spaces too. A through-wind scurried litter along the dirty landing. One floor lower was my guess. There, still more ruins, and one unpromising door. The door had not been cleaned, and was half-screened by a heap of broken railings. But it was, I estimated, in the right location, and the dirt was but a mask so that it would not stand out among the decay.

On close inspection, the door was solid indeed. Under the patina of grime, I could see some mark, a decorative pattern like the geometry of a spider's web. There were, just visible, hexafoil sigils etched in the ebony door frame.

I considered my approach. Another route in was unlikely. Sometimes, I reflected, directness is better than guile.

I knocked upon the door with the butt of my pistol.

'Hello?' I called. 'I have come to find you.'

To my surprise, a lock system clicked, and the door swung open. I saw pale light beyond.

'With your permission, I will enter,' I called out.

There was no reply.

'And the permission of your wards here,' I added.

'Let me know you, and they will let you pass,' replied a distant voice, speaking in Low Gothic. A woman. I did not recognise it.

'I am Beta Bequin,' I said.

'You are known.'

I took a deep breath, and stepped inside. No secret pain dropped me on the threshold. There was warmth beyond, and a clean, almost perfumed air. Inside the door, the short hallway was screened by wrought-iron panels, where the ironwork had been bent and fashioned into cobweb patterns of great symmetry and craft.

I advanced. Light filtered through a high gate at the end, a gate which also had been worked from black iron in web patterns. The light cast the shadows of that pattern back across the floor to me, covering the hallway's rich Selgioni rug with elongated cobweb shapes.

'I come in good faith,' I called out.

'You come with weapon drawn,' the voice answered.

I holstered my gun.

'This building has its hazards,' I replied, 'but my intent is true. I have heard you are in need of help. Of an ally. I think you have reached out to me already, in the hope that I might render assistance to you.'

'Assistance against what?'

'Against that which haunts us all,' I said. 'Against that which, until recently, you had spent years serving, and which now refuses you reward and recognition.'

'What is it you speak of?'

'Not what but whom. The King in Yellow.'

I had reached the inner gate.

'In what manner did I reach to you?' the voice asked.

'At the Lengmur Salon,' I replied. 'By way of the voicer, who was silenced for her efforts.'

'I reached to a person I knew once,' said the voice, 'and who aligned with a man who I thought trustworthy.'

'You would trust a heretic?'

A light laugh.

'Heretics are the only ones worth trusting,' the voice said, 'for they have everything to gain and everything to lose. But you are not that person any more, I fear. You have altered your path, and you side with those I fear I cannot trust at all.'

'Because?'

'Because the Inquisition is not a subtle instrument. It cannot modify its attitude to the likes of me to accommodate my existence.'

'I beg to differ,' I said. 'The Inquisition as a whole, yes. But I will vouch for the man I work for. Accommodation may be found. We can help you, in return for your help. A mutual arrangement. I am authorised by his command to make you this offer.'

'The Ordos will say anything to get their way,' the voice replied.

'Perhaps,' I said, 'but let us at least say those things face to face.'

There was a lengthy pause.

'Come, then. But turn on that limiter.'

I adjusted my cuff and slid the gate open.

The apartment was large and very fine. It had once been a stateroom dwelling for wealthy visitors, perhaps a grand duke or margrave. The long wall of south-facing windows had been tinted to reduce the glare of the afternoon sun, and the air swam with a cool, green light. Beyond the windows, a terrace overlooked the city sprawl.

It was a broad, spacious and well-appointed situation. The cobweb motif was repeated on the dark wallpaper, the carpet and even the soft furnishings. It was etched into the glass of the wall mirrors, of which there were very many. They were of many shapes and designs, as if collected by an enthusiast. Some were dim and foxed with age, where the silver backing the glass had corroded. Others were bright and crystal fresh. Incense burned in a gold tray on an onyx side table.

She sat facing me in a very high-backed porter's chair of brown leather. Her hair was deep red, and she wore a rust-coloured gown, just as she had the last time I had seen her in the side doorway of Lengmur's. As then, she looked nothing like herself. She was Timurlin's Zoya Farnessa, whoever 'Zoya' was.

But now I saw her, with all faculty of awareness, I could read through her disguise, and cast away her expert function. It was Mam Mordaunt, mentor of the Maze Undue.

'Hello, Beta,' she said.

She smiled at me. The exquisite chrome xenos-tech pistol she was aiming at me did not.

CHAPTER 21

Which is of quizzing and reflection

'I believed you dead for the longest while,' I said. I tried to express no fear or trepidation, despite the weapon levelled at me. It would have disappointed her.

'The Maze fell,' she replied. 'We executed *Hajara*. We wash up where we may, wearing other faces. You, Beta, have worn many.'

'You've been watching me.' This was not a question. At the Maze Undue, we had used the quizzing glass to study our assigned targets and prepare. I had no doubt these mirrors were of that strange nature, for Mam Mordaunt had been an expert in such espial craft.

'You presume that from my looking glasses?' she asked.

'I was told that by your perfecti, Verner.'

She mused on this.

'Is he coming back?' she asked.

'No, mam.'

She sighed. 'Did you kill him?'

'He tried to kill me,' I replied. 'But, no. It was done by another.'

'And done with artistry,' she said, 'for he gave up his true name.'

'He had little choice, in the end.'

Her eyes, ever dark, seemed darker.

'Then... Ravenor killed him.'

I shook my head. 'Ravenor took the truth from him, but Thaddeus killed him.'

I watched her face for reaction. There was none.

'I have seen,' she said mildly, 'that Saur walks with you. Such a false soul. A turncoat.'

'I do not know what he is,' I said. 'He doesn't either. His memory has been redacted. What was done to him?'

'Nothing I know of,' she replied. 'I last saw him in the turmoil of the Maze's destruction. We were all fleeing. Thaddeus is a master of both attack and defence. I remember him saying... years ago now... that he had trained in certain disciplines that would fortify his mind if he was ever captured. Synaptic countermeasures that he could trigger by means of a key phrase or mantra in extremis. They would sterilise his memories and wipe his thoughts, so he had literally nothing to tell, not even under torture. I suspect, Beta, Saur did it to himself.'

'He made himself forget, then forgot he'd done so?'

'He was captured, wasn't he?' she said. 'Captured by the enemy he feared the most, one he knew would show him no mercy. So yes, I imagine so. Synaptic countermeasures are not subtle. They would wipe even the memory of his own forgetting. I imagine he may be pitied, and forgiven. But you went to the enemy rather more willingly.'

'There was duress,' I replied. 'I was alone and forsaken. I was hunted by many. I made my own path and my own choices, the best choices I could.'

'To become a servant of the cruel Inquisition?'

'Mam, my whole life I believed I was a servant of the Ordos,' I said. 'You raised me that way. It did not seem such a great step.'

Her painted eyebrows rose slightly, and she pursed her lips.

'I suppose not,' she replied. 'So you may be forgiven also.'

'I didn't come here for your forgiveness,' I replied. 'I came because you are the one alone and forsaken, hiding in fear of your life. He that you served has turned his back on you, taken your secrets, and left you with nothing. You need an ally, or you will not leave Sancour alive. More than that, I believe you need revenge.'

'My, Verner did talk a lot, didn't he?'

'Is it not so, mam?'

She sat back in the tall chair, her face passing into green shadow. Her weapon lowered, resting on her lap, but I did not relax. It could rise and find me again in a moment. I knew her capabilities.

'I find myself disadvantaged,' she said quietly. 'All has gone to ruination, and past friends have turned away. The plans I have been part of are undone, or wrested from my grasp. And yes, beyond survival, I think I do yearn for some payback. There is a spite in me. The King in Yellow has usurped the Cognitae's ambitions, and distorts them for his own means. We had a great plan, Beta, one centuries in the making, and about to bear fruit, but the King has taken it from us, along with all our methods and technical accomplishments, and debased it into something monstrous. My desire to see him punished for that is very great. But I do not think you can offer me anything I need. I am glad to see you, Beta. Glad to see you alive. And I am touched that your concern for me was so great that you came to find me at no little risk. I have enjoyed this visit. But our paths from here are very different.'

'I don't think they are,' I said. 'And, with respect, this is no social call. We hunt for the King. We can offer you protection in return for your inside knowledge. You have information that would be vital to us. It will take us where we need to go, and bring you the payback you hanker for.'

'I cannot see me collaborating with the Inquisition, can you?' she asked, a tiny smirk on her lips. 'At the side of Gideon Ravenor? I don't think so.'

'But you could with Eisenhorn? Who, if anything, has been a greater foe of the Cognitae down the years?'

'He was different,' she said sullenly. 'An enemy, yes. But a heretic too. I know things about him, child. The things that happened to him on Gershom. The things that made him smile again. He was an outlier, for whom rules and laws no longer applied. I despised him, but he would have seen the merit of my participation, and he would have made an excellent instrument of vengeance.'

'He's dead,' I said.

'More's the pity. And Ravenor lives. The more noble man, and the harder to like. I cannot side with him, Beta. And I don't think you should trust him either.'

'I don't believe you have many alternatives, mam,' I replied.

'Is that a threat, Beta?' she asked, amusement oozing into her voice.

'An observation,' I said. 'Queen Mab is hardly overflowing with viable allies.'

'Not at all,' she said. 'I am considering several felicitous options. There are many parties in play, some with great power behind them.'

'I've met several,' I said. I wandered over to the nearest wall of mirrors and gazed into their surfaces. There was my face, many times over, small and large, clear or clouded, distorted by old glass or convex forms, run through with fractures and crazing spiderweb cracks. But beyond my face, beyond the room behind me, shadows lurked in some of the glasses, the quizzed images of far places and other rooms. A shadow in a chair, another at a desk, another pacing a high room. Little shadow-plays of animation, like the picture-box flickers of dim zoetropes.

'You have collected a great number of quizzing glasses,' I said.

'A hobby,' she murmured. 'They entertain me. Quizzing glasses, scrying plates of obsidian, flect shards from the Mergent Worlds...'

'They are more than entertainment, mam,' I said. 'You're watching your prospects, just as you watched me. Evaluating the best candidates to side with.'

She laughed, and rose. I had forgotten how tall she was, how elegant her motion. She joined me, the pistol in her hand, and stared at the mirrors. I could smell her perfume, though it was not hers, not the fragrance she had worn of old. It was something new, something of chypre or fougere, chosen to suit her new function. Behind it, though, I detected the slight smell of lho-sticks. She had always smoked, though never in our sight, a vice she had clearly maintained, though it was not part of her newly constructed persona named Zoya. I saw it as a flaw, a tiny weakness. She had assumed a new function almost perfectly, shaming the skill of her pupils like me, yet she had not been able to quit her habit. I imagined her alone in this apartment, smoking to steady her nerves, afraid of the whole world.

I had just seen through the mask she had always worn.

'What do you think, Beta? Anything promising?'

'I can scarcely make them out,' I replied.

'Look closer, child. You know how to work a glass, or was my tuition so poor?'

I looked. The shadows were just shadows, tiny quivering shapes making barely significant motions, filmed by age and wear and foxed silver. Then one, the one at the desk, turned slightly, perhaps to speak to someone beyond the frame of the mirror, and the light caught his face for a second.

'Blackwards,' I said.

'Balthus Blackwards,' she said.

'So he yet lives,' I said. 'You would consider him?'

'Unlikely,' she replied, 'for his fortunes have diminished since the incident at the basilica last year. But he is not without appeal. The Blackwards are in for their own gain, and commerce runs in their genes. They are mercenary, and thus more open than most to manipulation. I still have access to Cognitae reserves. I could buy his cooperation with a sum that would make him swoon.'

'Balthus perhaps,' I agreed, 'but not the devils he sides with.'

She glanced at me. 'And what would you know of them?'

'You've watched me, mam. You must know I was at the Basilica Saint Orphaeus that day. I saw them face to face. I do not think the Word Bearers are suitable partners to build a relationship with.'

'They are indeed unwholesome,' she admitted, 'and I doubt they can be trusted any further than your man Ravenor. They certainly can't be bought. And if they have a sudden change of mind, they would not be held by any deal Balthus could make.'

'I'm surprised he's still alive,' I said. I saw another image moving, remotely viewed in another frame. The partial glimpse of a face.

'That one I don't know,' I said, pointing.

'Really?' she said. 'I'm surprised. That's Naten Misrahi, seneschal to the Baron Prefect. I'm quite astonished your paths haven't crossed. The Baron Prefect is anxious to maintain his authority on Sancour, and it's slipping fast. He is out of sorts with the Ordos, and seeks alternate backing. Misrahi is his fixer. You should watch him.'

'I will,' I said. I gestured. 'Now *that* face I do know.'

In another frame, the figure pacing the high room had stopped, and daylight had sharpened her profile.

'Alace Quatorze,' I said. 'Of the Glaw dynasty. Also living, then. She was very knowledgeable, but I felt she was weak. No spine to her, no drive. Besides, mam, she has made unwise allies. The Emperor's Children are more vicious than might be imagined.'

have to imagine,' she said. 'I've met them. A brief encounter
ne named Teke. Thankfully, I was well warded. It was hard to
he wanted more – to kill me, or copulate with me.'

'Both, I should think. At the same time.'

That made her laugh. She raised her hand and gestured to an oval glass.

'Look there. Newcomers to the game just these last few weeks.'

I looked, and at first could not decipher the twitching shadows I was seeing. Then I saw proud crests and gleaming armour of high polish, and the passing flash of some chilling war-mask. It was not human.

'Is that–?' I began, amazed.

'It is.'

'Aeldari?' I whispered.

'Quite so. Matters here are now of such significance, even the xenos kinds are forced to step in.'

She looked at me. I had never seen such intent in her face.

'Beware them, Beta,' she said. 'Promise me you will. They cannot be beguiled by our skills the way humans and even transhumans can. Do not, under any circumstances, have anything to do with them.'

'As I presume you will not?'

She shook her head.

'There was another party,' I said. 'Your man Verner mentioned them. He said you had considered an alliance with them very seriously. They–'

'Do not speak their name, Beta.'

'I will not. I know better than to do so. They seemed to me no less dangerous than any visible here.'

'Oh, they're brutal creatures,' she said. 'But they have means and they have cunning, and they are a sight more intelligent than the Word Bearers or the Emperor's Children. I had contemplated them, aware of the risks. They await a reply from me, but I think it will be to decline.'

I paused for a moment.

'And… the Secretary?' I asked.

'Nastrand is dead. He died at the Maze, along with Murlees.'

'Then forgive me, mam. You show me faces in glasses, but not choices. It would be madness to link your interests with any of these. I think you are too bold when you say you have options.'

I turned to stare at her.

'I think you are very alone, and very afraid. I think it will be but a short time before the King, or one of these unholy forces, catches up with you. I think you should weigh my offer again.'

She turned away from me sharply, as though I had slapped her face.

'Still you ask!' she hissed. 'As if you know nothing! As if I had *taught* you nothing! I cannot change as easily as you did, Bequin!'

'I never changed,' I replied. 'And you have great fluidity of function, mam. You can change better than most. For Throne's sake, the alternative is death!'

'For *Throne's sake*? Hear yourself, child. I am Cognitae, and I stand against everything the Corpse-God represents. I would topple that Throne of yours. How could I stand with Ravenor?'

'Sometimes the threat is so grave, the worst of enemies must become the best of friends,' I said. 'You know better than me. How grave a threat is the King?'

Mam Mordaunt did not answer at once. She walked away from me, sat back down in the porter's chair and lit a lho-stick.

'What would he have me do?' she asked, in a small voice.

'Share the information you have,' I said.

'Such as?'

'The nature of the King's business. The full operation of the programme. The Cognitae's plan. Your name, perhaps?'

'My name?'

'Your true name.'

'You think I hide–'

'We all hide. Are you... Lilean Chase?'

She looked at me, and a smile flickered through her agitation.

'What a funny question,' she said.

'If you are,' I said, 'then you can help Gideon and me make sense of this.' I slipped the commonplace book out of my coat pocket and held it up.

'Goodness,' she breathed. 'You still have it?'

'I recovered it,' I said. 'Can you help me with the cipher? Explain 119?'

'Yes,' she said.

I put the book away again. As I did so, I said, 'The secrets of the Cognitae are seeping out, mam. I think they have been doing so for years as the Cognitae became increasingly unspun. Now is the time. Make sure those secrets go to the right places, where they can do most good.'

'Secrets...' she echoed.

'Yes, mam. The means to enter the extimate City of Dust. It is our primary goal.'

'You mean to get in there?'

'Yes. Do you know how it is done?'

'I do,' she said. 'I have crossed to it a few times. The method is known to me. But you've been there too. At Feverfugue.'

'I barely realised it at the time,' I said, 'and I have no idea how I did it or how I came back again.'

She regarded me with a curious frown.

'I think you do, Beta. I would think it obvious. You surprise me – so confident and so full of unexpected insight and knowledge, yet naive in the strangest ways on the most curious matters. Getting *in* isn't the problem.'

'It is, or I wouldn't be asking.'

'The problem, my child, is what you *do* once you're in.'

She stubbed out her lho-stick, half-smoked.

'I thought I had trained you well, Beta,' she said, 'but I see I must reinforce the most basic conditioning. Know yourself. Understand yourself. In this life, most answers lie within, or in plain view right in front of us. They can be seen with ease if you but take the time to look.'

'I'll remember that,' I said. 'Now will you describe the means to me, in return for the protection and cooperation of Gideon Ravenor and the Holy Ordos?'

I watched her think about it. I had no doubt it was a hard decision, for she had spent her days in such uncompromising opposition to the Inquisition that it had become like antimateria to her materia. One touch might annihilate her.

But I remembered the stale odour of lho that I had smelled on her before. That little imperfection in her otherwise perfect guise as Zoya Farnessa, that tiny flash of personal weakness, gave me hope, for it spoke to her fear and her desperation. I had an ounce of leverage. Ironically, the techniques of micro-psychological persuasion that I was employing were precisely those she had taught me so long before at the Maze Undue.

'Very well,' she said at last.

'Then tell me–'

She raised her hand and smiled.

'Beta,' she said, 'that information is my only insurance. I will share it with your Ravenor directly, once he has met my assurances. It is my currency. If I spend it now, you may simply kill me, for my worth would be gone.'

'I would not.'

'Even so. Go back to Ravenor. Secure for me a meeting with him, face to face. You will be at my side when that occurs, at all times, your limiter off. He will not strip my mind of its value. You will vouchsafe me in his company.'

I did not care for the arrangement, but I understood her demands. It was never going to be easy to gain and keep her confidence.

'Very well,' I replied, with reluctance. I had no wish to leave her, for this could all be a ruse to get me out of the way. The moment I was gone, she might just vanish again, more thoroughly.

'It might be better if you came with me,' I suggested.

'No.'

'Then, to arrange a meeting–'

'I will watch you, of course,' she said. 'I will be fully aware of the time and place you agree with Ravenor. And I will be there, provided he shows no hint of trickery.'

I suppose it was more than I could have hoped. She was willing to come in. She would be an asset of huge value.

I nodded my agreement.

'Is there,' I asked, 'a swift way down to street level? It is quite a trek otherwise. I'm sure you have your own secure means of entering and leaving this hiding place.'

She smiled.

'I have several,' she replied. 'For your convenience, I suggest you take the roof access into the port. A short walk, and we're too high up for the gangs. One of the freight elevators in the nearest cargo hall still functions, despite the look of it. It will carry you to the street dock on Childeric Pass.'

'How will I know which elevator?' I asked.

'I've marked it with a sign you'll recognise,' she said. She rose, crossed to a small ormolu side table, and slid open the top drawer. 'As for my witch-marks and wards, and any of my bonded gangers...'

She took something out of the drawer and tossed it to me. I caught it neatly. It was a moldavite pendant on a gold chain. In the tinted olive gloom of the apartment, the internal green lustre of the meteoric stone seemed so intense as to be alive. There was a hexafoil mark carved into one side of the gem.

'That will get you past them,' she said.

I was about to reply with a thank you when she turned abruptly. Something in the quizzing glasses had caught her attention.

'What is it?' I asked.

'Someone approaches,' she replied. 'Up the inner staircase.' She glanced at me, and I did not care for the look in her eyes.

'Have you betrayed me?' she asked. 'Told someone of this location?'

'I swear not. Let me look.'

The mirror that had caught her eyes was small and round, and seemed to show a foggy view of some chute, which I realised after some study was the black-iron staircase. Shapes – one, perhaps, or two – moved upon it, but they were mere ghosts in the poor light.

'Let me check,' I said. She seemed dubious. 'The deal is, the Inquisition will protect you,' I said. 'I will demonstrate the sincerity of our pledge.'

She paused, then nodded. The xenos pistol was still in her hand.

'If it is too much for you, retreat here,' she said. She raised her free hand, and peeled away the fine wig of rust-coloured hair. Beneath it, her own hair, black, was shaved back to almost nothing. 'This place is warded. We can make use of the defensive position.'

She had begun to unfasten the rust-coloured dress. Beneath it, I glimpsed a dark bodyglove. Despite the unfamiliar style in which her face was made up, she was already resembling the Cognitae Mistress I had known. I understood that, if a battle was coming, she intended to fight as Mordaunt, not Zoya Farnessa.

'Get to it,' she said. I stepped towards the chamber's iron gate. My first approach would be one of stealth. I flexed my right hand and felt the sudden and surprising weight of the blinksword as it manifested there.

'Verner's sword,' she said.

'Yes,' I replied.

'You've mastered the knack.'

In truth, it had been remarkably easy. Kara and I had examined Timurlin's weapon after his death. Its extimate nature seemed to be annealed into it. It was not a matter of concentration – in fact, concentrating too hard made the trick impossible to perform. But a gentle, almost subconscious act of will made the blade vanish in the hand, and then reappear by the same mode of thought. I had taken to it faster than Kara.

'Not everyone can do that,' said Mam Mordaunt, stepping out of her gown. 'I always thought you might climb to the rank of perfecti. Of course, the programme had another destiny in mind for you.'

I did not stop to pursue this comment, or even to consider its value as a compliment. I went out through the iron gate, and made my way back to the apartment's front door. The hall outside was as dark as before. An afternoon wind moaned up the stairwell, lifting zephyrs of dust from the filthy floor. I edged along with my back to the wall. Who was out there? Had they followed me?

In a moment or two, I discovered that 'they' had indeed done exactly that. Spying through the banister rail, I saw Renner and Saur, cautiously picking their way up the stairs. Saur led, his sword ready. Renner followed, gripping his assault gun. Both peered up into the darkness, wary.

'Penitent,' I called out, an over-loud whisper.

They froze.

'That you?' Saur called back.

'None other,' I replied. I stood up so they could see me, leaning out over the rail. 'Come up,' I ordered, 'but put up your weapons and make your peaceful approach apparent.'

Saur shrugged, and sheathed his severaka. Renner pulled the Mastoff onto his shoulder by the sling.

'What are you doing here?' I asked.

'Follow you, you said,' Renner replied. 'We followed you. It's a long way.'

'But the warded doorways?'

'Thaddeus found a work-around, didn't he?' said Renner. They joined me on the dirty landing.

'Those marks are wicked things,' said Saur, as though pleased with himself, 'but the frames they're carved on? Why, they're but old wood, and do not much survive the close action of an assault-auto.'

'He had me shoot a door frame out,' said Renner. 'Whole thing collapsed. The mark, it was still there on the frame, but the frame was lying on the floor, so we just walked straight through the space.'

I felt a little chastened by the simplicity of their approach. I had made use of an angel, summoned from the air. They had used brute force.

'Follow me,' I said, 'but make no sudden moves, and obey my instruction. You find me in a delicate position.'

I walked back to the apartment door, with them at my heels.

'You can stand down,' I called out. 'It is the others of my team. Friends. They have come to find me. Will you let them pass as you let me?'

'So I see,' I heard her reply from within. 'Yes.'

'I have reached a deal of sorts,' I told Renner and Saur as we entered through the iron-web hallway. 'Do nothing to disrupt it. I have a few last details to conclude, and we will be on our way.'

We entered the apartment. Mam Mordaunt stood beside the porter's chair, using its bulk as partial cover. She was now in a form-fitting bodyglove of soft black zoat-hide, and she had wiped the last traces of Zoya's identity from her face. A heavy satchel hung over one shoulder. She was aiming the pistol at us.

'This place is clearly compromised,' she said, relaxing her aim slightly. 'I will leave once you're gone, and not return. Don't worry. Our deal stands.'

She glanced at Saur.

'I was interested to see him face to face,' she said. I could tell from the puzzlement on Saur's frown that he did not know her at all, not even now she was more the Mam Mordaunt we had once known. I wondered if her long black hair back then had been a wig too, or if the short crop was a modern expediency. Had 'Mam Mordaunt' been just another function, one employed for years? I fancied I would never know her real self.

'Did I know you?' asked Saur. His eyes were more hooded than usual.

'You did. But that was another time, Thaddeus, and you are no longer yourself,' she replied. 'Still, it is reviving to see you, as it was to see Bequin. Old faces in a world where few faces are familiar or friendly.'

She looked at me.

'Hardly the demonstration of selfless support you promised,' she mocked.

'Let's be thankful for that,' I replied. I blinked the sword away, and stepped closer to her, drawing her aside. 'I trust we have an understanding,' I said quietly. 'I am staking a lot on this, perhaps even my life. If you renege and disappear, things could become very difficult for me.'

She looked almost wounded.

'I believe you think the Cognitae are just liars and tricksters, child,' she replied, 'that every word we speak, every promise, cannot be given value. We are as loyal and honest as any other order. More than most, I'd guess. More than the Ordos. To have existed as long as we have, we have needed to trust each other absolutely. To each other, our word is bond. The lies and tricks, Beta, are merely the outward guise we wear to protect ourselves from predators. You have my word, and you may trust it. I have to believe that your word is just as good.'

I assured her it was. She studied my face, then smiled and gently, momentarily, stroked my hair. How many times, as a child and as a pupil, had she made that gesture? It had always seemed empty, play-acting a maternal role and feigning concern. I had grown up thinking it a passive-aggressive display, a pretence of tenderness that was actually supposed to remind me that she held power over me.

Finally, and oddly, it felt genuine.

I confess, I wished the moment could have lasted longer, or that I could have set it in amber as a keepsake, but it was interrupted. Behind me, Renner had spoken Saur's name.

Saur stood there with a look of unfathomable mystery on his face. The slit of his mouth moved dumbly.

'What's the matter with him?' I asked. Renner shook his head. Saur glanced at me. I saw tears welling up in his eyes, and the sight shocked me. He was overcome with terrible grief, an emotion I never thought I'd see expressed by a brute like him.

'I...' he stammered hoarsely. He seemed helpless and lost. Teardrops trickled down the raw cliffs of his cheeks.

'He's remembering,' said Mam Mordaunt, stepping to my side to gaze on Saur. 'You're remembering, aren't you, Thaddeus?'

'A-all of it,' he sobbed. 'E-every part. In a flood...'

Whatever process had sealed his memory as a protective measure had lifted abruptly, and all those erased thoughts were re-collecting in his head with such speed and force it had unmanned him. He seemed so overtaken by them, he could barely stand. He took a few steps back and sat down in the porter's chair. He was shaking, wracked by a weeping fit.

'The sight of me, perhaps?' said Mam Mordaunt, showing no signs of sympathy. 'A recognition has triggered his memory block to release. He must have set certain mental keys to unlock his mind. My face, perhaps, maybe Nastrand's...'

She stopped to look him in the eyes.

'Is that it, Thaddeus? Was I a key for your mind fortress? You made yourself forget, and now the sight of me prompts you to remember?'

Saur shook still. He looked up at her with eyes red and streaming.

'My m-mind...?' he sobbed.

'You did it to yourself,' she said, 'for protection, and now–'

'I r-remember it,' he moaned.

'There, you see?' she replied.

'I remember it all,' he told her. His tears were so profuse they dripped from his jaw and chin, and spattered his oxblood bodyglove. 'Eusebe...'

'Hello again,' she said, with a cold smile. 'Collect yourself, please, Thaddeus. We–'

'Eusebe,' he wept, 'I remember. I d-did *not*. I did not d-do it to myself. It was done *to* me.'

Mam Mordaunt flinched back from him, her smile utterly gone.

'Oh shit,' she said.

'By whom?' I asked. 'By Gideon?' Ravenor had similarly caused Renner's mind to be edited.

'Was it Ravenor?' Mam Mordaunt demanded.

Saur shook his head. Tears flew out. He stared up at Mam Mordaunt, a pleading look on his stricken face.

'I'm sorry,' he said. '*Please*.'

Mam Mordaunt looked at him for a moment, then nodded. With chilling calm, she aimed her pistol at him.

'Quickly!' Saur said to her, looking her in the eye.

The xenos-tech weapon spat a brief beam of searing energy that passed through Saur's chest, the chair back, and the floor behind him. It left a gaping, smoking tunnel clean through the man and the furniture a full thumb's length in diameter. Saur's corpse folded forward in the seat, his face on his thighs, the backs of his hands on the floor beside his feet.

'Throne above!' I exclaimed in shock. 'Was that necessary?'

'He was a plant,' replied Mam Mordaunt, without emotion. 'An unwitting one. His mind had been wiped and set to reinstall on certain circumstantial cues. My presence, for example. I just pray I silenced the poor bastard fast enough, before–'

'I don't think you did, mam,' said Renner Lightburn quietly.

We all looked up. Through the long wall of green-tinted windows, we could see out across the balcony terrace and the wide city beyond. Stars had appeared in the hazy afternoon sky: small points of light, burning brightly. There were four of them, then five: one blue, two red, one yellow, one amber. They were rushing towards us across the city in loose formation, and at great velocity.

They were graels.

CHAPTER 22

In which the Eight descend

'We're dead,' said Mam Mordaunt.

'This is not my doing!' I protested.

'I know that, you foolish girl!' she snapped. 'The King was searching for me, and now he's found me.'

'What are they?' Lightburn asked, gazing at their approach through the windows with horrid fascination. 'Are they ships? The lights of ships?'

How could I explain a eudaemonic entity to him? How could I describe the merciless, implacable thought-form of a grael, its keening power, the etheric nature of its construction, the principles of the Eight? Any of that, to a man who had no knowledge of them, and scant experience of the warp? Could I say that it had been my intended destiny to become one? There was no point, and there was no time.

'If they have our location, we must flee,' I said.

Mam Mordaunt had already crossed to her quizzing glasses.

'There is no opportunity,' she said, surveying the mirrors' images. 'They come at us from all sides. I count twelve. One is already in the inner staircase.'

She looked at me.

'There'll be no fleeing,' she said. 'We must wish with all fervour that my defences are sufficient to the task.'

'Are they?' I asked.

Mam Mordaunt raised her xenos beam-gun and adjusted its setting.

'I have prepared long and hard for this emergency,' she replied. 'The chances of him discovering my whereabouts were always high. So, I hope so. But he sends so many...'

'What did you do?' I asked. 'What did you do that makes him hunt you so?'

'I exist,' she snarled. 'I know his secrets, and I am free to speak them.'

The first of the graels had reached us. They floated in across the terrace, slow, like dandelion heads on the wind. Each was a tiny bright star. We could hear the hiss and crackle of them through the glass.

'Renner and I have no means to fight them,' I said to her.

'You do,' she snapped back. 'Your black soul is some defence. Un-cuff.'

I did so, turning my limiter off. At once, the numb blankness of my pariah gene filled the apartment. Renner flinched. Mam Mordaunt curled her lip in distaste. I even felt myself, as though the many mirrors were reflecting the cold of my null state back at me.

Outside, the first graels fluttered back a little, sputtering and fizzling. Then they bobbed forward again towards the glass, seething bright as before.

'What else?' I demanded. 'We have but firearms and swords, and they'll be useless.'

'The bureau,' she replied, weapon in hand, her eyes not leaving the graels outside. 'Top drawer. What little I have...'

I ran to the polished bureau. I heard a fizzling crack from the hall outside, like a voltaic discharge, as a grael brushed against the warded outer door, seeking admission. A second later, there came another electrical spit as it tried again, applying more power.

The bureau's top drawer contained a few necklace charms and dog-eared notebooks, a drawstring purse of calfskin, a blondwood box that looked like a cutlery case, and two heavy, dark spheres of metal that I realised had to be frag grenades. They were old, and their dull casings were marked with a skull-and-cog motif. I put them in the hip pocket of my coat.

'The charms?' I called out.

'Forget them,' she replied. 'Just trifles. The box, and the bag!'

On the balcony, the graels – four of them now – had begun to buzz against the windows. As they touched the glass, there was a fierce crackle and flare as the wards rebuffed them. The graels shivered away, then pushed again, banging at the tinted panes like heavy insects, gusting showers of firefly sparks as they ground against the witch-marked barrier.

I opened the soft purse, which clinked as I picked it up. Inside were a handful of smooth-polished vitreous pebbles, like sea glass that might be found washed up on a beach after years of soft tumbling by the tides. Each one was a lustrous tobacco-brown, and engraved with a precise hexafoil design.

'What are these?' I called out.

Mam Mordaunt was still watching the windows, ready to raise her weapon in a two-handed grip.

'Flect missiles,' she hissed back. 'Projectiles. Throw them – carefully!'

I lifted the lid on the blondwood box. The interior was a shaped and cushioned pad of lurid pink satin. One shaped depression was empty, but the other nested a pistol, the twin of the chromed xenos-tech Mam Mordaunt clutched. I took it out. It felt disturbingly warm, as though it was a hot-blooded organism, and it was surprisingly light for such a carefully machined piece.

'Renner!' I called.

He was at my side.

'You can shoot. Take this.'

He accepted it from me tentatively, cupping it like an egg or a porcelain figurine that would shatter if it slipped from his grasp. He elbowed the heavy Mastoff around so it was slung across his back.

'You shouldn't trust me with a piece like this,' he murmured.

'Just take it,' I said. I had the purse in my hand, and took one of the glass pebbles out.

'The beamer has no kick,' Mam Mordaunt told Renner, 'and it is absolutely accurate. But it is a beam weapon, you understand, Curst? It will discharge collimated energy all the while the trigger is depressed. So squeeze gently, in the name of all the Warped Ones, then lift! Pulse it with a light finger or it will shred the room!'

I heard Renner make a grunt of displeasure. He gripped the weapon, and held it out at arm's length as though it might bite him.

'This is xenos shit,' he murmured. 'A stranger-race gun...'

'It is an Interex mauler,' Mam Mordaunt replied, with little patience.

'It uses kinebrach filament photonics. Just point it and shoot it, or you are no use to us!'

Six graels, each of a different incandescent hue, were now scraping and pushing at the windows. The glass shivered. Glowing coals of resistance flew from the balls of light and flurried out across the balcony terrace like sparks from a windblown bonfire. I could hear others, shrieking and scraping against the main door, and at the walls, and at the floor.

'The wards will not hold,' Mam Mordaunt murmured.

The witch-marks scribed on the sills and frames of the windows were already beginning to smoulder, spilling tufts of grey smoke into the air. The panes creaked and shifted. One grael, a malevolent acid yellow, swam backwards, and then rushed at the glass with furious intent. I heard the thump of the impact. There was a bloom of corposant, and a painful crack like lightning earthing, and the grael was thrown backwards again, shedding flecks of light. It seemed to simmer, hovering, to recover itself, then rushed the glass once more, with similar results.

The others battered and knocked, fizzling with malicious energy. Where some pressed with steady effort, the green tint of the glass began to bleach out, leaving pockmarks of clear glass through which hard, slanting beams of pale daylight began to spear the apartment.

The yellow grael struck at the barrier again. Another, fury-red, commenced the same approach, throwing itself at the glass with repeated indignation. More bleached spots appeared in the tinting, more rays of sunlight lanced into the room. The red grael impacted again, and this time the glass began to bubble, as if heated. Small cracks had begun to figure the panes. Three of the witch-marks on the frame caught fire, and started to dance with fierce little flames.

I caught Mam Mordaunt casting a look my way. She didn't speak. Her eyes were everything. I saw her anger, her fear and her blame. This was a doom she had evaded for months, since the fall of the Maze, and now it had found her because of me. I had brought this to her door, unwittingly perhaps, but most assuredly. And my bold claims that the Inquisition would protect her were worthless.

A violet grael flew at the windows, met resistance in a seething fluorescent halo for a second, and then broke clean through, sailing into the apartment, leaving a molten-edged hole the size of a fist in the glass behind it. It came at us, moving with shocking speed. Mam Mordaunt aimed, both arms straight, one eye closed, and fired. The searing pulse from her beam-gun struck it dead centre.

The grael expanded for a moment as it absorbed the massive energy load, like a billion-year time-lapse of a star growing swollen with age. Then it burst like a supernova.

There was a smack of shockwave as it did so. I recoiled, and felt the heat of it on my face. The grael blew apart, showering sparks of violet light in all directions. I saw some land, on furniture, on carpet, sizzling like firecrackers.

There was no moment of respite. The other graels, and there were nine outside now that I could see, redoubled their efforts on the breached glass. The yellow and red graels struck together, with raging force.

The windows exploded in at us. There was a hurricane rush of wind, and a blizzard of flying glass. I shielded my face, and felt shards cut at my coat and rebound off my raised arms.

Mam Mordaunt stood her ground, unflinching. Flying glass had cut her face in three places, drawing trickles of blood. Another fragment had sliced the bodyglove open across the outer curve of her left thigh, gashing the skin beneath. I saw the bright blood with great clarity. Cold daylight now bathed the room, replacing the cool green mood. I could smell the air from outside, the sharp, cold scent of the wind over Queen Mab.

She fired a second time, another tight pulse, and clipped the yellow grael before it could reach her. It spun away, wild and damaged, bleeding fans of sparks like a Saint Katarina's wheel. It hit the end wall and detonated, bringing down several of the quizzing glasses.

Renner fired too, aiming for the red grael. His first pulse from the unfamiliar weapon was tragically imprecise. It missed the grael entirely, and speared through the window frame and out into the sky. Renner yelped in dismay, the red grael rushing towards his face. Mam Mordaunt switched sideways and fired, tumbling the grael away from him with another clipping shot. Trailing energy, it veered and tried to steady itself. Renner re-aimed and shot it almost point-blank. Like the violet grael before it, the red one burst like a sun flare and showered writhing worms of neon-red power in every direction. The detonation threw Renner off his feet, and he crashed into the bureau.

I saw a third, an emerald-green orb, flying at me like a meteor. I tried to duck – a hopeless effort, I recognise in hindsight – but it swung away from me at the last moment, as if violently repulsed by my null aura. It rolled backwards in the air, crackling in a frenzy as it summoned more power to renew its attack.

Without conscious thought, on impulse alone, I flung the glass pebble in my palm at it. And I praised the God-Emperor of Mankind for making Thaddeus Saur, at whose mean hands I had been schooled and coached for many years, practising the skills of the throw-knife, the chakram, the shaken, the zaer, the francisca and the whirling iron in the alley-ranges of the drill until such skills had become instinctive muscle memory.

My pebble – a flect missile, as Mam Mordaunt had called it – hit the emerald grael squarely.

I have both heard and read of a device known, in the vernacular, as a *psyk-out* or psykanic negator. They are rare things, most usually made in the form of a hand-bomb or grenade. It is said the immortal Custodians make them, laced with dust brushed from the armrests of the Golden Throne itself, though that is quite fanciful, I'm sure, for why would there be dust on the Emperor's throne? Whatever, such devices deliver a potently negative anti-psyker charge, in effect a violently concentrated burst of the very essence of the pariah state I naturally radiate.

The flect missile seemed to create precisely that savage effect. As it struck the grael, the grael did not explode as the violet and red ones had, nor did it shower the area with disintegrating sparks. It simply distorted and folded in upon itself with a pop, like the sound of a cork blown from a bottle, that shattered the flect into dust. From that sudden implosion, the grael re-formed, as if from a pucker in the air itself, but now it was dull and colourless, without any trace of emerald green. A milky, lifeless sphere, it simply dropped to the floor, and rolled across the carpet, inert and cold as a doorknob. Without hesitation, I stamped on it, as I would stamp on some venomous insect, and it shattered like spun sugar under my heel, crushed into an ugly smear.

Another grael, this one vivid blue, buzzed past me, and I dodged aside as one might avoid a persistent hornet. I plucked another flect from the bag. For a moment, I thought we were gaining ground.

But just as Mam Mordaunt blew another grael out of the air with her xenos mauler, I saw that both the yellow and the violet graels, which I had believed obliterated, were re-forming. They rolled across the wide rug, glittering as they coalesced and spun with restored fury, and quickly became as bright as stars again.

However, they did not rise into the air. They grew instead.

The glowing orbs began to stretch and morph, as though they were losing cohesion, and then sprouted tendrils of energy up into the air. In just seconds, each had transformed from a bright sphere into the life-size shape of a human figure. Each was tall, vaguely masculine and powerful, and perhaps naked, though there was no detail to them and no features. They were human shapes, three dimensional, made of crackling violet and yellow light.

Another moment, and there was a red figure too, and an emerald-green one. Other graels, entering through the shattered gap of the windows, or carving the air around us, dropped to the floor and reassembled as human forms.

The grael figures stepped towards us, closing on us from three sides. They were silent except for the sizzle of their forms. Their footfalls singed the carpet.

I dragged Renner to his feet, and both he and Mam Mordaunt opened fire. Their pulsed shots punctured approaching forms, scattering them like flashes of sunlight on metal. But as quickly as they were burned down, they began to reshape, tatters of coloured energy that writhed on the floor, and melded and then repeated the slow, tendrilled growth into human form.

We were backing away from them, almost unconsciously, retreating towards the black iron gate of the hallspace. I think we had all reasoned that escape was our only option, however hopeless that was.

There was an explosive crash behind us. Other graels had finally overcome the wards of the apartment's main entrance, and blown that door asunder. They rushed in, three of them, still in orb form – one crimson, one lime, and one the deep blue of woad – coming at our backs. Escape, by any means, was a vain fancy.

I turned, raising a flect, to fend off the trio racing up at our heels. But Mam Mordaunt, firing a snap-pulse that vaporised another figure, yelled out a word command. It was a word that I did not know, though the very sound of it made me shudder with discomfort – yes, even on top of the fear and adrenaline already churning the very fibres of me. I am sure it was a word from the arcane language called Enuncia, for even as I heard it I could not then remember it.

The gate slammed behind us, and the ironwork cobweb patterns of the hall's arcade began to move. The metal twisted and flexed like soft liquorice, and lashed out, trapping the three graels in moving cobwebs of black iron. The web motif of her hallway had not been mere decoration. Caught within the creaking, twisting net of iron, the three grael orbs blazed with angry light, and started to push and burn against the enclosing bars. But as their forms touched a bar, or attempted to pass between them, there was a sharp, voltaic report, like the slap of a horsewhip, and they were flung backwards, as though they had been stung with a cattle prod.

The attack to our backs was momentarily blocked, but then so too was our only egress. I wondered, frantically, how much charge was in the xenos guns, and how many more flects were left in the calfskin purse. As fast as we disassembled the advancing figures – and our reactions were swift and unrelenting, scrambling them into puffs of aurora glare and motes of light – as fast as we fought, they were back and there were more. It was like the worst combat simulations in the drill, where the old practice cages threw holoform targets at you with increasing and unflinching speed, two for every one you bested, one from the left for every one from the right, until you were overwhelmed and overcome, and it was time for Saur, over the metal grind of the cage powering down, to tell you exactly how you had failed this time.

Except Mentor Saur would not debrief us this time. He was bent over, dead in the porter's chair with a hole in him so big I could have run my arm through him. There would be no debrief.

There would be no afterwards.

One touch of a reaching, grasping thought-form hand, and we would be made dead as simply and suddenly as old Mam Tontelle.

'There's no way out!' Renner yelled, firing a pulse with a little too much finger-squeeze. The beam demolished a pink figure and then burned on like a lance and entirely destroyed one upright of the window frame and the sill beneath it.

Mam Mordaunt knew he was right. By then, her options had reduced to almost nil, and she was working with desperation alone. Any fate was better than this inevitability. Anything that might be fought or negotiated was preferable.

So, as she fired her weapon again, she spoke the words. And those words were 'Immaterial College'.

CHAPTER 23

Six saviours

Called by name, they came. All six of them.

Can I fault Eusebe for that decision? In hindsight, I cannot, though what arrived was hardly salvation. Back in that moment, in the mirror-hung apartment high in Stanchion House, I might have tried to stop her, having had some modest experience of the rapacious threat the visitors presented. Increased peril is seldom a solution to imminent danger.

But there was no time, and the words were out of her mouth before I could deny her. The visitors always came, summoned by the arcane coding woven into their name. Just a chance utterance of it had brought them to us in the muniment room, and we had been unknown to them. Mam Mordaunt, by her own admission, had been building a connection to them, negotiating with them remotely – by quizzing glass, I am certain – for some time, contemplating a pact with them, despite the clear, inherent dangers of such a relationship. She was desperate, and needed their strength as allies; they sought her as a resource, prizing the confidential knowledge she possessed.

If she had brokered that deal, it would have ended badly for her. She knew that, which is why she had resolved not to take that step.

But now she was backed into a corner, in every sense, and with the grim pragmatism that seems to characterise the Cognitae, she had taken it anyway.

And it would end badly just the same.

So can I fault her? No. My life to that moment had been fraught with danger, and I had been too close to death too many times: in the chambers beneath the basilica, in the ghost halls of Feverfugue, in the pitchy depths of the Below... and those just begin my catalogue of near-lethal calamities. As the Golden Throne Above Us All is my witness, I believe that moment in Stanchion House was the closest I had come to extinction. It was *pandaemonium*, though not in the sense of the word as I would later understand it. The graels were deathless abominations. One alone was an insurmountable foe, and here were perhaps twenty of them, twenty unstoppable weapons of the Eight.

We were surrounded. We were trapped, and death was mere seconds or inches away. I was terrified, more terrified than I had ever been. There was no hope for us. So, no, I do not fault her. Something is always better than nothing.

The something that came... *Well.*

What had been pandaemonium became... There is no word. Words fail. When you are caught at a fever pitch of violent, chaotic jeopardy, the worst state you have ever known, and it becomes still *worse*, language simply runs out of superlatives and has nowhere to go.

First, then, there was a thunderclap.

No, no... *First* you must understand that everything that happened, happened fast. It had scarcely been a minute since the graels began their assault – a minute, if that. I have related these events to the best of my ability, but the very telling of it is a lifetime long compared to the flashing speed at which it occurred. So, to begin, know it was a blur of noise and turmoil in which even thought was incoherent until later recollection.

First, then, the fury of it. *Then*, the thunderclap. It shook the entire building. Later, I learned that the force of it had been so great, it had shaken loose some of the makeshift structures hanging from the girders of Stanchion House, and sent them plunging to the streets below, or left them swinging, cables fraying, their occupants clinging on and screaming. The whole building rocked. What was left of the glass in the breached casements blew in. Mirrors flew off their hooks, and smashed. The smack of air stung me. I tasted blood in my mouth.

A seething black cloud, the nimbus cap of a tempest, rolled in across the afternoon sky, and crowned the building. It did not move like weather, not even weather driven by a cyclone wind. It boiled in upon us, like black ink squirted through water, staining the sky in swirling, churning folds. Streaks of lightning stitched through it, golden threads woven into billowing black silk.

The visitors arrived together: two on the terrace outside, the other four in the room with us. They appeared, in the first instant, as glassy forms, just as they were when they had tried to push through the walls and doors of the muniment room, milky-glass things that seemed just vapours in humanoid form. But then the glassiness filled in, with colour and depth and detail, and they resolved into real, solid things. I believe they had manifested by some form of bilocation, an energetic transfer of matter from one place to another. It was not a teleport, though I know such rare and strange technology exists. It was an action of sublime sorcery, that moved animate material from a 'there' to a 'here'. The insolent use of such power wounded the world: the massing storm, the quake of the building... That was reality twitching in trauma as its fundamental laws were violated.

The moment they were whole, the visitors unleashed destruction. There was no hesitation. They had appeared among the advancing grael figures, and they knew them immediately as enemies. There was no warning, or challenge issued. They set to at once.

The graels reacted to the abrupt arrival before the first blow was even struck. They flinched, recoiling from each visitor that appeared in their midst. Though they had assumed human shapes, the graels had not, until that moment, betrayed any human response or emotional reaction. They had simply come at us with unfathomable, automaton intent. Now they baulked for an instant, exhibiting a flicker of body language: surprise, alarm, dismay, perhaps even fear or revulsion. It was disturbing, and passing strange to see the coloured phantoms display such human reactions.

I thought of my once-friend Judika. He had been a grael, raised to that state by the Maze Undue's programme. His blacksoul form had become a vessel – by means, I think, of some small, foul white spider-thing lodged in his throat – for a grael power, which he could manifest as a projection, a magent orb, that he could send out across distances. Had circumstances conspired that way, it would have been my fate too. I imagined then a picture of other nulls like Judika Sowl, trained and harvested by the Maze Undue and, perhaps, similar institutions, and sent to serve the King in Yellow. From his hand, they had taken the crackling albino spiders on their tongues like communion wafers, and become his templars, the *good daemons* who served as his foremost warriors. They had become of the Eight. *Eight for the legs. Eight for the points. Eight because that's what they ate.* Teke, the Smiling One, had crooned that like some nursery rhyme, but so it was. And Alace Quatorze had been quite wrong. The Eight were far more than that in number.

I thought of them, pariah children who had been like me, whose futures had been decided and their hopes excised, and who had then been harnessed as these things. Somewhere, perhaps somewhere in Queen Mab, or perhaps in the City of Dust, they sat, sending out these grael projections to destroy us, infused with boundless psykanic power and channelling the very warp, remotely guiding the graels as orbs, or human forms, or whatever, I imagine, they chose to conjure. They were dedicated, sworn to service, bound by faith, and immeasurably empowered to execute the King's will.

And now they flinched. Their thought-forms, for one unguarded instant, mimicked the reactions of their flesh bodies, far away, jumping in surprise and alarm, echoing and revealing the all-too-human responses of their guiding vessels. At the Basilica Saint Orphaeus, months before, Judika's grael form had been wounded by Scarpac the Word Bearer's cursed blade. Judika's flesh body had later shown that ghastly warp-wound upon it. That was sympathetic psychomagic, the flesh host suffering a reflection of the injury done to his projected thought-form. So then here, but in reverse, the thought-forms reflexively simulated the startled effect of their remote operators.

Though sublimely powerful, the graels had much to fear. The visitors, as Gideon had conjectured, were Adeptus Astartes. They were Space Marines, in full panoply of wargear. But, contrary to Gideon's theory, they were not all of the XV traitor host.

One was. Their chieftain, clearly. He was the tallest of them, a towering form, which manifested in the heart of the grael ranks. His warplate was gleaming lapis lazuli, quite the bluest blue I had ever seen. It was trimmed in burnished gold, and half-shrouded by a long, iridescent robe that flowed like oil. His warhelm, dashed with more lapis bands, was golden too, and fashioned to form the nemes headcloth and pschent double-crown of the Pharaonic kingdoms in ancient days. The crown's crest swooped high, adding to his stature, and it was as white as glacial ice. His face was a sculpted visor of snarling gold with cruel slits for frowning eyes and downturned mouth. This, as I was about to learn, was Senefuru, also named the Prosperine. In one fist, he held a rod of polished copper two metres long, capped by a silver finial in the form of a yowling feline's head. In the other, he brandished an ornate khopesh, the hooked sickle-sword of the Nilus Delta.

The instant he appeared, he swept the khopesh sideways with a fluid grace and precision that I would not have thought a figure encumbered by such massive warplate could have managed. It was deft, like the supple flick of a nimble assassin. It lopped the head off the grael to his right. The grael, a cobalt thing, fell to one knee and collapsed. This was not damage as we had rendered it, no temporary disruption of thought-form. This *cut*. I heard the vox-crackle howl of spider-pain. The severed stump of neck bled energy that flowed like water, spattering the floor. This liquid was white, like ichor.

Beside the magnificent Thousand Son was another Space Marine, not as tall, but quite the most massive of the six. His hulking plate was matt-grey, as though each weighty part of it had been cored from igneous magnetite. Its edges and panels were quite plain and without trim. The only decorations were the innumerable glyphs etched in it in gold leaf. They glowed in the smooth dull surfaces, as though lit from within by flames. He had the aspect of an auroch, of immense physical power, of hunched shoulders and pugnacious head. In his immense paws, he clutched a long-hafted war-flail with a studded, chain-hinged striking-head. He, beyond doubt, was of the indomitable IV Legion, so named the Iron Warriors.

With a tectonic roar, he began to swing the huge flail, two-handed, driving it into the graels within range. They ruptured, demolished and half-crushed, their coloured shapes deforming like mashed flesh, jetting sprays of ichor.

The sorcerer of the Thousand Sons spoke. He yelled across the chamber to Mam Mordaunt.

'You called to us, Zoya. Our name was spoken and we heard it.'

His was the voice at the muniment room door, a low, bass intonation with a hollow echo. Again, there was an accent to it, as though he was speaking in an unfamiliar tongue. He had called her Zoya. From this, I knew Mam Mordaunt had guarded her name, using that of her function, to block control over her, for the visitors possessed immeasurable influence through names.

'I pledge to you, Senefuru of Tizca!' she yelled back. 'As Zoya Farnessa, I pledge to your College, O Prosperine! Protect me as you promised!'

'And in return–'

'You'll get what you demanded! This is no time to specify terms!'

It was not. Carnage reigned, threatening to shred the room, the entire floor of the building.

'End them,' boomed the hollow voice of the magician-warrior to his brethren. They required no such instruction, for the miniature war had begun the instant they appeared. The graels were enemies to be neutralised on sight. The Iron Warrior's war-flail was matted with white sap-blood as he smashed graels aside, but they were rallying fast, and turning on him and his kind. Coloured thought-form hands reached out, and where they touched Astartes plate, searing sparks spat out, and the armoured warrior lurched back as though stung or shot.

'Uraeon Tancredo!' the Thousand Son howled. 'Contain the prize!'

I know little of the great Adeptus Astartes, except for what I was made to study in the secret books of the Maze Undue, but I knew that they were breeds apart, even to each other. To see an Iron Warrior work alongside one of the Thousand Sons, that was beyond explanation. Even the so-called Traitor Legions, who had turned against the Throne and fallen with the heretic Lupercal, seldom aligned. Their ambitions, and their private daemon-gods, were quite incompatible.

So it was with incredulity that I beheld the third of the visitors as, on the instruction of his mage-lord, he tore through the melee to reach Mam Mordaunt and secure her.

His plate was black, marked in white. Like the Iron Warrior, the armour was richly engraved with golden glyphs upon almost every surface. He wielded a golden fuscina, and his head was bare, except for a heavy rebreather that encased his nose, mouth and the lower half of his skull like a collar. His head was shaved, and inlaid with ghost lines of circuitry, and his glaring eyes seemed very old, as though they had seen too many endless wars.

His name, as the mage-lord had cried it, was Tancredo. And he was of the Iron Hands.

'Against the wall!' he ordered as he broke towards us. His bladed trident skewered a grael, and then hoisted it away over his shoulder, its limbs flailing as it tumbled. His voice was solemn and stern. It had been the one speaking from the end window of the muniment room the night before.

He came at Mam Mordaunt, ignoring both me and Renner. How could a loyal Astartes be standing with these others?

He was huge to us, like a noble god. He cursed and rocked as a crimson grael struck his ribs with a sparking touch, and punched it through the torso with the spike-end of the fuscina. It uttered a crackling wail as the haft wrenched out in a spray of white fluid, and fell to its hands and knees.

'Against the wall, I said!' Tancredo snarled.

'I am your ally, not your prisoner–' Mam Mordaunt yelled back.

He rammed the trident at her, and pinned her to the wall. The middle and left-hand blades of the fuscina's head were either side of her neck, the lunge-rest against her throat. Her eyes were wide with horror. The tines had drawn blood from both sides of her neck. A whisker either way, and it would have speared her through and killed her. Was this a measure of his skill, or a callous disregard?

She had been slammed into the wall, dislodging more mirrors.

'You do as you are told, Zoya Farnessa,' Tancredo hissed. He said it with particular intonation, as though the words alone would hold her in place as firmly as the trident. They would not, for that name had no power in it.

'Protect my friends too,' she gasped.

'This is no time to specify terms,' he replied, mocking her with her own words. He jerked the trident out, allowing her to lurch forward, and swung aside, driving the weapon at graels who surged to assault.

'This was a mistake,' she said, to us or to herself. She wiped blood away from her neck with the heel of her hand.

'No,' I said, 'it has borrowed back time from death.'

'A minute or two,' Renner muttered. He was looking towards the windows. Hundreds more graels were flying towards us, a twinkling constellation of coloured stars against the black storm. Surprised by the College, the Eight were flooding us with reinforcements. I had never imagined that so many could exist. The power of the visitors was humbling, but surely even the six of them could not combat this eudaemonic onslaught.

Perhaps Mam Mordaunt had known that when she called their name. Perhaps, all along, this had been her audacious attempt to wreak utter confusion during which we could effect escape. She had not let them have her name, so she was permitting them no permanent hold on her. She expected to break from their company.

But the visitors were implacable.

By then, the nature of the other three had become apparent, and each of them was just as fearsome as their kin. In the apartment chamber with Senefuru, Tancredo and the bestial Iron Warrior, was an Astartes in moss-green armour, covered with a long, cream, hooded surcoat. The surcoat, tied at the waist with a golden rope, was embroidered with eldritch glyphs like those engraved on the plate of Tancredo, and that of Perturabo's spawn. This cruel champion was most certainly a son of the Lion, of the First Legion Dark Angels. He swung an executioner's sword of such great length it seemed the size of a spear. The beheading sword's long grip was almost half the length of the weapon itself, and the long, straight, flat blade, double-edged, had a rounded, blunt tip.

On the terrace beyond the windows fought the remaining two, shredding the grael foe in the fulminous storm-light. One wore glyphed armour of sheened black, marked with white blazons. His black war-helm was snouted, like the beak of a great corvid. He fought with a brace of split-tipped swords, whose forks and serrated edges ravaged the psychomagical flesh of the foe. He had wings. They were full and huge, like the wings of Comus Nocturnus, but they were as glossy black as a crow's, and even from a distance I could tell they were not an organic part of him, as Comus' were. They were manifestations of psychomagic, ethereal wings fashioned in the void and fletched in the warp. Yet they seemed fully alive, beating as living things, an extension of his broad back.

He was of the silent XIX, the murderous Raven Guard. Like the Dark Angel and the proud Iron Hand, a loyalist, unless the old books lied.

I heard him cry out, the sharp call of a carrion bird. It was he who had perched and pecked at the chimney of the muniment room. He sprang aloft, his great black wings carrying him off the terrace into the lowering sky, to meet the onrushing waves of grael stars, head-on.

He left his companion to complete the killing on the terrace. His companion, the last of the six, was winged too, but his wings were bright, scarlet bones of shining psykanic energy. His armour was a lustrous, opalescent darkness: part midnight blue, part black, part Imperial purple, depending on how the light caught it. He made war with a vicious saintie, an ancient parrying weapon that I had found difficult to master. It was a rod, a short lance, with a spear tip at one end and a mace head on the other. In the mid-point of the haft there was a hand-grip covered by a guard loop. He whirled the thing, using the spear blade to stab and slash, and the mace head to break and shatter. With the guarded haft, he blocked and fended off any counter-attack. He wore no helmet, but his haggard face wore an expression of gleeful appetite. His hair was long, tousled and grey, his staring eyes black upon black. He was, I believed, a monstrous Night Lord of the VIII Legion Astartes, and a shunned traitor.

The skills of all six were monumental, but they had become the focus of the raging fight. The hulking Iron Warrior was doling out the worst of the killing, and the graels' priority had become to contain him. He was blasted by three graels simultaneously, and the surging rip of force threw him clean over.

'Onager is down!' the Dark Angel growled, a predatory rattle.

'To him, Anchisus!' Senefuru replied, and they both swung into the grael forces to cover the Iron Warrior while he regained his wits.

'Now,' snapped Mam Mordaunt to us. She made for the black iron hallway. This, while all forces were murderously engaged, was the moment to flee.

Mam Mordaunt used her xenos weapon on full beam to disintegrate the knotted network of wrought-iron webs, and clear a path. Her shots destroyed, temporarily, the three grael orbs still held in the web trap.

'Go! Go through!' she yelled at us. Renner was already clambering through the smoking, mangled wreckage of the ironwork, heading for the darkened hallway beyond.

I glanced back, and saw Tancredo, the Iron Hand, charging Mam

Mordaunt. He had seen, despite the turmoil, her effort to escape. She shot him with the mauler, the extreme power of the pulse boring into his chestplate and throwing him backwards. I turned to follow Renner, then looked back, expecting to see Mam Mordaunt at my heels.

But she was not. There was no sign of her. Tancredo was back on his feet, fuscina in hand, raging and looking around for a sight of her.

She was gone. Her, and her satchel too. The only clue that she had ever been there was her xenos pistol, which lay, burned-out and blackened, on the carpet between broken mirror glass and shattered frames. Had he slain her somehow? Had a grael vaporised her and left no trace? Had the xenos weapon misfired and disintegrated her? It was an utter mystery, and I had no time to fathom it, not if I hoped to live.

I stumbled out into the darkened landing. The uproar of the battle in the apartment was shaking the floor and the walls, and sifting dust and grit down from the ceiling above us.

Renner, scared out of his wits, began to go down the stairs, but I grabbed his arm.

'Up,' I said.

He looked at me as if I was mad.

'Down is too slow,' I said. 'Trust me.' Mam Mordaunt had told me of the faster and more discreet exit.

If I could trust her.

We ran up the stairs instead. We were on the second rising flight when we heard someone crash out onto the landing we had fled. It was the Iron Hand, hunting for us. Instinctively, I hugged back to the iron banister, and put myself between Renner and the Space Marine below.

Could he read or sense a null? Could I mask the trace of Renner?

Apparently I could, for at once he started down the staircase, his bulk shaking the whole frame of it. Then he stopped, and looked up. Right at me.

As he turned and began to thunder back up, I heard him snarl into a communication link.

'Two fugitives! Zephyr! Xarbia! The roof dock!'

At which point, the grenade I had simply dropped, like a stone down a wishing well, and struck the step beside him. It was one of the two from the drawer that I had stuffed into my coat pocket. I had expected a blast that might consume the entire stairwell, so I shoved Renner before me, bodily, sprawling on top of him on the filthy landing.

But the blast was *not* what I expected. Instead of belching flame, there was instead a soft gust of light. I thought the bomb's mechanism had resoundingly malfunctioned.

Tancredo, however, was not pursing us. He was still on the stairs, two flights down from us, rocking backwards onto one step and then forward onto the one above, over and over, the same exact motion. He was bathed in the pale flare of the erupting grenade.

I heard his voice.

'Zephyr! Xarbia! The roof–'

'Zephyr! Xarbia! The roof–'

'Zephyr! Xarbia! The roof–'

'Zephyr! Xarbia! The roof–'

The same precise intonation. The grenade, not an explosive munition, had been an ancient stasis bomb. The symbol on it must have indicated the enigmatic Machinekin of Mars, for only they, the books had hinted, had the means to manufacture such things, and only in ancient times.

Such a thing, on detonation, emitted a tight-looped stasis field, in which the same moment of space-time repeated itself, ad infinitum. Tancredo would take that step and say those words for as long as the blast zone endured.

I did not think that would be long.

I grabbed Renner's hand, and we ran up the staircase into the very summit of the ancient structure.

CHAPTER 24

Three killers

We ran, frantic, pell-mell. The highest levels of the structure, directly under the port, were dark, dank places, half-open to the weather. The walls ran with slime and rot, and the hallways were littered with trash and debris. We passed old machine rooms, and secondary holding spaces where ancient packets of freight waited in cage pens, never to be claimed. We did not break stride.

'I think,' Renner panted, 'I think you should hand it back.'

'Hand what back?'

'This life of yours,' he replied. 'Hand it back and ask for a replacement, for it is no good. It is broken and it is mad.'

'I didn't choose it, Renner,' I snapped, pausing to decide which way to turn next.

'Does anyone choose this life?' he asked.

Some did. I knew that. Gregor, Gideon…

I had no time for his foolery. The place was a rotting maze. I was trying to recall Mam Mordaunt's instructions.

'Shut up,' I said.

I suggest you take the roof access into the port. One of the freight elevators in the nearest cargo hall still functions, despite the look of it. It will carry you to the street dock on Childeric Pass.

'We're looking for the roof access,' I said. He gestured, and we started to run again.

Remembering Mam Mordaunt's words, I wondered again what had happened to her. Had she been destroyed or had she fled? If the latter, then by what means? I feared some misguided desperation, for desperation had driven her to summon the visitors as salvation. I was sure she'd brought them simply to provoke a terrible distraction that would allow her time to escape. But she had not followed us through the door, and how did one evade a charging Astartes of Medusa? Not by any sensible means. And if she had possessed another way out, why hadn't she used it before?

I reasoned that, whatever it was, it was even more unwise than summoning the visitors. Summoning them had seemed like a suicidal last resort, but perhaps there had been an even worse alternative, something unthinkable, that she had finally been unable to avoid.

I shuddered at the idea. Where was she? And how does someone escape from a place with no exits? What dire thing had she done? I sincerely hoped, for the sake of her soul, that she was simply dead, for the notion of some infernal, death-be-damned decision was too chilling to contemplate.

We followed a decayed serviceway, and found another flight of stairs that led up. On the wall, paint flaking, was Administratum signage listing security protocols and indicating port access.

From below us, the tumult of open warfare continued to resound. The whole building shivered every few seconds. There were crumps of explosions and other lesser detonations. Through gaps in the walls and through the windows we passed, we could see fierce flashes of light coming from below, each accompanied by a powerful vibration, and some of them hurling scraps of debris and flame out into view above the city. A huge plume of brown smoke was rising from the upper south face of Stanchion House. Mam Mordaunt's apartment lair was undoubtedly ablaze and devastated, and the fire was spreading to adjacent properties and the floors above and below. I could also hear sporadic chatter now: deep, shuddering bursts. That was definitely bolter fire. Attacked by swarms of graels, the Astartes visitors had resorted to their ranged weapons.

It was a conflict far beyond my mortal means, a clash of demigods and supernatural spirits. I could not predict the outcome, though I feared the forces of the Yellow King would triumph through numbers. But part of me wished the visitors would be victorious. I had seen the harm they had been able to inflict. In my mind sat vivid memories of the graels they had maimed and killed. I could not forget the sight of the crimson grael that Tancredo had speared right in front of us. I could see it crawling, broken, on its hands and knees, ichor pouring from its chest wound like wet oatmeal. With reason, I had been terrified of the graels, but that thing, even without face or features to convey expression, had been in hideous pain. I thought of its host vessel, wherever that vessel was: a pariah like me. Had he or she been crawling too, slowly and painfully dying from the mortal wound of sympathetic psychomagic? I winced at the savage tragedy of it. Had it been someone known to me, a friend or fellow from the Maze Undue? In another life, it could have been me. Renner was wrong. My life was broken and mad, but I would never exchange it for fear of getting something worse.

In that, I believe, my philosophy differed from Mam Mordaunt's, even though she had raised me to follow her mindset. Impulsive desperation is not your friend. Some choices are worse than death.

I feared we were on our own. Mam Mordaunt was gone, who knew where? And I could not make contact with Gideon on the link or by the wraithbone pendant. As we ran up the abandoned stairs, I opened Kara's perfume bottle in the hope that I could call the angel back to our side, but he did not appear. I wondered if even the likes of him would hesitate from approaching a site so fraught with violence and psychomagical wrath. He had escaped the King once: the scent of the King's graels, in such a multitude, and raging Astartes, would probably keep him at bay. The phial went back into my coat hastily, unstoppered, leaking its clotted, useless contents into the lining of the pocket.

Our way was slow, impeded by the wards Mam Mordaunt had left to guard the upper approaches. Almost every door and hatchway was bonded with a witch-mark. Renner nearly rushed through the first we came to, but I stopped him just in time when I spotted the scratched hexafoil. I went through first, protected by the moldavite charm she had given me, then tossed it back through the doorway to him, so he could put it on and follow me safely. We were obliged to repeat this relay pantomime several times, and our advance became a crawl.

This gave them time to find us.

We were caught in the final assembly hall, just in sight of the large roof access hatch. The hatch was jammed open. Beyond it, I could see the glowering sky and the rusted landscape of the roof docks. We began to sprint, but something landed in our path.

The Night Lord rose out of his crouch and smiled at us. His wings of skeletal red light were spread wide, and beat slowly like a billowing cloak. The black-on-black eyes fixed us with a terrible, hungry gaze.

'You should not run,' he said. His voice was a brittle, icy hiss, the one I had heard at the side door of the muniment room. 'You belong to us. You are chattels of the College. This was the deal.'

'I made no deal,' I replied, stricken with dread.

'Your mistress did,' he hissed. 'Where is she? She does not answer her name. You will tell us where she is hiding.'

Renner was carrying the xenos pistol in his hand. He simply jerked it up to shoot the monster.

Or tried to. The Night Lord was immeasurably faster than any human reflex. He snapped out with his saintie, just a blur, and the mace head smashed Renner's hand, hurling the pistol out of his grip and high into the air. I heard it clatter to rest in a distant corner of the hall.

Renner dropped to his knees in agony. The bones of his hand were broken. He clutched it to his chest, moaning with pain, his eyes screwed shut.

The Night Lord licked his lips with a dark, pointed tongue and tutted.

'Try not to be an idiot,' he said. He swirled the saintie, another blur, and brought it to rest smartly, upright against his right shoulder, his left hand low at his hip, fingers spread. The first position, or 'closed guard' in all the treatises on saintie form. I had never got the knack of it.

The Night Lord took a slow step towards us. I tried to pull Renner to his feet without taking my eyes off the menacing Astartes.

'I don't know you,' he said. He took another step closer, then suddenly recoiled, as though he had encountered a revolting odour. He had come close enough for the full measure of my blankness to affect him.

'I *do* know you,' he murmured, correcting himself. 'The blacksoul wretch. The pariah girl who cast us from the room last night.'

His saintie moved as a blur again, and stopped with the spear tip extended at my throat, as if he meant to chuck me under the chin with the blade. Seventh position, caution and restrain. I did not move.

'Are you Ordo?' he asked, in his brittle-glass voice. 'Are you Ordo, girl?'

'What would it matter if I was?' I replied. 'I do not think your brotherhood heeds the command of the Ordos.'

'Very much not,' he said. The blade at my neck did not waver. 'But I am interested. Interested in who you walk with, who you serve, and how you come to be in the company of Zoya Farnessa.'

Again, the name. It almost amused me. She had cheated them, and left them no hook to catch her with.

'You pursue her with great diligence,' I said.

'She is valuable.' He sniffed. 'Information. Precious secrets. The vulnerabilities of the Orphaeonic Tyrant. So begin with your name.'

'I know yours,' I said boldly.

'Do you indeed?' he replied. He kept the spear tip to my throat, but brushed his long grey hair back from his face with his left hand. The fingers were long, like claws. His black eyes gleamed with magpie curiosity.

'I know the name of your company,' I said, 'that which summons you out of the very air. And I know yours too.'

It was a fifty-fifty chance. I remembered the looping words Tancredo had spoken in the stasis field.

'Zephyr,' I said.

He frowned, disappointed.

'Or Xarbia. It's Xarbia.'

The Night Lord chuckled, and spun the saintie into sixteenth rest position across his shoulder.

'Sadoth Xarbia, once a lord of midnight,' he said, with the warmth of an ice floe, 'now of the Collegia Immateria.' He executed a mocking bow, but the resting saintie was ever a nanosecond away from third position, slicing sweep.

'I cannot imagine why you would stand with the likes of the Iron Tenth,' I said.

'I imagine there is much of everything you find unfathomable, pariah-girl,' he replied.

I had Renner upright. He was shaking with pain, but I kept my arm around him to steady him. This was possibly our chance. I had manoeuvred the Night Lord into giving me an edge.

'You will let us pass unharmed, Sadoth Xarbia,' I said.

His black-on-black eyes widened in surprise. He began to shake with bewilderment. Then he burst out laughing, a sound like icicles raked on tin.

'Did you think you had my name, and thus power over me? Power to command me?' he asked through his mirth. 'Sadoth Xarbia is not my true name. It has no force in it. No one gives their true name. Sadoth Xarbia is but the name I was given when I was inducted into the Collegia at the first degree through the rite of proposition.'

I tried not to let my disappointment show.

'And your fine institution boasts only the six of you?' I asked. 'Just a meagre six fellows?'

His face fell.

'There were more once,' he hissed. 'Time, and war with the Tyrant, take their toll. Few of us remain, but our bond is ancient. It was born from the ashes of Isstvan.'

'Yet... you are peculiarly composed in opposition,' I said.

'Opposition?' he scoffed. 'We can scarcely bear the reek of each other! But we are, all the same, blood-sons, are we not? Brothers born of one bastard line.'

'But brothers fight,' I pushed. 'Families squabble.'

'Not when the cause is united,' he began, 'and not when Tizcan sorcery compels the wills of those reluctant or–'

His sentence never finished. There was a brutal crack of bone, and Xarbia reeled aside, tumbling across the deck. The majestic Raven Guard Space Marine stood there, lowering one of his forked swords, glaring at the Night Lord in contempt. His massive crow wings furled against his back.

'You talk too much, Xarbia,' said the voice from his black beak of a helmet. 'You spill cursed secrets.'

Xarbia pulled himself up. The anger in his face was like a beacon fire. There was a bloody gash across his left cheek.

'It is not your place to chastise me, Zephyr,' he spat, and then became a blur entirely. His saintie, an extension of his form, lanced at the Raven Guard, who wrapped it away with a twist of his blade. Faster than the eye could follow, the two were trading blows, metal on metal.

'Move your arse, Lightburn!' I snapped.

I ran, leading the injured Renner down the deck in a rush towards the open hatch.

I looked back. The two visitors had already broken their violent brawl and seen our escape. They were cursing each other freely as they turned to pursue us. I hurled the remaining grenade, praying that I might catch them both in another stasis loop and snare them fast for a minute at least.

The grenade bounced and rolled along the deck to meet them. They both saw it coming and leapt back, wings opening to loft them away and clear.

The grenade went off.

It was not a stasis bomb.

The blast filled the centre part of the assembly hall with a slamming fireball that shredded the deck, and ripped a shockwave in all directions. Xarbia was blown I know not where, eclipsed by the outflung flames. The other, Zephyr, was thrown sideways like a fly swatted from the air, and struck a stack of freight containers. He crumpled their sides, fell, and they toppled onto him.

Though we were further from the epicentre, the searing blast felled us too. I was hurled clear through the open hatch onto the rusted platform outside. Renner was pummelled down by air-shock just inside the doorway. He cried out. He had landed badly on his broken hand, and renewed pain tore through him.

Dazed, I rose.

'Get up! Get up!' I yelled. I staggered back to reach him, but he was already on his feet, despite the crippling hurt. He shambled forward to catch me up.

'Wait!' I yelled, at the very last second. From outside, I could see the witch-marks on the hatch's corroded sill. I had the moldavite charm, Renner did not.

I fought to pull it off over my head. It caught on my coat's collar.

Renner waited, desperately repeating my name. Behind him, beside the pool of roaring flame left by the grenade, the toppled containers stirred. Zephyr clawed his way out from under them, tossing the wreckage aside.

I got the charm off, and threw it across the doorway to Renner. Encumbered by his broken hand, he missed the catch. The charm fell on the deck. He scrambled to grab it, gasping in pain, made awkward by his injury.

Ten metres behind him, Zephyr powered into a running jump, his carrion wings opening wide. He soared down the assembly hall towards us, dropping low to make the strike.

'Renner!'

His good hand found the charm, scooped it up, and then he threw himself forward through the hatchway. The Raven Guard was diving, just inches from his back.

But he did not pass through the doorway.

Without the charm on his person, Zephyr of the Raven Guard was arrested in mid-air, as though by an invisible net. He shrieked in agony as he was thrown backwards. The glyphs on his sheened backplate flared and went out, and his terrifying crow wings vanished in a blink. He hit the deck, his split-tip swords clattering away from him, and lay very still.

I pulled Renner to his feet. We didn't speak. His pain was so great his mouth was clamped tight. We fled.

The shipyard was a ruin, open to the sky. The sky above us was storm black, and clouds of smoke from the burning building below us poured up over the lip of the structure and blew back across the port. To either hand stood cadaverous cranes and derricks, the rusted bones of old machines, the decomposing carcasses of ancient vessels.

I saw the part-ruined cargo hall to our right – the closest, it seemed, to the roof access. That was how she'd described it. Inside, amid clutter and the slow collapse of decades, we found a bank of freight elevators. They were large, oblong cage cars, ribbed with steel bars and mesh, made for bulk cargoes. They stood inside iron frames, cages within cages, the heavy gearing filling the roof space above them. None of them looked like they worked.

'This?' Renner groaned in disbelief.

'One of them,' I promised. Unless she had lied.

I hurried along the line of them, searching for a mark or number. They were numbered, but only with the stamp-printed Administratum plates, most of which had become disfigured or illegible. Two cars were missing entirely, their empty shafts yawning into nothing. Broken cables hung like dead snakes, an alarming sign of neglect.

Then I saw it. One car, in the middle of the bank. Its plate number had been scratched at and altered to read '119'. The car's cage frame and collapsible metal gate were tagged with witch-marks.

'The charm!' I called. Renner, still hugging his fractured hand to his chest, tossed it to me carefully. I snatched it out of the air, put it on, and heaved the old outer gate open, its metal ribs concertinaing tight with a squeal of bare metal. Then I hauled the inner one open just the same.

'Renner! Come on!' I called.

He could not. Sadoth Xarbia had soared into the cargo hall and landed, silent as a butterfly, between us. He was blocking any chance Renner had of reaching me.

The Night Lord turned to regard me. His wings quivered, like the whirring of a moth. Their red, skeletal fans seemed to beat from within, like blood pulsing in capillaries. His grey hair was scorched. There were burns on the flesh of his face.

'You will not leave us without a proper goodbye,' he said.

He took a step towards me.

'You threw a bomb at me,' he hissed. 'I do not think our leave-taking will be friendly.'

Xarbia had lost his saintie. His long hands, at his sides, made a sound like spring-locks setting. Steel claws, each one a dagger, slotted out of his gauntlet-backs and covered his fingers, making the clawlike digits into true talons.

I had nothing left. My pistol, still holstered, would be useless against him, and I could hardly fight an Astartes armed only with a blinksword. There was nothing in my pockets except a leaking perfume bottle and a calfskin purse, now almost empty.

As he lunged at me, I wrenched out the purse and all but spilled the contents at him. The three or four glass pebbles remaining bounced off his face and chestplate. Two shattered.

Xarbia reeled backwards as though I had tossed acid in his face. He gurgled and hissed, and fell to one knee. The psykanic negation of the flects had stripped him of sorcerous trappings, and stricken him with pain. His opalescent armour lost its lustre and went dull, no matter how the light caught it. His great red wings winked away into nothing. He was choking, throttled by his own blood, which spilled out of his lips. I could smell the rancid, animal stink of him, now the glamour was gone.

I jumped into the elevator. Renner hurried to me, his face drained of all colour. I threw him the charm, and he put it on and stepped into the car beside me. Xarbia, on his knees, spat and hawked blood, and tried to get up.

I slammed the inner cage-gate. There was no time for the outer. Renner was trying to pull the lever that initiated power. I pushed him and his fumbling aside, yanked it across, and heard the hum and whirr of mechanisms engaging. I thumped the lowest marker of the elevator panel. The button lit, amber, then green.

There was a pause; the cage car shivered, swaying in the tight throat of the shaft. Then, with a lurch, the gears began to wind, and the car began to descend. It was a rapid plunge that put my heart in my mouth. I steadied myself, and saw a last glimpse of the crippled Xarbia, spewing blood in a hunched, foetal position, before the rising deck blocked him from view.

We rattled down the shaft, as though we were descending into hell. It was very dark, and the ancient mechanism was alarmingly noisy. Each floor passed with a strobe of cold twilight. Renner leant back against the cage wall of the car, barely able to stand. His hand – he clutched it by the wrist with the other to keep it clear of any impact – was buckled in the most horrible way. I looked at him, to say something encouraging.

There was a hard, metallic impact, and the whole car shook. Xarbia had landed on the roof of the descending elevator. He peered down at us through the cage roof, his talons scraping at the bars and mesh.

'A proper goodbye,' he hissed. There was murder in his black-on-black eyes. He began to tear and rake the mesh apart to get at us.

I drew the Tronsvasse, and emptied the entire magazine up through the roof of the cage. The gunfire was deafening in the confines of the shaft. Spent brass, hot as coals, spat from the slide and pinged off the bars and the floor. The cage roof stopped some of my shots. Others punched through and spanked off his warplate. He yelped and flinched, but I couldn't hit his face. With a cackle, he resumed his frantic clawing and sawing at the top of the plummeting car.

I kept control. I ejected the empty magazine from the Kal40's grip, and swiftly slotted in my pre-loaded spare. I resumed firing, aiming the gun up with both hands, but this time I was more selective. I fired single shots, shifting my feet to move position, trying to get a line on his head. He ducked and weaved, cursing me at every shot that flew out past him or flattened against his armour. His claws dug into the cage roof and began to peel it back.

I edged sideways, my eyes on him, and found a shot, clear at his brow. His taloned fist ripped down through the car's roof and seized the pistol as it fired, robbing my line. The Tronsvasse crumpled like foil as he squeezed.

I let go, of course. But I kept my right hand raised nevertheless, and urged the weight of the blinksword into it. The sword appeared, instantly stabbed through mangled ceiling, its conjured form taking precedence over existing matter. Xarbia yelped. The blade had blinked into place inside the reach of his down-stretched hand, through his right pauldron, and drawn an incision across his right cheek and ear. He wore a bloody scar to match the one Zephyr had given him.

His cursing became furious and grimly obscene. The Raven Guard had warned him for sharing secrets, but now he shared all of them, every last, bloody, appalling detail of how he planned to punish and dispose of me. He clawed down at me, almost all of his right arm inside the car. I tried to pull the sword free, but it was stuck fast through the indomitable ceramite of his shoulder guard. I held on. As he pulled and thrashed, I found myself briefly lifted off the floor of the car, clinging to the hilt.

His talons swung for me. I blinked the sword away, and dropped out of his reach.

I shouted for Renner. He still had the heavy Mastoff assault-auto slung across his back, a weapon with considerably more rounds and penetrative power than my pistol.

He staggered forwards, fighting the sway and shudder of the travelling lift, and tried to unship the weapon from his back, but with one hand useless, the strap and weight were tangling him. I grabbed him. I could not detach the gun from him, but I managed to twist the strap around his body so that it was in front of him. He raised it, bracing the barrel with his left hand, though his right hand was never going to fire it. I hugged myself to him, my chest to his back, and hooked my right arm under his, seizing the grip. He tilted the barrel up with his left hand, and I pulled the trigger. Locked together, just out of reach of Xarbia's grasping, scything hand, we fired it at the ceiling.

The pistol had been deafening. The Mastoff's throaty discharge made it feel as though we were inside a steam hammer. The muzzle leapt with barking gouts of orange flash. Spent casings showered the car like hailstones, rebounding from every surface. The furious fire-rate chewed into the roof, puncturing solid panels, and busting through the cage mesh. Xarbia howled in anguish as the pummelling gunfire, almost point-blank, hit him multiple times. His arm snapped back and out as he rolled on the moving roof, trying to evade.

Our shots also struck something structural. A gear, perhaps, or some cable support. Something snapped, and the entire car tilted significantly into one corner. We both reeled with it across the new slope, still clinging together. Misaligned now, out of its true fit in the tight channel of the shaft, the car, still descending at speed, began to rake the walls of the shaft with both its raised lower corner and, on the opposite side, its dropped upper corner. It did this with an unremitting screech of tortured, abrading metal, great flurries of sparks spraying from the grinding points of contact.

The Mastoff was spent. At frantic cross purpose, Renner and I struggled to remove the bulk magazine and replace it with the spare from his belt pouch. Over the scream of the scraping descent, I heard Xarbia laughing again. I got the bulk-mag, turned it, and tried to slot it into the Mastoff as Renner attempted to brace the weapon steady.

Xarbia tore the mangled lid of the car open, creating a hole large enough for his reaching arm, one shoulder, and his cackling head. He lunged down at us, talons carving close to our faces. There was no space to back up.

The whole car lurched and shivered again. Xarbia, just inches from us, wore a sudden look of surprise as he was plucked back through the hole in the roof. Something happened above us, a frenzied turmoil of movement and violence. I heard blows traded, and weight shifting with such force, the elevator rocked, rattled and swung, scraping other travelling edges and corners against the passing shaft.

Blood squirted down into the car at our feet. Then it dripped and came in other places. I broke from Renner, and stepped forward, staring up at the ceiling to try to make sense of what was happening. A torn white feather fluttered down through the hole towards my face.

I could see them now. Sadoth Xarbia and Comus Nocturnus locked in visceral conflict on the roof of the car. They grappled and clawed at each other in transhuman madness, the doubled might of two Astartes clashing to kill. Xarbia's talons dug into the angel's white flesh, and blood leaked down him. Comus' huge hands tore away the broken pauldron, and then swung it, striking Xarbia repeatedly in the side of the head. Xarbia punched, smashing Comus sideways into the car's main hoist mechanism. Shredded feathers flew. The car's roof began to buckle. Xarbia pinned Comus by the face, claws splayed, and tried to tear out the angel's throat with his teeth. Comus grabbed him by the neck, began to throttle him, then slammed his face into the hoist ironwork that Xarbia had pinned him against. Comus kicked the Night Lord away. The kick threw Xarbia across the car and into the wall of the shaft. But the car was still descending rapidly, and the shaft wall, moving past, was like a rockcrete treadmill. The impact carried Xarbia up for a second, then flipped him entirely, end over end. He landed flat on the car's roof, face down, blood streaming through the broken grille. The ferocious, abrasive impact with the wall had done great damage. His armour was scraped and chipped, and some parts had been torn clean off. In the strobing light, I saw his face pressed against the mesh, his pale cheek flattened and dimpled by the wire grille, one black-on-black eye staring down at me. I could not tell if he was alive or dead.

It hardly mattered. Braced for balance, Comus stooped over him, grabbed him, and threw him up again, right over his head. Again, the Night Lord struck the rising, rushing shaft wall. His limp form spiralled, like a broken doll, cartwheeling, spun by the impact force. As he turned, one arm caught the moving, fast-running main cables of the elevator, and they spun him wildly yet again, counter-rotating him in a brutal, helpless flip. He struck the shaft wall again with bone-cracking force, but did so as we dropped past another floor level. I saw him hit the rockcrete lip of the passing floor, carried past it into the open mouth of the floor's boarding chamber. I got one last glimpse of a leg, and one hand, draped lifelessly from the lip where he had come to rest, and then he was lost in the darkness above us.

Shrieking, the lift rattled on. Comus looked down at me through the torn roof. He was covered in gore.

'You came,' I called up.

'I smelled blood.'

'Plenty of that today,' I replied.

There was a thump, a bang of gears. The elevator shuddered, and then jolted us all as it suddenly softened its descent.

It came to rest.

Outside lay some dank and squalid cargo dock, strewn with garbage. I yanked open the inner and then outer cage gates, and stepped out. I tossed the charm back to Renner and stood, with blinksword drawn, on watch, as he put it on and limped out after me. The angel tore open the mesh side wall of the shaft's guard cage, and leapt down beside me.

'Can you fly?' I asked.

'Not in here,' he replied. He looked around. 'There's light ahead,' he said, though my eyes could not discern it. 'An exit to the street.'

'Childeric Pass,' I said.

Just as she had promised.

We turned to help Renner, and headed for the street.

CHAPTER 25

Be careful what you wish for

I crossed the courtyard of the Academy Hecula as light rain began to fall. It was early evening. Lightburn walked at my side. There were few students around. The incident at Stanchion House the previous day had thrown the whole city into consternation, and certain curfews and restrictions had been put in place by the authorities. The news sheets were full of wild stories: of invasion, of gang war, of insurgency, of misadventure. All were wrong. I doubted the authorities knew what had left Stanchion House burning, or who, if anyone, had walked away from the calamity alive.

For my part, I knew of only three: myself, Lightburn and the angel. I had no idea how the battle had been resolved, or who had prevailed. We had kept ourselves out of sight, not even risking a return to the nameless house in Feygate. There had been no contact from Gideon or the rest of his team. The district around Stanchion House had been evacuated and cordoned. There was a heavy presence of arbitrators and city watch in the streets, and talk of another war looming.

The cobbles of the wide courtyard gleamed wet in the trailing light. A handful of students hurried down the lamp-lit portico to find shelter from the rain. The clock above the yard sounded the quarter.

We entered via the lodge, and were directed to an upper reading room by a sleepy porter. We aroused no suspicion in him. We had cleaned up, and dressed decently. I wore a bodyglove and a long coat, Renner a set of pressed tan fatigues and a greatcoat, as one might expect of an ex-military lifeward escorting a young, female academic. Renner wore his right arm in a sling under his coat, the coat sleeve empty. I had done my best to clean, set and splint his broken hand. I am no medicae, but the essentials of battlefield aid had been part of my Cognitae schooling.

Our retreat from Stanchion House had been to the cargo-8 parked in a side street some way from the old port, the vehicle we had used to embark upon the mission. We stripped it of everything we could – medi-pack, clean clothes, a few small-arms, and then dumped it in a vacant lot behind Storax Place. We tried to break the thread of our progress as much as possible, in case anyone was following us.

Comus assured us no one was. He had stayed with us for a while, trudging the streets in our wake with, at my insistence, a dirty tarpaulin we had found in the cargo dock draped around him. He left us once we had reached the vehicle. I asked him to stay close, and he gave me a nod. The streets of Queen Mab were no place for a creature like him, but from the secret landscape of the rooftops, he could watch over us without being seen.

I had decided to press on with the leads I had left.

'Violetta, my dear,' said Mam Matichek, rising from her seat as we entered the reading room. She was, as ever, disposed in a black crepe dress and lace gloves, but over this she wore the purple gown and untied white cravat of a tutor-fellow.

It was a pleasant enough room, comfortable and inviting, lined floor to ceiling with shelves of books and manuscripts. There were several old, leather club chairs, with side tables, and the room was warmed by a fire burning in the grate. She had lit the table lamps and closed the shutters against the approaching night. The smell of her lho-sticks hung in the air. The chamber shared the same musty, scholarly feel that pervaded the entire Academy. It was the city's oldest and most respected seat of learning.

'I apologise, mam,' I said, squeezing her proffered hand, 'that I was unable to make our appointment yesterday.'

'And no wonder,' she replied sardonically. 'Whatever was that business at the old port? The whole city is a-chatter. The King stirs.'

'I'm sorry?'

'My dear, the old battle hymn? "When plight upon Angelus falls, King Orphaeus stirs from sanctum deep..." la dum dee da dee dum.'

'Oh, that.'

'Patriotic legends offer us reassurance,' she said. 'Well, not me. But the common folk lap it up. I've heard it sung three times today. Orphaeus will rise from his eternal rest and come to save us from the approaching war, whoever we're fighting this time. I honestly don't think anyone remembers who the enemy was *last* time. Anyway, a derelict building burns down, and there are mysterious explosions, and everyone decides a war's under way and Orphaeus will come to save us, as he always does. Stops them rioting in the streets, I suppose. You look different today.'

She had placed her hands on my shoulders to look me up and down. She didn't seem to disapprove so much as be surprised. I certainly looked nothing like the Violetta Flyde she had met twice before.

'I like your hair short,' she remarked. 'The coat and bodyglove are quite masculine, though you pull it off. I have no idea of fashions these days. I have worn the same cut of gown for the last thirty years. And my hair, though it was once auburn. Too wet for a dress, is it?'

'I decided–'

'What have you done to your hand, young man?' she said, cutting me off, and crossing to Renner, who was waiting by the door.

'Oh, a little... altercation, mam,' Renner mumbled.

Mam Matichek looked sharply at me.

'Do you come in disguise, Violetta?' she asked. 'Are you in some sort of trouble?'

'I could not make our appointment yesterday,' I replied gently. 'But you were kind enough to give me your card, and courteous enough to respond to my message that we reschedule.'

'I'm simply worried about Freddy,' she said. 'These are strange days. Yesterday's goings-on troubled him.'

'Do you know what happened in The Shoulder that night?' I asked.

'Oh, some brawl in the public bar, I hear,' she replied, lighting a lho-stick in her silver pinch-holder. 'I stay out of it. Though I hear it was Timurlin. Drunk again, no doubt. He is such a troublemaker. No wonder we've seen neither hide nor hair of him since. I didn't see *you* again, though. Did you witness it?'

'My bodyguards escorted me away,' I replied. 'Public brawls are no place for a respectable married lady. So, Freddy? Is he here?'

She nodded.

'I persuaded him to come. Well, Unvence and I did. Come through.'

She drew aside a panelled partition door and led us into an adjoining room. This too was lit by hearth and lamps, though the lamps were shrouded with felt cloths and provided only under-light. There was a long, polished table, set with several chairs and stacked with several piles of books. At the end of the room was a large bay window, with a beautiful antique astronomy scope set up on the bay-step. The shutters were open, and twilight hung outside.

Unvence got up from his seat at the table as I entered, and bowed his ungainly form at me with unnecessary formality. Freddy Dance, rather dishevelled, was sitting at the table too, but he did not rise. He was turning the pages of an astral gazetteer that he couldn't possibly read, a glass of amasec close by him.

'How is he?' I asked.

'Agitated, mam,' said Unvence solemnly.

'As ever,' said Mam Matichek. 'We're quite concerned for his mental wellbeing.'

'I'll see what I can do,' I said. I crossed to the table and sat down beside Freddy Dance. He seemed oblivious to me. Mam Matichek and Unvence looked on, with Renner, from the doorway.

'Sir?' I said, quietly, leaning close to him. 'It's Violetta. Do you remember me?'

Dance cocked his head, turning to me with his ears and not his eyes.

'Mamzel Flyde,' he said, in a tiny voice. 'Quite a puzzle, quite a puzzle.'

'I am sorry that my casual enquiry has thrown you into such confusion, sir.'

'No,' he said. 'No. No, mamzel. A puzzle is welcome. A distraction. I have not been distracted by anything for a long time. Not by anything good. Your aunt died. At one hundred and eighteen.'

'She did, sir.'

'One hundred and eighteen,' he said, tilting his head again and turning the pages of the book. 'Not the number in question. Fascinating in its own right, of course. One hundred and eighteen was the precise number of treatises written, in his lifetime, by Saint Corustine, upon all matters of philosophy, natural and miraculous–'

'I hear my question has confounded you and become an obsession, sir,' I said. 'Your friends worry for you. You take no food–'

He raised a hand.

'Knowledge is nourishment,' he said. 'It feeds us. A fine feast of facts and figures. I am sustained, Mamzel Flyde. And I am glad you have come. I am not confounded. No, not at all. I have written it all down.'

He laid his hands on the open pages of the star atlas, and stroked them with his fingertips.

'In my notebook here, you see?' he said. I bit my lip.

'Did you build me a cipher, sir? A key?'

'You are the key, mamzel.'

'I am?'

He sat back, staring upwards with his blind eyes, smiling, his head switching to and fro.

'I have made a start, as you may see from my notebook,' he said. 'But I cannot build a complete key without further information, without context, you see? Which only you can provide.'

'I understand,' I said. 'And I think I may be able to do that. But before I do, tell me what you have fathomed so far. I fear I will need to concentrate to keep up with your reasoning. I am no scholar of maths.'

I was cautious still. Freddy Dance might be a mad genius, or simply mad, and I was reluctant to share the book with him until I had decided which. Further, I had no wish to break the clearly secret confidence between him and Unvence in front of witnesses.

Dance put his gnarled hand on mine gently, as if he sensed my unease and wished to reassure me.

'Not just mathematics, dear child,' he murmured. 'Symbolism, secrets, many things.'

'Many things?'

'Yes. I have considered it carefully, and I believe 119 does not mean anything. It means *many* things. All at once. It is a mystic symbol, in numeric form. It is a hypersigil. Do you know that term?'

'I do, sir,' I replied warily.

'Then you know more than you appear to know, Mamzel Flyde,' he said. The old fellow seemed impressed with me. 'A hypersigil, or hyperglyph, compresses many significances into one concentrated form,' he said. 'It binds multiple meanings into one.'

'I would be happy, sir,' I said, 'with just one meaning.'

'Well,' he laughed, 'that is hard to provide, for they are inextricably bonded to each other. You desire a key for your cipher, but to have a functioning key, the *right* key, one must, so to speak, know every cut and notch on it. We must untie the sigil, you see? Let me do that for you, little by little. First, let us consider prime numbers. A prime number is simply a number, greater than one, that is divisible only by itself and one. Prime numbers hold an exquisite fascination for scholars like me. They obsess us and, yes, I know I am more prone to obsession than many.

'Why do they do so? Well, the definition of a prime number is deceptively simple. As you count up from one, it's impossible to predict when the next prime number is going to occur, and as the numbers grow very big, it actually becomes more and more difficult even to determine if a given number is actually prime. Prime numbers underpin the Imperium in some quite significant ways. Since before the Dark Age of Technology, the encryption used to protect communication, financial transactions and data transfer has made use of prime numbers, although in very different ways over the millennia. Prime numbers allow you, in theory, to encode all the knowledge in the universe in a single very large number... Though I haven't done it myself, I understand the means.'

'You... do?'

A smile crossed his face. Though he could not see me, no flicker of a smile crossed mine. He had just described a process of encoding that was strikingly similar to the way Enuncia had been explained to me.

'The thing is, mamzel,' he said, 'most mathematically inclined people have an instinct for whether a number is a prime or not. And, instinctively, 119 looks *very* much like a prime number. An unusual number of totatives. But here's the rub. Every other combination of those three digits is prime. 911 is prime. 191 is prime. 119611 – combining 119 with itself, turned upside down, you see? – is prime. But 119, that tricky deceiver, is *not*. 119 equals 17 times 7. Are you following?'

'I am,' I said.

'So... 119 looks like a number of great power, part of the mysterious brotherhood of primes. But it's an imposter. It's a semiprime number *posing* as a prime number. It's a mathematical oddity.'

'And that's important?'

'Any oddity in the field of mathematics is important. Now, come, come.' He rose to his feet, unsteady, and I rose too, taking him by the arm to support and guide him, though he was most certainly leading the way. He walked me over to the fine astronomical telescope in the window bay, reaching out his hands blindly to locate it, then grasp it, then caress it as a reassuring object.

'This is my scope,' he said. 'I did almost all of my significant work with this. Even the observations that led to my disgrace.'

'You mean *Of the Stars in the Heaven, with ephemeris*?' I asked.

'Yes,' he chuckled. 'That.'

'Pardon me, sir, but you cannot see. How did you make observations?'

'The glass never lies,' he said, and stooped to peer through the eyepiece. 'I do not see conventionally, not any more. The observations for that book, my masterwork, eroded my sight. They were *other* stars, you see? Stars of elsewhere, yet here.'

'And where might that elsewhere be, sir?' I asked, with a great effort to sound innocent.

'The King's realm,' replied Freddy Dance.

I have, in telling you this story, mentioned the King many times, so many, I am sure, that you are overfamiliar with the name. However, I feel I need to stress the importance of his remark. For many months, I had been in the company of people who spoke of the King, or referred to him, as a fact. But they had all been agents of the Inquisition, or the Cognitae, or otherwise privy to the dark secrets of Sancour. We accepted it, just as the course of this narrative has persuaded *you* to accept it. Yet to the common folk of Sancour, even educated persons like Freddy Dance, or Mamzel Matichek, the King in Yellow was no more than a fairy tale, if they had heard of him at all.

Here now was a man, mad though he might be, firmly speaking of the King as matter-of-fact, and connecting the name to a wealth of clues that had not yet been unscrambled.

It was his tone, I think, the surety in his voice. Freddy Dance was not a madman who had accidentally glimpsed the truth. He was a man who had discovered a truth that had *driven* him mad. I understood his madness, and feared that it might be my fate too one day, and the fate of all of us pursuing that truth. The answers, when they came, might be more than our minds could bear.

So Violetta Flyde faltered at that moment, hearing those words from him. Penitent, the novice inquisitor, yearned to step forward and formally take control of the moment. Yet Mam Matichek was there, and Unvence, and I was keenly aware of the bafflement and disapproval with which they were watching me. I wanted to protect myself, and Freddy too, but the truth, which had remained so elusive to me, and to Gregor and to Gideon, seemed at last to be in grasping distance. I made my choice.

Softly, I said, 'The King?'

Dance continued to stare through the eyepiece. 'Yes, mamzel. The King in Yellow. I find, as the years pass, that everything leads back to him, sooner or later.'

'So the stars you saw, and wrote of in your book,' I said carefully, 'these stars of elsewhere... Might they be the stars of an extimate space?'

He straightened up again, with a quizzical expression.

'Quite so. Quite so. Extimate space. My dear, you are a puzzle to be unlocked too, if you know of such things.'

'I believe I am,' I said. 'Your observations, sir? They ended your sight... And your career?'

'They didn't like it,' he replied, neglecting to specify who 'they' were. 'None of them. Told me I was mad, seeing firmaments that were not present, but I knew the real reason. They didn't like that I'd seen them. They didn't like that I'd spied into the King's private heavens.'

'Mamzel Flyde,' Mam Matichek hissed from across the room. 'I wonder at you! You indulge him with such nonsense! I fear you are overexciting–'

I held up an index finger in her direction, instructing silence.

'Continue please, sir,' I said to Dance.

'Happily. You see the scope here?' Dance asked me. He reached for my hands, and I allowed him to place them on the apparatus. Below the main scope was an ancient mechanical keyboard by which coordinates and angles might be pre-set.

'The keyboard?' he asked me. 'You feel it there?'

'I do, sir.'

'So then,' he said, 'I mentioned archaic technologies just now. I am fascinated by the way aspects of old technology survive, and sometimes get carried forward even after the technology itself is obsolete or forgotten. Especially here on Sancour. Tell me, what are the values on the keys there, from the top left?'

I began to read them, 'Q, W, E, R… as it is on all keyboards.'

Dance nodded. 'That arrangement of keys was devised so *long* ago, it would shock you. Long before the Dark Age of Technology. It was designed for mechanical writing machines, and we still use it because of familiarity and convenience. The symbol on our vox-devices that means "end link" is based on an old, wired communication system. And distress signals, such as 999 and 911, and 119, to this day, are based on the old mechanisms in telephonic exchanges. To this very day! A trio combination of three 1s or 9s still means "distress" or "emergency" in so very many aspects of our culture.'

'So…' I began, '119 could be an ancient warning symbol, a coded distress call, a reference to an all-but-forgotten expression for "emergency"?'

'Yes, my dear.'

'That's what it is? That's what 119 is?'

'Yes. In part,' he assured me. 'As I told you, it is but one aspect of the sigil. A significant one, I believe. But let us now consider the number in binary form.'

'Binary?' I felt a certain unease. Did this touch on the Mechanicus suspicion of mine?

'Yes, my dear,' he said. 'In binary, 119 is 1110111. The moment I visualised the binary, I regarded the central "0" and exclaimed "the eye"! It is a very compelling visual pattern. And of course, you can have longer and shorter versions – 5 equals 101, 27 equals 11011, 119 equals 1110111, 495 equals 111101111, 2,015 equals 11111011111–'

'Yes,' I interrupted. 'But an eye? You said "the eye".'

'Deeply symbolic,' he admitted. 'The eye has many mytho-symbolic meanings all of its own, but there is one of course, a terrible one, that has a great and menacing bearing on all Imperial fortune.'

Before I could stop to consider this, and contemplate the ramifications of the Eye of Terror, and the warp, and the Traitor Legions stalking the very planet on which we stood, he had moved on yet again.

'That binary pattern of 1s surrounding a zero eye, mamzel, is a pattern that strongly reminded me of another something – *telomeres*.'

'Telomeres?' I asked.

'I'll simplify,' he said, with a wry little chuckle. 'When the cells that make up your body divide, which they do all the time to reproduce, their DNA is copied into the new cell. But the copying process doesn't copy *all* of the DNA chromosome – it leaves out the very ends. So your chromosomes have lots of redundant sequences at each end. These are called telomeres. Every time your DNA is copied, you lose a telomere from each end of each chromosome. So as you get older, the number of telomeres in your cells reduces. This is part of the ageing process. If a cell has too few telomeres, it means it has been copied too many times, which means it may include transcription errors in its DNA. So, the cell is no longer allowed to reproduce.'

'So you think 119 is also a coded reference to genetic copies?' I asked. 'To clones and–'

'Genetic technologies have been fundamental to the Imperium since the Unification Wars of prehistory,' he said. 'They underpin mankind's martial strength.'

And hold a very personal significance to me, I wanted to say, but I refrained.

'I pictured the 1s around the zero as telomeres,' Dance said, 'and perceived a kind of countdown. As you go from 32,639 to 8,127 to 2,015, in the binary form, the number of 1s around the zero decreases as I just described. When you throw away the last pair, you go from 101 to 0. The end. *Death*. Perhaps someone has been counting down generations, using this code. Maybe your 119 is just a step in the countdown. Or maybe it's just a way of measuring the time or generations left until some cataclysm, or some kind of death. 119 is only three steps away from the end...'

I stepped back from him for a moment, and breathed deeply to centre myself. An encoding of universal knowledge was the alleged function of Enuncia, which had been sought by so many for so long. I had witnessed the power of just a fraction of it, a word. It was the grammar, the *grimoire*, from which creation could be spelled out. Had someone transmuted it, or hidden it, in a numerical form? Numbers, I had always been told, were a more efficient medium than words.

My mind swam. Dance had deftly connected a process akin to Enuncia with ideas of ancient distress, a warning, the symbol of the eye, of replicating and eroding genetics, and of a countdown. Gideon had said time was short, and Verner Chase had warned that the hour of the King in Yellow's triumph was almost upon us.

I had been a seeker of the truth of things, all my life long, it seemed, desperate to grasp some genuine meaning. And here was meaning at last, here was true learning, all at once in a great torrent, meaning upon meaning, in such quantity as might bowl me down and wash me away. I felt overwhelmed.

'Then we may consider the other meanings,' said Dance merrily, oblivious to my dazzled affect. He limped back to his chair, took a sip of his drink, and then sat down. 'The individual numerals in 119. 1 and 9 are both square numbers. So 119 represents three squares, two small ones – 1 times 1 – followed by a much larger one – 3 times 3. Visually, what might that represent? Two sons standing at the right hand of their father? Two daughters standing at the right hand of their mother? In numerology, 9 represents love and self-sacrifice. 11, however, is the mythical Iscariot number, the number of betrayal in ancient world-lore. In the Terran proto-religions, a messianic figure called Yeshu was betrayed by his eleventh disciple. But even that is curious, for mythologically, that betrayal was essential. It was, in fact, a pre-ordained act of loyal sacrifice, for without the betrayal, the divinity of the messiah would not have been recognised. I'll come back to that. 9 has other meanings, as I'm sure you know, mamzel–'

'Nine Sons who stood, and Nine who turned,' I said, by rote. *'Nine for the Eight, and Nine against the Eight, Eighteen all to make the Great Cosmos or bring it crashing down.'*

'Aha! You know your Heretikhameron!' Dance exclaimed with delight. 'Exactly. In 9, we see the primarchs, and like the Iscariot number it symbolises simultaneous sacrifice and betrayal. And so to 19. That, like 11, is laden with mystery. For it is whispered that there were once *twenty* immortal primarchs, twenty sons, but two were somehow lost. They have never been named or accounted for. They are, some might reckon, the nineteenth and the twentieth. Although, in fact, by designation they were the second and eleventh. 19, strictly speaking, in Legion order formulation, is the number of Corax of the Raven Guard, and it was also once used as an honorary designation for the original master of the Adeptus Custodes, who in the time of wicked Heresy was reckoned an equal and unofficial primarch. And also, of course, the great Militarum General Lexander Chigurin was affectionately dubbed the "Nineteenth Primarch" after his illustrious campaign of victories during the Scouring. But hermetically, mamzel, *hermetically* 19 is most usually reserved to indicate the missing primarchs. Either of them. It is the number-signifier of the lost, the unmentioned, the nameless, the unspoken, the forgotten.'

I sat down beside him.

'Do you believe, sir,' I asked carefully, hiding the fear in my voice, for this was proscribed knowledge of the most dangerous kind, 'that 119, in some coded way, represents one of the lost primarchs?'

'My dear,' he said, 'for various reasons, I am convinced that the hyper-sigil 119 represents the King in Yellow, and offers a clue to his identity.'

'A missing primarch, sir? Is that what you're saying?'

'I believe I am,' he replied.

CHAPTER 26

Configuration 6,337,338

'That,' said Mam Matichek, 'is quite enough.'

She came to me, all of an agitation, and almost yanked me out of my seat by the sleeve, drawing me aside.

'I hoped you might be a calming influence on him,' she whispered at me, her voice pitched low so that Freddy could not overhear, though I was sure his friends quite underestimated the sharpness of his hearing. 'I requested that you come here and soothe him. My friend is *very* fragile. But instead you yammer at him and make him worse. *Make him speak of heresy.*'

This last she hissed through clenched teeth, almost soundless in its ferocity. 'I think you should go now,' she said.

'That's interesting,' I replied.

'What's interesting?' she asked.

'That you *know* it's heresy,' I said. 'That you know, therefore, that what he speaks of is actually dangerous, and not the mere drivel of a madman.'

Her eyes widened in alarm.

'I didn't say anything–'

'Precisely,' I said. 'You didn't speak to that. Just now, you urged me not to agitate him. But you didn't *question* his agitation. You did not ask, for example, "who is the King?" when Freddy spoke of him.'

'I know the myth,' she answered indignantly. 'We all know the myth. You cannot live in Queen Mab and not know the myth!'

She looked to Unvence for support. The long-limbed clerk had almost plaited himself up in an attitude of discomfort.

'That is true,' he mumbled. 'A myth, no more.'

'No, no,' I countered. 'You both know it's more than that. I believe, *truly*, you're both worried about Freddy's health, but you're also worried what he might say.'

'Well, mam, I don't care what you believe,' said Mam Matichek. 'I think you should go now. I do not think *you* are what you appear to be at all. I took you for a nice young lady with a passing interest in the esoteric, but today – look at you – you come to us barely in that disguise. I see through you, and I will not have it.'

'I think my friend will be the one who decides when it's enough,' said Renner. He remained by the door, his tone just the right side of warning.

'What are you?' Unvence asked us, trembling. 'Are you Magistratum? Are you of the Baron's bureau of investigators? Are we to face charges?'

'We've done nothing wrong, Lynel,' Mam Matichek said. 'We've merely tried to provide some easement to a good friend, and instead–'

She looked at me.

'Please leave, before I summon the bursar and have you removed.'

'My burdener friend is right,' I said, remaining calm. 'I'll leave when I'm done. I bear no ill will towards you, mam, nor to Mr Unvence. For that reason, I will make things plain to you, though I fear it may alarm you more.'

I took the wallet from my coat pocket, opened it, and laid it on the table where they both could see it. Mam Matichek and Unvence gazed at the rosette in quiet terror.

'I am Bequin,' I said. 'I serve the Holy Ordos at the command of the Throne. I require your cooperation, and that cooperation will be noted in my report.'

Unvence covered his gasping mouth with a steeple made of both hands, and took a step back. Mam Matichek uttered a small sound, and sagged as if she might faint. Lightburn helped her to a chair.

'We're ruined,' she murmured.

'You are not ruined,' I said. 'Your cooperation is required, and I... hereby deputise you as my assistants. Now, how do you know of the King in Yellow?'

'One does not,' muttered Mam Matichek, gazing at the rosette, 'frequent such circles as the crowd at Lengmur's, or keep such company as Oztin Crookley, without hearing of such things. Without learning there is some truth behind the silly myths. We meet, we drink, we... talk of secret lore and magics until we quite believe it. It is all in fun, the illicit thrill of transgressive discourse.'

She looked up at me.

'Are we all to be burned for our foolishness?' she asked.

I shook my head.

She sighed. 'I always thought Oztin such a faker, a boaster, a charlatan, pretending he knew forbidden things–'

'He *is* a charlatan,' I said. 'But he, and you, and everyone in this city, I fancy, have stumbled on the truth. More than you know. It is woven into the stones and streets all around us. I seek that truth.'

I looked at Freddy. He was carefully refilling his glass from the decanter, trying to guide one to the other with his hands. I went to him, took the glass and the bottle, and poured it for him.

'You are an inquisitor?' he said.

'Does that frighten you?' I asked.

'Of course. But I'm relieved. You are taking me seriously. No one ever has. I have been mocked and disgraced and accused of madness. But you know. You *know* it's not that. You've come at last, to take this burden from me, and I am glad to give it up. This is the balm my mind needed, Aelsa, not your coddling, though I know you mean it kindly. This young woman knows I am not mad, and I will answer any question she asks, for she is freeing me from my long struggle with my own soul.'

'How do you know?' I asked him. 'How did you connect this to the King in Yellow, Mr Dance? I did not mention his name.'

'You did not have to,' he replied. 'He is real, and he is in everything that we are here, woven into the stones and streets, just as you said. But you speak now, of *speaking*, Mamzel Bequin. You said, "mention his name". As has been established, I am blind. I visualise numbers, for they matter to me and have always been my friends, but I hear them – of course – as words. One-one-nine. You said that to me, in the Two

Gogs. In those words, "one-one-nine". Inevitably, I have considered another approach, one that can only be appreciated by someone *hearing* numbers spoken.'

He grinned, his eyes elsewhere.

'If one expresses one-one-nine as words, mam, it allows us to contemplate an alphabetical order. If you alphabetise all numbers – *all* numbers – as words, do you know which is first on the list?'

I tried to think. 'Tell me.'

'Eight,' he said.

'Eight?' I echoed.

'Eight,' he insisted. 'Eight becomes one, for it is the first place upon the alphabetical list. When numbers are ordered as words, eight becomes one. Now Eight, as we both know, is the name given to those who serve the King. Those who slew Mam Tontelle.'

'So they are known to you too?' I asked.

'Only as a rumour,' said Mam Matichek, appearing at my shoulder. 'It's a most dangerous secret, and no one speaks of it, or pretends to know, but in our quiet circle...' She sighed and looked at me. Her expression was a mix of resignation and sadness. 'Dear Freddy should not be speaking of them aloud.' She patted the old astronomer's shoulder reassuringly. 'These are things that we, even in our private coterie, tend to avoid and ignore for fear of terrible retribution.'

'The Eight killed Mam Tontelle,' I confirmed. 'That was them.'

Unvence let out a little whimper.

'Eight is a number of such significance,' said Dance. 'More even than 9 or 19.'

'Eight for the legs. Eight for the points. Eight because that's what they ate,' I said. 'Eight because it is the symbol-mark of the Archenemy.'

Dance nodded.

'So that's coded there too,' I said. 'Hidden in plain sight in the number 119.'

'Twice,' said Dance, 'suggesting perhaps a mathematical process. One to the power of one, representing, symbolically, eight to the power of eight.'

'Chaos to the power of Chaos?'

'A number not to be taken lightly,' he said.

'So what of the 9?' I asked. 'If 1 and 1 are eight and eight, what is the phonetic value of nine? Where does that place in your alphabetical list?'

'Well, Mamzel Inquisitor,' he replied, 'that depends on the *length* of the list. Eight is always the first on the list, no matter *how* many numbers are included. But the position of nine varies, as does nineteen and one hundred and nineteen. We need to know the length of the list to be certain.'

'Of course,' I said, feeling rather stupid. 'The alphabetical placement changes the more numbers you include. So where would it fall on a list of numbers between, say, one and one hundred and nineteen?'

'You think too small, mam,' he replied. '119 is a hypersigil that is *meant* to be decoded. The number entire, one hundred and nineteen, is perhaps too obvious. Whoever made the sigil expects us to use the parts of it that we *can* unlock to unlock the rest. And the pair of 1s are constants. If they each represent eight, then they are *always* eight. Their place on the list never changes. So we can trust them. And multiply them as I suggested. Eight to the power of eight.'

'Giving us?'

'A very large number,' he said. 'Sixteen million, seven hundred and seventy-seven thousand, two hundred and sixteen. That's not a prime number. In binary, it's 1 followed by twenty-four 0s. It's about as unprime as a number can be. In fact, to the magos mathematicae, it's known as a humble number. If the alphabetical list is that long, and I think it is, then nine comes at…'

He paused, for a very brief moment, as he thought.

'At the six million, three hundred and thirty-seven thousand, three hundred and thirty-eighth place.'

'And the significance of that?' I asked, trying not to be fazed by the speed at which he had made that computation in his head.

'Well, it's not prime,' he replied, with a shrug. 'Beyond that I don't know. I think it's time for me to see your cipher, mam. The mystery text to which 119 is the key. Perhaps I can determine the significance from that.'

'I've brought it with me,' I said, and took the commonplace book out of my coat. Dance took it eagerly, running his hands around it, and putting it to his nose to sniff it.

'Freddy can't read, my dear,' Mam Matichek called out.

'I know,' I said, and glanced at the old astronomer. He was still quite occupied with the book. 'He can't read the book, I agree,' I replied, 'but Mr Unvence can.'

'What good is that going to do?' Mam Matichek asked.

I looked at Unvence.

'Let us not, for now, dwell on how I come to know this,' I said, 'but I am aware of your connection to Mr Dance.'

Unvence frowned at me, dubious and scared in equal measure.

'I won't tell a soul,' I promised, 'but I do need your help, sir.'

'What does she mean?' Mam Matichek asked. 'Lynel? What does she mean?'

'Lynel,' I began, with a look towards Unvence, 'may I call you Lynel, sir? Lynel is Freddy's way of seeing, and has been for a long time. Aren't you, Lynel?'

Unvence seemed ready to bolt for the door.

'Type D-theta-D, passive and singular,' I said. 'You were never tested, were you?'

The shipping clerk couldn't bring himself to reply.

'No one needs to know,' I said. 'You have my word. The word of the Ordos. Will you help me?'

Lynel Unvence cleared his throat. He was, when it came to it, remarkably brave, or else remarkably devoted to his friend. Mam Matichek was looking from him to me and back, in turn, quite fuming.

'I will, mamzel,' said Unvence.

'Thank you,' I replied.

'Help her *how*? Lynel?'

I placed my hand on her arm to gently restrain her, and we watched as Unvence sat in the chair beside his friend. He arranged his long legs as comfortably as the table-height would allow, produced his pince-nez from his pocket, and put them on. Then he took the commonplace book from Freddy's hands, and set it on the table in front of him. He opened it and regarded the inside cover.

'Lilean Chase. Lilean Chase,' said Dance, almost immediately, staring off into nothing. 'There is the "L" and the "C" at once, you see? The "L" and the "C" and the "1" and the "1" and the "9", just as poor Mam Tontelle said. And it is blue. She said that too.'

Unvence gazed at the first intricate page of text. It, like all the other pages, was just a dense block of handwritten and impenetrable glyphs. This I knew from my fruitless study of it.

'What is happening?' Mam Matichek whispered to me.

'Lynel is reading it for him,' I replied.

'I declare everyone has gone mad,' she said.

'Is it written in binaric?' I asked.

'No,' said Dance. 'But that's a good guess, mam.'

'I'm glad you can see why I asked,' I replied, 'and why I was startled by your talk of binary interpretations. I feared it was a connection to the Adeptus Mechanicus.'

'Oh, it is,' he said.

'Tell me how, please? And how you know that?'

'I knew a man,' he said. 'A friend of sorts. He was once a visiting scholar at the Universitariate of Petropolis, on Eustis Majoris, when I was the Reader in Astromathematicae there. This was many, many years ago. We bonded over our mutual love of numbers. I think he quite admired my facility with them, which was flattering. He never said, but I believe he had some past association with the Priesthood of Mars. Perhaps a renegade, an apostate run from their flock. I don't know. I haven't seen him in six decades. At the time we became friends, he quizzed me much about binary notation, and other codes used by machine systems. His name was Godman Stylas.'

'You have never spoken of him, Freddy,' said Mam Matichek.

'I have little cause to bring his memory to mind, Aelsa,' said Dance. 'This was years ago, and he was only around for a matter of months. Very private, very quiet. Very inquisitive, so to speak. But he told me something of the Mechanicus. Taught me things. He claimed the Adeptus used binaric for primary communication, but that they had another language. A secret one, a *sacred* one, I suppose. He called it Hexad. Binary, you see, is a little cumbersome. And our conventional "hundreds-tens-units" notation for numbers is *also* cumbersome, because it doesn't easily convert into binary, and it doesn't conveniently fit into bits and bytes. For fluency, in terms of cogitation machines, it is better to use hexadecimal, or *base-sixteen*, notation. Hex is trivially easy to convert to binary and vice versa. It's a convenient compromise, easy for both people and machines to read. Hexad is a hexadecimally based language the Adeptus Mechanicus uses for its more intimate and secret scriptures. For its spiritual lore, and its holiest texts, those of an Omnissianic nature, if you follow? Godman showed me how it was notated in written form.'

He pointed to the book in Unvence's hands.

'This, Mamzel Bequin, is Hexad. Your cipher is written in the most sacred and consecrated machine-code of the Adeptus Mechanicus.'

'Are you sure, Mr Dance?'

'Oh, yes. I know these glyphs. Few outside the Martian Priesthood do. Besides, there is a symmetry. Suppose 119 is not a decimal number, but a hex number. Well, 119 in hex is 281 decimal. And 281 is deliciously interesting, because to a mathematician like me, it looks obvious that it's not a prime number. But, aha, it is! *Another* imposter. And another part of your hypersigil. The sum of the digits of 119 is 11. The sum of the digits of 281 is also 11.'

'Can you translate the text?' I asked. 'Can you make the key fit?'

'It will take me some time,' said Dance, 'but I believe I can. Hexad is composed in a number of divine configurations. This is how the Mechanicus encrypts its deepest gospels. One has to know which configuration the Hexad is written in, and I think the key tells us. The 1 and the 1, irrefutable, give us the value for 9, and the value for 9 is 6,337,338. This is Hexad Configuration six-three-three-seven-three-three-eight. I can unravel it from that.'

He turned his head in our direction.

'A copy of Trefwell's Tables of Hexadecimal Concordance would make things a little easier,' he said.

'There are copies of that in the library,' said Mam Matichek. 'I'll fetch one at once.' She hurried to the door that led back to the reading room, pulling from her robes a set of keys for the Academy's main library.

'That would certainly speed up my work, Aelsa,' said Dance.

'And what work might that be?' asked a sneering voice.

'Oh shit!' Renner exclaimed. Mam Matichek had slid open the door into the reading room. Oztin Crookley, flushed and clearly foul-tempered, stood behind it, staring in at us. Mam Matichek made to close the door and keep him out, but Crookley pushed past her. I could see Aulay hovering outside in the reading room, peering in.

'Well, this is a fine little assembly,' said Crookley, looking at us all. He stuck his hands in the pockets of his embroidered, high-throated waistcoat, and puffed out his chest like a disapproving scholam-master surprising miscreants after lights-out. But I could see the slight sway in him, and smell the alcohol sweating from his pores.

'Very nice, very cosy,' he remarked unpleasantly.

'This conversation is private,' said Renner.

'Screw your private,' Crookley retorted, glancing at Renner with disdain. 'The Two Gogs has reopened. We were all to meet. Aulay and I have been there two hours, and not a sign of you. Not a sign of you! My own *friends*.'

I had heard stories of Crookley's foul moods, especially when in his cups. His charming charisma could turn on a knife-edge and become boorish and petulant, especially when he felt he was not the centre of attention he believed he should be.

'A little private meeting of friends, is it?' he asked. 'A little rendezvous of pals, all together, prattling secrets to each other behind my back? Why wasn't I invited? Why d'you leave me and Aulay sitting in the Gogs like a pair of spare eunuchs at an orgy?'

He looked at me.

'You'd steal my friends from me, would you, Mamzel Flyde?' he asked.

'That's not her name, Oztin,' Mam Matichek cut in.

'I don't shitting care what her name is,' he replied. He stared at me, making an effort to focus. 'I invite you into my circle, you little tart, you and that strange husband of yours, I offer you the hand of bloody friendship, and this is what you do? Steal my friends away as your own little retinue?'

'Stop it, Oztin,' said Mam Matichek.

'I bloody won't,' said Crookley, and advanced towards me.

'I suggest, Mr Crookley, you calm down,' I said.

'I suggest you–' He paused, then waved his hand, unable to form a suitably biting retort. Instead, he pushed past me, took up Freddy's drink, and knocked it back in one. 'What's your game then, "Violetta"? Eh? Eh? What have you been saying about me behind my back?'

'Step out, sir,' I said. 'Step out, or shut up.'

'Wooooo!' he said, play-acting scared. 'Or what? Or what, eh? You going to hurt me, are you? You or that one-armed ninker you call a lifeward? I've broken young fillies bigger than you, my girl. I've spanked them for disobedience, and they've thanked me for it.'

'Oztin!' Mam Matichek almost shrieked. He looked at her, and she glared meaningfully at the rosette still open on the table. 'Don't be such a Throne-damned idiot,' she whispered, 'or you'll wind up in more trouble than you could know.'

Crookley swayed for a moment. He cleared his throat. Then he walked to the table, stared at the rosette, and slowly picked it up.

'Is this a joke?' he asked.

'No,' I said.

'These... these can be faked,' he said, with contempt.

'They can,' I said. 'But that's real.'

He stared at the rosette for a moment longer. I could almost see his mind working. Then he put it down very suddenly, as though it had become too heavy, or too hot, to hold.

'Chair,' I said.

Renner dragged a chair into place just in time to support Crookley's sudden and unsteady descent. It creaked under his weight. He gazed at the fire in the grate and wiped his mouth with the back of his hand. In the doorway, Aulay looked on, his face as pale as paper.

'Shit,' murmured Crookley. 'I... That is to say... Shit. Am I... Am I condemned? Have you come for me at last?'

'What?' asked Renner.

'Is this why you... You take my friends to one side, for private interview?' asked Crookley. 'To gather evidence? Incriminating accounts? I... I've always walked a line, I know. I am a magus, I make no secret of it. I knew, one day, the bloody Ordos would come a-knocking, jealous of my liberated power, my force of will, my deep initiatic knowledge. I thought I had a few more years. Ah, there's so much I would have done...'

'They're not here for you, you silly old goat,' said Mam Matichek.

'We could be,' said Renner.

'Yes, we could,' I said. 'But we're not. Unless there's something you'd like to confess?'

Crookley turned pasty.

'I've done many things,' he murmured. 'Heinous things. In... in the Herrat, when the daemon-simurghs came for me, I gave myself to them, body and soul. I was their plaything, surrendering my flesh in return for their secrets. The humiliation, the obscene depravity...'

'How drunk were you at the time?' I asked mildly.

He paused, and glanced at me.

'Quite a little bit,' he admitted. Mam Matichek snorted, and tried to cover her laughter with a cough.

Crookley flushed blotchy red.

'You all mock me?' he asked. He got up. 'Is this about your number, mamzel?' he asked me. 'The number puzzle you set old Freddy? I heard all about that. Is that why you inveigled your way into my set of friends?'

'I came because of the book Freddy wrote,' I said. 'The one that made him blind and drove him to disgrace, the one that made everyone believe he was mad. But that led to the number. I apologise for abusing your hospitality–'

'No, you don't,' said Renner.

I frowned at him.

'She's a bloody inquisitor,' Renner told Crookley. 'She doesn't have to apologise for anything. She does the Emperor's work. So you just please-and-thank-you her for sparing your life, all right? And know that Mr Dance, and Mam Matichek, and Mr Unvence are all here sworn to the discretion of the Ordos, on pain of death. They are deputised to service, to render their skills as savants and linguists and what-not to the Holy Inquisition. So you, sir, and your friend in the doorway there, you will not betray them or that confidence.'

I was touched by Renner's fierce defence of me, and by the zeal with which he had played the part in character.

'My colleague is correct, Oztin Crookley,' I said. 'You and Aulay may consider yourselves bound by that order too. One word, one solitary word to anyone, and you'll burn for it. Am I clear? Your mouth is always too loose, Crookley. At least Aulay says little. From this moment, you must learn to be as quiet as him. This is not a story you can tell your friends, or blurt out over a shared bottle to impress some poor girl and get in her drawers. Do we have a plain understanding?'

Crookley nodded frantically.

I had Renner take Crookley and Aulay back into the reading room, and settle them quietly, out of earshot, dispensing to them glasses of joiliq and the sort of look of fatigued disparagement that Lightburn seemed to have perfected. I would have preferred them further away, or sober, or both, but it made sense to keep watch on them and mollify them with alcohol. I was becoming aware that the work of the Ordos was not black and white, not merely Throne versus Chaos. There was a problematic grey area in the middle where the eternal struggle crossed paths with civilians, even aggravating ones like Crookley. I am sure that seasoned inquisitors – Gregor, I imagine – would pile onwards, heedless of public safety and public lives, in the name of the greater good. If he had been here, would he have simply executed the miscreants, or chided me for not doing so? I hardly cared. Protecting the Throne was protecting the Imperium, and the Imperium was its citizens. What was our purpose, when all was said and done, if not to safeguard them?

Yet as I stood in the doorway, watching Freddy and Unvence work, as I awaited Mam Matichek's return from the Academy's library, I wondered if anyone was truly innocent. Freddy Dance and I had agreed that everything, and everyone, in Queen Mab and Sancour, and perhaps beyond and outward across the Angelus Subsector, was woven into the immense schemes of the King in Yellow. *He is in everything that we are here*, Freddy had said.

I feared that now more than ever. I wondered if we were all minuscule component parts of the King's plan, and if we had always been so. What Freddy had told me, what he had revealed by dismantling that simple three-digit number, was a staggering consequence. As I have oftentimes remarked, I had spent what felt like my entire life grubbing for the truth, trying to make sense of myself and the world around me, and here was such profound sense that I felt as though I had plunged into a pool of truth so deep and cold that it might shock me and drown me. I could see so much, so suddenly, as though I had abruptly gained a clear and uninterrupted view out across the city, where every detail of the streets and rooftops was magnificently revealed... But only because I was diving from the parapet of a high place and observing it all as I hurtled to the ground.

The number encoded the secret name of the King in Yellow. The text of the book, I was sure, would reveal his identity in greater and more specific detail. He would be known to me, perhaps with such intimate precision I could have power over him. He was some great being, who in all other regard, reduced me to microscopic insignificance. But his secret might be in my grasp.

And that secret, unspeakable and heretical though it seemed, might be that he was one of the founding figures of the Imperium, a living myth, a demigod who had once helped oversee the creation of human civilisation.

A lost primarch.

There was, I believed, promising sense in this. The King in Yellow both consorted with, and utilised, the power of the warp, to such a level of mastery he was feared and hunted by loyalist and traitor factions alike. The Traitor primarchs, those that had fallen so long ago, were also adepts of the warp. Their heresy and fall to Chaos had caused them to be shunned and outlawed for millennia, their names damned as obscenities.

Of the two missing primarchs of legend, nothing at all was known, not even their names, to be spat on and damned. What monstrous level of crime must they have committed to be redacted so? Something greater even than the genocidal sins of Horus himself, for though Horus Lupercal was considered the greatest of all evils, his name was yet remembered.

Theirs were not. What breach had they made that was so terrible they could not, like Horus the damned, even be named?

The warp. It could only be the warp. They had transgressed even further than Horus, if that could be imagined, past redemption, past infamy, past death and eternal condemnation, past even identity itself, erased forever for being more unspeakable than the greatest heretic.

No wonder the unspoken name was coded.

And they were not dead. Not gone. One of them still existed, in a City of Dust just behind reality. One of them was here.

The notion was terrifying. I am sure the notion even alarms you, reading this account after the fact. As I watched Freddy work, I felt the tremble in my limbs, the ringing in my nerves, as my entire being tried to rationalise the significance of what we were learning. I felt my heart flutter in the cage of my ribs as if it wished to burst free, and escape and flee this place.

Then I realised that the flutter upon my breastbone was not merely my racing heart. The wraithbone pendant was twitching fitfully, like a moth weary from beating against an unyielding pane.

I excused myself quickly, and went through the reading room into the corridor beyond. The hall was dark, quiet and cold. The Academy had been shut down for the evening. I hurried through the shadows to the seclusion of a small alcove facing the lamp-lit stone steps down to the main library chambers.

'Gideon?'

+Talon wishes Penitent.+

'Penitent acquires Talon. Where have you been?'

+Talon wishes Penitent, in nameless walls, required.+

'Cease with the Glossia,' I whispered. 'Where have you been?'

+Get here. You know where.+

'I am occupied,' I said. 'I have in hand matters of profound importance. I can't just leave–'

+You must. Matters arise that cannot be postponed. I need you, and your expertise.+

'Gideon, I assure you. I would not hesitate but for the most vital reasons–'

+I'm sorry. I need you here.+

I took a breath.

'Half an hour,' I said.

I walked back to the reading room, and called Renner to the door.

'I have to go.'

He raised an eyebrow.

'I have no choice,' I said. 'Ravenor's returned, and I am summoned. Stay here, Renner. Watch over Freddy. Comus is watching you, so call him if you need help. Contact me on the link if Freddy makes any headway, or reveals anything about that text.'

Lightburn nodded. He checked the function of his micro-bead link.

'How long will you be?' he asked.

'I don't know,' I replied frankly. 'I think as soon as I tell Gideon what we're on to here, he'll want to come himself. Just keep watch. And if anything happens, get Freddy, Unvence and Mam Matichek somewhere secure and lay low.'

'Like where?'

'The safe house in Shorthalls. And if that proves unsafe, wherever your wits can find. But use the Shorthalls site as a drop. Check it regularly, and I'll look for you there. Or send Comus to me. Just... Guard that book with your life. Oh, and keep an eye on Crookley and his friend. Don't let them interfere.'

'I can handle them,' he said. 'I'm plying them with drink. They'll both be asleep soon, I reckon.'

'Good,' I said, but glanced past him into the reading room. 'Where the hell is Aulay?'

'Stepped out for a piss,' said Renner. 'And to get a spot of fresh air. He'll be back. He doesn't go anywhere without Crookley.'

I nodded, then briefly squeezed his arm.

'Be careful,' I said.

'You too,' he replied.

I left, reluctant, and hurried through the quiet and gloomy Academy. The lamps were on in the porter's lodge, the porter asleep over his day book. Outside, light rain hissed across the blue darkness of the courtyard. I followed the cloistered walks towards the outer gate, the smell of night air and cold, rain-washed stone in my lungs.

A figure lurked in a cloister arch ahead of me, collar pulled up, smoking a lho-stick. He saw me approaching. It was Aulay.

'Get back upstairs, please,' I said.

He shrugged, and gave a nod.

'I thought you were going to expose everything,' he said. It was quite the longest thing he had ever said to me.

'What do you mean?'

'Don't play games,' he said. 'In front of the others, maybe, but here? I appreciate your circumspection, but we can be honest, can't we?'

'Let's,' I said.

He reached into his coat pocket, fumbled, and pulled something out.

'Waltur Aulay,' he said, holding the rosette so the light could catch it, 'Ordo Malleus.'

CHAPTER 27

Void-hearted

A night filled with steady rain had overtaken Queen Mab.

The city seemed to jolt and rumble past, moving, half-seen, through the darkness and the rain as if on its way somewhere, anywhere, to some undisclosed destination, to some secret destiny, using the rain and the night as a cloak to disguise its identity. It seemed determined not to be found out.

Raindrops struck the little window of the moving fly and settled briefly, quivering, before sliding away. Each one caught the passing lights of the city, and glittered like a star. Whole constellations, each one unique and never seen before, formed on the glass, then shifted, then re-formed. The fly rattled on at a lick, its springs jarring over invisible cobbles. I had told the cabman to make best haste for Feygate, and I could hear him urging the flyhorse on.

I sat in the darkness of the fly's cab, watching the brief stars on the window. I suppose I had intended to watch the city as it passed by, but that was impossible, for there was scarcely anything visible, so my vacant focus fixed on the raindrops instead. I merely imagined the route: Hecuba Parade from the Academy Yards, where I had hailed the fly, up Antium Hill, past the war memorial at Iprus Circle, then down Paterpath Row, through Tallyhouses and Stall's Cross and onto the highroad where it met Acremile Street. The fly shook like a child's rattle, the wheels clattered and splashed on the road. Stardrops came and went on the glass.

I considered Waltur Aulay's sorry tale. He had been filled with shame and regret. Fear too, I suppose. I had imagined many endings for Ordo careers – death in service, removal from office, heretical decline – but his had come as a miserable surprise. Just a slow erasure of what he had once been.

He was Ordo Malleus, or had been. A novice inquisitor of some promise. This is what he had told me there, in the shadows of the Academy cloisters. He had come to Sancour forty years earlier, on an assignment to identify a notorious heretic. That's all he said. A notorious heretic. Aulay – and this part of his reluctant confession had seemed the hardest to admit – could now not even remember the name of the heretic he had come looking for.

I wondered if he could remember his own name either. He had come into the city, clandestine, earnest Inquisitor Aulay, adopting the guise of a talented engraver, so as to mix in the louche artistic circles of Queen Mab that, even forty years ago, had been thriving and growing. He had played his part well, immersing himself in the lifestyle, following this lead and that, and he had chosen his role to make use of certain talents he possessed; Aulay had some interest in the work of engraving, a profession to which he had been apprenticed before recruitment into the Ordos. Some interest, some flair, and over the years that became a trade that he prospered at, winning acclaim and commissions to fortify his cover identity and broker introduction into the highest noble houses. He had fallen in with the rakish Crookley.

He had become himself. He had lived the part so deeply and with such gusto, that each element of his original self had slowly been replaced, as minerals in the earth slowly substitute for buried bones and turn them into fossils. Aulay had been, I suppose, seduced, not by the contamination of the warp, as one might expect, but by the debauched and heady lives he had committed to. Crookley's wayward behaviour was infamous. Aulay had become dependent on drink, until every day of his life passed by in a fuddled alcoholic haze. He had tagged along with Crookley and Crookley's associates, and thrown himself into the city's esoteric underlife, and consorted with hermetics, and secret orders, and private societies, and all those who dwelt in the liminal areas of the city culture. He had long since lost contact with his handlers, and those of his conclave he was supposed to report to.

Aulay told me that Crookley went too far, too often. From his story, I believed Aulay's delinquency had ceased, at some unfathomable point, to be an act by which he got close to malcontents he hunted, and the reverse had become true. Some vague notion that he was doing 'important Ordo business' became the excuse for his depravity.

Aulay, with pain in his eyes, told me that he now barely remembered the man he had been. The sight of my rosette had been a shock, a stirring up of old, thick sediment. Waltur Aulay had not been afraid that some secret heresies had been found out. He had been afraid that the Ordos had finally come to find him, to rebuke him and chastise him for the desecration of his sworn path.

And then punish him for the multitude of venal crimes and miserable transgressions he had committed in that wise.

I had assured Aulay that was not my purpose. I had told him, in strict terms, that I would turn a blind eye to his dismal behaviour, but only if he kept out of the way. He was not to get involved, not to meddle, not to even speak of what had occurred. I felt certain that, between them, Renner and the angel could keep the pair out of mischief, but I made Aulay promise to keep Crookley in check. Or, I said, I would reveal Aulay to the Ordo authorities, without hesitation, as a miserable and weak recidivist who had betrayed the honour and dignity of the service.

Not through gross crimes. Not through wild heresy or diabolis extremis. But through simple, pitiful human weakness. The Ordos would liquidate him.

His story had chastened me. I felt listless and bleak. I knew too well how complete the immersion in a function could be. I had been, in my life, so many other people. I had worn different names, different faces, different histories, sometimes for weeks or months at a time. I had answered, subconsciously, to other names, without thinking. Some of those guises, I think, I could have sunk into and never reappeared.

For there was no 'me' to be revealed. I had never known my true self, I was but an accumulation of unanswered questions. I almost despised Aulay for that: he had possessed a true identity, an original self, and he had willingly and carelessly lost it, so that any later glimpse of it was a shameful shock. He had owned a real life and he had thrown it away.

Rocked by the motion of the cab, I reassured myself that truths were finally in my grasp. In the past few hours, the last day or two, answers had begun to emerge, some of preposterous magnitude and significance. I felt I was approaching a point of conjunction, as when stars finally align after many years, and patterns emerge.

Most of this truth, of course, concerned the King in Yellow, and the great and secret war we fought. These were answers that would matter to many, to every soul in the God-Emperor's Imperium, perhaps. They were answers that might change the fate of worlds.

But some were mine. These were small, and only concerned me, and only mattered to me. But those answers, oddly, seemed the keenest. I could barely credit the sudden sense of freedom I had felt at showing my rosette to Unvence and Mam Matichek, and saying my name aloud. I had cast Violetta Flyde aside, Violetta and every other guise I had worn. I had revealed the truth of myself. I was Beta Bequin, a servant of the Ordos. No more masks, no more pretence.

It had been liberating. For the first time in my peculiar life, I had a real identity.

And a real purpose too. Though I worried what had befallen Gideon, and what had caused him to summon me with such urgency, I knew I was coming to him with findings of real value. All that I had learned from Mam Mordaunt and the events at Stanchion House, and everything I was learning from Freddy Dance. I had not prised open the truth fully, not yet, but I had made more progress than either Gideon or Gregor in all the years they had worked at it.

And what a truth it was.

I watched the raindrop stars moving on the fly's window. Specks of light on the glass. I had seen through the mystery at last, perhaps far enough to see some of those extimate stars, those constellations that blind Freddy had observed through his glass. The other heavens, the other place, the other reality that was, I was now sure, more solid and important than this one, even though it was hidden.

And that, I think, is when the notion hit me. The only subliminal prompt was the impenetrable darkness outside, the false rain-bead stars, the dirty glass. I thought of Freddy Dance, blind yet seeing. I thought of him placing his sightless eyes to the glass of the telescope, and witnessing, against all probability, a truth that no one else had been able to see. I thought of his words to me: 'The glass never lies.'

I felt a fire in me, a certainty. I could scarcely wait for the fly to reach its destination. By the time it rattled to a halt in the street outside the nameless house in Feygate, the horse snorting and steaming from effort, I already had the fare ready in my hand, eager to spring out, to run inside.

Eager to tell Gideon the secret I had been blind to, but which my mind had finally shown me.

I entered the property through the back gate, into the overgrown gardens. Harlon Nayl was sitting in the darkness on a low wall, as though he had been posted to wait for me. He rose, lowering the lasrifle that had been cradled across his lap.

'Good to see you intact,' he said.

'What's going on?' I asked. 'Where have you been?'

He didn't answer.

'Go on in,' he said, 'but tread carefully.'

I frowned at him.

'What have you been up to?' he asked. 'Any results? What the hell happened at Stanchion House?'

It was my turn not to answer a direct question. I was brimming with the urge to share all the things I had learned, and the notion that had just lately sprung into my head, but I held back. I felt uneasy and unsure. The nameless house was quiet and seemed unlit, and there was a sense of foreboding. I felt almost as though I was walking into a trap.

'I'll make my account, Harlon,' I said. 'Is he inside?'

'Yes, but hold back until he's done–'

I moved past him towards the back door.

'I mean it,' he growled after me. 'Don't disturb things.'

I moved on without acknowledging, and he caught my arm gently and made me pause.

'Listen,' Nayl said, his voice dropping low. 'Beta, just... just don't react, all right? When the moment comes, don't react or do anything rash. Do you understand me?'

'I don't know what you mean,' I said.

'You'll know,' he said. 'Please, Beta. If we have any kind of friendship,

I'm asking you not to act out. You'll want to be angry. Hold it in, for Throne's sake. There's too much at stake.'

I looked at him, then disengaged my arm from his grip, and continued on to the door. He followed me.

Inside, the rear hallway was a narrow, wood-panelled space. Two lumen globes had been lit, but turned down very low. Kys stood at the end of the passage, leaning against the wall, her arms folded. She had her back to me, but I could feel she was radiating hostility.

I walked down the hall. Nayl came in behind me, and secured the back door. Kys turned to glare at me as I passed her.

'Stay here,' she told me.

'He summoned me,' I said.

'Don't be an idiot,' she said. 'We're all here for a reason.'

'What's the matter with you?' I asked.

Her eyes were narrowed, belligerent, but I sensed it was not an anger meant for me. She was just in a foul mood.

'I thought we were in a bad place,' said Kys. 'That was yesterday. Now I know we're in a worse place.'

I stepped past her, and walked into the main hall. She made no effort to follow me.

Lamps had been lit in the main drawing room of the house. I could see their soft amber glow through the door, which had been left half-open. I could hear voices, speaking softly. Kara was standing in the door's shadow out of the shaft of escaping light. She was listening and watching through the gap. Her body language spoke of concern.

I slowed my bold advance, and crept up beside her. She glanced aside, saw it was me, and gave me a brief, tight hug.

'Happy to see you,' she whispered. 'Where's Mr Lightburn?'

'Minding some business on my behalf,' I whispered back. 'What's going on, Kara?'

She nodded towards the half-open door. I could smell something, a spice perhaps, like cloves or salo rind. It was almost medicinal. I stepped in close beside her so I could also peer through the gap.

In the large room, I could see the Chair. Ravenor had positioned himself near the fireplace. There were lamps set on the mantelpiece. He was talking to someone, but that person or persons remained quite out of sight from my angle. I couldn't hear what was being said.

I moved a little, to get a wider view through the door. Kara gripped my arm to stop me, but I edged over anyway.

Now I could see who Gideon was talking to.

Two figures, both standing, both tall. The moment I saw them, my heart pinched cold with fear. The moment I saw them, they could also see me, and one turned to look directly at me.

Its face was a mask, the ornate visor of a plumed warhelm, gleaming in the lamplight like abalone. The design, the features, and the eyes that gazed straight at me from the deep slit of the visor, were in no way human.

They were warriors of the aeldari.

The moment seemed to draw out. I felt I should move, but I could not. I could smell the curious, astringent spice. I could hear the soft purr of their respirator systems. The wraithbone pendant around my neck vibrated frantically like the heart of a tiny mammal. I thought of Mam Mordaunt beseeching me not, in any circumstances, to have dealings with the ancient xenos, and now, it seemed to me, Harlon's words of caution made sense. He had been warning me not to react to this.

The warrior gazing upon me then said something, though I did not understand the words. The tone of its voice was like a wire brush against velvet.

'This is Beta, one of my people,' Gideon said in response. 'She means no disrespect, and does not intend to intrude.'

I was about to bow and back away, but the aeldari spoke again.

'Yes, she is one of the void-hearted,' said Gideon. 'We call them nulls. She will not trouble you–'

The other aeldari spoke.

'I confess she was manufactured by the King,' said Gideon calmly, 'but she holds no allegiance to him, and she stands with us. I vouch for her loyalty.'

The aeldari who had spoken first took a step towards me. Its gaze had not left me.

'Grael,' it said.

'No, sir–' I replied.

'Crafted to be a grael vessel,' it said, and took another step closer. It spoke Low Gothic as though the words did not quite fit its mouth, as if the breath of them made unfamiliar shapes.

'Perhaps,' I said. 'That was a fate I escaped.'

'You look so alike,' it said. I did not understand. The xenos being was not the first to make such a remark, nor, I thought, would it be the last time I would be told such a thing. But the implication was that, somehow, this creature had known Alizebeth Bequin, or was at least familiar with her likeness. How could that be? All along there had been hints that Gideon Ravenor had had some dealings with aeldari kind in the past. This suggested a long and complicated involvement.

The warrior turned away from me, and returned its gaze to Ravenor. As it moved, the cabochon gems set in its pearl armour caught the lamplight and twinkled like stars or, as it occurred to me, raindrops on glass.

It spoke again, slipping back into the impenetrable cant of its kind.

'I urge that you give me longer than that,' said Gideon in response. 'A month–'

The other uttered something, cutting him off.

'I plead this, in light of our long association and friendship,' Gideon said. 'We have accomplished many things together. Your proposed course of action would end that. I could not condone it, or argue its merit to my superiors. Moreover, the consequences would be catastrophic for both our species. Your autarchs have warned, from the earliest ages, against allowing Kaela Mensha Khaine to guide the Ai'elethra, for that way leads only to Ynnaed's realm.'

The aeldari spoke, both of them, in quick succession.

'I don't dispute the extent of the danger,' Gideon replied. 'But there may still be less heavy-handed ways of denying it. In the space of a month I might yet–'

Dry, wire-on-velvet words interrupted him.

'A week,' said Gideon. 'Very well. If that's all you will compromise. I am disappointed. I fear our relationship will not be the same afterwards, and that is lamentable. You have few friends on my side of the line. I trust you will not break your word.'

They did not respond. And then, they were suddenly not there any more.

I started slightly. Their departure had not been visible. They had simply, silently, vanished.

'Do not be concerned,' said Gideon. 'They were a projected telepresence. Pyskanically manifested thought-forms.'

'I could smell them,' I said. 'I still can.'

'Their visitations are precise and fully sensory,' he said. 'Asuryani technology–'

'That's not what concerns me,' I said, turning to him, and stepping more fully into the room. 'This is what delayed you? Why you abandoned me to conclude the business at Stanchion House?'

'Yes, Beta. The envoys made contact some short while after you set out. One does not deny a formal request for audience from ambassadors of the Ancient Empire. Especially when affairs are so critically balanced.'

The Chair turned slowly to face me.

'But that is not what concerns you either,' he said.

Mam Mordaunt's stern advice was still in the forefront of my mind, but even without it, I would have been sorely troubled.

'You consort with xenos kind,' I said.

'Consort is a charged word,' he said.

'Whatever word you care to use, it seems ill-judged,' I replied. 'It seems in conflict with your station and office.'

'We have had this conversation,' he said. 'Inquisitors are obliged to bend the rules.'

'We have had the conversation indeed, but never to any satisfactory conclusion. The very basis of your pursuit of Eisenhorn was that he had transgressed. Yet you are capable of significant transgression too.'

'Are you suggesting hypocrisy?' he asked. 'Beta, the judgement against Gregor was the Ordos' not mine.'

'Yet you upheld it, and acted upon it.'

'For greater ends–'

'So you claim,' I said. 'You told me yourself that your pursuit of Eisenhorn was in part an attempt to regain the favour of the Ordos. Because, clearly, you were in some disgrace. Due to unwise associations, it would seem.'

'The aeldari are categorised as enemies of mankind,' he said. 'Certainly their goals and ambitions are not entirely compatible with ours. But there is overlap. Their conatus is not always at odds with our own, their enemies are often our enemies too. Early in my career, I encountered agents of the empire, and we bonded over mutual interests. I am not prepared to make an account of those dealings to you, but the outcome was of lasting benefit to humanity. Things were accomplished and threats turned back. I do not regret brokering that cooperation. And the cordial bonds of respect established back then have endured.'

I admit I felt betrayed. It felt as though I had discovered a trusted family member had been conducting a torrid affair.

'I have not had dealings with them for many years,' Gideon said. 'Many years, Beta. As you remark, the Inquisition looks unfavourably on such connections and I am required to conduct myself without blemish. But the aeldari made contact with me yesterday–'

'Matters on Sancour have now reached such a dire pitch, even the xenos kind are forced to become involved,' I said. 'Yes, this much I have learned for myself.'

'Really?' He seemed intrigued.

'I have been told as much. Shown as much.'

'By whom? I would know more of this. What did you achieve at the port? Clearly, it was fraught.'

'I located Eusebe dea Mordaunt, and learned a number of things from her. She was willing to cooperate, to a degree. But we were surprised, and I don't know if she is now living or dead. Saur certainly is dead. Lightburn is currently watching over some significant interests that I believe will be revelatory, while I attend you, according to your summons. I have left my work unfinished. And you left me to finish it. It was indeed fraught.'

'I had no choice,' he said.

'I believe you always have choices,' I replied.

'The aeldari contacted me when you were already on your way,' he said. I could tell I had annoyed him a little. 'They did so as a courtesy to me, in light of our history. The contact was urgent and, besides, it is unwise to rebuff the formal overtures of their kind.'

'So you left me to it?'

'I told you that you were quite at liberty to disengage.'

'So were you.'

'He's spent the last day and a half in audience with their envoys,' said Kara. She had entered the room behind me. 'Six meetings, like this one, some of them lasting hours.'

'There were delicate matters to negotiate that could not have waited,' said Gideon.

'Even though all of your own people are clearly bothered by this interaction?' I asked. I looked at Kara. She had none of Kys' anger or disgust, but the worry in her was clear.

'Eltahec. Ulthwé. Nyatho. Alaitoc. Olhn-Tann,' he said.

'Xenos words,' I snapped. 'What are you saying?'

'The envoys communicated to me that their kind has become increasingly aware of the King's activities,' Gideon said. 'Over the last few years, their concerns have grown, to the point where they have classified him *Iyanic Kaelas*, which means an object that must be vanquished. What we might term a Priority Alpha threat. They have tracked him to this quadrant, and have begun operations against him. But they hoped, it is clear to me, that we would deal with it.'

'Why?'

'Because the threat originates from our territories, and thus lies in our jurisdiction. They were reluctant to embark upon action that would risk the fragile peace between empires.'

'They don't want to provoke an open war with the Imperium?'

'They do not.'

'*Did* not, rather,' I said. 'They have run out of patience, haven't they?'

'They believe the threat is greater than we have assessed, and they are despondent at the progress the Imperium is making in its efforts to contain it. They believe we have badly underestimated the danger. Thus they feel they are obliged to undertake their own measures, despite the risk of war. Eltahec. Ulthwé. Nyatho. Alaitoc. Olhn-Tann.'

'Again, those words–'

'They are the names of craftworlds, Beta. Five craftworlds, currently converging on the Sancour region. An unprecedented assembly of aeldari strength in peacetime. They are about to unleash their combined wrath upon the Sancour System.'

'This world is going to die?'

'This entire system is likely to die,' he said. 'And whatever the outcome, whatever the success of their sanctioning assault, it is likely to trigger an era of savage and widescale hostilities with the aeldari.'

'If they would risk that, then the King in Yellow's menace must be very great indeed,' said Kara quietly.

'They gave you a week's grace,' I said to Gideon.

'I asked for a month–'

'And they gave you a week. They seem to set little store by your past association.'

'A week was a gain, the result of long negotiation. They were intent on commencing deployment tomorrow. And notifying me was a courtesy anyway–'

'Not a great deal of courtesy,' I suggested.

'It is decided,' he replied. 'What was urgent is now imperative. All secondary investigations are suspended. We will move immediately, and with singular purpose, to affect an entry to the King's realm via the King Door.'

'I do not believe that is viable,' I said. 'I have told you this repeatedly. I don't believe it is viable or survivable.'

'And your opinion has been noted,' he said. 'This is my decision.'

'Sir, I believe I am on the verge of finding an alternative means of entering–'

'The verge is not close enough, Beta,' Gideon said. 'Not any more. I commend you for the efforts you've made and the work you've done. There is no longer any time for speculation or enquiry.'

At that moment, I was going to tell him directly of the startling notion that had come to me on my way there. But I hesitated. I was not withholding, but I had reservations. Yet again, I felt my trust in him was tested. He had professed openness from the start, but in too many small ways he had not been straight with me. He had shared my thoughts without permission, he had abandoned a plan and left me alone without a word of explanation. His connection to the xenos aeldari had been a bitter blow. He was too often closed to me. This, I reflected, was only to be expected. He was the inquisitor and I was but his associate. I accepted that. His were the decisions to make, and his orders were mine to follow. My notion would require time to be assessed and tested, and he would not tolerate further delay.

Yet still I felt, as a certainty, he was making a mistake, an error of judgement forced upon him by circumstances. So I drew a breath, and decided to risk his anger by telling him anyway.

But then someone spoke for me.

'I think you should listen to her, Gideon.'

The voice came from the doorway behind me. I turned.

It was Eisenhorn.

CHAPTER 28

There is ruthless, and there is them

I felt the Chair's weapon systems begin to charge.

Eisenhorn made a vague gesture with his hand.

'Let's not, shall we, Gideon?' he said. 'I haven't come to fight.'

'I am required by order to detain you as *Extremis Diabolus*,' Ravenor replied.

'Then we will curtail such disagreement,' said Eisenhorn.

The floor in front of Ravenor's chair bubbled and blistered briefly as something retched up out of the ground in a gust of smoke. It unfurled from the molten flagstones like a banner.

The daemonhost Cherubael manifested before Ravenor, chains trailing, steam fuming off his taut flesh.

'Hello, little thing,' he said to Ravenor, his smile all teeth. 'Would you like to try me?'

The doors at the far end of the chamber burst open, little slivers of wood flying off the sheared latch. The vast and shadowed shape of Deathrow stood in the doorway, aiming a boltgun at the Chair. I saw the red dot of the targeting system settle, steady, on the Chair's armoured skin. Deathrow's mangy cattle dog trotted in beside his master, and stood, teeth bared, a low mumbling growl issuing from its throat.

Kara, displaying immense courage in the face of all this, started to move, her hand reaching for the gun in her rig. She stopped quickly as she felt the muzzle of a weapon brush the back of her head.

Medea had entered silently behind Eisenhorn. She held a Glavian needlegun in her red-gloved hand, pressed to Kara's skull.

'Please don't move, Kara,' she said. Kara clenched her jaw and slowly raised her hands.

Medea looked at me. I hadn't moved at all.

'Hello, Beta,' she said.

'I thought you were gone,' I said to her, but to Eisenhorn too. My throat was tight. My hands were shaking.

'I am so sorry about that,' said Medea. 'So very sorry.'

'There's one more,' said Eisenhorn, apparently not sorry at all. He stepped aside as Kys walked in from the hall. Her face wore quite the most murderous expression I have ever seen. Her fingers were laced across the back of her head.

Nayl walked behind her, nudging her in the spine with the barrel of his lasgun.

'She's contained,' he said to Eisenhorn. Nayl glanced at me, a bleak and apologetic look.

It hadn't been the aeldari at all. *This* was the moment he had warned me of. This betrayal was the thing he had begged me not to react to, because it would make me angry.

He had been right.

'How long?' I asked him. 'Since the start?'

Nayl seemed about to answer, but Eisenhorn cut him off.

'That's not the conversation we're here to have,' he said. 'Get over your feelings. There's more at stake. That applies to all of you.'

He looked at the Chair.

'Gideon, you could still resist. I know that. But understand it will be your people who suffer if you do. So... We'll open a dialogue.'

'If you wanted to talk,' said Ravenor, 'there were less confrontational ways of achieving that. And countless prior opportunities.'

'Actually, there weren't,' said Eisenhorn. His clothes and boots were scuffed and dusty, as though he had been through recent, rough travails. He walked, quite casually, across the wide drawing room, apparently oblivious to the tense stand-off, slid a farthingale chair out from under a corner table, and sat on it with his back to the panelled wall.

'I know you, Gideon,' he said. 'Too well. I know the orders you're saddled with. If I'd shown my face, you'd have been obliged to act.'

'I still am,' said Ravenor.

'You are, but this is a more propitious moment. We need to work together. We should have been working together from the moment you got here. But you are a resistant bastard. So I had to engineer a way we could collaborate without you realising it.'

'Bequin,' said Ravenor.

'Yes, Bequin,' Eisenhorn replied. 'Oh, she had no idea. No blame can be attached. But I had to get her in with you in a way that couldn't be questioned.'

'To learn what I knew?'

'And to share what I knew,' said Eisenhorn. 'We both had pieces of the puzzle, incomplete and useless. Through her, they could be fitted together.'

'You got the book to Dance?' he asked me.

'Yes.'

'Translation?'

'Another few hours.'

Eisenhorn's gaze returned to Ravenor.

'You see?' he said. 'More progress than either one of us has managed in years. And you have a way in, too? A way into the extimate realm?'

Ravenor did not respond.

'Potentially,' said Nayl. 'Not a good one. Hazardous, to any mortal.'

'I have a daemonhost and an Astartes,' said Eisenhorn, 'so I bring that to the table. We should discuss strategy.'

'We should?' Ravenor began. His voice trailed off. If he had possessed any capacity for human affect, I am sure he would have been shaking his head and laughing in bitter disbelief.

'Let me rephrase,' said Eisenhorn. 'This is a fleeting chance to set aside the pathetic game we are playing and do something of significance. I would like you all onside. Kara, Patience... and you, Gideon. So let's discuss how that may be achieved.'

Ravenor didn't reply. Kara glanced at the Chair nervously. Kys glared at the floor.

Eisenhorn sighed. He looked at Kara.

'Will you talk some sense into him?' he requested.

She shook her head.

'For Throne's sake, Swole.' Eisenhorn sniffed. 'You're not stupid.'

'I am not,' Kara replied. She looked Eisenhorn in the eyes, something very few people were bold enough to do. 'I do as he instructs. I see the merit of what you suggest, *if* your word can be trusted. But I act on his command. No other.'

Eisenhorn frowned. I wondered if he was not slightly impressed. He turned his attention to Kys.

'No point asking you, I suppose?' he said.

'None at all,' she replied.

'Thought so.'

'But I have a suggestion,' she added.

'Which is?'

Kys stared at him, and slowly unlaced her fingers and lowered her arms.

'You could die,' she said.

Telekine force smashed Nayl backwards into the hall. His lasgun tumbled in mid-air and flew directly into Kys' waiting hands as though drawn by wires. Her kine blades were already streaking like bullets towards Eisenhorn's face.

Eisenhorn did not move. He remained seated, almost at ease. The whistling blades parted at the last moment, diverted to either side of Eisenhorn's head, and speared the wall panels behind him. Kys froze, her body locked, unable to fire her captured weapon.

'No,' said Ravenor. 'Not like this.'

Kys moaned, paralysed.

'Not like this, Patience,' Ravenor repeated. Deathrow's target dot was now painting Kys' temple. The daemonhost put his hand around her throat, ready to squeeze. Medea took Nayl's lasgun from Kys' rigid grip.

'Is that a choice made, then?' Eisenhorn said to Ravenor. 'A decision?'

'If everyone stands down,' said Ravenor. 'I mean everyone.'

Eisenhorn stared at him for a moment, then nodded.

Medea lowered her pistol. Cherubael uttered a disappointed whimper, let go of Kys, and drifted away towards the ceiling. The red dot flicked off, and Deathrow put up his weapon.

'As equals, or not at all,' said Ravenor. He released Kys from the psykanic vice he had seized her in, and she fell forward with a gasp.

'Help her, Beta,' said Ravenor. I was moving to Kys anyway. She tried to shake me off, but she was too weak. I got her into a chair. Medea holstered her weapon, and went into the hall to check on Nayl.

'Funny,' I said, 'through all of that, you never asked me.'

Eisenhorn looked at me.

'What?'

'You never asked me which side I would stand on.'

'I...' he began, then regarded me with an even deeper frown, as though the question quite confused him.

'Did you stage it?' I asked.

'Stage...?'

'Your death. Did you stage it? You knew my hope to infiltrate Gideon's team and regain the book wouldn't work, because Gideon would see through it. He'd need to see my mind, in order to trust me, and so he'd see the truth. But if I truly believed you were dead, and turned to him in desperation to help, there'd be nothing in my mind to hide.'

'You had to go to him clean,' said Eisenhorn. 'You're a good actor. But gaining his trust was beyond any function.'

'So you staged it?'

'No,' said Medea. She had reappeared in the doorway and was regarding me with great regret. 'Beta, we were attacked. We were conducting the auto-séance, and the graels came for us. They razed Bifrost. That was genuine.'

'But you got out?' I said.

'Barely,' she replied.

'And then–'

'I realised it was expedient for you to think us dead,' said Eisenhorn.

'Expedient?'

'I knew you'd turn to Gideon. He would be your only option.'

'Then Harlon didn't know either?' I asked. 'Or surely his mind–'

'He thought we were dead too,' said Medea.

'I reached out to him only an hour ago,' said Eisenhorn. 'Told him to be ready, and to unward and unlock this house.'

'Harlon grieved for you,' I said. 'The thought of your death almost broke him.'

'He's strong,' said Eisenhorn dismissively.

'He was also right,' I said. 'He said, in the end, inquisitors don't care for the people loyal to them, the people close to them. He said inquisitors were ruthless and cruel, and, ultimately, would use anything and anyone to achieve their goals.'

I looked at Ravenor.

'All of them.'

'This concept comes as a surprise, Beta?' Ravenor asked.

Eisenhorn's lips curled with an almost-smile.

'It's never a surprise,' said Medea quietly. 'It's just *always* a disappointment.'

Eisenhorn glanced at her, then looked away sharply. His almost-smile faded.

'It's not a criticism, Gregor,' Medea said. 'I've been with you too long for that. We're all cruel, all of us. Kara, can you help me with Harlon? I think his ribs are broken.'

Kara nodded.

I heard Kys murmur, 'Good.'

Medea went to her. Kys was hunched in the chair, shivering. The shock of Ravenor suddenly waring her had left psyk-trauma.

'Are you all right?' Medea asked.

'Fine,' said Kys.

'You're very brave, very loyal, and very dangerous,' said Medea.

'And very dead, if she tries that again,' said Cherubael.

'She won't,' said Ravenor. 'A truce. For now.'

Medea and Kara left the room to tend to Nayl.

'I'm on the verge of finding an alternative means of entering the City of Dust,' Ravenor said to me. 'Your words, Beta. Gregor said I should heed you. I am now listening.'

'I'm not certain,' I replied. 'Just a notion that occurred to me belatedly, but if I'm right, it would be a better alternative than the King Door.'

'Go on,' said Eisenhorn.

'You told me that on Gershom, you entered one of the Cognitae's extimate spaces using Enuncia.'

'That doesn't work here,' said Eisenhorn. 'I've tried it multiple times.'

'Because we've been looking for a permanent door where just a process would operate as a key,' I said. 'The King Door is perhaps just that, but I think it's too dangerous to try. However, I believe there may be temporary doors, which is to say doors that may be conjured or summoned.

I think I did that accidentally, in Feverfugue House. I think the Cognitae knew the method, which is why they could pass freely between cities until the King denied them.'

I saw the surprise on Eisenhorn's face.

'Yes, the Cognitae and the King are no longer allies,' I told him. 'He has dispensed with their services, and they are on the run from him. From one of them, indirectly, I believe I have learned their method.'

'From Mordaunt?' Ravenor asked.

'From Mam Mordaunt, yes.'

'What method?' asked Eisenhorn. 'What do you need?'

'Can you give me an hour to test my theory?' I asked. 'I want to be sure. I'd rather not look like an idiot in front of either of you. If I'm wrong, and that's entirely possible, we will have to go with Gideon's plan and risk the King Door.'

'An hour?' asked Eisenhorn.

'If that. I know time is precariously short.'

'What do you mean?' Eisenhorn said.

'The King's scheme, whatever it may be, is about to come to fruition,' said Ravenor. 'A matter of days or hours. This I discovered from a Cognitae perfecti.'

'And not just that,' I added.

'What does *that* mean?' Eisenhorn growled.

'It means the aeldari,' hissed Kys.

'Oh, *that's* the stink in here,' said Cherubael. 'I could *not* place it.'

'What the hell have you done?' Eisenhorn asked Ravenor.

'I needed allies,' said Ravenor.

'You had one right here!' Eisenhorn snarled, slapping his own chest.

'Don't pretend for a moment–'

Eisenhorn rose sharply and strode across the room to face the Chair. 'We are allies now, barely, because I engineered it. But you could have extended your hand to me any time. *Any* time. I was the fugitive, you were the hunter. The truce was yours to call. The help was yours to ask for. You know I would have responded. But no, you call on your xenos friends?'

'I needed allies,' said Ravenor. 'The Ordos have no reach here. I contacted the Ancient Empire ten months ago and informed them of my concerns–'

'That's not what you told us,' said Kys. Her eyes were narrow.

'Ruthless,' I murmured. 'Even with the truth.'

'I told them of my concerns,' Ravenor continued. 'And they sent assistance, according to an old agreement. But–'

'But?' asked Eisenhorn.

'They have taken the initiative,' said Kys. She got to her feet. 'They agree with the threat assessment, and have embarked on action of their own. And he can't call them off.'

Kys looked at Ravenor with almost as much loathing as she had Eisenhorn.

'Can you?' she asked.

'We have a week,' said Ravenor.

'Until what?' asked Eisenhorn.

'Five craftworlds,' I said.

'Mother of shit,' said Cherubael, and bobbed closer to the ceiling.

'I do not command the aeldari,' said Ravenor. 'They operate on their own recognisance. This is a threat to them too.'

'You don't command them, but you call them and they come,' said Eisenhorn. 'Throne of Terra, Gideon. Did you learn nothing from me?'

'Too much,' said Ravenor.

'You were always such a cocksure little–'

The cattle dog barked loudly. From the end of the room, Deathrow said something I couldn't make out.

Eisenhorn nodded. 'Yes, you're right. Bequin, go test your theory. You don't have to be present while we continue this discussion.'

'And I have no wish to witness it,' I replied. 'I could use Patience's help.'

Kys seemed surprised.

'Go with her,' said Eisenhorn.

Kys looked at him with an unfathomable expression. Her kine blades sucked out of the wood panels where they were embedded, and flew back to neatly pin her chignon. She followed me to the door. As we left, we heard the voices of Eisenhorn and Ravenor rising in heated debate.

In the hall, Nayl was sitting awkwardly on a ladderback chair as Kara bound his ribs.

'What's going on in there?' asked Medea.

'The same thing that's been going on for years, I'd imagine,' I replied. 'I'd stay out of the way for a while.'

'I'm sorry, Beta,' Medea said to me. 'I'm sorry I hurt you. The pretence–'

'I'm sorry too,' I replied, without a smile.

'I didn't know,' Nayl said through pain-gritted teeth. His eyes were pleading with me. 'I really didn't. Beta...'

'Leave her be,' Kys said to him. 'For the record, I'm not sorry I hurt you. How many times have you changed sides now?'

He lowered his face to avoid her stare.

'Come with me,' I said to Kys.

I began to clear away the little scent bottles and jars that stood in front of the oval mirror. We were in the small upstairs room beside my little bedroom, where Kara had helped me prepare to perform as Violetta Flyde for the final time.

'What do you want my help with?' Kys asked, watching me from the doorway.

'Not much. But I wanted to get you out of that room. I was afraid if you stayed, you'd try to kill someone again.'

'Hah,' she said, saying a laugh rather than laughing. 'I told you Nayl would be the weak link,' she remarked. 'I told you. Still too much the heretic's man.'

'And I told you that you misjudge the quality of his loyalty,' I replied. 'He didn't know, until an hour past...'

'And how quickly did he turn, eh?' she asked. She snapped her fingers. 'He could have warned Ravenor. He could have warned us all. But no. One word from his old master, and he disarms the house to let them in.'

'Nayl's old enough to see the merit of a collaboration,' I said. 'And he's in a difficult position. Torn–'

'We're all torn,' said Kys with contempt. 'You're all torn. Kara, even Ravenor. Eisenhorn looms, and you all bow in his shadow. Yet you see what he brings with him? A daemon. A traitor-bastard of the Alpha Legion.'

'Gideon's hands are hardly clean either,' I said.

She sighed.

'A whole life spent in his devoted service, and he still dismays me,' she said quietly. 'Aeldari xenos? For Throne's sake. They are as bad as each other, I think. I have used up my days believing I serve the Throne above all, but this is the filth I am dragged into.'

'Me too,' I said. 'That's something I might have said of my own life.

Nothing wears an honest face. Those we admire disappoint us, or betray us. What truth may be found is uglier and more cruel than our worst expectations.'

'You sound more cynical than I do,' she said.

I looked at her. 'You have been made uneasy by Gideon for a long time, haven't you? You're loyal to him, but you struggle with his approach.'

'He uses people,' she said. 'Literally. And because of that armoured shell that houses him, one easily and often forgets that he is all too human.'

Angry voices echoed from the house below us.

'Listen to them,' she growled. 'Friends, enemies, both at once. Each of them knows that time is fleeting, yet they waste it in argument, about this and that, and a long and stupid history that matters to no one except them.'

'I am the one that will keep you true,' I said.

'What?'

'You said that to me. As we walked to the Gogs. It struck me so, I remembered it clearly. No matter what, you are true... to the Throne, if nothing else. Like me. Like, in his way, Harlon. Kara is too loyal to Gideon, and Medea too bound to Gregor. And it is impossible to define the loyalty of an enslaved daemon, or an Alpharian twin with his own agenda.'

'What are you saying?' she asked, stepping forward, curious.

'I'm saying we were both born orphans, Patience Kys. We have never known true parents to honour or obey. We've both had surrogates, and they have been fallible, and so we have learned to answer to ourselves before anything.'

'I do not even know my real name,' she said.

'Nor I,' I said.

'So... How do we proceed, no-name?' she asked.

'As before,' I said. 'We find the truth, however ugly. We find it for the sake of the Emperor. And once we have it, we present it to our warring masters and, perhaps, the stark truth of it will be enough to shake them out of their damned squabble so they might stand together and face down the darkness.'

'How can I help?' she asked.

'You can help me clear these bottles away from the mirror,' I said.

She made a quick gesture with her hand, and the many bottles, phials and jars rose off the dressing table as one. Another flick of her hand, and they all flew sideways and scattered in the corner of the room. Some smashed, filling the air with intense perfumes.

'Next?' she said.

I sighed. 'Never mind,' I said.

I sat down in front of the mirror, and ran my hands around its frame.

'You learned something, didn't you?' Kys asked, standing at my shoulder and watching me. 'From Dance?'

'And from Mam Mordaunt.'

'More than you've told them?'

'I want to be sure,' I said. 'A life submerged in lies has made me reluctant to speak of something until I know it to be true.'

'How... how stark and ugly is this truth?'

I glanced at her face in the mirror.

'The King in Yellow may be one of the mythical lost primarchs,' I said.

I watched her reflected reaction.

'Throne save us all,' she whispered. 'But you're not certain?'

'Not yet.'

'So what's this game with the mirror about?'

'The other part of the conundrum,' I replied. 'The way into the City of Dust. Mam Mordaunt, and the Cognitae... and many others, I imagine... make use of quizzing glasses to spy and gather intelligence. We did so at the Maze Undue.'

'Mirrors?'

'Mirrors, glass, lenses,' I said. 'Freddy Dance is blind, yet through the perfect lens of an astronomical scope he saw other stars. That's what made me think of it. With the correct glass, one may see truly, not with the eye, but with the mind. In Feverfugue House, I chanced briefly on the City of Dust. I could never repeat the feat. But the night I did it, I was using a cursed sighting glass that showed me the way. *The glass never lies.*'

'What, now?'

'Something Dance said.'

'Mirrors, glass, lenses,' she mused. 'You think they'll show you the truth?'

'No, more than that,' I said. 'I think some glasses do more than quiz. I think they open doorways. I think that is the method we have been missing all along.'

Kys seemed impressed.

'Glass can have properties,' she admitted. 'Cursed glass. Glass tempered by the warp. Like flects.'

'You know of those?'

'I have had some experience,' she replied.

'I found Mam Mordaunt in Stanchion House,' I said. 'She had many quizzing glasses there, a collection. They were how she surveilled and remained so well informed. But confusion overtook us, and in the midst of it, she vanished. I thought at first she was dead. Disintegrated. But I now think she escaped, using a means familiar to her.'

'Through a quizzing glass?'

I nodded.

'And you think that why?'

'She claimed to have two methods of exit, one she was loath to employ. But in the end, I think she was forced to take it. Her life was imperilled. If she had a means to flee, to step away, why was she afraid to use it?'

'Because of where it led?'

'Because of where it led,' I agreed. 'She could step through a glass and leave Stanchion House, but only to the City of Dust. The King has renounced the Cognitae, and seeks to purge them, so the City of Dust is the last place she wanted to go.'

'In all ways, the last place,' Kys said.

I sat back in frustration.

'What is it?' asked Kys.

'This glass is no good,' I said. 'I know a little of the craft of quizzing, and this glass won't work. It is, I fear, just an ordinary mirror, and it won't respond.'

'So we need... a special one? One made for such work?'

I rose to my feet.

'Yes,' I said. 'And I think I know where one may be found.'

We went back downstairs. The house had fallen silent, the argument subsided.

There was no sign of the daemon or Deathrow. Through a side door I saw Kara, sitting silently as she watched over Nayl. He was coiled on a couch, fast asleep.

Kara didn't see us. With Kys at my heels, I walked down to the drawing room. We would tell them what we knew. It would be enough, I hoped.

In the drawing room, Eisenhorn stood facing the Chair. Both were entirely silent and still, as though some divine force had set them fast as statues. I noticed a rime of frost glittering on the carpet and the upper surfaces of some furniture. I stepped towards Eisenhorn.

'Do not disturb them.'

Medea stood in the hallway behind us.

'Don't,' she advised. 'Their vicious argument continues. They have merely taken it to a psykanic plane.'

'They are arguing still?' I asked.

'Fiercely,' Medea said.

'Idiots,' said Kys.

'They have many matters to unpick,' said Medea sadly. 'Lifetimes of friendship and enmity, trusts broken, crimes imagined and real. They cannot work as one until things are swept clear between them.'

'They're still idiots,' said Kys.

'And they will never resolve it, not in a hundred years of rowing,' I said. 'For they are too alike, and yet too different. One bound by a code of duty, the other by a higher calling, one Throne-loyal yet unwise, one heretical yet true.'

'And both idiots,' said Kys. 'And they lack trust of any kind. They trust no one, not even themselves, for they are shamefully aware of their own transgressions. This is what the Ordos do to men. They cannot trust each other. They will never trust each other, and this dispute will never be resolved.'

'More importantly, they're wasting time,' I said.

'I know,' said Medea.

I turned to her. 'You will not interrupt them?' I asked her.

'Frankly, I dare not,' she said.

'Then when they stop – *if* they stop – tell them Kys and I have gone to run an errand. We won't be long.'

'What errand, Beta?'

'It's important. Tell them that. Tell them to contact us with all urgency if we have not returned by the time they are done with this... this... pointlessness.'

'You are leaving the house?' Medea asked, surprised.

'Yes.'

Her face hardened.

'I can't permit that, Beta,' she said. 'I forbid it.'

'Medea,' I replied, 'I say this with the greatest affection, but you are in no way my mother to forbid me anything.'

We left through the back door, through the overgrown tumble of the rear garden. The rain had stopped, and the stars were out.

'Where to?' asked Kys.

'Highgate Hill.'

'The holloways, then,' she said. 'The quickest route.'

We descended into the shadows of the Footstep Lane holloway. Almost at once, we became aware of a figure behind us.

The cattle dog growled. As ever, his master was an unresponsive slice of darkness save for the buzz of his visor and the fidget of the amber cursor in the visor's optic trench.

'Deathrow,' I said. I could feel Kys tense beside me, her telekine power fluttering to life.

The dog growled again. *Beta.*

'We know each other's names,' I said. 'I do not think your fine hound needs to speak for you any more.'

The visor buzzed.

'Are you sent to stop us?' I asked. 'To prevent us leaving?'

Deathrow raised a hand, and removed his battered visor and mask. His face, the mere suggestion of a handsome, noble countenance quite at odds with his brutal garb, was still masked by shadows. I fancied it would be so, even in broad daylight.

'I am charged to watch the rear of the property,' he said. 'To watch for intruders. Are you intruders?'

'How can we be?' I asked. 'We are leaving, not coming in.'

'Then you are not in my purview, Beta,' he said.

'Thank you,' I replied. 'I am pleased to make your acquaintance again this day.'

He walked away, past us, down the holloway, the old dog trotting at his side.

'I was sure he'd been sent to stop us,' said Kys, watching him go. 'Why didn't he?'

'He may have been. Who knows what agenda he truly follows?'

'Because he is Eisenhorn's?' she asked.

I shook my head.

'Because he is Alpharius,' I said.

In just a little over an hour, after brisk walking, and with the night still deep upon us, we reached Highgate Hill, and walked up the cobbles of Low Highgate Lane. Above us, looking out across the wastes of the great Sunderland, stood the ruins of the Maze Undue.

The last time Kys and I had been there together, the last time we had been there at all, we had been trying to kill each other.

And I thought I had succeeded.

CHAPTER 29

A-mazed in the House of God

'Renner? Renner?'

For a moment, he didn't answer. Then the micro-bead's vox-link crackled.

'I'm here,' he said. *'Where are you?'*

'Working,' I replied. 'I'm just checking in. Are you safe? How is it going?'

'We're safe enough,' Lightburn's voice came back, tinny and hollow over the link. *'Still where you left us. The old boy's working, decoding. I think he's making progress.'*

'A translation?'

'Getting there, I think. Dance is tired, but he's keeping at it.'

'Stay in touch. Contact me the moment he gets something solid.'

I shut the link down, and walked through the crumbling archway, leaving one ruined, empty room for another. Kys stood waiting for me, a scatter of broken roof tiles under her feet.

'Where do we look?' she asked.

'Further in. These are just the skirts. If there's anything left, of course. Your raid punished this old place badly.'

'And weather's done the rest in the months since,' she replied.

'This old place' was, of course, the building that had been my home for the greater part of my childhood. My life, in fact. The Maze Undue, a scholam said to be a training house for Inquisitional prospects, but in truth a Cognitae facility used to raise the products of their breeding programme.

Products like me. Blacksoul nulls.

If you were not a pupil there, or if you have not visited the Highgate part of the city, then know that the building faces the dusty north-east on the top of Highgate Hill, and that the side of the building is permanently stained by the grey murk of the Sunderland. Even in my time, parts of the site were no longer fit for habitation. Now, more than ever, it was a broken shell, a heap of rubble open to the elements.

It adjoins the orphanage, the Scholam Orbus, a companion faith school. The orphanage faces west and north, confronting – from its position on the edge of the Highgate Hill crag – the black threat of the Mountains. It is now closed too, shut down, I imagined, after the Ordo raid.

The buildings once leant together for support, stone pile against stone pile, their definitions blurred, but the Maze was now virtually collapsed. As Kys and I made our way through the wreck, I glanced up, imagining floors and staircases that were long gone, the vacant air where once had stood the candidates' rooms. Mine had been there, Judika's, Faria's, Corlam's...

The robing room, the refectory and the washrooms were gone too, but part of the main pile still stood, just about: the remains of the staff room and the library. Above them, I hoped, some vestige of the top room still existed.

We picked our way through the skirts, which had been Mentor Saur's domain. The skirts had been our term for the outlying and largely ruined parts of the Maze Undue along the eastern wing, where physical training and combat practice took place. Rainwater pattered from the shattered roofs. The night breeze gusted through bare doorways and blind windows, fidgeting the rubbish that had blown in to litter the rubble-strewn floors.

Kys led me into a large chamber that had once been weatherproofed and lit. We had called this the drill. The railed rings for sparring were still there, half-buried in fallen slates. To the left were the practice dummies, sad ghosts in the twilight, and a row of pegs where once had hung pavis shields and ceramite bucklers. To the right was the smashed debris of the two mechanical sparring machines.

'You trained here?' Kys asked.

I nodded. 'Saur trained me here. And this is where he killed Voriet.'

'He was our way in,' she said. 'He found Eisenhorn, led us to him. But for Voriet, we wouldn't be here.'

'He didn't deserve to die for that,' I said.

'No one does.'

I believe the Maze Undue had been, for a long time, a playhouse, because there had been the traces of an arched stage in the hall, and other evidence of an unsuccessful theatrical past. But like all of the play-acting trade, it had known many functions. Originally, I think, it had been a place of worship.

As a child and a candidate, I had guessed this from the name. Maze Undue. I had studied texts of Old Terra in works kept in the datastacks of the library, and acquired some grasp of Old Franc. I once mentioned to Mentor Murlees, who was the savant and librarian of the house in my time, that Maze Undue could easily be a corruption of the Old Franc phrase *maison dieu*, or 'house of god'.

He had smiled at the thought of it and nodded.

He had said, 'Indeed, there is no maze, Beta.'

I knew better now. There was indeed a maze, and for the most part it was the convoluted pathway of my life. At least I still had a life. Murlees, like so many of them, was dead now.

'We need to find a route to the top room, if it's there still,' I told Kys. 'This way.'

The top room was where the briefings had taken place. There, candidates had been prepared for their functions. Part of that preparation was to observe and read the lives of those we were going to deceive.

For that purpose, the mentors had kept a quizzing glass there.

We found a staircase, every third or fourth step gone, and made our way up. The ruin seemed to shift and creak beneath us, its weight uneasy. Steadying herself against a wall, Kys glanced at me grimly.

'You think a mirror will have survived this?' she asked.

Increasingly, I did not.

The floor gave way without warning, in a splintering crash of dust and rubble.

Kys' mind caught me as I went down, and suspended me above the pitch-black plunge that had opened up. She hauled me onto the relative safety of the remaining stairs.

'You could fall to your death here,' she said.

We were near the top when our wraithbone pendants began to tingle.

'He wants us,' she said. 'He's discovered we've gone.'

'He can wait,' I said.

We took the pendants off, and left them at the top of the stairs where we could find them again later. Kys seemed amused by this, to be liberated from Gideon's beck and call.

'If he knows we've gone,' she said, 'he's finished his damn argument.'

'Which means they've reached some kind of agreement,' I said.

'Or Eisenhorn's dead,' she said.

'He isn't,' I said.

'How do you know?'

I pointed.

We had entered the upper hallway, at the end of which the top room was located. The roof was gone, blown out, the rafters left like a ribcage. Ahead of us, a figure floated in the night air.

'He sent him,' I said.

Cherubael drifted into the hallway like a lost kite.

'You ran away, little things,' said the daemon. 'He's very cross about it. They both are.'

'And you've been sent to fetch us?' I asked.

The daemon shrugged, bobbing in the breeze.

'He insisted,' he said. 'I hardly care what you do, but he insisted. I think he wonders about you. Wonders what you're doing here, wonders if you can be trusted. You're not up to no good are you?'

'No, daemon,' I said.

'Ah, but you'd say that if you were. I know I would.'

'I'm doing his work,' I said.

'Are you? Or are you doing the work of the Cognitae that made you? Work you may have been doing *all along*?'

'We'll finish what we've come here to do,' said Kys.

'No, little things, you'll come along back with me. I'm sent to fetch you. No arguments.'

Kys lowered her head slightly, her feet planting a little wider. The kine blades slipped out of her hair, and flashed up to hover either side of her.

'We will finish what we've come here to do,' she repeated.

Cherubael snorted with amusement, and then began to laugh so hard, and with such helpless mirth, I thought his tight flesh might burst. The wracking laughter wobbled him from side to side in the air. The sound of daemon hilarity was unpleasant, a maniac peal that I would not choose to hear again.

'That's just darling, little thing,' he giggled, recovering a little composure. 'So very funny. You? Fight me? You don't want to do that.'

'Kys does,' I said. 'But she shouldn't. She'd lose. I don't want to.'

'Then don't,' the daemon said. His smile faded. 'I have become quite fond of you, Beta. I'd hate to hurt you.'

'I think that's a lie.'

He looked offended.

'It's not,' he said, clutching a clawed hand to his breast as if offended. 'I *am* fond of you.'

'I think you are, in your own strange way,' I said. 'No, the other part. That was a lie. I think you'd like to hurt me.'

'Oh, I'd love to hurt you,' he said, with worrying relish. 'Both of you. In a lingering fashion. But I am instructed merely to fetch you, not harm you. Although, if you resist and put up a fight, injuries may unavoidably occur.'

'Go back,' I said. 'Tell him we'll return before long. We are not finished here.'

'I'm a daemonhost, little thing,' he said. 'I don't do nuance. I am a chained slave-soul. I am given an instruction, I perform it. He told me to fetch you. I must fetch you. I don't get to argue with the instructions. So are you coming, or not?'

'Not,' said Kys. Her kine blades shivered in the air, ready to fly.

The daemon smiled.

'All right, then,' he said, making an attempt at reluctance, but unable to disguise his glee.

'You don't want a fight, daemon,' I said.

'Why?' he asked.

I plucked one of Kys' blades out of the air with my right hand and quickly dug the tip into my left palm. Beads of blood spilled onto the floor, and away into the night wind.

'Because it won't be with us,' I said.

Uttering a wail, the daemon flew at us, arms wide to snatch us up in his embrace. Kys pushed me to the left with her kine-force, throwing me out of the way, as she executed an impossibly high somersault over the onrushing fiend.

I sprawled clear. Cherubael overshot me, and the end of the ruin's ledge, then turned back in mid-air to swoop again. Kys, still airborne, caught a passing rafter, spun her bodyweight around it like a gymnast on asymmetric bars, and landed on her feet on the hall floorboards. Everything was shaking and creaking.

Kys was facing the charging daemon. I tried to scramble out of the way. Kys dropped into a crouch, extending her arms in front of her, hands cupped one over the other. The kine blades spat past her on either side and met the daemon, burying themselves side by side in his chest.

He writhed in the air, let out a shriek of outrage, and wrenched the blades from his torso. Sticky black gore, the texture of my dreams, oozed off the spikes.

He came at us again.

I conjured the blinksword into my hand. If I could time a strike...

He was so fast.

He was an inch from me when Comus took him in his arms, then through a wall, then through part of the eaves, then out across the broken roofscape of the Scholam Orbus. The angel had arrived like a thunderbolt.

The two of them tumbled away into the night, angel and daemon, light and dark, locked together in a savage tearing, biting, clawing brawl, each quite as terrible as the other. They fell, together, grappling, and smashed through the roof of the scholam below us. We could hear the fight continuing, now out of sight: tiles rippling, walls quivering, sudden sprays of pulverised brick and mortar. We could hear the sounds of inhuman blows, and the daemon screeching in pain and delight.

'You all right?' I asked Kys.

She nodded.

'Quickly then, while we have the chance.'

I picked myself up, and began to hurry to the top room.

'Will they... destroy each other?' Kys asked, looking back.

'They may. I imagine Cherubael may win. But Comus is singularly savage. He has a rage in him. A thirst. I think he was purpose-built to fight daemons.'

'You signal him... and then send him to what will almost certainly be his death to protect yourself?' she asked.

'He fights for the God-Emperor, not me,' I said. 'But, yes. I did that.'

She raised her eyebrows.

'I know,' I said miserably. 'I already have all the makings of a true inquisitor, haven't I?'

Somehow, the mirror had survived the doom of the Maze Undue.

It had fallen from its stand, and lay in the dust and dirt with a great crack across it.

'I'm amazed,' said Kys.

'It's a quizzing glass,' I said. 'Perhaps hardier than normal glass. Let's not question our luck.'

'How much luck can a broken mirror afford us?' she asked.

We took it up between us, and dragged it upright to lean it against the rain-eaten bricks of the wall. A few slivers of silvered glass fell out.

I stared into it. The ghost of my face looked back, dirty, wet with rain. I had seen myself in its surface so many times down the years. So many versions of myself, and so many other lives besides.

Daemon screams bubbled up from far below.

'Will it work?' Kys asked.

'I know how to quiz it, at least. Wait.'

'What if it works?' she added.

'Now you ask *that*?'

'Never mind,' she said. 'How will we know if it works?'

'We'll know,' I assured her.

She didn't reply. Because it had worked, and she was no longer there.

Or, rather, I was no longer here.

CHAPTER 30

Finding myself in the Palace of Thaumeizin

There was no sense of change or transfer, no stammer or edit of reality. Upon a drawn breath, I was in the cold and dark and damp of the ruined Maze Undue; upon the exhalation, I was in a place of warm daylight.

I was still staring at a mirror. It was square and plain, but impossibly pure, manufactured with incredible precision. It was hanging on a wall of polished amber tiles. I could see myself in it: the dirt on my cheeks, the drops of Queen Mab rain in my hair, the surprise in my expression. In the reflection, the room behind me was tiled from floor to ceiling.

I stepped away from the mirror, and turned. The room was square and very plain, tiled entirely in gleaming amber. My boots left muddy smears on their perfection. I didn't know how they had been set: there seemed to be no mortar or cement, but I could not have slid a leaf of paper between the lustrous tiles. Above me, the ceiling was domed, and the tiles followed the curve of that dome until they met at the apex without blemish or irregularity. There was one door, an archway, facing the wall on which the mirror hung. It seemed that the entire purpose of the room was the mirror.

'Patience?' I called softly. There was no answer. I clicked my micro-bead, but the link was dead. I walked towards the arch.

Beyond it, a long tiled hallway flanked with sleek charcoal pillars. If this was the City of Dust, then it was not what I expected. It seemed clean to the point of sterility.

The air was warm. Strong sunlight shone in through the pillared arches, casting long, hard shadows of the columns across the floor, like italicised numerals on the face of a clock. The quality of the light was strange. It was so pure and fierce, and so directional.

The hallway, like the chamber with the mirror, was tiled in amber. They held a rich inner warmth, glowing where the sunlight touched them. I looked at the tiles on the wall beside me: again, so perfectly fitted. Close to, I realised there was a mark upon them, a tiny pattern repeated in delicate rows across the surface of every single tile. It was the numeral '8', over and over again, each one no bigger than the tip of a pencil. But the numerals were aligned on their sides, forming bands or chains. They were not eights at all. They were the lemniscate, the geometric symbol for infinity. They were the limitless apeiron, the tail-biting double-circle of ouroboros.

I stepped back.

I could hear nothing, but there was a sensation of music, or at least a harmonic vibration just at the edge of hearing. The air smelled of perfume, but then I realised it was me. It was the splashes of Kara's fragrances that had spotted my clothes when Kys tossed aside the bottles in the nameless house. A faint trace, but it smelled so strong because the place smelled of absolutely nothing.

Place. *Palace*. The scale was great. I sensed I was in a small part of something vast. I started to walk, then paused. I realised there was a word in my head that had not been there before. It was a word of forbidden Enuncia that I had forgotten the instant I spoke it. I had only remembered it when I passed into the extimate space at Feverfugue. To remember it again, suddenly, here... It seemed to prove that this was extimate space too.

I walked. Through the open archways, I could see a city below. The wonder of it stopped me dead. A great city, of towers and domes, all gleaming grey and white, steel and corundum, some topped with crests and spires of glinting auramite and orichalcum. Beyond the city, concentric rings of walls, built strong for defence, like cliffs, and as majestic as the towers. The sky above was the deepest black, in stark contrast to the brilliantly lit city. I leaned out a little beside a charcoal pillar, and looked up. I glimpsed the sun, the source of the blazing light. But it was not the sun – it was a supermassive star, not of the same system. Set in the blackness, it glowed numinous white. Around its haloed glare, other stars twinkled, an infinite scape of unfamiliar patterns and strange constellations that I was sure Freddy Dance would recognise at once. Closer, like phantoms in the perpetual dark, I saw the rims and crescents of primordial exoplanets, some very large, timeless and inscrutable in the King's private heavens.

I steadied my breathing. How big was this palace, this city? A hundred leagues across? A thousand? The mighty walls seemed so far away, yet I could see them sharply, just like the innumerable stars, for the air was so clear and there was no light pollution.

And there was no one there.

The emptiness was eerie. I wandered the amber halls for a while, and found a staircase, wide and of burnished marble, and followed it upwards. I reached a much higher level, emerging into the unforgiving starlight and onto a great platform of white stone, lined with huge statues, each one a giant winged man of noble aspect hewn from alabaster.

The likeness of every one of them, crafted by a master sculptor, was that of Comus Nocturnus.

I thought I was high up in the palace, but the platform I had reached, larger than any grand plaza in Queen Mab, was merely the foot of greater towers that soared above me, strong-lit against the blackness, their white ethercite radiant. Just looking up and trying to comprehend their height made me giddy.

I looked away, back at the city below. I had a greater vantage now. I could see the plan of it, the perfect plan. It wove in spirals and graceful curves obeying, in both macro and micro scheme, the universal harmony of the Golden or Divine Ratio. The streets seemed wound like the coiled cells of a sectioned nautilus. What place was this, what mind could have conceived it?

From this height, I could see beyond the distant walls. I could see a bone-white shoreline, a beach perhaps a kilometre deep and as wide as the horizon. Beyond that, an ocean, boundless and black beneath the starred black sky, lapping endlessly against the bone-shore. Despite the space of distance, I could hear its rolling surge. I thought I could even hear the clack and tinkle of the shells and pebbles on the tidal edge.

It was the ocean sound I had heard in the Below. This, I felt with great certainty, was the other side of that same sea, the far shore of the vista I had glimpsed through the King Door. It could not be crossed or navigated, and even if it could, one would then only face the insurmountable walls of the city. Ravenor was wrong, Eisenhorn too. The King Door could be no mortal access to this place. They had not even begun to imagine the scale of the other side.

For it wasn't a sea at all. The city was a great, shining island, and the sea was the immaterium, calmed and majestic, but as infinite and absolute as the apeiron pattern on the amber tiles. I had no idea why the great empyrean wasn't washing me away, me and the place I stood in.

What Comus must have done to cross it...

I began to walk across the platform, intending to skirt the base of the vast towers and take in the view on the other side, but I was still underestimating the scale. What looked like a walk of five minutes was so much more, for in five minutes I had barely begun to cross even a part of it. I realised how huge these cyclopean towers were, and thus how impossibly vast those distant walls must be, how titanic the bone-white shore, how truly endless the sea. The sunlight – the starlight – was fierce, for there was no shade. I felt but mild heat, but the skin of my cheek began to burn. There was no shield of atmosphere, no sky, but something kept the air I breathed from escaping into the void above.

I kept walking anyway. My footsteps, the only sound, were as tiny as me. Whenever I stopped, and turned to look at the city, the towers had subtly adjusted themselves, as though turned by a photogravitational influence. I wondered if they were following the slow track of the giant star across the heavens, as flowers follow the sun. I saw birds, twice, far away above the ocean shore, the white dots of seabirds soaring in the black sky.

I knew they were not birds.

I began to feel afraid. The wonder of the place was so great, it teetered on the edge of terror.

At last, after walking for longer than I was able to accurately calculate, except that my legs sorely ached, I began to round the corner of the tower base. I leant to rest against the warm, white ethercite. I saw the sprawl of the city that had been obscured from my view, and I saw what filled the black heavens above it, but had been eclipsed by the high towers.

A baleful scar slit the blackness diagonally. A cosmic manifestation, a puckered whorl of starlight and warp, shot through with crimson, pink and traces of flame. It was bigger than the local star. It was light years across, a galactic wound. It dominated the bowl of space, the entire psychocosm. Skeins of tiny stars, some bright as ice flakes, some raw as cinders, slowly tumbled into its yawning abyss of fluorescent nebula gas and bloodshot light. Their fall was glacial, the supreme progress of Long Time. The scar seemed to gaze down upon the city like a burning, disfigured eye. Then I felt terror, true terror, for that was what it was.

The *Ocularis Terribus*. The Eye of Terror.

Below its numbing horror, a war was raging, far away. From the distant walls of the city, from towers and fortifications greater than the greatest cathedrals, darts and spears of electrocorporeal light lanced up into the sky, and some were answered by red beams that flickered from the high darkness beneath the Eye's glare. I saw bright flashes quiver and throb below the horizon, coming and going, speaking of colossal destruction and annihilation beyond my range of sight. I could hear nothing, not even a faint roar. These were world-shaking detonations, city-destroying blasts of searing bombardment, and I could hear nothing.

I saw flights of angels, dots far away, like snowy blossom on the wind, lifting from the far battlements in formations a thousand strong, setting out into the blackness. I saw golden barges and burnished warships hanging silently, hanging impossibly, in the darkness above the city, prows facing outwards, ready to embark. One passed overhead as I watched. I do not know where it had come from, but its shadow crossed me and crossed the tower I leant against. I looked up to see its golden form, the detail of its plating, its finials, its gun ports and engines, the slow flutter of its banners, the masts of its forward lances, piping and ducts of its gargantuan keel. All wrought of gold, every part of it. Its passage was completely noiseless, and it seemed to go on forever as it crawled past overhead.

I watched it go. I slid down the wall, my back to it, until I was seated on the ground. I watched it go until it was just one of many on station over the shimmering walls.

What had I expected of this place? A decayed shadow of Queen Mab, perhaps. A ruined relic choked in dust and desert. An arcane lair. A furtive King, lurking in a dismal hall, hidden from the real world while he plotted and schemed.

Not this.

Never this.

We had imagined much, but we had fallen so far short it was laughable. This was beyond anything, a realm that contained itself in utter metaphysical perfection and atomically precise engineering, that constrained and harnessed the very ether as a barrier defence. No wonder that all who heard of this feared it. No wonder that warriors of all fealty, traitor and loyalist alike, and sundry great warlords of other species, gathered feverishly at Sancour. This realm of Orphaeus was a threat to all things, or an answer to all prayers. It had to be stopped, or it had to be joined for fear of being left on the side that opposed it, for that side would surely lose.

I think, at that moment, I may have lost my mind.

When I became aware of things again, I found myself back inside the palace. I presume I must have walked, numb and insensible, all the way back across the platform and descended the stairs into the amber hallway. I did not even know if it was the same hallway I had started from. The tiles all looked the same, for they were. I could still hear the hiss of the distant empyrean ocean washing the faraway shore.

I found myself, sitting on the floor at the base of a pillar, exhausted and dazed. The amber tiles were sun-warmed beneath me. I had been crying. My hands trembled. I had no idea how long I had been there.

'It will be all right,' said a voice.

I looked up. A young man was standing over me, a look of concern and comfort on his face. He was wearing an austere white uniform that recalled the ceremonial dress of the Imperial Battlefleet, topped by a rich blue robe edged in auramite thread. Upon his tunic breast, collar and sleeves, the repeated symbol of the lemniscate was embroidered in gold. I could see complex tattoos upon his throat, and across the side and base of his shaved head.

I knew his face.

'Judika?'

'No, that's not my name.'

'But you have his face.'

He laughed, as if to say *of course*. He helped me to my feet. I glimpsed a cuff as he raised me. Gold, but otherwise like mine. He was a null.

'Are you new here?' Not-Judika asked.

'Yes.'

'We found you by chance. Others have gone for help. Newly arrived, then?'

'Yes.'

'Then no wonder you are in a state,' he said solemnly. 'You should have been received. Nothing was scheduled. You should have been greeted. The Palace can be overwhelming to those who have not seen it.'

'The Palace...'

'Thaumeizin. The Palace of Thaumeizin.'

'Is that his name?' I asked.

'Is that whose name?' He frowned. There was a slight but distinctive crackle in the texture of his voice, like the prickle of vox static. 'You need water, and rest. You are clearly unwell. I know I was when I first arrived, and I was received and cared for. Have you been wandering around alone?'

I nodded.

'Throne save you!' he cried. 'It's a wonder you're not mad. There is induction, to acclimate you. Neuroanatomical treatment. You should have been taken to the adytum for initiatic processing.'

'Thaumeizin...' I said.

'Yes,' he replied.

'Not a name?'

'Yes, the name of here,' he said. 'This is the Mote. It is all things here and all we are. It is bounded by the Sea of Souls. It commands Pandaemonium. You were told this?'

'No.'

'No one told you this?' Not-Judika asked. 'How were you sent to the Mote without being told this?'

'I'm not sure,' I said. 'Of anything.'

'This is the Palace of Thaumeizin. Thaumeizin means wonder, for all things begin in wonder. So it is said in the earliest Eleniki philosophy, for it is the wonder at a puzzle that drives us towards knowledge. Have you not been taught any of this?'

'Knowledge?' I began. I was very dizzy.

'Knowledge translates to power...' he said, slowly but lightly, as though it was a refrain I should know and join in with.

He studied me uneasily, frowning.

'Who are you?' he asked. He was looking at my clothes, the dirt on my hands and face, the mud that had dried on my boots.

'I'm new,' I said.

'What's your name?' His tone had changed. He had become wary and guarded. He had been steadying me, but he took his hands away.

I tried to think.

'Violetta,' I said, striving for an identity.

'What kind of name is that?' he asked.

'Penitent,' I said quickly.

'We are all penitents before the King,' he said.

'The King?'

'You'll have to be brought to him,' he said. I heard the crackle again. 'The custodians will examine you first, but you'll have to be brought before him. You're… you're either not right at all, or you are not what you seem.'

'What do I seem?' I asked.

He glared at me, suspicious.

'Like an intruder,' he said. 'Like you do not belong here, or are not meant for here. Like you came here by mistake.'

'I came here on purpose,' I said.

'Not like the rest. An interloper.'

I was about to protest, but I heard footsteps. Three people approached along the hallway, three more young people like Not-Judika. Two women and a man, heads shaved. They wore the same white uniforms and gold-edged robes as him. One of the women wore a blue over-robe, like Not-Judika, the other a robe of deep cochineal red, and the man's was a pale absinthe green.

'Is she all right?' one asked. 'Is she better now?'

'I don't know what to make of her,' Not-Judika replied.

'Help is coming,' said the man in the green robe. 'The custodians have been summoned.'

I looked at him. He wore green, yes, but more distressingly, he *also* wore the face of Judika Sowl. A different pattern of tattoos covered his throat. Two Not-Judikas stared at me. I stepped back, until the pillar behind me stopped me.

'What's wrong with her?' asked one of the girls. The crackle, sharper, was in her voice too. Her face… Her face was that of Faria who, like Judika, had been a candidate with me at the Maze Undue.

'Faria?' I asked.

She frowned at me.

'Why does she call me that? I think you're right. I think there's something wrong with her.'

'Yes,' said the Judika in green. 'Look at her clothes. She's not meant to be here.'

'No,' said the other girl. 'She is. Look at her face.'

And I looked at *her* face, the face of the girl wearing cochineal red.

It was mine.

It was as looking in a mirror. Her head was shaved, and inked sigils covered her neck and the back of her head. But her face belonged to me.

'She's programme,' she said. 'Look at her. Her hair's too long, and she's covered in dirt, but look at her. Alizebeth genome. Like me, see?'

'I thought so,' said Judika-in-blue. 'But she is acting strange. She hasn't passed through initiatic. I don't like it.'

'Hush! She's simply scared,' the other me said. 'You're scared, aren't you? Don't be. We are alike.'

'Too alike,' I whispered.

'It's all right,' she said. 'We are Alizebeth genome siblings. Sisters. Made whole from the same dust.' She smiled. My smile. She reached out to me. I could not bear the thought of her touching me.

'Please, don't.'

'It's all right,' she insisted. Her tone was soft and kind, but the crackle was lodged in it.

'Don't!' I snapped, and brushed her hands away.

More people were hurrying down the amber to join us. More young people in white uniforms and coloured robes. More Judikas. Another Faria. Four Corlams.

And at least three more who owned my face.

'Please,' I mumbled. 'Stay away from me. Stay away.'

'Where are the custodians?' Judika-in-green called to those just arriving. 'She must be detained.'

'I can calm her,' the other me in cochineal red told him. She was facing me still, smiling still.

I blinked the sword into my hand. They all stepped back sharply.

'She's damn well armed,' said Not-Faria.

'Custodians!' Judika-in-blue shouted.

'She won't hurt us,' the other me insisted. 'You won't hurt me, will you? You wouldn't hurt me, no more than you'd hurt yourself?'

She stepped towards me again. I raised the sword, but she was right. I could not bring myself to strike at her.

So I said the word instead.

CHAPTER 31

Named

The world exploded. The word exploded. The word exploded the world.

I don't know.

I was thrown backwards with great force as though I had been hit by a siege ram. I flew, in a spinning shower of broken glass. The ground caught me from behind, hard. It was wet and cold.

'Bequin?' Kys said, scared.

I swallowed. I could not speak. I felt word-burn in my mouth, my lips. I was lying on my back in the top room of the Maze Undue, the night sky above me, full of familiar stars. Drops of rain falling on my face.

I sat up. Splinters of glass slid off me and tinkled onto the floor. I was facing the quizzing glass. It was just an old and broken frame, the glass blown out of it. Pieces of mirror littered me and the floor around me.

Kys crouched beside me.

'The hell?' she said. She tried to help me, to comfort me, but she was not very good at it.

'How long?' I murmured.

'What?'

'How long was I gone?'

'Five minutes,' she said.

'Then?'

'You came back,' said Kys. 'Out of the glass, backwards. You flew out like you'd been thrown. Shattered the mirror, but not the frame. Like some damn carnival trick.'

I nodded.

'Help me up,' I said. She hauled me to my feet with her hands and a jolt of telekine force.

I swayed. She propped me with her shoulder, then turned my face with her fingers so I was looking into her eyes.

'Where did you go?' she asked.

'There,' I said. 'The City.'

'The City of Dust?'

'It's not a good name for it,' I said.

'What did you see?'

'Everything,' I replied.

She let go of me. I stood, unaided, badly.

'I found myself in the City of Dust,' I said.

'And?'

'No, Patience, I *found myself*.'

'Well, good for you,' she sneered.

'Not at all,' I said. 'We must go back. Go back to Gregor and Gideon. Will you help me?'

'Yes, but will you tell me nothing?' she asked.

'I'll tell you everything,' I replied. 'Give me a moment. I'll tell it all to them too. They've made a terrible mistake. It is so much worse than they could have imagined. He has built an empire. He controls his reality. He shackles the empyrean itself. He rules Pandaemonium.'

Kys looked at me as though I were raving.

'This is the King?' she asked. 'You mean the King in Yellow?'

I nodded.

'You know who he is? One of the lost sons? What is his name?'

'I don't know,' I said. 'But we are fools to think we can fight him. He is not some heretic warlord. He is…'

I felt my voice fade.

'What? He's what?'

'I have no word for it,' I said.

'But you got in? Through the quizzing glass?'

I nodded again.

'Well then,' said Kys, 'we have that. That's something. A way in. Gideon and Eisenhorn, they will thank you for that.'

'I don't think they will,' I said. 'Not when I tell them the rest.'

It took us a while to make our way down through the ruin of the Maze Undue. I was tired, sore, cut and unsteady. Everything seemed so grey and lightless, so dirty and old, and stained with shadow.

By the time we reached the street, Low Highgate Lane, they were waiting for us. They stood in the street, solemn, like some estranged, dysfunctional family unwillingly assembled to pose for a group portrait. Eisenhorn stood, haggard and sullen, a violet light in his eyes, and the Chair waited ominously to his right. Kara, Medea and Deathrow flanked them. Kara's hands were in her pockets, and she eyed me warily. Medea's red-gloved hands were clasped in front of her and her face was expressionless. Deathrow was hooded, his face invisible, the dog sprawled at his heels. Nayl waited nearby, stiff and hunched in pain.

Of the daemon and the angel, there was no sign.

'An explanation,' said Eisenhorn. 'You defied us.'

'She did your work for you,' said Kys. It came out as a snarl. 'She's found the way in. A door to the City of Dust, and she can do it again. So temper your demands with gratitude, heretic.'

'Watch your tone, Patience,' said Ravenor.

'I don't think I will,' said Kys.

'We have come to an arrangement,' said Ravenor. 'A truce, so we can work together. You will show Gregor respect.'

'No,' said Kys.

'We have come to an *arrangement...*' said Ravenor.

'I'm happy for you,' said Kys.

I put my hand on Kys' arm.

'Stop,' I whispered to her.

'You found a way in, Beta?' asked Medea. She was wearing a formal black suit with a high collar, as though she expected to attend a funeral. The red of her gloves was a brutal splash of colour.

'Yes,' I said.

'And the King?' asked Kara. 'What of the King?'

I started to answer. I wanted to unburden myself and tell it all, every last part of it, as I have done in this narrative. But there were voices in my head, whispers that hissed and scratched at my ears, and prevented me from focusing. A crackle, a prickle...

I realised it was my micro-bead. It was the tinny voice of Renner Lightburn, calling my name, over and over again, as though there were many of me to greet.

'Wait,' I said to the glaring warband. I held up my hand to silence them while I fumbled with the earpiece. Eisenhorn glowered.

'Lightburn?' I said.

'Why the hell didn't you answer?' he said. *'I've been calling you.'*

'I'm here now,' I said. 'What's the matter? Do you have news?'

'The old boy's got a translation,' Lightburn said. *'Part of one, at least. The start. The book is a name. The whole damn book. A single name, written in that Hexad code thing, thousands of characters long. What–'*

He broke off. I heard muffled voices away from the link.

'Renner?' I called.

He came back on. *'All right. Freddy says millions of characters. I was wrong. He wanted me to be precise. He gave me an actual number, but I'm not being* that *precise.'*

'Renner, just tell me!'

'It's the true name of the King in Yellow,' Lightburn said. *'He's sure of it. That's what the book is. I can give you the start of it, the bit he's translated.'*

'Please do.'

'Hold on. I've written it down here.'

I waited. I looked at Eisenhorn.

'We have his name,' I said. His jaw clenched. He glanced at the Chair. Like me, they were both expecting the worst. The name of a lost primarch-son. The name of a daemon. The name of a god. The name of the Emperor above all, whose true name, once known and spoken, might pull reality apart or command the cosmos.

Renner Lightburn's voice returned.

'I have it here,' he said. *'Beta, the name begins as follows...'*

I listened. I nodded. I turned to the warband.

'The name of the King is Constantin Valdor,' I said.

Beta Bequin will return in the final volume of this trilogy, which is called PANDAEMONIUM

ABOUT THE AUTHOR

Dan Abnett has written over fifty novels, including *Anarch*, the latest instalment in the acclaimed Gaunt's Ghosts series. He has also written the Ravenor, Eisenhorn and Bequin books, the most recent of which is *Penitent*. For the Horus Heresy, he is the author of the Siege of Terra novel *Saturnine*, as well as *Horus Rising, Legion, The Unremembered Empire, Know No Fear* and *Prospero Burns*, the last two of which were both *New York Times* bestsellers. He also scripted *Macragge's Honour*, the first Horus Heresy graphic novel, as well as numerous Black Library audio dramas. Many of his short stories have been collected into the volume *Lord of the Dark Millennium*. He lives and works in Maidstone, Kent.

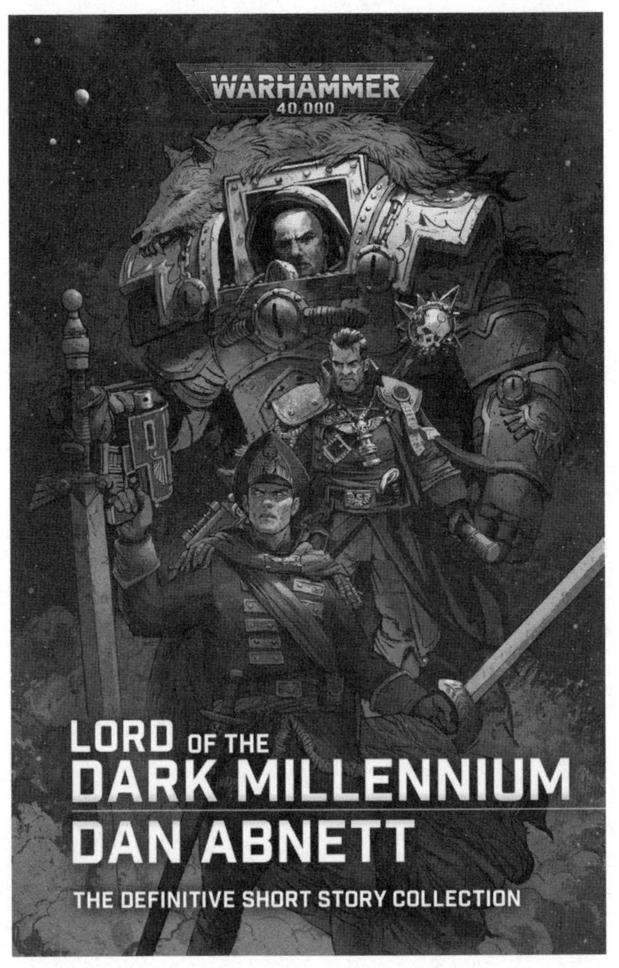

LORD OF THE DARK MILLENNIUM
by Dan Abnett

For more than twenty years, Dan Abnett has been writing tales about the grim darkness of the far future. For the first time, more than 30 of these legendary stories have been brought together in one amazing collection to celebrate Dan's Warhammer 40,000 and Horus Heresy legacy.